Praise for Allison Amend's

Enchanted Islands

fascinating rumination on identity, friendship and love. . . .
Amend] vividly evokes Duluth's bleakness, Chicago's sparkling
ustle, rural Nebraska's quietude and San Francisco's sophistication.
Most enticing of all is the otherworldliness of the Galápagos."
— *San Francisco Chronicle*

"Dazzling." — *Travel + Leisure*

"Amend's novel manages to encompass a woman's life, the story of a
marriage, a tense standoff between Allied and Axis operatives, and a
sensitive examination of women's friendship."
— *Minneapolis Star Tribune*

"Allison Amend is a wonderful writer—generous and psychologically
astute—and *Enchanted Islands* is both a sweeping epic and a moving
exploration of the intricacies of friendship. This is a beautiful novel
hat will stay with me for a long time." — Molly Antopol,
author of *The UnAmericans*

Absorbing. . . . Amend's spirited rendition of [Frances Conway's] life
reads less like a memoir and more like Jane Austen. It has acute inter-
personal observations and subjective flights of fancy." — *BookPage*

'In *Enchanted Islands*, Allison Amend distills the entire life of Frances
Conway—one of, if not *the*, most fully realized characters I've encoun-
red in the last decade—into a captivating narrative. . . . Brilliant."
— Jill Alexander Essbaum,
New York Times bestselling author of *Hausfrau*

"Mesmerizing and captivating. . . . The kind of book that will make you want to renew your passport." —*Bustle*

"Secrets, lies, and spies on a faraway island. . . . Appealing characters and vivid local color make for an entertaining read." —*Kirkus Reviews*

"In this shrewdly textured yet directly told tale of an unorthodox life, Amend fills Fanny's worlds of poverty, intrigue, and indignant old age with rewarding vibrancy and touching vulnerability." —*Booklist*

"A taut, powerful tale of human relationships and the sacrifices people make to maintain their balance." —*Publishers Weekly*

"In this compulsively readable novel, exotic locales and international espionage bend before the greatest intrigue of all: the life of a captivating mind. . . . *Enchanted Islands* is as moving as it is impossible to put down." —Matthew Thomas, *New York Times* bestselling author of *We Are Not Ourselves*

ALLISON AMEND

ENCHANTED ISLANDS

Allison Amend, a graduate of the Iowa Writers' Workshop, is the author of the novels *A Nearly Perfect Copy* and *Stations West*, which was a finalist for the 2011 Sami Rohr Prize for Jewish Literature and the Oklahoma Book Award. She is also the author of the Independent Publisher Book Award–winning short story collection *Things That Pass for Love*. She lives in New York City, where she teaches creative writing.

www.allisonamend.com

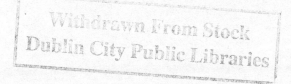

ENCHANTED ISLANDS

Enchanted Islands

A NOVEL

ALLISON AMEND

Leabharlanna Poiblí Chathair Baile Átha Cliath
Dublin City Public Libraries

ANCHOR BOOKS

A DIVISION OF PENGUIN RANDOM HOUSE LLC

NEW YORK

FIRST ANCHOR BOOKS EDITION, APRIL 2017

The Library of Congress has cataloged the Nan A. Talese /
Doubleday edition as follows:
Amend, Allison.
Enchanted Islands : a novel / Allison Amend.—First edition.
pages ; cm
I. Title.
PS3601.M464E53 2016   813'.6—dc23   2015023460

Anchor Books Trade Paperback ISBN: 978-0-8041-7204-2
eBook ISBN: 978-0-385-53907-4

www.anchorbooks.com

Printed in the United States of America
10 9 8 7 6 5 4 3 2 1

Az me ken nit vi me vil, tut men vi me ken.
If you can't do as you wish, do as you can.

—YIDDISH PROVERB

The Galápagos have a malign spell which repels all efforts
at colonizing . . . The Galápagos are only for the few . . .
And so I warn the readers of this book to remain away
from the Islands of Enchantment.

—SIDNEY HOWARD, *ISLES OF ESCAPE*

Everywhere nothing living. Only the wind blowing, the
seas breaking—all alien, all self-contained, all indifferent.
And dead though my surroundings seemed, there was
nevertheless something alive in the emptiness and dead-
ness. Something alive that was totally unmindful of me
yet, paradoxically, threatening. The indifference itself was
the menace. Anything could happen to me, and the island
and the sea would remain imperturbed, as if nothing had
happened. I was not needed, not wanted, not noticed.

—FRANCES CONWAY, *RETURN TO THE ISLAND*

Part One

CHAPTER ONE

You're not allowed to read this—I'm not even really allowed to write it. But now that Ainslie is gone and I will surely follow before too long, I don't see that much is the harm. I suppose the government will censor what it will.

A curious effect of childlessness is that your story disappears with you. Of course, everyone's does eventually, but the suddenness with which my history will be extinguished causes me much consternation. I am of the generation who came of age in the new century, though my formative years were spent in the last—I am therefore pulled between the past and the present.

That my life will be of interest to readers I dare not assume. But it is an unusual one, and for that reason alone record should be made of it.

*

It is the usual manner with these memoirs to begin at the beginning and head toward the end, so I will start with my name: Frances Conway. It was not always thus. Still, this is the name you will read on the placard that is outside my room. I was born on August 3, 1882. I will save you the math—I am eighty-two. It is only thanks to Rosalie's largesse that I can spend my last years in relative comfort in a private "retirement home" rather than one of those paupers' adult day cares.

At mealtimes I am supposed to go to the dining hall where the Mexican nurses serve food that is inoffensive to any palate, which is to say, offensive to all. They are surprised that I speak Spanish. I am in complete possession of my faculties, as much as I ever was. It is merely the corporeal situation that is in disrepair—my hands twisted like *muyuyo* branches and my back as bent as a burro's. I have to wait for someone to push me in my wheelchair if I want to go anywhere, and that stands in contrast to my days in the Galápagos when it was nothing to walk three or four hours for a chat or to get the mail.

Rosalie is already waiting for me at our table, her walker at attention like an obedient dog beside her. She has started on her soup, and I can hear the slurping from here, an annoying habit she picked up after getting dentures. She waits for me to get situated, but I can tell she has something to say. Her head is cocked toward me, her eyes unnaturally bright.

Lourdes puts an identical plate of soup in front of me, but then, seeing the glare I give her, takes it away.

"Sleep all right?" Rosalie asks.

"Fine," I say. "You?"

"Listen, Fanny, you'll never guess, but there's a ceremony for me!"

"What kind?"

Lourdes returns with a plate of what must be food, though its origins are mysterious. Chicken? Potatoes? I pick up my fork and poke at it.

"I'm to be honored." Rosalie has a bit of soup on her chin. I motion to her to wipe it and she does so, without breaking her story. "Hadassah of Northern California. They want to celebrate my war work."

"War work?" I ask. I never knew that Rosalie ever worked, especially not for the war.

"It's the twentieth anniversary of the end of the war. Can you believe it? Twenty years already."

"What are they honoring you for?" I ask.

"Fanny, pay attention!" Rosalie drops her soup spoon into the bowl. It clatters, causing those with the mobility to swivel their heads in our direction. "Do we need to get you an ear trumpet?"

I frown at her. "But I don't understand what you did in the war that deserves honoring."

"You were there," she says. "You were there at all those fund-raising parties for Israel. Do you think that state just appeared out of thin air?"

I put down my fork. I'm not going to eat this mush. "Throwing parties is war work?" I see Gloria making her hobbling way toward our table. "Incoming!" I whisper.

"Who?" Rosalie leans toward me. Her vision is not the greatest.

"Gloria."

"Oh Christ." Rosalie sighs. "We're waiting for Jemmie, tell her."

"You tell her," I whisper back.

"Huh?" Rosalie says I need an ear trumpet, but it's her hearing that gets worse at convenient times.

"Gloria," I say, "so nice to see you. Sorry you can't join us. We're supposed to have a meeting with Jemmie."

I feel a bit bad for Gloria as her face falls in disappointment. But I can't sit through another meal with her dribbling food into her lap and hearing about her successful grandchildren who are always planning to see her but then never quite make it. Here in the retirement home we are nearly all women. The few men in residence are even more decrepit than we old hens. They are cocks of the walk. The younger women mill about, fawning over these toothless skeletons as though they were meat worth catching.

"A meeting for what?" Gloria is from New York, and sounds like she's a carnival barker.

Rosalie has turned back to her soup, leaving me to deal with the consequences. "For the . . ." I rack my brain. "Rosalie, what's the name of it again? My memory fails me."

Rosalie says, "Huh?," but I know she hears me.

"The name of the committee. The official name. You know, of the committee we're meeting about."

"Oh, the CFC. The Condolence Flower Committee." Rosalie has always been good with a quick lie.

Gloria has already begun to turn away, a process not unlike that of a giant tortoise, as she says, "Well, I'll leave you to it." No one wants to be on any committee that has the word *condolence* in it. Not in Chelonia Manor.

We call it that because the first day, after witnessing the interminable shuffle to get to the dining hall, I said, "It's a chelonian stampede."

"What's that?" Rosalie asked.

"Chelonian. Turtles."

Rosalie thought this was hysterical, and from then on we lived at Chelonia Manor.

When Gloria's finally out of earshot, Rosalie giggles.

I shush her. "What if she hears? Now we have to form a Condolence Bouquet Committee."

"Flower," Rosalie says. "No we don't. She'll forget. Can you please pass the bread?"

Rosalie has become quite plump since we moved in here. I, on the other hand, am my usual skin and bones and tendons. The last time I saw Rosalie heavy was when we were children. Since then, she's always been vain about her appearance.

I take a piece of bread for myself. It's a generic white biscuit, but I'll put some butter on it. Unsalted butter, of course.

"Ay, Señora Conway, pero, no come nada!" Lourdes says to me in mock concern. I tell her my plate is still full because the food is tasteless, artificial, though it pains me after those years of near starvation to waste even a morsel. She tells me in a stage whisper that they have beans and rice in the kitchen for the *empleados*. She brings me a plate. It is not in the style of Ecuadorian food, but at least it was growing recently, and it is nice and salty.

"No se lo diga a nadie," Lourdes warns. Really, who cares if someone my age eats salt or doesn't?

Rosalie and I have lived at the Chelonia in Los Gatos, California, near San Francisco, for two years. We both survived our husbands, though mine was more than a decade younger than I. When Rosalie fell and broke her hip, her son insisted she move in here. So I did too.

It is one of nature's great injustices that once you have carried out your purpose on earth you are not worth feeding anymore. We saw this daily in the Galápagos, where animals gave their elderly parents no more thought than the bones of the animal they'd just licked clean.

I don't want to let Rosalie's announcement go. "I didn't see you do anything during the war that you weren't already doing before the war or that you didn't continue to do after the war."

"Then you weren't paying attention. Clarence and I brought over several refugees from Europe. And I knitted. I was constantly knitting."

I have no memory of Rosalie knitting. I do have a memory of helping her and the maid put up bunting for VE Day, which apparently is twenty years ago next month.

A belch of jealousy burbles up inside me. Rosalie is to be honored. It was always thus, that Rosalie was in the spotlight while I sat in the wings, but this in particular galls me. I am the one who truly served my country during the war. I am the one who stayed in a marriage for the sake of my country, who came close to losing my life for it. And I can tell no one.

"Congratulations," I say. "Is it a party?" I suspect that Rosalie hears the green-eyed monster in my voice, but she has seventy-five years of practice ignoring my uncharitable sentiments.

"A ceremony at the synagogue. They're sending a car for me. I hope it's a limousine. I'd love to see these old biddies' faces when I drive off in a limousine." Actually, I'd like to see that too. I had no idea that a nursing home would have more cliques than a middle school. "Of course you'll come, Fanny. I'll insist. They wanted me to give a speech, but I told them I couldn't possibly. They nearly insisted until I explained I can't stand for long because of my hip."

"You're not that hip," I say, and Rosalie, quick as ever, laughs at the joke.

*

Once a month, Rosalie's Dan comes to see us. We have lunch in a diner and then he takes us to visit Ainslie's and Clarence's graves. I would prefer to go to Muir Woods or the ocean. But I don't know how to tell him and Rosalie this. Nor do I imagine I could do anything at Muir Woods other than sit in the car enjoying the parking lot.

Dan always has flowers for both of us and kisses my cheeks when he comes in my room.

"How are you, Fanny?" he asks. He has Rosalie's charm, her lively eyes. I think Dan has gotten even bigger since I last saw him. His stomach hangs below his belt, billowing out as if he's stuffed a pillow in there. When he walks it jiggles to his mid-thighs.

Without asking, he stands behind me and wheels me out of the room. I don't like being moved without my permission. Being confined to a wheelchair should not turn you into a child. But the wheelchair's resemblance to a stroller is undeniable. Oh the infantilization of old age!

When we get outside, Rosalie is already situated in the front seat, which I suppose is her right, as it's her son who is taking us out, but it would be nice if occasionally she would relinquish it to me.

It is a process, always, to get me in a vehicle. I must stand on my own weight, then launch into the seat, hoping I've judged the proper trajectory. Dan's low car does not help the situation. It's bright red, hard to miss. It is new since his divorce.

The radio blares when he turns the key—rock 'n' roll. I got used to silence on the islands, and that's what I like now, the sound of living things going about their living. But it's his car and he finally turns down the volume, telling us the latest about his children, who seem to be spending more time outside school than in.

Dan drops us both off at the entrance to the diner. He parks the car and then comes to wheel me inside. Rosalie performs what she calls her "soft shoe," the shuffle-step-step that is her gait. We make our way like a misfit parade to a table. I'd like to sit in a booth, but the logistics seem insurmountable.

I order the saltiest thing I can think of, lox, or as they call it here, smoked salmon, and Rosalie orders tongue, which I think tastes like shoe leather. Dan gets a corned beef sandwich. Rosalie has passed on her messy eating habits: While Dan's still chewing he takes a bite of pickle. I watch the juice run down the corner of his mouth like water from a hole in a cliff face. He says nothing while he eats, makes no attempt at conversation the way he did in the car. I take a couple of bites of my fish, but his eating has put me off mine.

When he is done, he hits his chest twice with his fist as if to knock the food farther into his stomach or dislodge a gas bubble. Then he crumples his napkin and throws it on his plate amid the bits of crust and beef. It still seems a shame to waste food, even though I know we live in a time and place of plenty.

Rosalie, too, has turned quiet, like she always does when we take this trip, like she does when she's dreading something. I, on the other hand, am happy. Happy to be out of the Chelonia, happy to eat sodium, happy to visit Ainslie.

We visit Clarence's grave first. I stay in the car, and Dan helps Rosalie to the gravesite. I watch as they pick up rocks and place them on the tombstone, bow their heads for a prayer. The sun has gone behind a cloud and the wind is picking up the leaves.

Dan comes back to the car, giving Rosalie her space. When he gets in, the car bounces. "Cold out there," he says, blowing on his hands. "Listen, Fanny, I have something serious to discuss with you."

I straighten up. He attempts to turn so he can see me, but there's not much room between his belly and the steering wheel.

"It's about, well, it's about what no one wants to discuss, mortality."

"I'd rather discuss it than experience it," I say.

He laughs. Though he said he is cold, he is sweating profusely, round dark circles appearing on his short-sleeved shirt under his arms.

"It's about the burial plot."

"Oh," I say. I'm caught up short.

"You'll have to choose," he says. "Ainslie's not in the Jewish section, so if you want to be buried Jewish—"

"I bought the plot next to him," I say. "It's there in the papers."

"I know," Dan says. "I just thought you might want to think about it. It bothers Mom, thinking of you with the Gentiles."

"So now I have to worry about your mother's eternal rest?"

Dan holds his hands up in a gesture of retreat. "It's your choice. I'm just giving you the options. You can think about it."

I look down. There's an age spot on my thumb. How long has it been there?

*

Dan wheels me to Ainslie's grave. He stands a discreet distance away so I can converse with Ainslie's headstone. Of course, I don't believe

I need to be here to speak to him, and I suspect that I'm just talking to myself anyway, but I do feel closer to him here, where there are few buildings. It's like we're back on the islands.

I tell Ainslie what Dan said about the religious burial. I tell him I wish he were here to ask his opinion. Then I smile because I know that I would never have to ask. He would give it, asked or not.

I look around at the willow trees, the combed grass. I am always grateful to be out of doors, but today something makes me feel lonely, like the only blade of grass in a clover field. I refuse to feel pity for myself, and I try to straighten up in my chair the best I can with this humped back.

Then I tell Ainslie that Rosalie is being honored for her war work. I tell him how unfair it is that our story goes untold while hers gets inflated. Ainslie tells me in my head (not really, I'm not that divorced from reality) that the negativity I feel is jealousy, and that I need to get over it. It was part of the deal, this secrecy. Still, I wish he were here to commiserate. He was always so good at validating whatever emotion I needed corroborated. And then there is nothing more to tell him unless I start to relate the gossip from the Chelonia, which bores even me. I tell him I love him and I'll be with him eventually, though I don't really believe there is any kind of afterlife. I wave at Dan, and he comes over.

"All set?"

I nod. He bends down, not without difficulty, picks up a rock, and puts it on Ainslie's tombstone. In contrast to the Jewish section, it is the only rock sitting atop all the marble, though there are plenty of wilted flowers. The rock looks a little like a tortoise, swaybacked.

"Want a rock?" he asks.

"I'll share yours," I say.

He stands up and turns to me. "Ainslie would have loved this spot."

I nod, though I think that Ainslie would rather be alive than buried anywhere. Wouldn't we all?

*

I used to be so busy, not a moment to stop and rest. And now it is moments of activity that punctuate my sedentariness. I have swimming for physical therapy two times a week. It is odd to think that I have a sensual life again after so many years of emptiness. It may seem strange, too, for a woman my age to experience physical pleasure, but I am not dead, yet. Patricia comes to my room and lays me out on my bed. I'm embarrassed when she removes my clothes, and think it's ridiculous when she puts me in a black swimsuit. My breasts have never been much to look at, but between my crooked back and gravity, they seem to be heading to the grave faster than the rest of me.

Then Patricia wheels me to the pool. I love the heat and the smell of chlorine. It's usually quiet in there; only the sound of therapists whispering instruction and limbs moving through water. She straps me into the harness and then winches me down. I feel the water rise to meet me. It's cool and silky. She unstraps me and holds me under my arms like I'm a child, but even with that point of contact I can feel the water loosen my limbs. My legs begin to kick with muscle memory. They're free in the water. For a minute, I can pretend that I'm back in the islands, that it's ocean tide lapping at me, not the splashes created by other residents.

Sometimes Rosalie and I attend the morning lecture in the atrium. Today there is a woman from the San Francisco Opera, talking to us about *Don Giovanni*. I enjoy these lectures, most of the time. I like to see the slide shows of African safaris, take a virtual tour of the Hermitage, watch a second-rate magic show. It passes the time. Rosalie and I sit together, giggling and making trouble like schoolgirls. Once, the attendant shushed us, which set me into a laughing fit so strong they had to wheel me back to my room to calm me down.

This woman is a singer, part of the opera's Merola program. She is young and thin. How can anyone sing opera so young, so thin? How does she know about real love? How can that small rib cage fill an auditorium?

She speaks about breath control. I remember seeing this opera, with Ainslie, in Golden Gate Park one summer night. He took off his jacket and put it around my shoulders, and though he finished the entire flask of gin he'd brought to the picnic, eating little as usual, he seemed sober, listening to the music attentively and humming it on the way home.

I listen now not to the music but to the silence before the young woman presses the button on the record player. The quiet, when the

music ends, is dirty with the rustling of old people's wheezing, the click-
ing of the phonograph needle bobbing against the label, the distant
kitchen clanging. It sounds like the islands then, so silent, more silent
than you can even imagine, and yet so noisy.

*

They don't send a limo; they send a young person to pick us up in her
enormous car, which is covered in bits of food and children's books.

"Sorry," she says. "I drive the carpool and the kids are slobs. I'm
Susie." I shake her hand; my bones rub together painfully. "Are you
Rosalie Fischer?"

"No, I'm the friend," I say. Susie's hair is tremendously long, down
past her waist, where it grows straggly like a passionflower vine. She
is dressed in a wood sprite's flouncy skirt and a ruffled blouse with no
sleeves.

She looks disappointed. "You look so much like my aunt," she says.
"You are Mrs. . . . ?"

"Just call me Frances, please."

"Okay, how are we going to do this?" She opens the front passenger
door, at which I am surprised. I assumed I'd be riding in the back of the
beast, which is elongated like a hearse. I decide to get in quickly before
Rosalie arrives. Rosalie can take her turn on the way home. I want to see
the world for once, instead of the back of Rosalie's head.

I heave myself onto my feet, but I've done it too quickly and my legs
wobble. Susie grabs me at my armpits. She is surprisingly strong for a
wood sprite, and she lowers me into the seat carefully.

My fancy dress has ridden up, exposing the tops of my knee stockings
and my old-lady thighs. Impossible to smooth it down. I place my jacket
on top.

I would like to see the look on Rosalie's face when she realizes she's
sitting in the back with the compost. But I can't turn around. After
Susie greets her and gets her situated, I say, "You can have the front on
the way home."

"Thank you, Frances," she says, using my full name so I know she's
mad at me.

The ceremony is to be held in the synagogue's ballroom. When Rosalie and I enter, all the women stand to clap. I am handed a glass of wine, which I drink, and then another, which I also drink, not wanting to be rude, and then the afternoon becomes like a blanket of fog settling in a valley. I'm vaguely aware of Rosalie receiving a medal, of her posing for pictures.

Susie sits down next to me and offers me a piece of cake. Why not? I take a huge forkful, much larger than my mouth, and laugh when it doesn't fit.

"What did you do during the war, Frances?" Susie asks. I want to tell her what I did, what Ainslie and I did, how I played my own small but significant role, but I have been sworn to secrecy. Still, I wonder, what would be the harm now, when so many are gone? How long until a secret is no longer a secret?

"Oh, I was a secretary," I say.

"It must have been a fascinating time." Susie helps herself to a piece of my cake, and instead of thinking she has bad manners, I enjoy the intimacy. Is this what having a daughter would have been like?

"That's one word for it."

Susie laughs. "You and Rosalie have obviously been friends for a long time. You share the same emanations."

I have no idea what this is. "Since we were eight years old."

Susie shakes her head in mock disbelief. "You must have some stories to tell."

"You have no idea," I say.

*

Later, in bed, a slight headache from the wine, I think about Rosalie. How many nights have I done so, my own version of counting sheep? So we share the same emanations. How could we not, after all these years together? It's always ever been me and Rosalie, so it should not surprise me that here at the end we are the two left standing, fighting our own biology. Spouse, sibling, these connections seem more tenuous than whatever emanation holds Rosalie and me together.

Friendship between women is complicated. We can be kind to the world, but where other women are concerned, we often show our basest selves. We who have grown up in an age such as mine—where women start to wear trousers and leave off girdles, where we can have careers and be perfectly productive members of society without marrying or bearing children—have no excuse for our lack of sorority.

As I lie here—I sleep very little—my thoughts turn to my stories. Rosalie's have been told and live on through her children, her awards and deeds (because I will admit, now that I am being honest, now that I am being charitable, she has done some good with the enormous amount of money Clarence made). But I have no children, no visible contributions. I will tell my story, then, official secrecy act be damned, and then something I've done will live on, and I can move on from this world.

CHAPTER TWO

I was born in Duluth, Minnesota, the second in a family of four girls and three boys. Non-farming families did not generally have so many children, but my parents were fertile. I suspect my mother got pregnant as a way of keeping my father at bay for eleven months out of the year. They hated each other. The marriage was semi-arranged in Poland; they had only met twice before their wedding. A hasty weekend and then Papa left for America. He was there a year before he saved enough to send for her and the baby, my brother Joe, the only one of us born in the old country.

Mama took in sewing and washing. Papa stocked the shelves in a grocery store. I never heard a kind word between them. But they did encourage me to read, and made my brother take me often to the newly built public library, which is where I met Rosalie Mendler. She had beautiful tight curly hair, light brown with golden highlights. She was a small girl, and she had a funny sort of cross-eyed look that glasses later straightened out.

My brother Joe was eager to get back—he had arranged to play a game of stickball. "Let's go, Fanny," he said. "Don't dance around looking for the perfect book. Just pick one you like the cover of."

I ignored him, smiling shyly at the little girl, whose mother was sitting primly at a table nearby, a stack of books in front of her like a club sandwich she was going to eat. Rosalie pretended not to notice me, but I saw she picked the same book out twice.

"I read that last year," I said. "It's for second graders."

"I'm in third," she said, putting it back on the shelf.

"Me too," I said. That exhausted the conversation. I browsed the shelves some more. "Here," I handed her *Robinson Crusoe*. "This is a good one for third grade."

"I read it," she said. "Have you read *Gulliver's Travels?*"

"Uh-huh," I lied. I had checked it out of the library but found it impenetrable.

"I couldn't get through it," Rosalie told me. "It was soooo boring."

I wanted to admit my lie, but now I couldn't see a way to do so. I had wanted to befriend this bookish girl, but I had gone about it the wrong way. I searched for something to say.

"I liked *Little Women*," I said. "I like books about girls."

"It was so sad, in the end," Rosalie said. "I just about bawled my eyes out."

"My little sister told me I was being a baby," I said. It felt so good to meet a kindred soul.

"One should never apologize for sentiment," Rosalie said, obviously quoting her mother, who looked up from her book and put her finger to her mouth to shush us. We giggled.

Joe said, "Fanny, we're leaving. Now."

I took the first book that was in reach as Joe pulled me toward the checkout desk. I turned to wave, but Rosalie already had her head in a book. When I got home, I realized I'd selected a mystery book for boys.

I made sure to run into her again, and soon Rosalie became my constant companion. I was over at her house every day after school. We'd play pretend, or read, or sit with her mother while she brushed our hair. Rosalie's family was from Germany, and her house was filled with books. I often stayed to supper and her mother served meat, real meat, not just chicken. Rosalie and her little brother and I got to eat all we wanted, but Mr. and Mrs. Mendler didn't put any on their plates. When cleaning up, though, I noticed Rosalie's mother ate any leftovers while she stood in front of the sink.

Rosalie's house was a sharp contrast to mine. At the Mendlers' the radio could be heard, while at my house someone was always yelling or crying. Rosalie got her own room, with a sign saying KEEP OUT OR

ELSE, whereas all the children were piled into the one bedroom in our apartment, my parents on the sofa in the living room with the newest baby. Our house was always damp with hanging laundry, though it was nice and warm in the winter—Mama had to keep the iron going.

Rosalie's and my parents met just once, a disaster. My parents spoke only the most rudimentary English. Plus they were dowdy and round like dumplings, and I was embarrassed of them. My father walked with a limp whose origins he refused to relate. Rosalie's family was thin and tall, and it was only later that I understood the irony that my family's discontent hid an undercurrent of, if not happiness, then satisfaction. Rosalie's, meanwhile, was comprised of a thin veneer of contentment covering up a lake of disappointment and deception. Her mother's face was lined, as if she had permanently just received bad news. When she smiled, her teeth showed, top and bottom touching each other, as if creating a white wall against intruders.

*

When I turned fourteen, my parents informed me that I'd had enough school, and that I would go to work. I was devastated. I loved school. Rosalie helped convince my parents that I should at least attend secretarial school, and it was there I went for the first day of what should have been my high-school career, toting paper for the typewriter and a steno pad.

Secretarial school had me yawning by lunchtime of the first day. We sat in rows in front of typewriters and practiced putting our hands on the right keys. Then we pressed a succession of vowels, AAAA, EEEE, IIII, etc. Consonants would have to wait for tomorrow. Steno class was equally as uninspiring. First we were to practice handwriting. Mine had always been abominable, no matter how steady I held my hand. The teacher, an overweight man whose pants were held up by suspenders, strode up and down the rows, clucking or cooing at our lines of letters.

Class was dismissed at noon, so I walked across town to Rosalie's high school to wait for her. The unimaginatively named Central High School was an enormous building that looked more like a bank or a government office. I opened one of the big doors and went inside in search of a bubbler, and just then a bell rang. Students streamed out of classrooms, a storm moving in from Lake Superior, fast and windy. I got swept up in the crowd and found myself in a classroom. Before I could leave, the teacher closed the door and began to take roll.

The perspiration under my arms began to spread as the teacher moved down the list. The names were a mix of ethnicities, German and Hungarian and Finnish and Irish and Polish, and she got to the end of the list and asked, "Is there anyone whose name I haven't called?"

Five or six students raised their hands.

"Please come up and add your name to the roster," the teacher said. So I stood up with the rest of them and added "Frances Frankowski" in my spindly handwriting. Then I sat back down and took out my steno pad. Everyone else had a composition notebook.

The teacher wrote her name on the board: Mrs. Hanson. I copied it down in the book. Then she added "History." I copied that down too.

"What is history?" she wrote under her name. Then she turned around. "Well, class?" she asked. "What is history?"

A boy in front raised his hand. Mrs. Hanson nodded at him. "Say your name first," she said.

His voice broke as he spoke, but Mrs. Hanson suppressed the giggles with a look. "Johnson, Peter. History is what happened in the past."

Mrs. Hanson nodded, considering the answer. "Good. What's the oldest history book you can think of?"

A small blond girl raised her hand, sitting on the edge of her chair. "Joanne Macintosh," she said. "I mean, Macintosh, Joanne. The Bible." I happened to know that there were books written by Greeks and Romans much older than the Bible, but I didn't correct her.

"Okay," said Mrs. Hanson. "How do you know it's so old?"

"Because God wrote it," she said proudly.

"I see," said Mrs. Hanson. The words hung in the air for a minute. Then a girl I recognized from the neighborhood raised her hand.

"Actually, wasn't it written by Moses? And then the other books in it were written by the people who have their names on them?"

"Very good. What was your name?"

"Sohnen, Jessica."

"Miss?" A boy who was too tall for his desk raised his hand and spoke at the same time. "I don't want to be impudent, but isn't there separation of church and state?"

There was a murmur of agreement from the class.

"Your name," Mrs. Hanson demanded.

"Järvi? Lars?" He spoke tentatively.

Mrs. Hanson considered. I tried to decide how old she was. Young, maybe in her twenties. Did she have children, I wondered. She wore a simple gold band around her ring finger, but no other jewelry.

"You're right to bring it up," she said, and I could see Lars sag with relief. "But we're talking about the Bible as a popular book, not as a religious treatise. Let's go back to Jessica. Where does the Bible start?"

"Sohnen, Jessica," she said again. The class laughed and Jessica's face grew red. "Genesis," she added in a small voice. "In the beginning."

"Ah," Mrs. Hanson said, as though this were news to her. "What day, according to the Bible as a text, was man created?"

Two dozen hands went up. Mrs. Hanson called on someone in the back row. "The sixth," he said, not providing his name.

Mrs. Hanson said nothing. "I'm waiting for you to draw a conclusion," she said, after a while. "That's what this class will be about, your conclusions rather than mine."

The class was silent. I understood what she wanted to say. I had already come across this paradox in synagogue, and I began to think maybe I could express it. Before I could convince myself not to do it, my hand shot up.

"Frankowski, Frances, but everyone calls me Fanny," I said. "Since the Bible is writing about a time before there was man, man obviously was not present to see creation. So how does man know about it?" Now that I was on a roll, I doubt much but an earthquake would have stopped me. "And there are books that are older than the Bible."

"Good, Fanny." Mrs. Hanson turned to the blackboard and I flushed with pride. She wrote "perspective" on the board. Then she wrote, "History is the oral or written interpretation of the past." She underlined *interpretation*. I wrote this down. "Very good. We'll be studying the Crusades first." She wrote "Crusades, 1095–1291" on the board. "Now who can tell me," she perched on the edge of her desk, "why the Crusades happened?"

I wished that stenography class had actually covered stenography because I wrote furiously to keep up with Mrs. Hanson's bombardment of facts. When the bell rang I had filled three pages with notes. I followed Jessica out the door and down the hall. She went into a classroom and I sat down next to her. "We have biology together too?" she asked me.

"I suppose we do!" I said, enthusiastically.

But my career as a hidden high-school student hit a roadblock. Mr. Spark read the roll, and told everyone who wasn't on it to go straight to the office to register. I followed the other five students out the door and around the corner to the main office, where, in order to not make waves, I registered as a student.

Rosalie was delighted when she found out. She told me that I shouldn't feel guilty about deceiving my parents. I could go to secretarial school just often enough to be counted. I could buy a book and practice on my own. I could use Rosalie's family's typewriter to practice. And then I would receive my certificate *and* my high-school diploma. It would be difficult but she would help me. I threw my arms around her, smelling her hair—wood smoke and fried potatoes.

*

My parents didn't find out about high school until the following year. I had passed my secretarial exam, but told them I had one more year to earn an extra certificate. Then came a letter to the house from Central High containing my report card (all As, I'll have you know) and I wasn't home to intercept it. Though my parents were barely literate and spoke little English, they knew enough to figure out my ruse.

My mother sat at the table crying and sewing. She sewed constantly, while cooking, bathing the younger kids; it would not have surprised me to wake in the middle of the night to find her sewing in her sleep. My father paced the floor. Pretty soon the people below us would hit the ceiling with a broom.

"How could you do this to us, lie?" my father asked.

I said nothing.

"Fifteen years we've taken care of you," he continued. "Now it's your turn to help."

I looked around the small room. From the kitchen I could see into the living room where my parents slept and into the girls' bedroom. I could smell the ache of cabbage on the stove. The wood floor, swept too many times, strained to hold our furniture. I knew then that I would not be living in this apartment much longer. I thought that I was moving on to bigger and better things. I know now that I was just moving on.

*

Rosalie hid me at her house in plain sight for three days before her mother realized it. Rosalie ruled the roost chez Mendler. Her parents deferred to her in almost all cases, catering to her whims. Sometimes she tested how far she could push them, demanding money for sweets or forcing her mother to make an additional dinner when the one she prepared was not to Rosalie's liking. It was curious, because to everyone else Rosalie was respectful and kind, sycophantic; my parents thought she was snobby. I found this side of her distasteful, but there were things she didn't always like about me, she said, one night in a bull session, where we critiqued each other's shortcomings. I was too judgmental, too rigid. I never dreamed, never let myself be a silly young woman. So I let her spoiledness be the thing I didn't like about her. And the fact that she was always late to whatever we'd planned.

When I showed up for dinner for the third straight evening, Mrs. Mendler finally caught on. I explained why I couldn't go home.

"Dear, you need to respect your parents' wishes."

"I can't be a secretary," I said. "I want to go to school."

"There are lots of things I want," Mrs. Mendler said. "But there's a thing called duty and we need to respect it."

She smiled her white wall smile. Her tone was so stern, so matter-of-fact, that I returned home, quit school, got a job, and did what I was supposed to do.

*

I went to work for a business at the local port, answering correspondence and fetching coffee. The boss was impressed with my typing
skills, I think. In any event he stood over me quite frequently while I
typed. It couldn't have been to look down my blouse, I don't think. I
was always buttoned up, and often wore a cravat, which was the style.

I saw Rosalie mostly on weekends, but once, on a day with no school,
Rosalie came to meet me for lunch, and we ate on a bench by the port,
sticky buns that she had purchased on the way over, still warm from the
oven.

I stayed at her house most Saturday nights. My parents were
relieved—one less mouth to feed one night a week. Rosalie was in love
with a boy from school, Melvin Shumwitz, a basketball star and one of
the only Jewish boys in her class, who did not notice the adoration of
the brainy girl in braids whose chest was still flat. On Saturday evenings,
Rosalie and I would read the women's magazines, especially the advice
columns. "My wife don't cook good, what should I do?" "How do I get
a man to notice me?" "Would you marry a girl with one leg shorter than
the other?"

Rosalie always answered the questions by supposing that she and
Melvin were an old married couple. "Well, when Melvin proposed to
me, he was on one knee at the carousel in Central Park."

"In New York?" I asked, incredulous.

"Yes, in New York, where we both live. I am a famous Broadway
actress and Melvin is . . . a banker."

"Oh a banker. With his marks." I scoffed.

"Yes, a banker." Rosalie was adamant.

After she drifted off to sleep, I pored over her schoolbooks, reading
the notes she took in class with her meticulous handwriting and copying down the assignments. I read the books she read, Herodotus and
Dreiser, Defoe and Eliot, staying up late into the night, tilting the lamp
away from her side of the bed so she wouldn't notice. But one night,
after a couple of months, I saw that there were two copies of each of her
schoolbooks, the second with the dog-eared corners of secondhand use,
and I understood that one set was mine, to read alongside her.

*

Sometimes, on Sundays, a storm gathered around Rosalie. She would wake up with her usual good humor, but directly after breakfast, often with crumbs still hovering around her mouth, she would begin to slink away emotionally, until noon brought with it a blank stare. On these days, her parents and I left at lunchtime, Rosalie's melancholy unspoken of. Rosalie's only chore in her house, apparently, was to deliver the rent to the landlord every week. I never saw her do a dish, or sweep, or hang laundry. When her parents left, she'd tell me I had to go, shooing me out the door. Occasionally they took me with them for tea or a walk. More frequently, I went home to help my mother.

One Sunday morning, Rosalie shook me awake and asked me to pretend to go home when her parents left. "But come back right away, all right?"

"All right," I said, too drowsy to question her.

We ate breakfast as usual. Rosalie picked at her toast and barely sipped her tea, fidgeting around in her seat like she had to use the toilet. Her parents took no notice, reading the Sunday paper, wordlessly exchanging sections. Her little brother scanned the funny pages, laughing at the stupid jokes.

"Well," her father said finally. "It's a nice day. Let's go look at the ships. Fanny? You up for it? Rosalie, you'll wait for the landlord."

"I don't think so," I said. "It's a busy week and my mother could use some help with the ironing." It occurred to me how odd their family was, the parents and brother going out, never asking Rosalie if she wanted to come, almost like Rosalie had to stay home as punishment for some transgression. I tried to meet her father's eyes, but he turned back to the paper.

"Everybody up and ready," her mother said brightly. Had I never noticed the false levity in her voice, a stage actress playing the role of mother? "Getting late."

Rosalie closed the door behind us and I accompanied her family to the end of Lake Street. I said goodbye and turned my customary right up the hill. But once they were out of sight, I doubled back, running to Rosalie's house.

She was pacing the first floor, wringing her hands like Lady Macbeth. She was so agitated that I didn't want to upset her by asking what was wrong. When there was a knock on the door, she jumped.

"Here," she handed me an envelope, whispering. "Open the door just wide enough to give it to him. Pretend you don't speak English."

Even back then I was motivated by the excitement of espionage, and I should have learned that it is inevitably disappointing. I opened the door a bit. Their landlord was an Irishman with thick hands. He rocked back and forth on the balls of his feet. Had he ever washed his hair? At his side rested a large well-worn leather case.

"Where is she, then?" he asked.

I answered in my best thick Polish accent. "Out," I said. "Family is out. Rent here. Here, rent."

He looked disappointed, took the envelope, and went on his way. "Stupid Polack," I heard him say. "Dumb Mick," I thought back.

I closed the door and watched as Rosalie's face transformed into a smile. "Thanks, Fan. You're a real pal."

"Always," I said, not sure what I'd done.

I find it hard to believe now that I didn't understand what was happening. But I was so sheltered and so young. Most of my waking thoughts were about myself. Would I grow curvy? Would I have the courage to quit my job and run away from home? What should I do with my limp, drab hair?

When I thought about Rosalie—which I did, in my defense, often—I decided she was simply irrational and showed signs of nervous behavior that she would most likely outgrow.

*

Though we all anxiously awaited signs of maturity, Rosalie had a desire to start menstruation that bordered on the obsessive. I was scared as well as excited—from what I'd heard at school, the monthly was unpleasant at best, messy and uncomfortable. I worried it would hurt, that it would start while I was at work and I couldn't do anything about it. But Rosalie scanned her underwear each day for signs, took every upset stomach as a precursor to cramps. When the pain would go away, she'd burst into tears, so forlorn that nothing I could say would calm her.

Right after my fifteenth birthday, it finally happened to me, a bright spot of blood when I got home from work. When I whispered to my mother what had happened (I didn't know the Yiddish or the Polish; I told her I was passing blood), she knocked on my forehead three times. Then she wordlessly showed me how to fasten the bulky pads to the belt around my waist, and I felt like a child with a diaper, the sensation of having liquid seep out of me strange.

When I told her that weekend, Rosalie began to cry. I was angry that she was so selfish. Couldn't she celebrate my womanhood with me? But she refused to speak, indeed refused to come out of her room, so I ate dinner with her parents without her, and then went home to spend the night without my books.

I considered not going to see her the following weekend. I was angry with her and wanted her to know it. But the lure of the books was strong—I wanted to hear what her teacher said in the lecture about the Industrial Revolution, and I wanted to finish *Pride and Prejudice*.

So I arrived at her house at our typical time, and Rosalie received me like nothing had changed. We ate, then listened to a radio program, though Rosalie was silent. Then she went to bed while I stayed up reading her notebooks.

I thought she'd gone to sleep but her voice emerged, reed-thin, from between the covers. "Fanny? What's it like?"

I closed the notebook. I knew exactly what she was talking about. I tried to explain to her how it drips out over several days, describing the diaper padding to her.

She nodded at me, sitting up. "But is it different?"

"Different than what?"

"I mean . . ." I heard the sharp intake of her breath. "Are you different?"

"Is that what you're worried about?" I asked. "I'm the same me. I'm your friend, always, Rosie." She hated when I called her that.

She waved her hand at me like I was a silly fly. "It's not that. I want to be different. I want to be . . ." She let the thought trail off.

"We will be," I said. "We'll grow bosoms and get boys and get married and everything."

Rosalie smiled sadly, as though she meant the opposite.

*

Rosalie was not far behind me in becoming a woman. It may have been the only thing I ever beat her to, and I can't say that this didn't give me a small satisfaction, which I took pains to conceal but probably didn't do a very good job of. When she was finally "visited," as we used to say, she met me at the door bright-eyed with happiness, and we sang until her mother banged on the door and told us to keep it down. I didn't understand her elation—so far it had been the curse its name promised to be—but her excitement was infectious.

The next morning, Rosalie woke early, and I heard voices from downstairs. She, her mother, and her father were having a heated discussion. Occasionally her father's voice would emerge from the floorboards, loud and angry, but I could not make out the words, and Rosalie's mother hushed him.

When I came downstairs, Rosalie was in her Sunday funk, and I understood that I was to leave directly after breakfast.

"Would you like to come with us?" her mother asked. "Rosalie has to wait for the landlord."

"No, thank you, Mrs. Mendler." Rosalie avoided my gaze.

She walked me to the door. "Want me to stay and do it?" I asked.

"No," she said, her tone so icy that I let it drop. I thought she was sore that her family left her, and I could see how dealing with that man would put anyone in a bad mood, but Rosalie was always so dramatic that I assumed she was exaggerating her displeasure for effect.

The following Saturday, I found that Rosalie's mood was still sour. She'd stayed in bed most of the week, with a vague complaint of a headache and stomach pains. Her mother called the doctor (a luxury in which no one in my family had ever indulged) but he was unconcerned.

I sat by her side. Her mother said she'd barely spoken or eaten in the last few days. "Rosie," I said, "you have to tell me what's wrong."

"I can't," she said hoarsely. "There aren't words for it." I was hurt that she wouldn't confide in me.

I nursed her that night, sitting on the bed and reading to her from *The Castle of Otranto*. Every so often she sighed, and once she got up to use the toilet and drink some juice.

When she woke up the next day, Rosalie was close to her normal, if morose, Sunday self. She came downstairs in her dressing gown for breakfast, and I completed her English assignment for her (a paragraph on symbols of nature in Dickens).

"I'll go along home then," I said, after the breakfast chatter had died down.

"You needn't go yet," said Rosalie's mother, looking up at the wall clock.

"I have things to do," I replied, "since Rosalie is feeling better."

Rosalie heard the chill in my voice. She walked me to the front door, where a cold wind forced its way between the door and the jamb.

"You really are my best friend," she said. "And no one could ever have a better one. Just remember that you've always been a perfect friend to me."

"You sound like you're dying," I said, anxious to lighten her tone. She hugged me. The display of affection made me blush.

"We're all dying," she said. "Every moment."

"Thanks for the reminder," I said. And then I walked down her front steps in ignorance.

*

Part of my worry was that I wasn't good enough for Rosalie's family. After all, we were Eastern European immigrants. The Germans who arrived earlier were our superiors in every way, a sentiment the Germans and we both shared. They were educated, wealthy. They spoke impeccable English, even those who just came over, and often worked the same jobs they had held back in Germany—professor, banker, lawyer, pharmacist. Even the ones who practiced a trade had their own shops and often hired others to work in them.

We Poles, on the other hand, were peasants. Most of my parents' generation couldn't read. Someone had to teach us to sign our own names. And we barely scraped by, taking in washing, like my mother, or serving as maids. The men worked in the factories or on the docks, or, like my father, stacking stock, manual labor. Our English was stilted, clipped, and simplistic. And we were squat, dark people, with curly hair and brown eyes (I was the anomalous straight-haired giant). The Germans were tall, often blond, and held themselves erect, lithe like the Westerners they were. Yes, they deigned to help us, monetarily, in the name of our shared religion, but they were the beneficent ones, we the supplicants.

Rosalie's family never treated me that way, kindly looking the other way when my table manners were not up to snuff, or I encountered a new vegetable that I approached in the wrong way (artichokes come to mind—at some point I'll be able to tell without blushing how I tried to eat the whole leaf, struggling with my knife and fork). But I worried that their goodwill had an end date, when they would no longer tolerate their Tarzan experiment and return me to my natural habitat to be raised by apes.

Naturally, I placed Rosalie's family on a pedestal. They were wealthier than we were, better-dressed, better-spoken, much better-fed. They placed a premium on education; they encouraged reading. Around the table, they had active political discussions, opinions on the Zionist movement's president, David Wolffsohn, and whether or not Germany should intervene in the revolution in Turkey. It was expected that their children attend university, whereas no amount of begging could persuade my parents to let me reenroll in high school. I felt sometimes that I had been switched as a baby at the hospital, that somewhere my *real* parents were stuck with a short, frizzy-haired child, wondering where on earth she had come from.

I didn't understand until later how important appearances were to the Mendlers, that even in front of me they had to pretend. Their wealth was gold foil, shabby wood underneath. They took off their shoes indoors not to avoid dirtying the carpet but to get more wear out of them. Mr. and Mrs. Mendler didn't eat meat because there wasn't enough money to buy a portion for everyone. The furnishings Mrs. Mendler was divesting of were not discarded for reasons of style but rather sold for cash.

I say all this to explain, and perhaps to excuse, my lack of action. It simply didn't occur to me that something bad could happen to Rosalie.

*

Unlike me, Rosalie did change when she became a woman. She grew calmer and sadder somehow, her flights of drama subdued and rehearsed. I wondered if she was finally growing up. In January she had finals to take, and I'll admit now what I wouldn't then—that I was too jealous to help her study. Plus, it was a busy time at work, and I went in on occasional Sundays to help with the books for taxes, so we let a few weeks slip by with minimal contact.

That spring, Rosalie grew breasts, her chest swelling in a way that looked painful. Mine remained the meager acorns they would resemble my entire life. Her hips filled out, she grew soft in her arms and legs, her face nestled in a pillow of chubbiness.

One Sunday morning, her skirt no longer fit around her waist.

I helped her pin it closed. "You'll need to start reducing," I said. "Unless you're getting ready to grow."

The following week one of my brothers became a bar mitzvah. No one in Rosalie's set was religious enough to follow this custom, but in our house it was an important rite of passage. My mother had been baking all week for the small reception in the synagogue after the ceremony. We would serve wine. It was thanks to my salary that my parents had enough money to furnish this small luxury, and I was a bit resentful that I had worked so hard for a sibling's celebration, when no celebration was ever held in my honor.

I invited Rosalie to the service, but she claimed to have nothing to wear. "I guess I'm getting ready for that growth spurt," she said. Her mother was going to take her shopping that weekend. I was not unhappy that she wouldn't be there. She had grown so distant, so sad, that I constantly had to cheer her up, which was exhausting. She never wanted to do anything; we never laughed anymore, just studied in near silence. I assumed at the time that she didn't want to come to our poor, conservative place of worship, so different from her own. I wonder now if she declined because there wasn't enough money for a gift.

My brother's ceremony was fine, the reception elegant by my family's standards. Several people came up to me and said how proud my mother was that I was able to contribute to the family's savings. I was a good girl, they said.

One yenta was going to look around for a suitable boy for me to marry. The idea made my fingers go cold, that I would be stuck in Duluth, married to some boy from my parents' village in Poland. It must have registered on my face, because the woman put a hand on my arm and laughed. "Not for a while yet, dear. Not until you're eighteen."

Eighteen. It wasn't so far away.

*

Rosalie's mother answered the door. "Rosalie's up in bed," she said. "She's sick. Very weak. She won't be able to see you today."

"That's all right," I said. "I'm sure she won't get me sick." I took a step forward to brush past her. She blocked me. I hadn't realized how imposing Rosalie's mother could be.

"You've been a very good friend to Rosalie," she said. "But she needs a bit of space now. Perhaps you could postpone your visits for a month or so? Just until she gets her strength back. And then it will be like old times between you. Just think, almost summer. You'll be able to play all day, the way girls do."

Had she forgotten that my life didn't have summer? I worked all year round, a day off each for Christmas, New Year's, and Good Friday. On winter Fridays, I arrived home after Shabbat had begun, to a plate that had cooled since sundown. I no longer played like a little girl. And it had been quite some time since Rosalie had either.

Her mother wore a faraway look, imagining a scene taking place beyond me in the little square of garden over my shoulder. "It's what Rosalie wants," her mother said.

After that I stopped going to Rosalie's house, certain that my suspicions that I was too low-class for her family were the reason. No wonder they didn't want their daughter to spend time with the likes of me.

We went a long time without seeing each other. My mother was happy for the help around the house, but I missed Rosalie terribly. I felt as if I had been rejected by a suitor, and I cried in my shared bed, sobbing quietly so as not to wake my sisters. I started again on my small library of gift books I'd received from Rosalie's family over the years. I picked up *Little Women* and made it only as far as when Jo, out of anger, almost lets Amy drown when she falls through the ice and then is deeply regretful, when I realized I had to contact Rosalie.

*

I woke early and stopped by Central High School, waiting until I saw someone Rosalie and I knew, a girl named Shilah.

"Hello, Fanny!" she said. "Whatever happened to you? Someone said you joined the merchant marines, but I said, 'Girls can't join the marines.' You didn't join the marines, did you?"

"No," I said, reluctant to tell her that I'd begun to work for a living. "I transferred to a high school for gifted girls."

"Oh," Shilah said, unimpressed.

"Can you do me a favor and give this letter to Rosalie? It came to my house by mistake."

Shilah accepted the unlikely story unquestioningly. "Can I tell everyone that you joined the circus?"

"You can tell anyone whatever you like, just don't forget. I think it might be from her beau," I lied. I wished I could take it back. What if Shilah opened it, her curiosity piqued?

What did the letter say? I no longer remember, but I'm sure, knowing me at the time, that it was long, overwritten, and flowery, full of youthful longing and pledging several things. I'm sure Rosalie disposed of the letter years ago. Yet I kept every letter she ever sent to me and have them still in a box under my bed.

All day at work I wondered if Rosalie had received the letter, if she would respond. A chasm had grown between us; she'd had some sort of experience I couldn't understand. I feared she'd leave me behind.

The next day I received a letter in the morning delivery, which made the senior secretary cluck, "We are not a post office, Miss Frankowski." It read:

Dearest Fanny,

I was so glad to get your letter. I feared that you'd been put off our friendship after the last few months.
  Know that you are my truest friend, and that you have always acted selflessly. I will cherish that, as should you, when I am no longer here.
  Adieu, mon amie. I love you with all my beating heart.

Rosalie

At the bottom, she had drawn a rose. I would have laughed at the note's histrionics if it hadn't sat oddly, like I'd eaten turned meat for lunch. What had she meant by "when I am no longer here"? Was she thinking of harming herself? I had a sudden chill that my mother described as someone walking over your grave. But what if it wasn't *my* grave but rather Rosalie's?

I strode into the front office and demanded to use the telephone. We were one of the few Duluth businesses that had one—essential for communicating with the East Coast. The head secretary, Mrs. Peck, protested—it was not for employees' use, but I insisted it was an emergency. It was only when I was holding the receiver in my hand that I realized there was no one to call. Rosalie's family didn't have a telephone, and though the neighbor had one, I would be unable to explain myself. If I called the police, I'd have similar trouble. I'd gotten a letter from a friend that said what? That we were good friends? How was I to explain its tone?

The operator came on and I asked for an invented extension, buying time. How would Rosalie do it? There was no building high enough to throw herself from. "There's no such number," the operator said.

"Yes, thank you," I said. It was unlikely that Rosalie knew how to tie a noose.

"I said, I can't connect you. Do you have the proper extension?"

"Hello, Mother," I said. "What's that? Of course, I'll come right away." The operator hung up, and I turned my face into a rictus of tragedy.

"My brother's had an accident in the mill," I said, a ruse I'd picked up from the novel I'd been reading. "I have to go home at once."

"Oh you poor dear," Mrs. Peck said dryly. The logic of me calling my house to receive emergency bad news was clearly preposterous. Plus, there was no possibility of my family having a telephone. "Is it very bad?"

"The worst," I said, and I grabbed my jacket and ran all the way to Rosalie's house.

*

I found Rosalie in the water closet, bringing up her lunch. From the look of it, she'd had something with rice. "Oh Fanny," she moaned. "I tried the aspirin, but I don't think I did it right."

"No, I don't think you did," I said, "and thank God for it. What were you thinking?"

"I can't do it anymore." She slunk back against the wall, her hair disheveled. She had bits of vomit around her mouth, and one strand of hair was twisted with it. I took a washcloth and wet it in the basin, wiping her mouth and her forehead. "I can't, Fanny."

"Can't do what?" I wiped around the toilet and flushed the sick down.

"Can't go on," she retched again, vaulting toward the toilet. Nothing came up, though she heaved several times. "Can't," she said again. She turned to face me, her eyes bright and feverish. "Let's run away, Fanny."

"What?" I said. "You're hilarious."

"We've talked about it a million times. Let's go to New York. I'll be an actress. I'll support us while you go to high school, and then you can work while I go. We can both go to university, to Barnard."

I laughed, wringing out the soiled washcloth.

"I'm serious, Fan." She grabbed my forearm, her fingers digging into the skin.

"You're scaring me," I said. "I don't know what you're talking about."

"Listen, Fanny, I've saved a little money, enough to get us there. We can do this."

"What about your parents?" I asked. "You can't leave them."

"Just watch me," she said. "They've used me up enough."

"You're being ridiculous," I said. I must have let the annoyance creep into my voice because she recoiled. I had neither looks nor education, and for Rosalie to tease me this way was cruel. It was all fine for her to pretend that she had a way out, but I was as stuck in this life as Arthur's sword of legend was in its stone, growing rustier by the year.

CHAPTER THREE

May arrived, and I hoped the changing weather would improve Rosalie's mood. Frankly, I was afraid. Between her weight gain, her suicide attempt, and her permanent melancholy, so different from her flamboyantly pouty moods before, she was a different and dangerous person. I had the sense that we both were simply going through the motions of a friendship that had burned its candle to a stub.

We resumed our weekend patterns, but there was a shift in our relationship. Rosalie held herself away from me, as if she were my tutor rather than my friend. I stopped telling her about the funny things my boss did, imitating his wide waddle and beady stare. She stopped telling me about her week at school. She adopted a listless air that I found affected, and I frequently caught her staring blankly at the wall above the desk when she was supposed to be studying.

I most likely would not have had the courage I mustered had I not been reading Kipling's *Kim*. In addition to being madly in love with India, I imagined myself an intrepid orphan. Espionage's odor was enticing (the subsequent spy-novel craze tells me I was not the only one to fall into its clutches), and I decided to investigate what I considered Rosalie's Dangerous Game.

One Sunday, when the lake refused to acquiesce to spring and was blowing a chilly wind across its surface onto the shore, I left Rosalie's parents and doubled back to her house. Rosalie answered after my first knock, as though she had been waiting in the hallway. "Fanny?" she gasped, her features bunched in confusion. "You can't be here. You have to go away."

"I'm not leaving," I said. I barged inside.

"You have to." She pushed me toward the door but I pulled away from her. She was still wearing her robe.

"You need to explain to me what's happening."

"The landlord's coming today," she said. "You can't be here." There was a pleading in her voice, a desperation that scared me. She tightened the robe's belt.

"I was here before. I saw him," I said.

"And I got in trouble for that. I know you're trying to help, but you'll just make it worse. Leave now."

"No," I said. I thought I was taking a stand.

"Please," she said.

There was a knock at the door. Rosalie shivered.

I noticed money on the front hall table. "Is that it?" I said. "Give it here." I swiped the bills and headed for the door.

There stood the same landlord I'd seen before, same unwashed hair, same pocked nose. When he saw me, he scowled. "Where is she?" he demanded.

"There's your rent," I said, holding the money in his face. "That's what you're here for."

He looked at me like I was stupid. "Fucking hell. Where is she?" I recoiled at the swear. He set down the suitcase he was holding, a worn leather trunk. "I won't be sold the illness shite again."

"She's not here," I said. "She's gone out." I couldn't risk a glance behind me.

"I don't believe you." He pushed the door open violently, and I fell back onto the floor. "Rose," he called. "Where are you, my flower?"

Rosalie was standing where I left her, as still as a rock. He turned to me. "I'll just use your little Polack friend then, shall I? Maybe she won't pull those faces."

He grabbed me by my braid and hauled me to my feet. Pain tore at my scalp. Then he put his hand on my cheek. It was callused, the nails ragged and dirty. I screamed, and that roused Rosalie from her stupor. She smiled falsely. A wall of white teeth. Her mother's smile.

"I'm right here, Mr. O'Rourke, right here."

O'Rourke dropped me like a cigarette he'd finished. I slumped to the floor, rubbing my head. I noticed now that O'Rourke walked with a limp similar to my father's, dragging his right foot as his knee wouldn't bend properly.

Rosalie had forgotten I was there. She'd turned her back and was walking up the stairs, O'Rourke following her, carrying the trunk. He was silent now, docile.

I ran toward the stairs, and Rosalie took them quickly, leading O'Rourke by the hand. They got to her room and Rosalie closed the door, locking it. I pounded on it.

"Will you shut her up?" I heard O'Rourke say.

"She'll leave," Rosalie said.

"I won't, I'll never leave you," I screamed.

I heard Rosalie's footsteps near the door. "You have to," she whispered. "This isn't a magazine story. This is my life."

I slumped down against the door. I still held the rent money in my hand. I noticed now that it was three one dollar bills. How could they rent that whole house for twelve dollars a month?

"Maybe she wants to be in the photos too." O'Rourke chuckled. I couldn't hear what Rosalie said back to him. Then there was silence followed by a series of pops and the burned-metal smell of flash-powder. I had never had my photo taken, but I knew that the flash made that noise. What kind of photos was he taking? I heard Rosalie wince; she let out a small cry. I could hear O'Rourke laugh. They were in there for a while, and then the door opened, and he stepped out over me. "Told you she wanted to watch." He put his case down and bent over to take the money from my limp hand. He had a cigarette already lit and the smoke trailed behind him as he went down the stairs and closed the door.

I could hear Rosalie moving around the room behind me; she opened the door and stepped over me on the way to the bathroom, her robe open, her breasts swinging. I struggled to speak, to move, to do anything, but my limbs were disconnected from my body. I was paralyzed. *Move!* I urged myself. *Move!* I was terrified; all the bravery I'd summoned when I followed them up the stairs and pounded on the door had left me.

I worried I'd had a stroke, but no, if I concentrated I could move my pinkie finger. Then I worked on my hand, my wrist, until I was sitting up, my breathing righted. The bathroom door was closed and I knocked softly.

"Rosalie?"

"I'm washing," she said, from behind the door. I heard the toilet flush. Then she came out of the room, the old Rosalie restored. I saw how quickly she recovered, how practiced she was at acting.

I grabbed her by the shoulders. "How long?"

"How long what?" She wouldn't meet my eyes.

"How long has this been happening?" I grabbed her chin, forced her to face me.

"Oh, years. Years and years and years."

"Rosalie." I began to cry. "I didn't know. You didn't tell me."

"Yes, well," she said. She was businesslike, firm.

"What does he make . . . what do you do?"

"At first, it was just pictures, when I was a girl. Then it was bathing costumes and then nothing at all. And then with boys sometimes, and sometimes with . . . things . . . inside."

I gasped.

"I thought maybe when I became a woman he wouldn't want those pictures anymore, but . . . And then maybe if I got fat . . ."

I was overwhelmed with sympathy for her. I wanted to draw her to me, but her arms were stiff at her sides. I was still gripping her face; I acted on impulse, kissing her lips. It was not a sensual kiss, and when I pulled back I saw it hadn't affected her at all. She remained stolid.

"You have to tell your mother. You have to," I said. She stared at me, her eyes narrowing in incredulity. I understood. Her mother knew. Her mother had arranged it.

*

I left before her parents came home. I didn't know what else to do. I wandered around by the port. Though it was spring, the wind was icy off the lake. I turned up the collar of my thin coat for warmth.

How could I have been so stupid, not seen what was happening? How else could Rosalie's family have afforded that grand house? What did it feel like, I wondered, having the camera on her, his eyes. Knowing that other people looked at photographs of her naked, vulnerable. I couldn't even imagine putting something inside of me there (I knew so little of my own anatomy). I touched my cheek where his rough hand had lain.

But Rosalie hadn't even protested. She was used to it. And perhaps that was what broke my heart most. It had become banal for her to be violated.

Reading this with modern eyes, you may wonder why I didn't go to the police. But it was a different time, a different place. People would have blamed Rosalie. She would be damaged goods. No one would marry her. She'd be disgraced.

How could her parents have sold her like that? Though mine were overly strict and old-fashioned, I knew my mother would have died before she let anything like that happen to me. She would have protected me with her own body, would avenge anyone who hurt me. And yet the people who were supposed to protect Rosalie were the ones who hurt her, who allowed that animal to hurt her over and over again.

I decided then that we should run away together. Rosalie's plan, though far-fetched, could be hatched. I was already working. I could be a secretary anywhere and support us.

Should I tell my parents I was going to leave? They'd try to convince me to stay, surely. Out of love or necessity? If they would just let me fin-ish school, I could make something of myself and send money home. If I stayed, our situation would never get any better. They would marry me off to whomever the yenta chose, like we were still in the old country. Might they be relieved, I wondered, if there was one less person in the cramped apartment? One less set of clothes to wash, meals to prepare, turns to wait for the communal lavatory? Possibly. They would keep me home out of fear of the unknown, the immigrant's clinging to old-fashioned ways, conservative ideals. But this was America! We'd come for opportunity, and now they wanted to waste it by being timid, afraid. I wasn't afraid.

By the time I got home I had decided. And our little apartment, three floors up with the makeshift kitchen, the crammed rooms, the laundry hanging like dour bunting on lines strung across the room, draped on every chair and table, made my decision seem right. I would tell my mother that they were late with payroll this week, and we could be gone before the first of the month, before the rent was due.

*

I marched over to Rosalie's house the following weekend. I had been preparing my speech all week and had honed it to what I considered a supreme example of rhetoric and accusation, whose ultimate purpose was to . . . I wasn't sure, but I knew I had righteous indignation I had to get off my chest.

When her mother answered the door, however, her blond hair swept back and her apron tied primly around her waist, I completely deviated from the script.

"How could you?" I demanded. "How could you let that man take pictures of Rosalie?"

"Excuse me?" she said. "I'm sorry, what are you talking about, Frances? Your face is all red."

"You let O'Rourke take pictures of Rosalie, dirty pictures."

"Dirty pictures?" She laughed. "Hardly. He has a line of women's fans and Rosalie models them for the catalog."

I was struck dumb. Was it possible that she didn't know? I knew her to be a kind person, a cultured person, an intelligent person. She must have understood. Rosalie must have told her what the pictures really were. The look Rosalie had given me in the bathroom confirmed it.

"That's not true," I said. "That's not what it's like. The pictures . . . they're . . ." I didn't have the vocabulary to say what those photos were.

"Look, Frances, are you coming inside? I don't know what Rosalie has said, you know her and her stories. That one is ready for the stage."

"But, have you seen—"

"Rosalie, Frances is here." She swept me inside, our conversation over.

Rosalie grabbed my arm, pulling me into her room and closing the door. "I heard you. With my mother. What do you think you're doing?"

"Someone has to confront her," I said. "This can't go on. How can she pretend not to know?"

"Oh, she knows," Rosalie said, her hands bunching at her sides. "But she doesn't *know*."

My face must have shown my confusion.

"She knows what's going on, but she can pretend she doesn't know. And then she can convince herself that it's all innocent so that it's not her fault."

"But why don't you just tell her you're not going to do it anymore?"

"We'll lose our home," Rosalie said. "We'll be out on the street! I'll be ruined. I can't believe you told her. You've destroyed me."

Surely she was being a bit grandiose. "You were so upset."

"I'm always like that right afterward and then it passes. For God's sake, Fanny, you're like gully-fluff. Just leave," she said. "I can't look at you right now."

I wasn't familiar with the word *gully-fluff,* but I certainly understood its context.

*

I went to Rosalie's house the next afternoon, ready to apologize. She was right. It was not my place to tell or not tell. I was planning to beg her forgiveness. I had even brought her a sticky bun, which I knew she liked. I knocked on the door, and when no one answered I pounded on it. Finally Rosalie opened it. I could sense rather than see her mother behind her.

"I can't see you anymore," she said.

"What?"

"I said, we can't be friends anymore."

"Because . . ."

"Because we can't." She was cold, all business, pale.

I opened my mouth but no sound came out. I was too stunned even to feel hurt.

"Goodbye, Frances." She closed the door in my face.

*

Each day before work I went by Rosalie's house. It was early, and her household wasn't yet stirring. But I made a little pyramid of stones where she would surely see them from her window when she looked out in the morning to judge the weather. By the next morning they were gone, whether by Rosalie's hand or by someone else's I didn't know.

After a week, I stood outside the window and waited for Rosalie's face to appear. When it did, she didn't seem surprised to see me there. She looked paler than before and thinner. She had rouged her cheeks in a way that made her look exaggerated, like an acrobat in the circus. I waved. She dropped the curtain back into place.

After waiting for her for three days, during which her curtain never moved, I stopped going to Rosalie's house. I wasn't sure what her silence meant, but it cut me, to stand there in the dawn looking vainly as if for a lover. I began to plan my own solo escape. When I had $100, I told myself, I would catch a train east. I decided on Hartford, a city enough like Duluth. I would be sixteen by then, and I could easily pass for eighteen and take a room in a boardinghouse somewhere. I could get a job in the evenings washing dishes or caring for children or even taking in laundry. And then I could enroll in high school. Hopefully I wouldn't be too far behind; I'd been keeping up with my studies through Rosalie until recently. I could pretend to be an orphan. The fantasy was romantic enough to sustain me as I added two dollars, now three, to my savings, walking with my head down looking for fallen pennies, buying no books or sweets, just saving for the day when I'd catch the train.

Each day I ate lunch on the bench where we once shared sticky buns, hoping Rosalie would come and see me. It was late May now, and the weather wasn't too cool. I ate my sandwich while scanning the crowd for Rosalie's form among the fishmongers, the roasted-nut salesgirls, the inevitable port girls for rent.

If I wasn't allowed to see her, how could I convince Rosalie that running away was not only her only option but my only option too? In imagining our life together, I began to find my own situation completely untenable, crying at work on a regular basis when the boss criticized me, whereas before his criticism fell around me as though I had a protective umbrella. My file grew thick with demerits. I knew that I would soon be fired.

At home I so exasperated my mother that she hit my arm with the laundry brush, the first time she'd ever taken her hand to me. She was more upset than I was, begging my forgiveness and kissing the spot repeatedly, her tears wetting the skin. I forgave her. I wanted to hit someone too, to kick and lash out.

I told her they had reduced my hours at work and docked my pay accordingly. I began to save the extra money instead of putting it in the jar above the icebox. I kept it in a small pouch I'd sewn one night and which I pinned into the waistband of my skirt every day. My money was always with me then. It would be too risky to hide it in the small apartment, where there were many hands that might discover it. I felt bad about the deception, but justified it as a penalty for the slap. I told my mother that with my free afternoons, I was looking for work downtown.

Then, on the last day of May, there Rosalie was, carrying a large carpetbag. I'd nearly forgotten that's why I sat there every day. Yet it was so natural to see her finally approach me, as if we'd been meeting there for years. She threw her arms around me, and I let myself lean into the hug. I wanted to tell her everything, and then I understood how lonely I'd been without her.

She held me at arm's length and then we hugged again.

"Oh Fanny, I've missed you so!" she said.

"Me too. Awfully. Please say you can be my friend again."

"I'm going away." Rosalie stared over my head out onto Lake Superior. The large barges were just arriving from Canada to discharge their loads of coal and fish and textiles.

"What? When?" I sputtered. "I'm going away too. I have thirty dollars saved. We'll go together. As soon as I have a hundred."

"You can't come with me. I'm ruined." She spoke so softly, her voice was almost too small to hear.

"No, Rosie."

Rosalie continued to look out on the water. A breeze came up and the harbor grew frothy. "It's true, I'm damaged, worthless."

"It's just pictures. It's not—"

"I've done other things too," she said. "Not everything, but most of it. And once I bled, so I don't think I'm . . . intact." She turned to me. Her face was eerily blank, the bruising around her eye a mauve that blended in to her ashen skin.

I slumped, examining the worn sleeves of my coat. Rosalie's life was worse than I could ever have imagined. And I had been feeling so sorry for myself for having to quit school to work. Rosalie in pictures, with boys, with objects, doing things . . . it was too horrible.

"We'll start over, somewhere else," I said. "It doesn't have to count."

Rosalie noticed I was crying. "Don't," she said. "Just don't." She stood up. "Goodbye, Fanny. You've been a true friend. My best friend. I love you. Try to forget what you saw. Try to forget me."

"Please," I begged. "Please let me come with you. We can go to Hartford, I have it all planned out."

"Hartford?" Rosalie asked. "Why on earth would we go there? Chicago. It's closer."

I heard her say "we." I didn't care where we went.

"I'm going today," Rosalie said. "If you want to come with me it has to be today." She pointed to the carpetbag, which I could see now was stuffed with clothing. I began to protest. I couldn't leave today. I didn't have my things. I needed to write a letter to my family, give notice to my job . . . Rosalie just sat in front of me saying nothing and I saw how feeble my excuses were, how they were just fears.

Finally I said, "Yes, all right, today."

"You get paid today, right? It's Friday. Then ask for an advance on next week's pay."

"They'll never do that."

"Try. Tell them your mother has to see the doctor, or your baby sister needs medicine. Meet me at the station at five fifteen and we'll catch the five thirty. It'll be busy at the train station then; no one will notice us."

"But my clothes—" I began. Rosalie gave me a stern look. It was one of the things she teased me about, the horrible state of the hand-me-down rags I wore. My mother made them out of discarded fabric or forgotten washing. Surely I would not need any of this for my new life.

And then I said the easiest word in the world, the word I was to say so many times without thinking through the consequences. I said, "Yes."

*

I waited nervously for four forty-five, when they handed out pay for the week. When the senior secretary called my name, I garbled the sentence I'd been planning. "That's highly irregular," she said. "You'll have to ask Mr. Narrins."

I knocked softly on his door and waited for him to say, "Come in."

"Hello, sir. I was wondering if I could have an advance on my pay, just a week. You see my sister, she's a baby, and she needs to go to the doctor."

Mr. Narrins took his pipe from his mouth. "The doctor. What are her symptoms?"

"She's been listless, feverish. She can't keep anything down."

"It sounds like the flu," Mr. Narrins said. "In which case the doctor will do you no good, and you'll be wise to keep your money."

"No, sir," I said. "My brother had it before, and the doctor gave him some very good medicine that cured him quickly."

"Come on, Miss Frankowski, tell me what it's really for."

"What?" I asked, acutely aware that he was staring at me.

"What is the true purpose of the money you'd like to be advanced?"

"The doctor, sir, as I said."

"I have to say, Miss Frankowski, you lie about as well as you type."

I nearly protested that I typed very well. I searched my mind for a plausible reason I needed the money. "School fees, sir. For correspondence courses."

"Right," he said. "I have a feeling, Miss Frankowski, that we won't be seeing you anymore."

"No sir." I shook my head. "I'll continue on, the same way I've been. I like my job. I value it."

"Here." He wrote something on a piece of paper. "Tell Mrs. Peck to advance you half a week's pay. And Miss Frankowski"—he paused before he handed me the paper—"please do something worthwhile with yourself."

"Have a good weekend, Mr. Narrins. I'll see you on Monday."

"Have a good weekend, Frances," he responded, chuckling.

I danced my way back to Mrs. Peck's desk.

"Well, that is very irregular," she said again, reluctantly counting out the bills. I wanted to leave her with some parting words: Mrs. Peck, you are a cream-faced loon (apologies to Shakespeare); or, Mrs. Peck, you are a goopy goldbricking grousing gasbag (apologies to the English language). But I held my tongue. It would only have given me a moment's satisfaction, and I would regret it later, if I knew myself at all.

*

As I rode the tram, packed with people going home from work, I began to worry. What if Rosalie wasn't really going to meet me? What if she changed her mind? What if it was a trap set by her mother to see if I really was the bad influence she claimed? I tried to brush the thoughts from my mind. Rosalie would be there and we would run away together to the life we were meant to live. After all, my parents left Poland for the unknown. Now my New World would be Chicago.

I arrived at the train station with fifteen minutes to spare and waited as directed under the large clock. The minutes were long, and I searched every hurrying person for Rosalie's face. But that one was old, that one a man, this one fair. Each moment made me doubt myself and our journey more. Surely this was a fool's errand, some fancy of youth that we would greatly regret. Maybe Rosalie had already come to that conclusion and decided not to meet me. Maybe her mother had locked her up.

From there my mind began to spiral as it does when anxiety takes hold. Rosalie didn't love me. No one would ever love me. My life would be a barren wasteland of loneliness, witness to the love and companionship of others, a joy that would be denied to me. I was thinking in that vein when Rosalie's face appeared, red from hurry. Late, as always. She didn't even pause but grabbed me by the hand, and we took off running for the train.

We hopped aboard as the whistle blew and went from car to car searching for our compartment. I was breathless from running, from excitement. Rosalie consulted our tickets and then purposefully marched through the cars, until we found Cabin F, places 2 and 3. She grabbed the door handle and pulled, then pulled again. Behind us, the conductor unlatched the door and it slid easily. Rosalie flashed him a smile, and he took her bag and put it in the overhead rack.

She slumped into her seat and began to fan herself with the tickets. I sat next to her and tried to calm my beating heart by examining our fellow passengers. One was a young man, perhaps a bit older than we were. He was dressed very smartly in a suit too warm for summer. He'd taken off his hat and his hair stood up in all directions, a multitude of colors from brown to blond. He had a friendly face but was absorbed in his book, either to give us time to compose ourselves or because he really was not interested. I saw the title, a religious treatise on the nature of sin, and imagined that Rosalie and I were temptation. Also in our cabin were two older women, already at their knitting, with a basket of food that smelled strongly of sausages. They were chatting in a Scandinavian language. There was no one in the last place, and after a bit Rosalie set her handbag on the empty seat.

The train groaned out of the station and the tension left Rosalie. I wondered if she was worried her parents had followed her to the train. As we sat, my excitement began to leak like gas from a balloon, and I filled up with nervousness. I looked at my hands and found little half moons of white where my nails dug in. Rosalie and I dared not speak to each other. I know I would have burst into terrified tears had she said a word or even looked at me.

After a while, the city behind us and the fields of wheat stretching out on all sides like I imagined a vast ocean would, Rosalie said, "Would you like some water?"

It wasn't until then that I realized I was desperately thirsty. "Yes, please," I said, adopting her overly formal diction.

Rosalie reached into her bag and pulled out a stoppered bottle. I drank deeply and handed it back, and Rosalie sipped from it. Then she pulled out a deck of cards. "Shall we play?"

We played war on the arm of the seat between us, and as usual, Rosalie beat me. We played a second game, and it began to get dark. I wondered where we would sleep, but Rosalie did not appear to be worried, so I tried to adopt her air of confident traveler. I'd never been farther than out on the lake in a canoe, but Rosalie had been to Milwaukee, so she knew better than I what a train trip entailed.

At nine we reached Florence Junction. The young man gathered his belongings. "I wish you a good day, ladies," he said, his first words to us, with the hint of an Eastern European accent. I wished I'd had the courage to speak to him.

The conductor came around to do up the beds. What an ingenious contraption: The benches became a bed, and two more berths were lowered from the ceiling to form bunk beds. Rosalie and I volunteered to take the top bunks; the Norwegian ladies were much too stout and old to climb. I was relieved because I was worried that the beds might fall on me in the middle of the night.

"Keep your belongings on your body," Rosalie whispered. "I've heard stories."

"What stories?"

"That at night, they drug the cabins and steal everyone's money."

I gasped. Could this be true?

Rosalie saw my face. "I'm sure it's just a story," she said. "Otherwise, people would stop traveling by train if it happened lots, right?"

I climbed into my bunk and shivered beneath the thin covers. The train pitched and tossed, and I was afraid that I would roll out of the berth should I fall asleep. So I stayed awake until the very wee hours, when I heard from Rosalie's breathing that she wasn't sleeping either.

"Rosie," I whispered. "Are you awake?"

"Come over, then," she completed my thought. I climbed in next to her. Her familiar wood scent calmed me, and I curled up next to her for warmth.

"Oh, Fanny." She sighed. "What have we done?"

"We've rescued ourselves," I said.

CHAPTER FOUR

The train station in Chicago held more people than I'd ever seen. I gripped Rosalie's hand tightly as we looked around.

"What now?" I asked quietly.

"What's that?" she said.

"What now?"

Rosalie didn't answer, though I know she heard me.

"This way," she said finally.

Rosalie amazed me with her resourcefulness. She went straight to the Rock Island ticket counter and asked the woman where we might find lodging. She concocted a story on the spot that we were going to visit our aunt but wanted to stay in Chicago for the night to wash off the train grime. The woman smiled and told us where we might find a room for the night, someplace respectable but cheap. Had Rosalie been thinking about this falsehood, or did her mind spin tales that quickly? I might have found it chilling had I not been so afraid. I was trembling with anxiety, and I would have gotten straight back on a train for home if I thought I'd have any chance of figuring out which was the right one.

We walked the few short blocks and found the place. If the reception clerk wondered at two young women traveling alone, he did not let it show. Instead, he gave us the keys to a small bedroom on the third floor, sparsely furnished, with one bed that we were to share. There was a washbasin, a lavatory down the hall. The room's one window looked across the alley to a brick wall, and so the threadbare curtain was unnecessary. Rosalie and I both agreed without speaking that it would do just fine.

*

The next morning Rosalie bought us coffee and a bun each from the little shop in the bottom of the hotel. We were both on edge, and I was even a little cross. "Let's have a day of sightseeing," she said. "We can go see the Columbian Exposition buildings. We'll look for work tomorrow."

We had the hotel manager draw us a map and headed down to the lake. Like our own Lake Superior, Lake Michigan gave off a cool breeze and we had to bend into the wind to make our way. Once we reached Michigan Avenue, though, the wind tapered off and the views opened up. It was beautiful. In the distance, down the wide road, was a gleaming white building, like the Parthenon must have been when it was newly built.

"That must be it," Rosalie said.

We paid admission to the art museum and wandered around, never moving far from each other. Here were pictures I'd only ever seen in books, and those in black and white at that. Here were Degas, Turner, Renoir. We went to see the Greek statues, and I blushed at the naked men, but Rosalie stared with the interest of a physician. As we walked among the art, my apprehension that we'd made a mistake evaporated. Here is where we were meant to be, side by side, studying the great artistic achievements of man.

My heart opened, the way it does when you are filled with the sense of potential. My steps were buoyed, and I let my imagination proclaim me university professor, artist. I imagined Rosalie and me, our houses adjacent, our broods playing together, even perhaps with the same governess, while we pursued our Great Works (what these would be, exactly, was nebulous, but forgive a poor young girl her reveries). I remember, even now, the wonderful lightness of spirit, which produced an equal lightness of body. I might have floated off with contentment. When one is low, one feels bogged down, weighed by forces that tie one to the earth. To the very spot. And yet in the museum I felt myself equal to the high-hung pictures, lost in their swirls and dots, reflected in their mirrors, and enveloped in their abstractions.

Rosalie and I had a small lunch at a diner and seriously discussed our options. First, we pooled our money. Rosalie had twenty-three dollars, and I had twenty-one (after train tickets and food and the week's lodging). We had enough, we thought, for four weeks, if we lived frugally. I made a list of all the jobs Rosalie might do.

Childminder. Though Rosalie had a little brother, she had never had to take care of him, whereas I had wiped enough of my siblings' bottoms to last a lifetime.

Secretary. Again, the experience was mine.

Maid. I was more likely to be successful at this, since I had the experience with washing and helping my mother with chores, whereas Rosalie had never so much as even folded a dressing gown.

Apprentice to a trade. This was a bit nebulous, as we didn't know which trade would accept unskilled apprentices.

Waitress. This seemed the most likely prospect for Rosalie, as she was pretty and personable, and all the other professions were dominated by my meager skills.

We discussed, seriously, the issue of school. It was now late May and Rosalie had forfeited her term by leaving when she did. She was reasonably confident, though, that she could easily pass an entrance exam, perhaps even skip a year and enter her senior year of high school. I could teach her typing and shorthand in the evenings, and she could be ready to work in one year. In the meantime, I would have to sacrifice and earn our living, and then it would be my turn. And who knows, perhaps I could pass a diploma equivalency exam and enter university at the same time Rosalie did. I was doubtful of this; it had already been two years since I'd been at a regular school, but I played along to buoy her spirits.

We purchased a paper and turned to the help wanted ads, circling the most promising. I bought a map and several tokens for the elevated railroad and we went to bed that night full of excitement, believing that our new lives would soon begin.

What a bitter disappointment the following day. I spent most of it in the downtown area, applying for secretarial jobs. But as soon as I introduced myself they said the position had been taken, or told me to leave my information and they'd call me. It must have been my last name, Frankowski. In Chicago, the Polish immigration had been particularly strong, and I wasn't sure if being Polish or being Jewish was the greater sin. In any event, I decided to turn my sights to Jewish firms in the port area, since I had more than a passing familiarity with the terms and issues thereof. There weren't any positions listed in the paper. Perhaps these things weren't advertised but rather passed on via word of mouth. I'd have to arrive at the right time, and slot myself into a place before word got out.

By now it was past one and I was hungry. I bought a hot dog from a vendor and ate it greedily. It wasn't until after I'd swallowed the last bite that I realized it was most likely not kosher and contained swine. The thought brought it back up into a garbage can on the corner of State and Madison, and I wiped my mouth, looking around to make sure no one had seen me get sick.

"Are you all right, dear?" a voice asked, and an elderly woman put her hand on my forearm. This expression of kindness brought tears to my eyes. "Can I help, at all?" I could hear from her voice she was Irish.

"No, thank you," I managed. I ran, the tears streaming freely now. I was embarrassed, and disappointed in myself. Perhaps I was, after all, still a girl.

I ended up in the West Loop where the buildings petered out into tenements, and then, when I crossed a bridge over the river, into warehouses and derelict buildings. I turned around and walked back—like in Duluth, you could always orient yourself by the lake, where the buildings stopped abruptly like they were playing a game of Grandmother's Footsteps.

It had begun to rain, and I didn't have a jacket or umbrella. Or anything, really, besides the skirt Rosalie had loaned me, which was too large. I had taken it in with embroidery thread, which was coming loose, and I clenched it to my body to make sure it didn't fall down as I walked.

I hoped, for her sake, Rosalie had had better luck, but when I entered our hotel room she was sitting on the bed, her head in her hands. I laughed, even though I wanted to cry, because it was rather funny, me bedraggled from the rain, holding up a skirt that didn't fit and her assuming the position of Rodin's *Thinker*. Rosalie didn't know why I was laughing, but she joined in until we were both on the floor rolling around.

Such an extremity of emotions. I now understand that it was a response to anxiety, but then it just was the way things were, tragic and funny all at the same time.

*

It was Rosalie who, the following day, hit upon the idea to go to a synagogue in the morning to see if perhaps our co-religionists could help us.

"Rosalie, you're brilliant."

"At the very least maybe they'll have some clothes for you so you don't have to walk around holding your waist all the time."

But how to find a synagogue? Our hotel clerk wouldn't know, that was obvious. I suggested we look for a directory, and that we would probably find one in the library.

The main library in Chicago was a grand thing, on a much bigger scale than our little house of learning in Duluth. I tried to walk softly. Rosalie asked the librarian where we could find a directory.

"You'll have to speak up, dear," she said.

"A directory," she repeated. Another librarian shushed her.

The deaf librarian brought over an enormous volume. "Here you go. You can look at it on that table there, then bring it back here."

We spread it on the table. The type was tiny. Rosalie looked under "Synagogues." There was no listing.

"Try 'Houses of Worship.' Or 'Worship,'" I offered. But there was nothing there either.

"Temples," Rosalie said. And there was a list, of all the synagogues in the world, well over fifty. I could hear Rosalie gasp too. There were four synagogues in Duluth, and everyone knew which one everyone attended (or didn't attend, as the case often was).

We split up the copying, and I started from the bottom. "I'm tempted," Rosalie said after a while, "to take the page."

"How?" I asked.

"You make a coughing noise and that masks the sound of the page ripping."

"Rosalie!" I was shocked.

"I just said I was tempted," she said. "Don't be so censorious."

I made a note on my piece of paper to look up the word.

Finally we finished our list. Rosalie turned the pages of the directory to the listings of residents.

"What are you looking for?" I asked.

"Nothing." Rosalie had become more secretive since we got to Chicago, seeming to draw her own conclusions and neglecting to share them with me. I didn't want to say anything to her for fear of upsetting her further.

We went straightaway to the closest synagogue on the list, but it was a run-down building and two men sitting on its steps glared at us. The next one looked like a school. It was plain and nondescript, hardly an inspiration for worshipping the Almighty. But by that point I wanted to use the toilet, so we went inside.

The receptionist looked us over and was obviously unimpressed. Rosalie explained our presence patiently, saying that we were cousins, recently orphaned, who were looking for work and to finish school. When she stopped talking, the woman didn't respond.

"May we speak with the rabbi?" Rosalie asked.

The woman shook her head slowly. "I don't think we can bother him with this."

"May I at least use your toilet?" I asked.

The woman pointed down the hall behind her, as if words were too expensive to waste on directions. I left Rosalie to work her charms and proceeded down a tiled hallway with unmarked windowed doors. The rooms were all dark. Finally I found a door marked "Girls," cementing my suspicion that this had once been a school. I used the toilet and was washing my hands when the door opened and a woman about my mother's age walked in.

"Oh!" she said. "You startled me. I thought I was the only one here."

I smiled in apology.

"I've just come in to loosen my girdle a bit. For some reason I can't breathe today. It might be that the reason is the cookies I had yesterday."

I smiled again.

"Do you think you could help me?" she asked. "I can do it myself but it involves a lot of twisting and turning around."

"All right," I said.

She put her back to me. "No one is around today. I thought the Aid Society meeting was today, but I got the date wrong, it's on Thursday, and now I've come all the way downtown for nothing."

I nodded, then realized she couldn't see me. "Oh."

She untucked her blouse from her skirt and I could see the stays of the corset digging into her flesh. She had cinched it way too tight.

I undid the knot and her lungs filled with air. "This is barbaric, what we do to ourselves, but it's almost worth it for the relief you feel when it's over, isn't it? Now tie it back up, tight, but not too tight, there's a dear."

I had never tied a corset before. In Duluth women rarely wore them. But it didn't seem too hard. Just pull on the strings and tie a knot. Knots I could do. The woman had a mole on her right shoulder, an angry brown stub.

"There you go," I said.

"Thank you," she said. "What's your name, dear? Why aren't you at the rally?"

"Fanny—Frances."

"I'm Mrs. Bloomfeld. Who are your people?"

I was confused by the question. Then I realized she was asking my last name. I opened my mouth and without even thinking about it, I said, "Frank," leaving off the Polish "owski."

"I think I know them. Bankers, right?"

"I'm not sure," I answered. "We might be from a different part of the family."

"All the young people have gone to the rally. Why aren't you with them?"

"I didn't know about it," I said. I looked at our reflection in the mirror. Mrs. Bloomfeld's hair was curly around her face and long in the back where she'd gathered it into a tail. She smoothed it with her fingers.

"My cousin and I just arrived in town a few days ago," I said. "We're orphans."

Mrs. Bloomfeld revealed herself neither impressed nor particularly sorry for our plight. Maybe lots of "orphans" passed through the synagogue.

"Maybe if you hear of some work," I said.

She smiled at herself in the mirror, turning her chin back and forth.

"Where are you staying?" she asked. I gave the name of the hotel.

"Oh that's terrible," she said, but gave no further comment. "Well, nice to meet you, Frances Frank. Thanks for the help with the laces."

When I returned to the entrance, Rosalie had indeed charmed the receptionist, who was pouring through a synagogue directory. I stood back and let them look, their heads bent together, whispering. That's how Rosalie and I must have looked, I realized, when we were studying. When Rosalie and the woman were done conferring, Rosalie kissed her on the cheek and promised to come and see her soon. I waved goodbye.

"Oh, she was nice." Rosalie linked her arm with mine. "We are to come to the Young Ladies' Aid Society meeting on Thursday. And I think I shouldn't bother to look for any work before then."

I was not convinced that we should give up our search, but I let myself be persuaded by Rosalie's good mood to go to Oak Street Beach, where we lay in the sun in our shirtsleeves and had an ice cream. Rosalie bunched her skirt up to her knees and took off her stockings to "get some sun on my legs," but we were too close to the buildings to really feel we were at the beach. City rules applied, not beach lawlessness. Rosalie had always suffered from a lack of modesty. Now, in light of what I knew about her, I wondered which was her natural inclination and which a response to her circumstances. We never spoke about what had happened. I took Rosalie's lead, and it was clear she never meant to discuss it.

*

The next day burned hot. My clothes were instantly soaked with sweat when I took to the streets, and they had begun to smell, though I rinsed them nightly with soap. Thank God Thursday was just a day away.

We arrived in plenty of time for the meeting, and Rosalie greeted the receptionist, Lillian, warmly, introducing me as her cousin.

"That's a pretty name," I said, which made her smile, the first sign she didn't hate me.

She led us to a room where two dozen women were assembled. They were all nicely dressed and coiffed, and some had elaborate hairdos which announced the fact that their hair was plaited by servants. They turned and stared at us, but Mrs. Bloomfeld, who was running the meeting, didn't pause. "Next piece of business," she said.

Lillian pointed to two chairs and we sat down as quietly as we could.

"The Sukkot committee will need to be chosen by the end of the month. Please consider volunteering, either to chair the event or to work on a subcommittee. Traditionally, these have been delivering meals to the homebound, feeding poor children, and helping to plan the celebration.

"Also, it has come to my attention that the account from which we give boys their siddurim when they become bar mitzvah is sadly low. We'll need to have a fund drive to replenish it. So if anyone has any ideas, please let me know."

Next to Mrs. Bloomfeld, another woman was taking down minutes, scribbling furiously. She obviously didn't know shorthand, and I knew that she would invariably miss some of what was said if she tried to record it word for word.

"And now we have . . . your name again, dear?"

"Frances Frank, Mrs. Bloomfeld," I supplied, before Rosalie could answer, which surprised her. "Nice to see you again."

"And you," she said. "This is your cousin?"

"Rosalie," I said. We had agreed that Rosalie would plead our case, as she could talk a polar bear into moving to Florida, but she was struck dumb, and I already knew Mrs. Bloomfeld.

"Ladies," I said. "We are orphaned cousins, just arrived from . . . Minneapolis." I didn't want to give our real hometown in case someone had relatives there. You never knew. "We are looking for work. And a home. And also, I don't have any clothes." This was inelegant, I knew, but I wasn't a gifted orator like Rosalie. In fact, this might have been the largest group of adults I'd ever spoken in front of. Luckily, my ineloquence jarred Rosalie out of her stupor and she took over.

Rosalie should have been a novelist. She wove a tale so subtly sad and moving that I nearly reached into my own empty pockets to donate money to us. The story involved Mr. O'Rourke, but it was Rosalie's mother who was the victim, and all in the service of providing an education for her daughter and niece (my mother was disposed of early). Rosalie's mother died dramatically—here she borrowed liberally from *Les Misérables*, and I hoped none of the women present had read it. Several were weeping by the end, and we had the offer of a place to live (in the fancy neighborhood of Douglas, no less) in exchange for Rosalie taking care of the woman's elderly mother, a Mrs. Klein, during the day. I was to come to a specific address the following afternoon where someone's daughter had piles of clothes that should fit me. (Was she built like a roofing board as well, I wondered?)

We heard a lot of "You poor dears," and many cakes were shoved at us, as though we were Dickensian street urchins who had never been properly fed. I had never known a day of hunger in my life, and Rosalie never knew an hour of it, but she ate greedily to keep up appearances.

We left laughing and jolly, excited at our new lives.

*

Mrs. Klein's home was dreary to say the least. Heavy drapes covered the front windows. When I drew them back, they opened to a shower of dust, little bits floating in the lamplight, dancing on the currents. The house was enormous, seven bedrooms with at least as many bathrooms. I went upstairs only once. Its eerie silence and stillness (I had never heard a house so quiet) spooked me.

And yet Rosalie and I were crowded into the maid's room near the kitchen. "Never mind," Rosalie said. "We can sneak out the back stairs and we have our privacy. And our own bathroom!"

I had never shared a bathroom with just one person. Always there was someone knocking at the door, anxious to take his turn. The three families on our floor shared two communal commodes. There was one bathtub, and we had a once-a-week family rotation.

Mrs. Klein's, though, had unlimited hot water. The kitchen was a dream, with a new gas oven and a large sink that held all the dinner's dishes for washing. There was even an entire room devoted to laundry, with another basin large enough to contain a washboard, and a pulley system that held damp clothing up in the air where the warmth sped it dry. The hallway was so long you might have played basketball in it, with smooth shiny boards (that I hadn't realized I'd have to polish). The bathrooms were ornately tiled, with a border of engraved porcelain that spanned the entire length of the room. Each had a claw-foot tub, and one even had a showerhead! I dared myself to try it one day when Mrs. Klein was out.

But Mrs. Klein never went out. Apparently, until recently, she'd been very active, attending luncheons and walking in the park. She had suffered an attack, though, which left her in the hospital for several weeks. She had full-time nursing care until recently, when her disagreeableness chased the last one out. Her daughter had convinced her she was doing us a favor, and hoped that the motivation of *tzedakah*—charity—might overcome her irritability.

Our room was wallpapered with tiny fleurs-de-lis, peeling near the one window. It looked out into the alley, across which other people slept in maids' rooms and other kitchens belched cooking smells and steam into the air. There was something comforting about the proximity, everyone going about their lives the same way we were.

We were only half a mile from the lake, and I walked there daily to look at the water, which changed, like Rosalie's moods, now frothy and violent, now placid, crystalline.

*

Our lodging settled, I had to resume looking for a job. I spent the next day down by the piers, stopping in at shipping companies and presenting myself as an experienced secretary. I went to the smartest company first, whose offices were neat and nicely appointed. They took up the entire upper floor of the warehouse.

It was noisy at the receptionist's desk, and I kept having to repeat myself. Finally I got it across that I was looking for work. She looked me up and down. "It's very hot," I said, by way of excuse, which must have struck a chord, for she replied, "Ya, ya, very hot it is," her words truncated by an accent I identified as Eastern European. Her features, too, looked like they might have been created in my parents' home village. I took a chance.

"*Tu bist ein Landsman?*" I whispered in Yiddish.

"*Vah?*" She leaned closer.

"*Landsman!*" I said, loudly. Literally, are you a countryman? Are you a fellow Jew?

"*Meir zeinen gants landsman aher,*" she said, matter-of-factly. We're all landsmen here. As if that weren't notable. She said, in English, they weren't looking for any girls at the moment, but she'd be glad to inform me if they had any work in the future.

I wrote down Mrs. Klein's address. As I turned to walk out, I heard her yell, "*Vartn oyf!*"

I turned.

"My sister-in-law Elsie works for a business that might be looking for someone," she said in Yiddish. "I'll write you down the address. I'll see her tonight and let her know you're coming if you want to stop by there in the morning tomorrow."

I was so grateful I nearly wept. "Thank you! This means so much, you have no idea . . ." I began to babble, but a loud buzzer rang and the woman snapped to her feet, gathering a pad and pencil at the same time. "Here," she thrust a sheet of paper at me.

That night, I told Rosalie about my lead.

"That's great. What's the business?"

"I couldn't ask," I said. "She was called away, but who cares?"

"What if it's a diamond-smuggling company?"

I laughed. "Or a private-investigation firm?"

"Lion-tamer training school."

I couldn't think of anything stranger than that, so I continued to laugh. "What did you do today?"

Rosalie's face drained of color and smile. "Nothing."

"Did something happen?" I asked.

Rosalie was like a different person. "No, nothing." She shook her head, trying to dislodge a thought.

Something had obviously happened. I couldn't even think about what it might have been, to make her turn to stone like this. When she did this, pulled away, she seemed so remote. She was leaving me, and I hated it. There were parts of Rosalie that would forever remain unknowable to me, perhaps to anyone, maybe even herself. It made her seem older, wiser.

I took off my blouse and skirt and hung them up, standing in only my chemise and slip, as we usually did inside to save the clothing. Only then did I notice that Rosalie was wrapped in a shawl. "It's so hot," she said, though she pulled it closer around her. "And I have a headache."

"Lie down," I said. "I'll get a cold cloth."

I ran a washcloth under the tap in our room and wrung it out. She lay on the bed with her eyes closed. I placed it on her forehead. She sighed deeply, and said, "Thank you, Bear," which is what she used to tease me with when we were children, because I wanted to add honey to everything. I kept changing the cloth until she fell asleep. I spent the evening reading quietly near the open window, hoping for a breeze.

*

The next morning I went as directed to see my Yiddish-speaking friend's sister-in-law, Elsie. She greeted me warmly. She had the curliest hair I'd ever seen, like a Negro's though hers was light brown, and eyes that were close set. She had rouged her cheeks, which I found tremendously chic. She spoke to me in English, and when I peppered my dialogue with Yiddish phrases, she looked at me strangely so that I understood that she knew none of the old tongue.

We sat in the lobby, on an uncomfortable bench. I had to turn awkwardly to face her. My new skirt had a tag that scratched my hip. I'd never had store-bought clothing before, and so far I was not overly impressed.

"If we take you on, it'll have to be a real commitment," she said. "You'll have to interview all the way up the ladder. Yes, even for a secretarial position."

The sign on the side of the building said MAYS SHIPPING. I asked her now what it was that the company shipped.

"Let's say paper. Yes, paper, in a way. You seem like a nice, bright girl. Where did you say you come from?"

"Duluth. I mean, Minneapolis."

"Which is it?" She smiled at me. "No, don't tell me. I don't really need to know. See? Now everything with me is on a need-to-know basis. I don't ask my husband any questions anymore, and you know what? Our marriage is the better for it, would you believe? And you went to secretarial school?"

I was surprised to learn she was old enough to be married. She looked so young. "My certificate was lost in a fire and the school has since closed, but I can prove to you that I know shorthand and typing. I worked at a shipping company before, so I can fill out manifests, reconcile inventories—"

"Here, take down what I'm saying." She proceeded to dictate the very speech we learned how to take shorthand on. So even though my shorthand was excellent, this demonstration of my talent was impeccable. Then she had me type a letter in carbon copy on the typewriter, which I did in two minutes and fourteen seconds. "Not a record, but quite respectable. And you corrected the spelling here. Nicely done."

I'd done it unconsciously. I smiled. I enjoyed the praise. I started to think that perhaps my parents hadn't done me such a disservice when they made me attend secretarial school. My chest clenched, a spasm of guilt about my parents. I pushed it down.

My next interview was with my direct supervisor. He didn't stand up, and when he extended his hand, his arm was so short I had to lean to reach across his desk. His skin was the same dull brown as his chair and his suit, so that he was camouflaged against it, sinking into the leather.

"Well, I'll leave you, Mr. Andrews. Will there be anything else?"

"No, thank you, Elsie."

She closed the door softly behind her. Mr. Andrews made no attempt at conversation. He turned back to the papers on his desk and began to organize them. I sat quietly, unsure what to do. This detente lasted a couple of minutes. Finally he spoke.

"Good, then, you can stand silences. I abhor people who can't stand silence. Silence is natural. Talking is what is unnatural. Don't you agree?"

I nodded.

"You can speak, though, yes?"

"Yes," I said. "Sir," I added.

"Splendid. What is your position on the Thirty Days' War?"

I'd never heard of the war he spoke of. "I have none," I said. "I tend to be interested in history rather than current events."

"Perfect. You may go. Obviously, I won't see you out."

I stood up, trying to display my disappointment. I noticed that the room was completely devoid of any photographs or portraits. The walls were covered with bookshelves and maps. One wall was bare, with a light rectangle where a picture must once have hung, and for some time, but there was nothing there now.

I returned to Elsie's desk. "How did it go?" she asked brightly.

"I'm not sure," I said. Obviously I hadn't gotten the job. Mr. Andrews thought I was an uninformed idiot.

"Don't ever ask about his legs. I should have told you that."

"What about them?"

The telephone rang. "Mays Shipping," Elsie answered. "How may I help you?" She nodded and wrote something down on her pad. "I'll let him know. Thank you for calling." She hung up. "I'll just stick my head in and see how it went. Can you answer the phone if it rings?" I nodded.

Elsie disappeared down the hall. I ran my fingers over her desk, solid mahogany. The feet were curved and decorated, the top inlaid with gold leaf. I would love to have a desk like this. My desire to be Elsie was so strong that I impulsively sat in her chair, held the edges of her paper.

Just as I was reaching for her pencil, the door burst open and in ran a young man about my age, very tall, dressed in dungarees, his fingers stained with ink. "Hello, who are you?" he asked. I struggled to determine how to answer, but he didn't give me a chance. "Are you the new girl?" he asked. "I need to see Mr. Andrews. Is he disposed?"

Without waiting for me to answer, he followed Elsie down the hall. I heard him knock on the door, then Mr. Andrews saying, "What is it?"

Elsie came back out. "Well, Mr. Andrews likes you, but why on earth did you let that boy barge in? Couldn't you have stopped him?"

Just then a very loud buzzing started, in pulsating bursts of deafening sound. I put my hands over my ears automatically. "Break time!" Elsie sang. "Come on, let's get a coffee."

She took my hand and pulled me down the stairs to a large canteen area where men were lining up for coffee and a roll. Elsie smiled and cut in front of one of the men near the head of the line. He pantomimed pinching her bottom, and I held my breath, but it appeared it was all in good fun because she turned and shook her finger. "Now you know I'm a married woman—"

"Marriage don't got nothing to do with it."

I was shocked. I had never heard anyone speak that way to a lady. But Elsie shook her head as though he were a little boy who had gotten into some harmless mischief. She whispered to me, "They're a bit rough here, but it's all talk. You'll get used to it."

When the coffee and roll were offered, I turned them down. "Come on," Elsie said. "It's free."

My surprise must have shown on my face.

"Here," Elsie said. "Sit and I'll explain."

We sat at a picnic table in the corner of the large room and ate our rolls. Elsie said, "Mr. Mays runs his company according to the principles of Adam Smith. Are you familiar with him?"

I shook my head no. The coffee was strong and hot. My hairline began to sweat.

"I'd never heard of him either. But we're all supposed to be reading him. Not that people do. Half of them can't read. And I couldn't follow it at all. It was like reading the telephone directory. But the gist is that workers and management are all on the same level, it's just that each one is doing what he does best. So, for example, I can't lift a heavy pallet, can I? But I can take shorthand. Jorgensen there can't write his name, but he can load a container so that no square inch of space is wasted. We each have our talents and mine is no better than his."

This made sense to me, though I had always been raised to understand that a life of the mind was infinitely more important and desirable than liveliness of body. The body was a mere vessel to contain the exalted mind. But why? Why was the mind so important? It can live without nourishment, when the body cannot.

"So," Elsie continued. "Every day at ten o'clock we break for coffee and a roll. At noon we have half an hour for lunch. That you have to bring. And at two thirty we get an apple and a cup of tea with milk. It's an expense, sure, but Mr. Mays has the loyalest workforce there is. Everyone is fed so everyone works hard. No one ever takes from him, no one ever shirks."

I looked around the canteen. Men were laughing and smoking, enjoying themselves. At work. My father always returned home beaten in both body and spirit.

"Mr. Mays is a bit of a . . . what's the word? He thinks we can achieve paradise here . . ."

"Idealist?" I offered.

"No, it's a strange word, foreign . . ."

"Utopia?"

"That's it!" Elsie said. "You're a smart one! Yes, he's trying to create a utopia."

"Admirable," I said.

"Yes." Elsie sighed. "He's really quite something. You'll meet him directly."

The loud buzzing noise sounded. "Back at it," Elsie said, getting up. She put her tin coffee cup on a table with the hundred or so other empty cups.

There was a great rush up the stairs, so that I couldn't speak to Elsie. I was afraid of losing her. It was like I had imprinted on her, a duckling on its mother, and now I would be motherless again if I lost sight of her. I also had questions. No one had yet told me what I was to do if I were hired here, nor what the wage would be, nor what exactly the Mays Company shipped.

When we got back to the desk, I could no longer contain my questions. "Wait, Elsie. You haven't told me, I mean, I don't know—"

"What you'll be doing, right." Elsie drew her face into a pout of concentration. "I'll let Mr. Mays tell you. Let me just see if he's ready."

I stood stock-still, a growing nervousness in my stomach. I imagined this Mr. Mays a political cartoon, a potbelly, three-piece suit, and porkpie hat. When Elsie poked her head around the corner and waved me into the office, I was surprised to see a young man who couldn't have been much older than my brother Joe. He was dressed in a casual suit, the buttons undone. He stuck out his hand to shake.

"I know, I'm young. The original Mr. Mays is retired," he said. "Please don't hold it against me. You're young too. How old are you?"

"Eighteen," I lied.

Elsie hovered by—a parent watching her baby meet a dog. I shook his hand.

"Now, Elsie, you can go on back to reception," Mr. Mays said. "The girl is perfectly safe."

"Of course she is," Elsie said. "Call me when you're done."

Mr. Mays walked to the little sitting area in front of his desk. He hitched his pants and sat down, stretching his arm out indicating that I should sit in the chair opposite. It was a tall chair, and when I sat my feet did not reach the floor. I was wearing borrowed shoes and the left one slid off my heel. I tried desperately to keep the right one on, flexing and pointing my toes, but it was no use. It slipped off, and I tried to decide if I should ignore it or if I should slide down to put it back on. It was this I worried about all through our interview.

"Ostensibly, Miss . . ."

"Franko—Frank," I supplied.

He nodded. "We are a paper-shipping company. We work on two legs of a piece of paper's journey. First, we transport logs to mills. Second, we distribute paper. This puts us in a unique position to distribute other things. I have a special fondness for a certain pet issue, and my position allows me to create and disseminate a regular broadsheet." He paused.

"Oh," I said, as something needed to be acknowledged.

"This is the part for which I'll need your discretion. You will mostly be assisting Elsie—she has too much to do, poor thing. But sometimes I'll ask you to take down articles for me, and these need to be kept to yourself, do you understand?"

I nodded. I was pleased, truth be told, to be trusted with a task that required discretion. I imagined hinting at the secret but keeping it from Rosalie. I wanted a secret too.

"Um," I began, not sure how to broach the topic. "What about the . . . rather . . . how often . . . or how much . . ."

"You want to know about salary," Mr. Mays said. He uncrossed and recrossed his legs with the other foot on top. I could just see the hint of a sock garter peeking out. "We'll pay $10 a week to start, and we'll reevaluate after three months. Will that be okay?"

Ten dollars a week? I could barely contain myself. I'd never even seen that much money. With that, Rosalie could finish high school and I might be able to take a night class or two. Maybe we could even get our own apartment soon. "I promise I'll do a good job."

"I'm sure you will," Mr. Mays said. He examined his nails. "Now go tell Elsie, and she'll get you started."

*

That evening I hurried back to the house. "Rosalie," I shouted, "Rosalie, guess what?"

But she wasn't in our room. I wandered down the hallway. The door to Mrs. Klein's room was ajar, and I could see her in her bed. For a minute I thought she was dead, but then I saw her chest move. I went to the kitchen where I warmed up a can of soup, which I ate sitting on our bed, wondering where Rosalie had gone.

I sat up as late as I could, worried that she'd been kidnapped or raped or sold into slavery, but then fatigue overcame me and I slipped into unconsciousness on top of the covers, stretched diagonally. I woke when Rosalie gently rolled me over, making herself some room.

"Where've you been?" I mumbled.

"Out," she said. "I'll tell you tomorrow."

"I got a job," I said, fighting through sleep to articulate the words.

"That's wonderful. Tell me in the morning."

But in the morning she was sound asleep, so I tiptoed out the back door. The day was hot already, the sidewalk giving off steam from the previous day, but it couldn't touch me. I had a real job!

CHAPTER FIVE

The tasks were no better or worse than what I did in Duluth. I did some filing for Elsie, typed up boring correspondence, a couple of bills, and a note to a lawyer. I had already learned not to read what I typed, just to make my fingers type the letters that appeared on the page in front of me. So I could easily know and not know the company's business.

Elsie promised to show me the switchboard after lunch, and we walked together down to the canteen. She pointed out people I should know, but all the names ran together in a cloud of Mikes, Johnnys, Pauls, Sols, Abes, etc.

Elsie took two coffees and two rolls. I smiled at her, acknowledging her greed. "They're for Mr. Andrews," she said.

"What does Mr. Andrews do?" I asked.

"Make my life difficult," Elsie said. "Oh, you mean what does he do for the company? Collections, I believe. Sometimes our customers are reluctant to pay, but Andrews is great at getting money from stones."

"Why doesn't he get his own coffee?" I asked.

Elsie looked at me disapprovingly. "That's not funny."

"I'm sorry, what did I say?"

"You saw his legs."

"I didn't," I said. "What's wrong with them?"

Elsie said, "You're not so observant then."

"They were hidden behind the desk."

"He was born without much of them," she said. "At least, I think he was born like that. They're like old dandelion stems, withered. He can walk on them, but barely, and only with crutches."

"Poor man," I said. "How does he live?"

"With his mother, I think," Elsie said. "But poor man nothing. He is the best collection agent this company has ever seen. People pity him, or fear him, like it's a disease they can catch, and they pay up to avoid contagion. Don't pity him, it's a huge mistake."

I nodded to say I understood. But how could I not pity him? Imagine if I couldn't walk. Even my father inspired pity, and he only had a limp. No wonder Mr. Andrews was so unpleasant.

*

Rosalie was out two nights in a row. I sat up until she came home, and I turned on the light right when she let herself in. "You have to tell me," I said. "You can't keep doing this."

She sighed heavily and sat down. "I was at the cinema."

"I don't believe you. What, every night at the movies?"

"I'm cooped up here all day, wiping her bottom," she hiss-whispered, "and you're out in the world, seeing people, it's not fair."

"It's not fair?" I asked. I tried to keep my voice down. "I'm working, I'm not out having tea and cakes."

"Let's not fight."

"I don't want to fight." I held my ground. "I want to know where you go."

Rosalie considered. "I've been taking acting lessons."

"Until midnight? Come on, Rosie, I'm not an idiot."

"After the lessons, in exchange for them, I go out dancing with the teacher."

I was no longer so naïve, and I could read between the lines. "You're his mistress."

"No," Rosalie said quickly. "Just out dancing, so he can show me off. Sometimes I sit on his knee or let him kiss my cheek or my hand but that's it. Honestly."

She saw my expression. Just a few months ago, any thought I had seemed sprung from Rosalie's mind as well. We used to be a hydra, and now we lived on different poles. It was the first time I realized that you could share a bed with someone and yet not know them at all. If I hadn't been so angry, I would have cried at the loss.

"Acting lessons," I said.

"Yes, he's great. Peter Leigh is his name, and he's taught the best. You know . . . Lillian Russell, Fanny Templeton . . ."

"Who?"

"Broadway actresses."

"Then why's he in Chicago?"

"Everyone starts here. It's widely known that Chicago has the best regional theater." Rosalie sounded like she was reading from a promotional poster. "It feeds into Broadway."

Rosalie's enthusiasm was infectious. I began to soften.

"And are you any good, Rosie?" I asked.

She paused. "I think maybe so," she said. "At least, Peter says I am. But then, he has ulterior motives." She giggled.

Then I smiled too. "But what would Melvin Shumwitz say?"

This made her stuff a pillow in her mouth not to laugh so loudly she'd wake Mrs. Klein. I laughed too, until tears began to stream down my face. It felt good.

*

I hadn't been working at Mays Shipping a dozen days when it fell to me to do some of Mr. Mays's "other work." The young man I'd seen earlier, the one wearing coveralls, with ink on his fingers, had a printing press in a room off the warehouse floor. I'd never have known it was there until Elsie showed me. It was hidden behind a shelf of bits and pieces of things, metal joints and odd curved pipes, which swung away neatly at a mere touch to reveal a door inside.

Elsie said, "Zeke, this is Frances Frank."

He didn't look up from his work. He was seated on a rolling stool, bowed over a beast of a machine whose purpose I could not discern in its large rolls and clamping jaws.

"Do you know how to use one of these?" he asked.

"I'm afraid not." I shook my head. I hoped Elsie would say something to prove my worthiness, but she had slipped out, closing the door behind her. The room was quiet, windowless, and smelled of ink and something musty I couldn't identify.

"Why does he send me these girls who can't use the press?" Zeke asked, a question that was not addressed to me.

"I'm a quick study, Mr. . . ."

He ignored my prompting for his name. "And me under deadline. Okay, here's what we'll do. You *do* know how to spell, right?" I refused to rise to the bait of his barb. I found him unpleasant, and that was the nicest adjective that came to mind. "Read the proof sheets against the master and tell me where I went wrong. I'd say, 'if I went wrong,' but there hasn't been an edition yet in which Mr. Mays hasn't pointed out a mistake. So here you are to correct my spelling like I'm back in the third grade."

Finally he looked at me. He had brown eyes beneath bushy eyebrows. They reflected off of a hidden light source and were smooth like he'd never set foot in the sun. His high cheekbones made him look intelligent, buoyed by all that he read.

"Don't stare," he said. "Didn't your mother tell you it's not polite? Here, read this." He thrust a broadsheet and a piece of typewritten paper into my hand. The broadsheet had just been printed; the ink was still damp. I looked around for a work surface. Zeke cleared off part of the table by sweeping his forearm across it, sending pieces of type and awls and a mallet to the other side of the desk. He straightened a chair for me.

"Mademoiselle," he said mockingly.

When I proofread, the whole of the piece barely registers. Instead I see the individual words on islands of their own and judge them accordingly. Sometimes I look for their neighbors, in the case of homonyms, but I leave a text as ignorant of its contents as before I approached it. So I had no idea what I was reading now, and I assumed all the foreign words—*Eretz Yisrael, Hovevei Tziyon*—were spelled properly in the original.

He sat glumly paring his nails while I worked, but I refused to hurry. This was going into print and I was still proving myself at the office.

I found three mistakes. At one point Zeke had set "the" as "teh"; he spelled "possibility" with only one "s"; and he had transposed two words.

I circled the errors with the pencil he provided and handed the pages back to him. He didn't say thank you, just sighed heavily. He pulled out the type and carefully rearranged the letters. The word "possibility" made him groan, then curse—it forced him to reset five lines of type until he could make up the space lost. All the while I stood there, waiting for further instructions. I'd never seen a printing press before and had never considered where newspapers came from. It made sense, now that I saw it. Put in letters, ink plates, pass a sheet of paper over it. How had it taken so long for civilization to invent it?

"Don't touch that," Zeke said, though I wasn't going to.

He neither looked at nor spoke to me while he ran through another sheet of paper. "Check this," he said.

By this time I was a little annoyed. "You could say 'please.'"

"I could," he said. And for the first time, I saw the edges of his mouth twitch in what might have been a grin, which made me warm to him a bit. I told him it was ready.

"Who reads this?" I asked him. "Where does it go?"

He didn't answer me, just cranked the handle. The machine roared to life, creating enough racket to be forging metal instead of merely pressing paper.

*

That became my regular chore, then, to proofread the broadsheets on Mondays before they went to print. I remained ignorant of their destination, if not their contents. I couldn't keep reading them without absorbing at least their subject matter, but I didn't ask questions.

Mr. Mays, and also Zeke, if I could tell by his grouchy enthusiasm for the task, were active in the Zionist movement. I knew a little bit about it from Rosalie's parents, who were followers of Nathan Birnbaum. That Mr. Mays had tendencies toward socialism, I could tell by the way he ran his company, but no one levied that charge against him. We were all happy with his largesse, his rolls and coffee and fair wages.

I got used to Rosalie's schedule and no longer woke up when she came in at night. She seemed happy. On Sundays we went to the municipal pool and swam lazy laps in the deep end, stopping by the soda fountain on the way home for brown cows, our only splurge. Other than that, it was cheese sandwiches and carrots most of the time, with occasional forays into the poorest cuts of lamb shank or bones for broth. Sometimes Rosalie would buy extra meat with the money she used for Mrs. Klein's food, and we ate it greedily. I would not call my days in Chicago enjoyable, exactly, but they were busy, which, as the old adage has it, keeps one from brooding too much.

At the end of July, Mr. Mays treated everyone to a picnic by the lake. The beach chosen was a short walk from the warehouse, and when the bell rang at one o'clock, we all tramped over there. Some men had been sent ahead to get the fire going, and it appeared they'd also got the keg tapped, for a few of them were already pretty jolly. The other occupants of the park were Negroes, who liked to spend time by the lake when the temperature rose. Usually when it was this warm, the Eastern Europeans and other Caucasians stayed indoors. There was a nice breeze off the lake, and I began to think the Negroes had it right.

Even Mr. Andrews had come out for the event. He had a chair with four wheels, two large ones in back and two smaller ones in front, and one of the men from the loading floor pushed him as he held on. I hadn't yet had the chance to see his legs, and they were as Elsie described them, like the last little shrunken carrots in the bin in the cellar when spring has already arrived. I looked away before he could see me cringe.

I had some lemonade and set out my dish, a melting gelatin mold with cream-cheese filling. Though I'd packed it with ice, the day was too hot. No one tasted it, and it sunk slowly until it was a soup on a plate.

"Which one's yours?" I heard a voice behind me. It was Zeke, grumpy and dismissive. But his interest in soliciting my opinion was new. I'd never seen him outside the printing room after that first day, though I'd spent plenty of time in there, and in the light he looked smaller somehow, less fierce. His eyes shone even brighter.

I turned as red as the gelatin and pointed to the failed dish.

He laughed and put his hand on the back of my shoulders, leading me to the other table. He showed me a noodle kugel, perfectly browned and golden with bits of sugar. "Wow," I said. "You made that?"

"My mother did," he admitted. "Not much of a pair of chefs, are we?" And something in me leaped to be included in his "we," like I'd stepped out into the sun, hot all over, but especially on the back of my neck where my braid draped. But just as soon as our moment of community began, it was over, and Zeke joined a group of men arguing heatedly over something that I knew could only be politics. I turned to look for Elsie. She had stripped down to a modest bathing costume, two straps leading to a dress, and she waved me over to join her. I didn't have anything to bathe in, but I waded in up to my knees, and the water was wonderfully cool. I shaded my eyes with my hand and watched Elsie frolic with some of the men who were also swimming, splashing them and giggling. I envied her ease. She looked to be having so much fun. Rosalie could act like that, but then Rosalie was a talented actress. Maybe Elsie was also acting the role of a carefree girl. As I was contemplating, I felt a hand on my shoulder. Before I could turn I was catapulted in the air and landed in the water, sputtering to catch my breath.

"Zeke," Elsie scolded. "You can't just throw someone in the water."

"I didn't," he said. "I threw Miss Frances."

I coughed meekly. I was embarrassed to stand up, knowing that my chemise would show through my thin cotton dress, so I sat in the shallow water. A powerful flash of hatred made me kick a wave of water toward Zeke, but he merely turned around, holding his pipe in the air, and laughed as he waded back to shore.

Elsie came up to me. "Are you all right?" she asked. "Men are like children."

"My dress will cling."

"I have a shawl you can wear until you dry."

I began to cry. Elsie took me in her clammy arms. "It's okay," she said. "It's just a dress. It'll dry." I couldn't articulate why I was crying. At that moment I missed my mother and Duluth so much. There my older brother would have defended me, would have picked up Zeke and dragged him out to sea until he said uncle. My mother would have a towel ready, and a nice tongue sandwich, and I could be far away from the world where men wrote secret newspapers and tossed poor young girls into the lake.

The day was ruined for me, so I sat apart from the others while my dress dried, and then went home, toting my ruined gelatin mold. When I got to Mrs. Klein's apartment, I was crying again. In the kitchen, I ate the whole thing with a spoon, then tipped the mold to my mouth to slurp down the rest of the juices. When I looked in the mirror my face was red around the mouth from the gelatin, like I'd put on clown makeup, and Rosalie of course wasn't home, so I put myself to bed.

*

On Monday, Elsie handed me a note when I walked in. She got there an hour before me and I stayed an hour later after she left, and in that way we covered the switchboard and Mr. Mays's extended hours. "What's this?" I asked. I opened it. I couldn't imagine who would be sending me notes, unless it was Mr. Mays with some sort of complaint. Our three-month trial was only two months in, but I thought he was satisfied with the work I'd been doing. The handwriting was crooked like I imagined Scrooge's writing in Dickens. I read the note, which I'll reproduce here, exaggerated spelling and syntax errors included:

Dear Miz Frances,

The boys telled me I have to pologize for my actshons. I pologoize.

Z. Gregor

Zeke. Trying to be funny.

"It's an apology note," I told Elsie, whose fake surprise told me that she'd been the "boys" to whom Zeke was referring.

"Well, now, that's nice," she said. "He's not a bad sort after all, is he?"

"No more than a rotten apple," I said, and Elsie laughed.

"I think," she said, "he's sweet on you."

Now it was my turn to laugh. "Funny way of showing it."

"Men." Elsie picked up her steno pad and walked down the hall. "As sweet as apples can be," she called over her shoulder.

"Or tart!" I yelled back, and I heard Mr. Andrews say "Shush" from his office.

*

But I began to wonder if she was right. The following week, at coffee time, Zeke asked Elsie and me an inane question that he already knew the answer to. "See?" she nudged me. "Sweet as an apple."

"Maybe he's sweet on *you*, did you ever think of that?" I teased back. The half roll I'd eaten turned to a lump in my stomach.

"Nope, he knows I'm married. And my husband's a hell of a lot bigger than he is." She laughed. I was no longer shocked at her language. In fact, some of it I'd begun to adopt unknowingly, swearing "dammit" under my breath when I mistyped.

The following day, as I was leaving work, I saw Zeke hurriedly stub out his cigarette and fall in step beside me. "Oh, you're leaving too?" he asked. "How's your route?"

"I take the El," I said.

"Which way?"

"South."

He nodded. "I'll walk you there, make sure no one bothers you."

No one had ever bothered me in the two months I'd been at Mays, but I let him walk beside me. Still, I made no attempt at conversation. Even though it was apparent that his brusqueness was a mask for some deeper feeling for me (whatever that was), it still smarted, and I wasn't about to give in to the sharp turnaround now.

About this time, Rosalie began to talk again about New York.

"But that's so far," I said.

"The train goes there." She was home for the rare evening and was engaged in brushing her hair. I hadn't noticed before how long it was; she had always kept it plaited at home.

"The train goes a lot of places. Siberia, for instance."

"Ah, but they don't have theater there," she said. She sighed. "Broadway. Dancing. Won't that be nice? Or California? Sunshine. Real ocean beaches."

I wasn't so sure. Chicago was already fairly overwhelming, and I could only imagine what New York would be like. California was Shangri-la—a desert island from the funny papers, palm trees and coconuts. I was wrong about both California and desert islands.

Zeke and I began to "go steady" or "court," which is what we called it back then, and he showed his softer side. We often went for long walks along the lake, where he would sometimes take my hand. His mother packed us picnic lunches, and we'd go to Jackson Park Beach, happily chatting and splashing each other.

I didn't tell Rosalie about Zeke. When she asked where I'd been, I said I'd gone to see a Scandinavian choral music ensemble. A couple of times I said I'd gone to Elsie's. A couple more she wasn't home to know I had gone out. I enjoyed keeping it from her, savoring the idea like a lollipop I was hiding, taking it out and licking it when she wasn't around. I would tell her soon, I thought. After all, she didn't tell me about Peter Leigh right away. Or I'd tell her when there was something to tell.

I wanted to tell my family. I did miss them and worried that I was causing them pain. I wanted, too, to prove to them how successful I'd been on my own—a job, a boyfriend. But letting them know where I was would be letting Rosalie's family know where she was, and I couldn't do that to her.

Though Zeke was occasionally gruff, he showed himself to be a patient teacher as he instructed me on how to work the printing press. He was passionate about his pamphlet, about the Zionist movement. I wasn't aware that there had been some sort of Congress in Europe, and I hid my ignorance from Zeke. I was always conscious of his education, his intelligence, and the large holes in what I knew.

One day as we walked near the lake, I asked him how he'd first gotten interested in Zionism. He'd become active in college. There was a group of intellectual Jews there, he said, mostly Marxists, who conceived of this utopia. They were followers of Theodor Herzl, who was advocating for a Jewish state in Palestine, calling themselves B'nai Zion.

"Don't people already live there?" I asked.

"Yes, but it really should be our land. We were the original settlers."

"By that logic," I said, "we should give Illinois back to the Indians."

"The movements have been compared," he admitted. "And some of the same people are fighting to keep Indian Territory for the Indians."

I didn't know exactly where Indian Territory was, and if you'd asked me I would have said it already belonged to the Indians, thus the name, but I held my tongue for fear of seeming stupid.

"And what would we do there, in Zion?"

"Oh, same as everywhere. Farm. Be tailors. Run newspapers. Ship products."

I held this thought in my mind for a second, imaging my mother in the desert washing clothes with sand, the sun beating down on her beturbaned head.

"There's a smaller part of the movement that wants to try out Marx's ideas on a small scale, called a kibbutz, where everyone lives communally and shares in the work."

"That's what my apartment was like where I grew up," I said. "We all shared one lavatory and we all did the work."

"Yes, but this would be voluntary," Zeke said. When he got excited, little bits of spittle collected in the corners of his mouth. "That's what's amazing. All these people banding together by choice to form a more perfect union. What the United States was supposed to be. And what it has failed to be."

This awoke in me an indignant sense of patriotism. "You think the United States is a failure?"

"Of democracy, yes. It's an oligarchy of rich people. We don't even have directly elected officials. For all the talk of liberty and equality and representation, we just appoint people to make our decisions for us."

Something was a bit wrong with this argument, but Zeke was so worked up that I thought it unwise to upset him further. His step quickened, and he bent over to pick up a rock and toss it into the lake, listening to it thump dully as it hit.

I picked up another, this one perfect for skimming, and set it shimmering across the calm surface. Zeke looked amazed. "How do you know how to do that?"

"My father taught me," I said. "Sometimes we'd go down to the water and we fished and skipped rocks."

"Do you know the physics behind it?" Zeke asked. He was showing off. He knew I wanted to go to college.

"I don't need to," I said. "It skips the same."

"It does." He laughed. "That it does."

And for the first time he bent over to kiss me. His lips were warm and slightly salty, wet from his saliva. He let them linger there for a second, then pulled away. My first kiss! I thought. Now I would have something to report to Rosalie.

Then he put his hand on my breast and I was so shocked I took a step back. Even safely away from him, I could feel the place he touched me grow hot—with shame? Desire? I didn't know which. I stepped back and he resumed walking as if nothing had happened. We continued awkwardly by the lake until we reached the back door of Mrs. Klein's house.

"Well," Zeke said. We'd been silent for the past fifteen minutes; the kiss had stolen our breath. He leaned forward and pecked my lips again. "That's okay, right?"

"Okay," I said.

He turned and took a step away. "See you at work tomorrow."

"Tomorrow's Saturday," I said.

"Right. See you Monday." He stumbled a little. I giggled and waved and didn't wait for him to go down to the end of the alley before I let myself in.

*

I would like to skip this part. But it's important, or the rest of my story won't make sense.

As the weeks went on, I got used to his touching me under my blouse, and his flattering happiness when I touched him back.

One afternoon, he and I took the train to the South Shore in Indiana. It was a relief to be out of the overheated city; the dunes undulating before us looked like our own planet. Lake Michigan is as big as an ocean, with waves to match. I was too afraid to get in over my waist, but Zeke dove through the waves like a dolphin. He'd grown up at the beach; his father believed in regular exercise, and they swam every day in the summer, though they lived on the Near West Side. Zeke came out of the water and stood over me, dripping. I laughed. I had purchased a bathing costume especially for this outing. It was the first new piece of clothing I had ever owned. I remember it: It was wool with a sailor collar and a skirt down past my knees. I was proud of it. The ties hid my lack of chest and the belt emphasized my waist. I felt beautiful.

The water fell off Zeke and he moved so that his body cast a shadow over mine like he was lying on top of me. "When can we, Fanny?"

I knew what he was asking me. It was what he'd been asking me since we started going steady. But I was barely sixteen and terrified. I wanted to, both because I too had urges and also because I wanted to make Zeke happy, but the consequences seemed potentially too dire. Every time he put his hands on me I could hear the warning of the flashbulb's pop, and I pushed him away.

"Do we have to be married, Fanny? Because I do want to marry you, when I'm a bit more settled." He smiled and knelt beside me, taking my hand and miming putting a ring on my finger. "*Ani l'dodi v'dodi li*," he said, the Hebrew wedding vow that tied a couple as beloveds.

I wanted to believe, but I couldn't. I didn't trust myself. "Soon," I said, meaning the opposite.

He growled in frustration and let my hand drop, lying back into the sun.

I had ruined our day. We rode back to the city in sunburned silence.

I felt terribly guilty. I was a tease, his stony face said as much, one of the worst things a girl could be called. I had no idea how to remedy this, other than to give in to his demands.

He met Rosalie that afternoon; we arrived back at the house at the same time.

"Well don't you look sun-kissed and rosy!" she said. "You must be Zeke." The wall of teeth.

He shook her hand. "You didn't tell me your cousin was so pretty," he

said. Rosalie smiled. I knew he meant it as the compliment one is supposed to give women when one meets them for the first time, but I felt
jealousy's sticky grip.

"Oh, stop! How was the beach?"

"Beachy keen!" I said. It was a terrible pun. Both Zeke and Rosalie
laughed tepidly, with politeness.

"Why don't we all go out, maybe next Saturday? I'd like to get to know
the man who is occupying all of Fanny's time." I was surprised to hear
Rosalie say this. Did she miss me? I hadn't even thought that she might
feel neglected. I assumed she was out with her acting teacher.

"Zeke observes Shabbos," I said.

"How's Sunday?" he said. "I can take you both out for ice cream. Bring
your beau," he told Rosalie.

"I would if I had one. Do you mind doing double duty?"

"A girl for each arm, I'm a lucky guy."

I wanted to interject myself into the conversation. "That sounds fun."

"Then it's decided. I'll call for you at two?"

"Perfect!" Rosalie said. "Nice to finally meet you, Zeke." She opened
the door.

"I'll be there in a minute," I said.

Zeke kissed me, holding me tight so I could feel how much he wanted
me. "Ow," I said as the embrace turned too forceful.

"Sorry." He backed away from me. "Bye."

I didn't turn back at the door to wave. I didn't want to see him and
feel bad about what I was denying him.

*

Zeke arrived on Sunday with a daisy for each of us, and we linked arms
as we walked toward the El. We went all the way up to Vogelsang's Drug
Store for a soda. What did we talk about? I don't remember exactly, but
fashion, probably, or our favorite foods. At the fountain we laughed and
drank Coca-Cola. We walked to nearby Lincoln Park and visited the zoo
and the conservatory, the glasshouse steamy and close. I don't remember anything in particular about that day, I just know that I felt so happy,

like I was part of a real family. I imagined us in fifteen years, Rosalie and her husband, our children with us. The future seemed certain.

When we were alone that night in bed, Rosalie said, "You're so lucky. I'm happy for you, Fanny. He's wonderful."

"I know," I said, "isn't he? I mean, he's a bit square and he can go on about Zionism, but I think he might be my Melvin Shumwitz."

Rosalie laughed. "Don't lose him, now."

I started. "Why? Do you think I'm doing something wrong?"

"No, no," Rosalie said. "I just mean, hang on to him."

"I don't know how," I said. "He wants . . . he wants to . . . you know."

"Of course he does." Rosalie's voice sounded loud in the dark. "They all want to."

"I'm afraid," I said.

"It's kind of fun."

I switched on the light and sat up. "Rosie, have you? Did you?"

She nodded, full of a secret. "With Peter."

"Your acting teacher? But he's married!" I laugh at myself now to think that that was what I was concerned with.

"He loves me," she said, wounded.

"And you   Aren't you worried about getting . . . You know?"

"He uses a French letter." Rosalie examined her fingernails.

"He reads to you in French?"

"No." Rosalie laughed condescendingly. "It's a sort of glove, over his thing. It makes you not have a baby."

I'd never heard of such a thing. "And it's fun?"

"Not at first, but then yes. And they are so appreciative."

They? I had nothing to say. Rosalie was again a thousand leagues in front of me. "I wouldn't know what to do."

"He will," Rosalie said confidently.

*

First Mr. Andrews fell sick, and we were all worried because his health was fragile. Then one of the clerks went down—he sent his son with a note excusing his absence using the most unnecessarily graphic descriptions of his symptoms. Then the men on the floor caught it, and production fell thirteen percent, a statistic that I painstakingly calculated with my mediocre math, so take it with a grain or sack of salt. Then one day Zeke didn't come to work.

At coffee time I felt a bit off, and my stomach had turned by noon so that I was racing into the lavatory every fifteen minutes, thinking I was going to lose my roll, only to sit facing the porcelain forlornly, wondering whether I would feel better if I got sick.

I emerged to find Elsie standing there. "I'm sorry to keep it occupied," I said.

"I don't have to use it," Elsie said. "I'm standing here to tell you to go home."

"I'm fine," I said, leaning against the wall. "I'll stay."

"Frances, you're positively green," she said. "You make grass look dull in comparison."

I had to agree that I was a bit woozy, and the room was tilting dangerously. So far I hadn't done much work and probably wouldn't be capable of any.

"Don't worry," Elsie said. "Mr. Mays gives two sick days a year."

I wanted to tell her I didn't need a sick day, but I felt the need to rush back into the lavatory and this time I was successful in my purging.

Then Elsie had no trouble convincing me that I should go home and lie down. She even gave me a dollar for a hansom cab, a luxury that I had trouble accepting but ended up taking, not even enjoying the plush velvet in my stupor. I had only been in a carriage a handful of times, and combined with the queasiness of my stomach, I had the sensation of flying, like my spirit had been released from my body and I was hovering above myself.

I let myself in; the house was silent. I checked the living room and the dining room, but Mrs. Klein was not in the sitting room nor eating lunch. The door to her room was closed, so I assumed she was napping. I walked down the long hallway and through the kitchen that led to Rosalie's and my room.

I heard then a loud groaning, which I thought might have come from me or my stomach. The walls got narrower in my vision and I so wanted to lie down that I had trouble making sense of what I saw when I entered the room.

Rosalie was on all fours on the floor, completely nude, and a man held her long braids up like the reins to a horse. He was still mostly clothed, his pants around his ankles and his shirt bunched up around his waist. They were facing the window and had their eyes closed and so didn't see me in the doorway. Rosalie moved away from him and his organ popped out red and angry and then he put it back in. Rosalie moaned, and the man spoke in a gruff, huffing voice. "Here it comes," and I realized the voice was familiar. Zeke.

I was frozen in the doorway the way I was paralyzed at Rosalie's house that afternoon. I willed my limbs to move but they refused to obey and held me there, captive to the scene. Zeke and Rosalie separated, and that was when she saw me.

"Fanny, what are you . . . ? Oh God, Fanny."

All that came out of my mouth was a squeak.

Zeke pulled up his pants hurriedly and tried to hide by turning his face away, like a child who thinks he is invisible if he closes his eyes. Another wave of nausea overtook me and I barely made it to the bathroom before vomiting up mostly bile into the bathtub. Rosalie followed me in. She was still unclothed and her breasts hung low, the nipples large. Her face was red from exertion and bits of sweat clung to her. Hers or Zeke's?

"Fanny, I can—" I brushed past her and heard Zeke say, "Wait!" I grabbed my small purse as I ran out the back door, tripping more than once and landing on my backside as I hurried down the stairs.

Once outside I began to run, my legs and lungs aching after only a minute or two. I ran to the lake, too confused to cry or even to think about what I'd witnessed. I ran until I thought I would black out, and then I sat on a bench. I was emptier than I ever have been, my stomach a vast pit of quicksand, an eddy, at the bottom of which only air swirled.

*

I was awakened by a woman out with her dog sometime later. I wasn't sure how long I'd slept, but it was obviously early evening. My shivering had calmed, though my fever had gotten worse, and I was very confused. From what they told me later, I had called the woman by Mrs. Bloomfeld's name, mistaking her fancy dress. Therefore, they took me to the Bloomfelds' house, though Mrs. Bloomfeld claims she barely recognized me, I was in such sorry shape. Luckily, no one had robbed me while I was unconscious; I had all my savings in that small purse.

Her maid helped me to the bathroom and changed me into a plush nightgown. I remember that it was the softest material I'd ever touched. I took a cup of tea with honey and fell asleep before I could drink it.

When I awoke, the first thing I saw was Rosalie's face, and I was very glad until I remembered why I was in need of nursing in the first place.

"Fanny," she said, and stroked my forehead with a wet cloth, but I turned so that my back faced her. I gathered Mrs. Bloomfeld's soft sheets, so much more luxurious than our own scratchy linens, so that Rosalie couldn't climb in next to me. If I could have plugged my ears I would have. But though I tried not to hear, I couldn't help it.

"I'm so sorry, Fanny. It's . . . hard to explain. Here, I'll try. I came home one night and I saw him outside the back door, smoking and pacing. He was very odd, as you said he could be, but then I saw that you had left him unsatisfied . . . He was saying that he wasn't going to see you anymore because he couldn't get married now, and what sort of modern girls wouldn't . . . finish what they'd started? And I knew how much you cared for him, Fanny, so I took care of it, and then we just sort of kept meeting. It was for you. I didn't mean to hurt you."

At the word "hurt," I recalled with vivid precision watching him put his thing there, inside her, and heard her groan, which was not one of complaint, and I pulled my legs into my chest and the covers over my head and it wasn't until I heard her footsteps leave the room that I allowed myself to straighten.

My fever broke for good the following day, and I had time to think about what Rosalie had said. A veil had been lifted. I heard the stupid logic of her tone. She was an actress, I reminded myself, capable of chameleon changes and personality subterfuge. She withheld from me all those years her family's arrangement with the landlord, and now I wondered if the scene at her house hadn't been for my benefit, if she had always planned to live off me while she worked her way to New York. I felt duped, angry. And foolish, one of the most painful emotions for a young person, when nearly every day brings a new humiliation born of inexperience.

I was angrier at her than at Zeke, though I had plenty of rancor for him as well. I had thought that we would be married. I fantasized about having children in Palestine, about bringing them up in a mango orchard, of making sacramental wine from grapes we'd grown ourselves. I had allowed him to seduce me mentally, even if I didn't relent physically. And now I wondered why I hadn't.

What was clear to me was that I couldn't face either of them, and yet I'd have to. How do you look someone in the face when you've seen them do what I saw them do to each other? How do you not see that same scene every time they hand you a coffee cup, or a broadsheet to proofread?

Here the momentary clarity wore off, and before I could think of where to go and what to do, I fell asleep again, dreaming of Mrs. Bloomfeld's daughter's dolls, whose shiny hair and white skin stared at me from their glass cabinet.

Mrs. Bloomfeld came in the following morning and drew the curtains herself. She put her hand on my forehead. "I think you're all right now," she said. "Rosalie said you've fought, though she won't tell me what about."

I said nothing, barely blinked. "Well, you'll have to make up," she said. "I know I fought with my cousins and sisters when I was your age, and it's all forgotten now."

"I don't think this is something I can forget," I said. My voice sounded hoarse from disuse.

"Well, if you won't tell me, then I can't agree or disagree." I let the silence build, though Mrs. Bloomfeld was obviously expecting an explanation, or at least an acknowledgment.

"You're very kind to care for me," I said, finally.

"Well, my daughter is away at school, and I would hope that if anything ever happened to her, someone would take her in as I've done you. But you can't stay here forever."

I wanted to hibernate eternally, curled up in Mrs. Bloomfeld's daughter's bed, surrounded by lush carpets, the desk, and occasional tables that were there for mere decoration, not just function.

"Can you eat some breakfast?" I nodded and Mrs. Bloomfeld said she'd have some sent in. I wished I knew her daughter. Rosalie was the only friend I had in the world. I thought of Elsie, but I knew that she was busy in her own world, and her friendship, while not false, was superficial, as well as new. Mrs. Bloomfeld was right. I would have to reconcile with Rosalie if I was going to continue to live with her. But how to forgive her? I never wanted to see either her or Zeke again.

As soon as I could put weight on my legs, I did what Rosalie would have done, and I imagined she was proud of her protégé. I dressed in one of Mrs. Bloomfeld's daughter's dresses that was hanging in the closet. I picked out two other worn ones that weren't likely to be sorely missed, and packed them in a satchel I found. I also borrowed some of her underthings. I didn't borrow them; I stole them. I told myself that I could mail them back when I got settled.

I snuck out the back door of the house when all was quiet and took the El to Union Station. I caught the first train that was going west. I didn't intend to ride it that far. I just wanted out.

Part Two

Part Two

CHAPTER SIX

The years passed. Time is like a dray horse—it follows its own will. It plods along when you wish it would speed, and then it runs away from you when you need it to stroll beside you. I ended up in Nebraska, working as a secretary for Mrs. Doris Keane, a wealthy farmer's wife and suffragist. My principal qualification for employment was my facility with the printing press, since she published voting rights pamphlets. In return, she let me live on the farm, adjusting my hours so that I could finish high school, then paying me a wage so I could attend college. I won't dwell on this part of my life. Just know that I remember it as one of the more peaceful moments in my existence. Though I was glad to leave Nebraska when the time came, I sometimes still miss its vastness, the placidity of the acres of farmland, the way you can see the weather rolling in, the polite way it warns you. I miss the flat plain faces and the way that nothing ever changed, except that polite weather.

My anger at Zeke and Rosalie, especially Rosalie, burned like persistent coals for months. When it waned, I fed it with the image of them together, fanned it with memories of Rosalie's betrayal with the man I loved. Did I love him? I don't know now. It was so long ago. And then gradually over the course of a year or so the anger left me and I was caught up in my new life. First hours, then days, and then weeks went by without Zeke or Rosalie crossing my mind. Daily life is consuming—it will mask unpleasant thoughts.

I learned all sorts of skills during that time which have proven to be useful in my later life; one can't live on a farm for six years and not pick up some basic knowledge of Nature's stingy largesse. I learned to trap and skin a rabbit without losing my lunch. I could grow a vegetable garden.

I also learned much about Mrs. Keane's enthusiasms. My very first day, Mrs. Keane gave me two pamphlets. One said "Give yourself to Christ" and the other said "Stand up and be counted." The connection between Christianity and suffrage was nebulous at best; I knew the Old Testament well enough to know that any quotations from it needed to be twisted if they were to support Mrs. Keane's cause. The Bible did not mention women's right to vote, and I doubt the New Testament spent much ink on it.

During my time with Mrs. Keane I became a convert (if a passive one) to her cause. Now it seems obvious that women should have the right to vote, but at that time, most people, if they didn't actively oppose it (on moral grounds, or on the grounds that it would be politically inexpedient), hadn't given the issue much thought at all. That's just the way it was.

Having seen the pamphlets, though, I was too afraid to mention that I was not a Christian. It wasn't that I lied. It was more that I never quite found a way to mention it, and then it was too late to mention it. Mrs. Keane thought pork was unclean, so it was never served at the farm, though we raised and slaughtered pigs. It was easy to forget about my religion.

But every September I would start to feel guilty. Some date in the month (I had no access to a Jewish calendar) would be Rosh Hashanah, followed ten days later by Yom Kippur, the two most important holidays. On Yom Kippur one is supposed to ask for forgiveness, and I had a barnful of people I needed to seek absolution from. I was sure my parents were worried; even if they were relieved that I was no longer dependent on them, they would most likely be happy to know that I was okay. I wanted to write Elsie and Mr. Mays as well, to excuse my flight. Maybe they wouldn't forgive me, but at least they'd have an explanation. And Mrs. Bloomfeld deserved a thank-you note for nursing me, and an apology for appropriating her daughter's clothing.

After two Yom Kippurs had passed, I sat down after breakfast one day with some blank paper and tried to pen those notes. It was hard going. I'd wronged all of them, selfishly. And though I had my reasons, which may even have been good reasons, I'd lied and even stolen, and I saw, just for a second, how Rosalie might have been able to justify her own misconduct. Would my parents write back? I'd never learned to write Yiddish, so I wrote in English. Would they even be able to read it? Would they consult someone, or would their shame about their poor English prevent them from doing so? Would they be proud of me for continuing my education, or would they think me frivolous and a liar?

Not three weeks later, a letter came from my parents. Nothing was mentioned about my precipitous disappearance for two years. We began a regular correspondence, quarterly letters that said nothing of importance. My brother wrote in English, using the plural first person so that I was never sure whose opinions on the weather and the price of chicken were being expressed. Elsie sent me a brief note; by her brevity I knew she was angry with me. I never heard back from Mrs. Bloomfeld, which did not surprise me.

Six months later, Mrs. Keane's maid told me that a letter had come for me, but I didn't go down to get it until suppertime, as I assumed it was from my family. I was writing a paper, I remember, for my eighteenth-century British literature class, the second one I was taking at the university, though I was also still attending high school to catch up on the math and science I'd missed.

The envelope sat on the entry table, and from the stairs I recognized the handwriting. Rosalie always had perfect penmanship, a trait that annoyed me, as I could not make my hands do anything so orderly and was often penalized for my messiness. My stomach flipped and the blood left my brain. I should have known she'd find me. It wasn't like I'd hidden that well. All three of the people I wrote to had my address. I debated whether to open it. Part of me wanted to throw it in the fireplace unread, a romantic gesture fueled no doubt by my current reading list. But another part was curious to see what she had to say. I put my thumb under the lid of the envelope, but just then I heard the maid calling me to supper. Mrs. Keane liked to eat with us when her husband was away, and she could not abide tardiness. So I shoved the letter into the pocket of my skirt and rushed to the table.

All through the meal, the mumbled grace, the "please pass," the conversations about the advance of autumn, the suffragist movement, the Indian question, the letter sat burning in my pocket like an iron hot to shoe the horses. I couldn't wait for the meal to end. Usually I helped with the dishes. I considered claiming a headache, but it seemed to me a cowardly thing to do. I hurried so through the washing up that the cook asked me if I had a beau waiting.

I imagined the contents of the letter a thousand different ways. She would apologize, beg forgiveness. She would tell me she and Zeke were getting married, that she'd landed a role in a movie, that she was expecting Peter's baby . . .

Even if I no longer thought of Rosalie every day, I had no other close friends, and I still longed for her company. Sometimes I talked to her in my mind about things that were troubling me or milestones I achieved. Even after I reminded myself that she and I were no longer in contact and of the circumstances that forced that breach, I still used her as a sort of mental diary, a repository of my innermost thoughts and challenges. So to actually receive a letter from her gave me the uneasy sensation of being talked to from beyond the grave.

Safe in my room, I tore the envelope and removed the letter. It was two pages long:

Dear Fanny,

I hope that you'll read this, though I suppose if you're reading this then you decided to read it . . . Fanny, how can I ever apologize? Or, rather, how can I beg your forgiveness? What do I have to do so that you'll grant it? Because I will do anything. I will beg anything.

Fanny, I made a terrible mistake. But that's what it was, a mistake. I thought I was helping. I see now that I was not. That doesn't excuse what I did, but maybe it explains it, a bit.

Fanny, I miss you so much. You're my only friend. You're the only one who knows my secret. Please don't judge me, Fanny. Instead, forgive me, your sister.

Maybe it will please you to learn that I've been suffering. You were not wrong; my acting teacher was not who he said he was, and dropped me suddenly, insulting me terribly in the process. Mrs. Klein's daughter asked me to leave. I'm ashamed to tell you how I put food in my mouth. Suffice to say that my punishment has fit my crime.

As you can see I've gotten back on my feet. I keep and clean a dance and acting studio downtown in exchange for classes, and they let me sleep on a cot in the back room. There are mice, of course, but it's not bad otherwise. I continue to go on auditions, but so far there's been very little work. I also dream of Broadway. Perhaps I'll get there one day.

Fanny, I pray you'll write me back and say that all is forgiven. How is it that you came to live in Nebraska? What's it like there? Are you in school? Working? Married? Engaged? I'm panting with anxiety to hear from you, and I only hope that your experience since we parted was as wonderful as you deserve, and not as abjectly miserable as mine has been, which I deserve.

Yours in love and humility,

Rosalie

I let the letter fall out of my hands onto the desk. It was what I had suspected, even what I had hoped for. Rosalie had taken the trouble to find me, to write me, to apologize. I even believed that she thought she was helping the situation when she began her relations with Zeke. Whatever became of him? Rosalie didn't say.

I won't hide that I felt a certain amount of satisfaction knowing that she'd been struggling while I fulfilled my dream of going to school. I wanted to write her back. I planned to do it a million times but there was always something more pressing that had to be done. I even started the letter and got as far as "Dear Rosalie," when I realized I didn't know what my next words would be. Did I forgive her? And what did I want from her?

While I considered what I wanted to say, the urgency to write her passed, and the months flew by in a blink. It felt like I had written her back already. Then when the school year finally ended I did put pen to paper and sent the letter off. In it, I told her she was forgiven, and that I was happy to hear from her. I told her a bit about my life and about school, and I included a rather graphic description of when I learned to kill and pluck a chicken.

When the letter came back to me marked "No Such Resident," I was sad I hadn't written immediately. Regret washed over me the way it always did in the aftermath of an impetuous action. Where had she gone? I hoped to New York. Or California. But this was back when people disappeared, when America was a vast swath of uncharted territory, and people were like pebbles tossed into the ocean.

Perhaps I wanted to continue to disappear, and that's why I moved to San Francisco when I graduated. Or maybe it's just because that's where I got a job, as a newly minted English teacher, diploma still fresh off the press.

*

I was a fourth-grade teacher for almost ten years, then a seventh-grade teacher for five, a teacher of English to Oriental immigrants' children for a dozen more. During that time, I lived in an apartment in the Fillmore with two other women. They got married, and I found two others to live with me, and when they, too, got married I decided that it was too much trouble and I moved into a boardinghouse near the school where I was then teaching.

Each year the students stayed the same while I aged, incrementally but undeniably. The girls in the boardinghouse left to get married, or to move back home, their fun in the big city done. I was courted a few times, and a few times thought that maybe I'd get married, but it never worked out, and then I got used to being who I was, and it was too late to find someone.

Most Friday afternoons, after school let out for the week, I would go to the cinema, to clear my mind of the children's problems and the politics of elementary education. There was a theater halfway between school and my house, and I could make the showing at five fifteen. I remember there was a Chinese man outside who sold grapes, a strange enough cinema snack that I always bought them. He had a jug of water that he'd pour over the grapes to clean them before he handed them to me, wrapped in harsh brown paper.

I never cared what I saw. They changed reels each Wednesday, so it was always something new. I was fond of adventure films, films in which animals appeared, and films set in Europe. I was less interested in the romances or comedies. They promised something false, something silly. I looked for Rosalie in the faces of the extras and the bit players. During the credits I'd look for her name, half hoping that I might see it. But I never did.

Milestones came and went with the suddenness of summer rain showers. My father died, and I sent more of my money home to my mother. My younger brother hurt his leg on the streetcar, and I sent a little more. And then my mother died of influenza and the money order I sent got sent back and I lost track of my siblings without realizing it. My thirtieth birthday took me by surprise. Not so my fortieth, which I had dreaded for so long that its actual occurrence was not nearly as bad as the anticipation.

One summer I took the train back to Nebraska to visit Mrs. Keane. There was a younger version of me doing my job. When we won the right to vote, I sent Mrs. Keane a card and it was this girl who wrote me back, a form letter thanking me for all my hard work for the movement.

My fiftieth birthday found me wanting a change. I had started to find the children irritating rather than endearing, and colleagues noticed I was burned out. I was sick of teaching the same thing every year, each new class simply a variation of the previous ones. I found the immigrants' lack of English annoying; my patience was razor thin. So I gave my notice and began to circle jobs in the want ads of the *San Francisco Chronicle*, the way I had done all those years ago in Chicago.

I applied for a number of secretarial jobs, including one that only vaguely described its purpose. I must have come across as discreet, for they hired me, and after only six months I was given basic security clearance and found myself working for the Twelfth District Office of Naval Intelligence.

It sounds like a glamorous job, but like all secretarial jobs it was mostly typing up reports and documents, answering phones, taking messages, and sending people on errands. My ability to read and not absorb communications served me well. I remained legitimately ignorant of what was going on. We had a small satellite office inside a nondescript office building downtown, a dingy back suite that had a heavy unmarked door. This suited me just fine. No real responsibilities, no one counting on me.

I have always been a rather quiet person, content to observe rather than participate, and my reticence grew with age so that by the time I reached my early fifties, an age at which women stopped being noticed, I blended into the scenery as neatly as a camouflaged iguana.

*

Ainslie had trouble opening the door. He was carrying a standard-issue briefcase, his hat in one hand and a large military duffel in the other. My first impression was that he was tall, incredibly tall, with a wide, matinee-idol mouth. His hair was pomaded neatly in place. He set the briefcase down to push the door. I wanted to help him out, but sometimes military men get embarrassed when a woman shows them how things work. Finally he pulled on the door and knocked the briefcase over. He tried to hold the door open with his leg while he reached for his case, but apparently he had never been to our outpost office before or he would have known that our door—reinforced iron-paneled—was notoriously heavy, and it closed on him.

I left my desk and gave the door a heave-ho with my meager body weight. Ainslie had bent to pick up his case, and like a Keystone Cops routine, I banged him in the head. His first words to me were, "Ouch, Lordy, that smarts."

I was horrified to see that a bright red welt was forming rapidly on his forehead, but he smiled. Everyone who has met Ainslie remembers his eyes, preternaturally focused and shiny, and he turned them on me while rubbing his forehead.

"Quite the bunker here."

He left the duffel in the hall and accepted my arm to take him to a chair. I mumbled apologies and said I'd send the boy for ice.

"If you could send him for some liver instead, that'll keep a lump from forming."

Right then, Director Childress came from his office. "Connie!" he said, extending his hand. "How the hell have you been?"

Ainslie shook his hand, pumping it hard. "Can't complain. I was fine until your girl here coldcocked me."

Childress looked at me with surprise and confusion. I could feel my face turn red.

"Sir, I'm sorry, I—"

But Childress laughed. "Good old Connie can take it, can't you, Lieutenant Commander?"

"I don't know, sir, she's got Kraut aim."

They went inside Childress's soundproof office. I opened our fortified entrance and pulled in his duffel. It weighed more than it appeared to, and it was all I could do to drag it inside. I kicked off my heels and bent over to pull it. I was thus engaged, my hind region high in the air, when Ainslie stuck his head out.

"The boy back with the meat yet?"

I straightened up hurriedly. "Sorry, I was just . . ."

Ainslie's forehead knot was a bright clown's nose above his eyes. "Let me know when it gets here."

"Yessir," I said.

Their meeting ended before the boy got back. Ainslie and Childress emerged, without the briefcase, and said their goodbyes. Ainslie slung the heavy duffel over his shoulder and, pretending to be afraid of my lethal force, took his leave. Not five minutes later, the boy came in with a piece of liver, which I ate for dinner that night, though I hate organ meat.

*

I thought nothing more of the handsome man who came to the office until the following week when Childress called me into his sanctum sanctorum. I brought my steno pad, my constant companion. Childress motioned with his chubby hand for me to sit. His office had no windows and curiously it always smelled of paste. He usually had a fan going to circulate the air, as he was always sweaty, and his hair swirled with its oscillations. It blew cold on my ankles.

"I have a strange proposition, Miss Frank." (I had kept my assumed name.)

I began to write the sentence down until I realized he was addressing me. I looked up. "There is an assignment . . . it's a strange one, and it requires a certain kind of person. Well, a female kind."

I couldn't imagine what he was about to ask me.

"Do you remember that man named Conway last week? The one you hit with the door?"

"I'm so sorry, sir. It was an accident. I was just—"

"It's not about that. He's . . . well, I can't tell you until you have the appropriate clearance, but let's just say he does some shadow work for us."

It is a testament to my ability to disassociate myself from my work that I wasn't sure what he was talking about.

"He's been assigned to a rather remote post, and part of his cover requires that he arrive with a wife."

My first thought was that Childress was going to ask me to find someone to marry Conway. I thought about the girls in my boardinghouse. There might be one on the second floor who would be appropriate. I didn't know much about her. Would she pass the background check?

Childress was waiting for some kind of response. "I can look around," I said. "But surely he can find his own wife. He's very handsome."

Childress cleared his throat. "Yes, well, he's a confirmed bachelor, and we need someone who will remember that the first duty is to the country rather than to some sentiment. It's sentiment that compromises, every time. Or greed, I suppose. Greed and sentiment. We thought that you might consider it, Miss Frank."

"Consider what? I'm sorry . . ."

"Marrying Conway and accompanying him on his mission."

I believe my jaw actually flopped open. My throat went dry.

"You have the clearance, no ties that I can see to anything or anyone in particular in the Bay Area. You are highly capable . . . And you said that you lived on a farm, so you're self-sufficient."

The proposal was so preposterous that I couldn't even articulate the reasons why I couldn't go.

"It's Floreana, one of the Galápagos Islands, in case you were wondering."

I had heard of them, of course, in relation to Darwin and his famous finch, but they might as well have been on a different planet for all I knew about their location and topography.

I was unable to muster the appropriate muscles to produce speech; even my brain was paralyzed.

"Pacific, off the coast of Ecuador. I have a map here somewhere." Childress began halfheartedly looking through the piles on his desk. He gave up after two piles. "It would just be for twelve months or so. Then you can come back here and get the marriage annulled and all will be as it was. Are you all right, Miss Frank? You look like you're in pain."

Throughout my life people have told me that when I'm not actively managing my features they screw up into a rictus. My brow furrows, my eyes narrow, and my nearly invisible lips retreat into the safety of my mouth. I can only assume I was wearing this expression now. I felt, as Ainslie liked to say, flummoxeled, a combination of flummoxed and frazzled.

I nodded, my tongue large in my mouth. I tasted, peculiarly, pennies. Looking at my reaction now, I understand that it was so extreme because I knew already that I would accept the mission. Still, Childress gave me two weeks to think about it, and arranged for me and Ainslie Conway to get together to discuss the nonclassified part of the arrangement.

Childress gave me a file folder that contained the following information (supplemented by a trip to the library and a 1935 *South American Handbook*).

The Galápagos, formerly known as Las Islas Encantadas, or the Enchanted Isles, are an archipelago formed by volcanoes about six hundred miles west of the Ecuadorian shore. They were the nationless playground of whalers and buccaneers until Ecuador annexed them in 1832. Darwin paid his famed visit in 1835. Still, they served mostly as a service station for passing ships in search of protected bays in which to repair ships, take on fresh water and coal, and capture tortoises (this can't have been good sport, for the tortoise's reputation for pokiness is well deserved, but they could live for months without water and provide fresh meat for those at sea). There were no more tortoises on Floreana, I was disappointed to learn; the sailors and pirates had eaten them all. The few that escaped were decimated by the introduced goat and rat population. Supposedly, also, pirates buried treasure there, though none had yet been found, so this must have been a romantic fantasy. Then the islands were the site of a penal colony, a coffee plantation (whose owner was so cruel to his employees that they killed him), various fisheries that failed, and occasional mutineers put ashore as punishment. It did not sound promising.

There were four inhabited islands, and we were to live on the south-ernmost of these: Floreana, a round island with two protrusions like fox ears. The first permanent European residents of Floreana were the Germans Dr. Friedrich Ritter and his partner, Dore Strauch. An odd pair, Ritter was an ascetic, a strict vegetarian, and by all accounts a taskmas-ter. He met Dore when she was his patient. They soon became lovers, though they were both married. Ritter had contrived his own philoso-phy, a mixture of Nietzsche and Kant and Ritter that emphasized self-sufficiency. Dore was an acolyte. The Galápagos seemed like the perfect place to test their theories, so they sat both their families down and convinced their respective spouses to unite just as Dore and Friedrich were uniting. And apparently the arrangement worked out.

The doctor was short, grouchy, and surly. Dore was subservient and of equally bad humor. I have known my fair share of vegetarians in my life, and there is something about those who choose to forgo meat when it is available that creates a particular type of misanthrope. Friedrich and Dore had no teeth; they had them pulled before leaving the Conti-nent to avoid dental problems. Why would vegetarians need teeth?

They had been on the island about five years when Margret and Heinz Wittmer arrived. Margret was pregnant at the time, and they had with them Heinz's son from his first marriage; the boy had rheumatic fever, which caused poor eyesight.

Margret's account of their arrival can be read in her book, *Floreana*, which in its own way is as redacted as mine. Much of it is her attempt to exonerate herself and her husband from the charges of murder.

Apparently there was no love lost between Dore and Friedrich and the Wittmers, though they shared a common language. Friedrich refused to help them, though he did eventually tend to Margret after she gave birth. She failed to deliver the placenta and would have died of septic shock had he not intervened.

In October 1832, an Austrian baroness arrived with her three lovers: an Austrian, a German, and an Ecuadorian who soon left the island. A diva in search of a stage, she established herself with the intention of starting a luxury resort. She told wild stories of her absent husband, a count, and their lavish lifestyle before she decided to travel the world.

The baroness was the worst kind of neighbor—she stole from the other colonists, and convinced stopping ships that they need not leave any extra supplies for the other residents. She beat Lorenz, the weakest of the lovers, savagely. He often escaped to Friedrich and Dore's in tears, begging for help. One day he arrived saying that the baroness and her German lover had left on a boat. No one ever saw the boat, and no trace was ever found of either of them. Did Lorenz murder them, finally driven to the brink by his mistreatment? Did Friedrich dispatch them with his bag of apothecary tricks, sick of their meddling? Or did the Wittmers do it? Maybe the baroness and her lover met with an accident, or maybe they actually did catch a ship that no one ever saw. Who knows?

But it was these kinds of antics that drew the attention of the press and the military. What were all these Germans doing on an island in the Pacific? And more were arriving. Add to that the fact that Friedrich died of meat poisoning (some vegetarian!) less than a year later and you have a real whodunit.

The report on the disappearances, I saw, was signed by Allan Hancock, whose name was familiar as an oil baron and amateur scientist. I wasn't aware he was working for the government. Included were a copy of his ship's log, with several photos of the sailors dressed as women and Roman gods to celebrate his first trip across the equator. "The Pollywogs and King Neptune" read the caption.

As for Floreana, the log showed several pictures of the deceased in livelier times (pun intended). I studied the baroness's house for a while. It was a scene from *Mutiny on the Bounty*, palm trees and gracefully draped platform beds and chairs. There was a rug on the ground, and the baroness was smiling, thin-lipped. In other photos, Hancock was holding a large iguana by its tail, and in still another he was laughing with Friedrich while Dore pet her donkey, Fleck.

I am never one to shy away from a challenge, and reading about the Galápagos I was being issued one. "You can't make it here," the literature said. "You are old and not up to the task."

"I'll show you," I said to myself. "I have homesteaded in Nebraska and joined the gold rush in San Francisco. A few brambles on an island don't scare me." Let it be known that I lived on a long-established farm in Nebraska and was half a century too late for the gold rush. The only panning I did was to search for a decently punctuated sentence among my students' papers. If you're going to have an imaginary debate, however, you might as well embellish the facts.

I will not deny that the idea of spending more time with matinee-idol Conway was a tick in the pro column. Yes, I was north of fifty, and though literature stops recording desire once the decrepitude of thirty sets in, real life does not immediately follow suit. I knew him not at all, but I liked the cut of his jib, as they used to say.

It is also worth remembering that I tend to make decisions impetuously where drastic life changes are concerned. It has always been a feature of my personality. Some would compliment me on my devil-may-care attitude. Others might disparage it as myopia and insanity. They would both, of course, be correct.

*

He was very, very handsome. After a separation, I was always struck breathless by his beauty as if seeing him for the first time. He was less intimidating sitting down, though the second he saw me, he stood and kissed me on the cheek, which made me blush. Luckily the supper club was dark enough that no one could see.

He pulled out my chair and pushed it in as I got settled. Then he motioned for the waiter. "What'll you have?" he asked.

"Um . . ." I rarely drank. "What are you having?"

The waiter stood at attention tableside. His white apron brushed the tablecloth.

"Manhattan." He raised his glass. "I'll take another."

"I'll have a Tom Collins," I said.

"So," Ainslie said, leaning forward. I took the slight tremble in his elbows for nervousness, which calmed me. "I don't know what I should ask you. What's your middle name?"

"I don't think I have one," I said.

"You don't know?" he said.

I did know, actually, but I didn't want to tell him. It was my Hebrew name, Franya. Yes, my parents named me Frances Franya Frankowski. I shrugged. "You?"

The waiter brought the drinks. I took the smallest of small sips. It was strong. Ainslie drank deeply.

"Ainslie actually *is* my middle name. Elmer is the first. It's also my father's name so I took the middle one." Then he said something that sounded like "Homely name."

"I don't think it's that homely," I said. "I've certainly heard worse names."

"Family name, I said. But good to know you think it's not too homely."

I could feel the heat spring to my cheeks. "Oh, I'm so sorry," I said. "I'm so embarrassed."

"Don't be. I happen to agree with you, which is why I go by Ainslie."

"I feel terrible." How had I made such a tremendous error during the first five minutes of our acquaintance?

"Nonsense. Here, I'll insult your name and we'll be even. Ummm . . ."

"I'll help. My nickname means . . . derriere."

Ainslie laughed. "And in England it means something worse."

"That's their word for taxes?"

"I don't get it," he said, leaning forward on his hand.

"'Taxes' is the only word worse than 'fanny.'"

He tossed his head back, guffawing.

"I'm going to like you, Fanny," he said, winking at me.

"I really thought I'd left that name in Duluth." The alcohol was taking effect and I was enjoying our banter.

"What shall I call you then? How's Franny?"

"I'll ask her."

He grimaced.

"That's fine. I answer to Franny."

"So, Franny, tell me about yourself. All I know is that you're from Duluth." I gave him an abbreviated and cleansed history of my travels, and asked him the same.

"Childhood on horseback in California, enrolled in the navy on my eighteenth birthday. Sent to the Philippines to fight Mohammedans. They always arrange their children's marriages. It seemed to work out all right, so I have good hopes for this one."

I laughed in nervousness. Ainslie took another sip of his drink so I tilted mine back and let the liquid touch my lips.

"Have you been married before?" I asked.

He shook his head. "Confirmed bachelor." He used the same words Childress had. "You?"

"Never."

"Well, then, neither of us will have expectations. I'm afraid I'm probably everything Childress told you. He and I go back to the Great War, when he plucked me out of my unit and drew me to his bosom. Every time I try to get out of the racket, he lures me back in."

"What's so enticing about this assignment?" I asked. "In fact, what is this assignment?"

"You're part of the draw, naturally," he flashed his teeth in a grin and signaled to the passing waiter for one more.

"Naturally," I said. It was kind of him to offer a compliment. He could hardly have been interested in me, eleven years his senior.

"But seriously, they haven't told you what we'd be doing?"

"My clearance hasn't . . . cleared."

"My God, the bureaucracy is maddening." His drink arrived and he plucked the cherry out of it with his fork and ate it. The waiter also set bread and butter on our table. Ainslie first tilted the basket toward me, but I was too nervous to eat. When I shook my head, he took a roll, ripped it in two, and slathered both halves generously with butter. He ate one and washed it down with half his drink. His fingers were long, too thick for the rest of his spindliness. "I've been told I have a prodigious appetite."

"I see," I said.

Ainslie finished the roll and brushed the crumbs into a neat pile near his plate. The waiter handed us our menus. Ainslie buried his face in his but continued talking to me. Later I would understand this was part of his training, to cover his mouth if talking about sensitive topics. I could still hear him over the din if I leaned in.

"I'll just tell you. It's hardly the stuff of spy thrillers. You know where the Galápagos are, I assume?"

I nodded.

"And you'll have read those *Time* and *Life* articles about the disappearances or murders—whatever you like."

Again I nodded.

"Did it strike you as odd, so many Germans living on a remote island?"

"It did. But I have known some Germans, and they like to do things in their own manner."

"True," Ainslie said. "I'll have the lamb chop." The waiter had materialized, and I hadn't noticed.

"The sole," I said.

"Very good, madam." He took our menus.

"And another round, please," Ainslie said, though my drink was almost as full as it had been when the waiter first brought it to the table. "We find it very suspicious, and by we I mean naval brass."

"Aren't they just living out their Swiss Family Robinson fantasies?"

"Maybe," Ainslie said. He ate another piece of bread. The butter was gone. "But I bet they're up to something. Maybe it's just residual suspicion from the Great War. I always think Krauts are the enemy."

"What would they be up to?"

"I'm talking with my mouth full on purpose," Ainslie said. "Don't think I'm rough. I'm a little rough, but mostly trained." He laughed, then choked a bit, grabbing for his drink and draining it. "Lean in, take my hands so we're sweethearts sharing intimate nothings." I did so. His hands were cool and smooth and I regretted not manicuring mine better. I have bony hands, and time has not been kind to them. "I'm not sure what the Germans are doing there," he said. "But someone should find out."

Our salads arrived, a mountain of green lettuce clinging leaf to leaf. Ainslie ordered a glass of red wine. "Do you want one? I got into the habit in France."

"Sure," I said. I liked wine.

"Make it a bottle," he said to the waiter. "We shouldn't talk about this here. Let's just get to know each other."

Ainslie told me about his upbringing in California. He was rather wild, rode a horse to school, joined the navy for adventure. What followed was a hilarious account of a stint in the Philippines followed by misadventures with the Rough Riders in Mexico. It was like a Charlie Chaplin movie with sound instead of vision, the verbal equivalent of pratfalls. Ainslie imitated a Mexican convincingly, and told me how he once delivered a baby. Then someone confused him with another Conway and he became a rifle instructor. He had no idea how to teach riflery, and faked his way through the first two months because it was easy duty until the officers found out and threw him in the brig. He was surprised to be sprung less than twelve hours later, by Childress, who had heard about his deception and decided he'd be perfect for intelligence. He worked his way up to lieutenant commander.

Thus he ended up in France. There was a little combat, which he didn't talk about, but mostly his job was to charm villagers, keep his ear to the ground.

"So you speak French?"

"Nah," he said. "Didn't need it. It made people more relaxed around me, talk more freely with each other."

"But it was in a language you didn't understand."

"That would be the essence of military intelligence." He poured the last of the wine into our glasses. I was a bit tight now. "As it happens, I did manage to pick up one piece that was interesting."

"What?" I leaned in, interested.

"Can't say," Ainslie said coyly.

"Come on, tell me!"

"Lips are eternally sealed." He held them together with his fingers until, infected by my laugh, he began to chuckle too hard. It was so funny. What was, exactly? I'm not sure, but I hadn't laughed so hard in ages. My stomach began to hurt and other people were giving us looks.

"Time to go," he said. "Let's have a nightcap. My place?"

I was completely enraptured. Ainslie had the uncanny ability to make you feel like you were the only person in the world, and that his attention, which could be bestowed on anyone, had alighted on you because you are so special. And having been invisible for so long, the spotlight was warm and inviting. A small feather tickled my lower stomach. It was something I hadn't felt in a long time.

*

Ainslie's apartment was not far. It was a small one-bedroom, neat as a pin, nary a personal touch in sight. It might have been a hotel room for all its personalization. He poured us two scotches and we sat on the sofa.

I set my glass on the coffee table. "Why on earth would you want to do this?" I asked, seriously.

"I like the taste," he said, and took a sip. I tilted my head at him and he smiled. "You're lovely," he said. He pretended to pinch my cheek.

"I'm old," I said. "I'm eleven years older than you. And don't you dare say something asinine like 'old is how you feel.'"

"I don't even know what that word means," he said. "See? That's the kind of thing I'd want my wife to say."

"This is crazy," I said.

"A lot of what I do is." He looked into my eyes, actually seeing me. His look was inscrutable. It wasn't desire . . . what was it? "What's the worst that could happen?"

"We could hate each other and be stranded on a desert island, wallowing in misery for the rest of our lives or killing each other in a murderous rage."

"That is a bad-case scenario," he agreed. "I have an idea. Let's go camping this week. I'll get Childress to give you three days. We'll go up to Humboldt, tool around in the mountains. I have a pair of pup tents we can use. Separate tents, of course. If we survive that, we'll know if it'll work."

There was no reason not to agree.

*

"I've never been camping," I admitted, as we were motoring over the Golden Gate Bridge out of the city. It was overcast, and I had my scarf around my ears for warmth. Per Ainslie's instructions I had donned my first trousers, and I had bought walking shoes, which made me feel like I was wearing a pair of ottomans.

"It's not hard," Ainslie said. "It's just living, only dirtier."

He turned the radio on and began to sing along to "Paris in the Spring." He sang horribly, off-key, making up his own lyrics. The wind was loud, so I joined in with my warbly alto and we disharmonically headed north.

On the other side of the bridge the sky cleared, and we wound around Route 1, getting glimpses of the Pacific as it reached the continent's cliffs. "Not so bad, is it?" Ainslie asked.

"Eh," I said, pretending to be unimpressed. "At least it's not raining."

The trip was a success in that I learned that I didn't mind camping, fortunate, since we were effectively about to spend eight years of our lives doing exactly that. Ainslie and I got along splendidly. We made each other laugh.

The first night, I woke up to see a tiny light outside my tent. I stuck my head out. Ainslie was smoking, looking at the sky.

"Contemplating our relative smallness in comparison to the vast universe?" I asked.

"Honestly?" Ainslie said. "Trying to decide if I want fried chicken or pasta when I get home."

I knew then that everything was going to be fine.

CHAPTER SEVEN

I took the rest of the week off to think. On Friday, I went to the movies; decisions were often clearer to me after I sat in the dark for an hour and a half eating grapes. Matinees had the benefit of being both cheap and never crowded. They liked to show movies that had already had their moments in theaters. Since I cared less about what I saw and more about the experience, I barely looked at the title before I went in. This was a comedy, I did register, something madcap and farcical. I had my book and my bag of grapes, and I didn't notice who else came into the theater behind me, only that I was not alone.

The movie, *Night and Day* (I remember the title for reasons that are about to become clear), was, as these things usually are, formulaic and moderately enjoyable. It took place in rural France, though obviously it was a Hollywood soundstage. At one point, behind me in the theater I heard someone whisper, "Watch closely, here it is," before an unremarkable scene in a café. I thought I heard giggling. And then a small voice said, "Where, Momma?," and someone replied, "Shhh, there, the waitress."

"That's you?" the voice asked.

"It was," she answered.

I looked at the waitress in the scene. She was dressed like an exaggerated French woman, all ruffles and flounces. She had small eyes that were hidden under bangs, and her dark hair fell over her chest. She had two lines in French that sounded even to my untrained ear like an American had learned them phonetically. Her lips were painted red to look larger than they were.

And then I got involved with the farce: bed-hopping and door-slamming, secret passageways and misunderstandings, and soon the lights were coming up. I saw the woman and her three children ahead of me—two almost grown and one smaller.

Outside it was raining, and the family stopped to arrange umbrellas and mackintoshes, and the woman bent to help the smallest child. When she stood up, I recognized the eyes, the impossibly white teeth. Rosalie.

Her mouth fell open and her eyes went wide. The umbrella dropped from her hand. She tilted her head forward as if to ask, *Is it you?* I nodded.

"Fanny!" She took a couple of running steps forward, then caught herself and walked slowly to me, taking me into a hug. Then she held me at arm's length. "Is it really you?"

"I suppose it is," I said.

Behind her the youngest child said, "Who's that?"

"This," Rosalie said, turning to the children, "is my oldest friend, Frances Frankowski. Say hello to Miss Frankowski." I didn't tell her that I was going by Frances Frank. She grabbed my hand and squeezed. "Barbara," she pointed to the older girl, a pretty brunette with Rosalie's striking eyes; "Dan," an awkward boy of about sixteen with a crew cut; "and Sylvie." Rosalie could see the confusion on my face. "My children."

"I'm a mistake," Sylvie said.

I laughed. "Surely not."

"How do you do," the two older ones said in unison.

"Very well, thanks."

Rosalie still hadn't let go of my hand. She was gripping it so hard it hurt a bit, but I said nothing. As if reading my thoughts she let go, but kept her arm against mine to prevent my running off.

"Frances," she said. "I can't believe it's really you, Fanny. It is you, isn't it?"

"Yes," I whispered. My throat was dry, my mind empty. All the times I had imagined our reunion, and now everything I wanted to say left me. "I . . ." I trailed off.

Rosalie laughed. "I know, I know!" Her laugh, the high-pitched peals of glee, brought me back to our childhood. Her laugh was always so joyful. I smiled. "Please come have a cup of coffee. Say yes, you have to!" She had the same insistence as she did when we were kids. "Children," she said, "go get some ice cream at Giulio's. Barbie, make sure Sylvie doesn't make a mess, yes? Wait for me there. I might be a while." She handed the children some money and they skipped off. I followed her to a nearby diner.

She ordered us coffees while I sat mutely. I watched her speak to the waitress. Her eyes had little showers of wrinkles emanating from the side, and I could see the gray at her temples. Her face was thin; she had pierced her ears.

"Tell me everything," she said.

I shrugged. "There's too much."

"I'll start, then. And I'll tell you the secret part too. First, I'm thirty-nine."

I furrowed my brow in confusion.

"If anyone asks, I'm thirty-nine. I'm always thirty-nine."

"Okay . . ." I always freely volunteered my age; it excused a lot. And though Rosalie looked good for almost fifty-five, thirty-nine was pushing credulity.

"I know," Rosalie said. "A child at forty-four. I thought I was done . . . with all that, but then Sylvie arrived. No, wait, I'll start at the beginning." Rosalie told me how after she sent that letter she made her way to New York where eventually she found an agent who took her to Hollywood. She had a few bit parts in silent movies, a couple of advertisements, some dancing scenes in a crowd, and then it became very clear to her that she was never going to make it as a star. She met and married Clarence Fischer, who owned an antique-reproduction furniture store in Union Square (she mentioned the store's name and I pretended familiarity). They also had a factory, which was put to use during the Great War. He moved into manufacturing, and they were doing well enough to weather the Depression. In fact, they made money, as they'd invested in real estate, which was safe enough. "And, you know, people have to sit and sleep on something." Rosalie didn't have to say it; she had ended up quite wealthy.

She was the same old frivolous Rosalie, interested in money and appearances. Still, my heart warmed. I knew no one from the past, and it was so good to be around a friend, an old friend, especially one for whom the world was usually sunny. I forgot, at that exact moment, why I'd been angry with her. Rather, I knew, but the sting was absent after all these years.

"Are you married, Fanny? Children?"

I suppose I made a natural spy, because here is where some small part of me took over my faculties. I was jealous of Rosalie, the way I had always been, the way I would always be. I wanted to one-up her, or at least even our status.

"Yes," I said, "I'm married. I'm Mrs. Ainslie Conway."

Once I said it, I had to marry him, because when you tell a lie to someone you haven't seen for almost forty years it's important to see it through. That is honestly how I made my decision.

"Oh that's wonderful!" Rosalie said. "Tell me all about him."

"He's very kind," I said. "And also tall. He's very tall. We've only been married a short time." I told her I was working as a secretary for the navy, and that Ainslie was an officer. She was sorry that my talents went to waste in secretarial work. I told her I used to be a teacher, and that I liked my job.

"I need to go find my children," she said. "But I don't want to let you out of my sight. And I want you to meet Clarence. Say you'll come to Shabbat dinner tonight?"

My shock must have registered on my face. "I know, I know," she said. "Clarence's family is religious, and I, well, I've grown to like the customs. Don't laugh, just say you'll be there." She handed me a card with her address and discreetly paid the check. Then she handed me a small mother-of-pearl-shafted pen and another card and made me write down my address and telephone. "I'm not losing you again," she said. She stood and kissed me hard on the cheek, bounding out of the diner like someone half her age.

I sat stunned. "Would you like anything else, miss?" the waitress asked, obviously anxious to have her table back.

"No, thank you," I said. "I just need to sit for a moment."

Was I dreaming? Rosalie was living in San Francisco? I shook my head to clear the fog.

Rosalie. I smiled, finally able to get my legs working again. Rosalie.

*

I primped carefully for my night in Pacific Heights. I actually bought a new dress, belted at the waist with puffed sleeves and a yoke collar that drew attention to itself and away from my meager bust. I paired it with my only cloche and the same T-straps I'd been wearing for years. I even rouged my cheeks a bit.

Though only a mile away, Rosalie's neighborhood was about as far from my shabby Fillmore apartment as one could get. The house was even grander than I expected. I thought she'd been exaggerating her wealth, but it turned out she'd described it modestly. She lived in a true mansion, at the top of a hill, painted brightly in lavender and aubergine. The grand stone staircase was decorated with flowering vases—hostas, ranunculus, hydrangeas. I climbed the stairs and was surprised when it was not Rosalie who answered the bell I rang but a maid.

"Mrs. Conway," she said. "Please come in, I'll take your coat."

My pumps echoed on the marble floor as I followed the woman into a drawing room. In my boardinghouse efficiency, I couldn't imagine having my own room just for sitting and chatting. The Regency furniture was upholstered velvet, and the ornately carved mantel framed a fire that crackled with warmth.

Rosalie was making herself a drink at the sideboard. She came up and hugged me, then wiped my bangs, wet from my walk in the rain, off my face.

"I was worried you wouldn't come," she said. "We'll have dinner and then you and I can chat privately. Melanie, what time is it?"

As if on cue, the grandfather clock chimed six fifteen.

"Rosie?" A lumbering step came down the front stairs and a large man stuck his head in the drawing room. "This her, then?"

"Clarence, meet Frances."

Clarence was a formerly thin man whose weight had settled in his belly. He had very little hair left, but what he did have he combed around in a circle to simulate hair. He had a wide bulbous nose and a sharp chin, but it made for a pleasant face, if not exactly a handsome one. He shook my hand vigorously.

"Kids," he yelled upstairs. "Let's go."

I heard a rush of footsteps down the stairs, and we all walked into the dining room for dinner.

Clarence said the prayer over the candles, wine, and bread, and we were served by two different people, one colored and one white, who never let the wine in the glasses dip below halfway. Even the two older children, who were about Rosalie's and my age when we left home, drank wine. When the meal was over and the plates were cleared, the family sang songs in Hebrew. I recognized some of them from Rosalie's house in Duluth as classic Zionist melodies.

Afterward, the children and Clarence disappeared upstairs. Rosalie waited patiently at the entrance to the living room, while the maid turned on the light. I looked at her. "Marriage does funny things, Fanny, as I'm sure you know."

We sat, and I could feel the wine show hot on my face.

"Fanny, did you ever get my letter?"

I knew immediately the one she was talking about, the apology that I received on the farm in Nebraska. I nodded.

"Can you ever forgive me?"

I'd been angry for years. At times, that anger fueled me. Other times it deeply saddened me. Now I looked inside myself, and all that bubbled up was laughter. "Rosie, that was a hundred years ago."

"Well, not that long, really." She looked a little offended.

"I can't still be mad at something that happened when we were children. Plus, it meant I got to go to Nebraska and finish school. It's hard to regret that at this point."

"I'm so glad," Rosalie said. "Every year on Yom Kippur I pray for your forgiveness."

I wanted to laugh again. Rosalie used to join me in condemning my parents as superstitious peasants. For her to have found religion in this way made me question if I knew her at all. Of course, I'd changed too.

"I can explain why—"

I cut her off. "Rosalie, there's no need. Tell me instead how you met Clarence."

She grew animated and told me a long story, which I didn't quite follow, about stepping on his glasses while serving as a cigarette girl in a club in Los Angeles. She was animated, waving her arms, and when the story finished, she got up and stood near the door. "Melanie!" she called.

The maid from earlier arrived. "Yes, ma'am?"

"Can you light me a cigarette, please?"

Melanie went over to the console where a small box held cigarettes and a match. She held the cigarette up to Rosalie's lips and lit the end while Rosalie breathed hard.

"Do you smoke?" she asked me.

"No," I said. When she pulled the cigarette away from her mouth it was ringed with red. How had she managed to keep her lipstick on during dinner? My lipstick always slid off my lips like a dolphin sheds water.

There was a silence. Rosalie grabbed my hand again, squeezing it to the point of pain. The fire had died down, and the room was dark except for the point of her cigarette. "Fanny," she said, "I'm desperate not to lose you again."

"You won't," I said. I had been so lonely, I hadn't realized.

"I don't want us to have any secrets," she said. I nodded. Yet I already had secrets. "But there are things between us that I want to keep between us. I'm sure you understand." I nodded again. Her husband must not know about her past. That was fine with me. The less I thought about the past, the better.

"Do you still see your parents?" she asked. "Are they alive?"

"Passed away nearly thirty years ago now. My older brother still lives in Duluth, I think, but I haven't had any letters from him in years."

"I'm back in touch with my mother. I know, it seems crazy, but someone sent her Clarence and my wedding announcement and we started corresponding. She actually lives over the bridge now, in Marin. She's widowed. Not from my father but from her second husband."

Will wonders never cease, I thought. "What happened," I ventured, "to Zeke?"

Rosalie's face was blank for a minute. Then realization swept across it. She stubbed her cigarette out in the ashtray. "Oh good Lord, that was the last time I saw him. Bad things were happening. They were going to get worse." Her brow furrowed and she looked at her hands. "But then they got better!" I had forgotten how Rosalie was able to clear a mood like sweeping a porch. It was an admirable quality, for those of us who tended to dwell in the land of grudge and funk.

Rosalie called again for the maid to light another cigarette.

"Should I build up the fire, ma'am?" she asked.

"No, that's all right," Rosalie replied. "Just let it burn down."

*

That Monday, I marched into Childress's office the minute I arrived and announced that I would marry Ainslie and go to the Galápagos. I never actually made the decision, but telling Rosalie made it a fait accompli. It was already done; we just had to go through the actions.

Childress fast-tracked my security clearance and by the middle of the next week, I was Mrs. Ainslie Conway.

Ainslie and I got married by the justice of the peace at the court-house in San Francisco. Childress was the witness and the girl down the hall from me at my boardinghouse agreed to come sign the paper in exchange for a meal out. At the St. Francis hotel, where the Office of Naval Intelligence had gotten us a room, we ordered prime rib and drank martinis like we'd lost something in the bottom of the glass. We all got a little sloppy. The girl, I remember now her name was Laura, got friendly with Childress. I watched her squirm on his lap as he pre-tended to drop an olive down her bodice, and tried not to think of Mrs. Childress, who called sometimes to remind Childress to take his pills or to not forget his doctor's appointment or to bring something home for dinner, nor of the Childress children, who perched in a photograph on his desk, as red-cheeked and chubby as their father.

Ainslie held my hand at dinner and occasionally rubbed my knee. He pecked me chastely on the cheek when Laura and Childress got to sneaking kisses. I drank more to quell my worry. What would our mar-riage night be like?

In the hotel room, I was as nervous as my first time, as though I weren't an old lady who was marrying for patriotism instead of love. Ainslie took his time in the bathroom, whistling. I heard the water running and the steam crept under the door and into the room like there was a fire in there. I had to urinate badly, but I didn't want to interrupt his ablutions. Finally he came out in his underwear and I brushed past him into the bathroom.

I was nervous that as I peed the sound would be too loud, too revealing, but I needn't have worried. When I emerged from the bathroom in the hotel's robe, a teddy underneath concealing my scrawny breasts and slack stomach, Ainslie's voice was thick with sleep.

"'Fraid I drank too much, pet. We'll do the marriage bed tomorrow, yes? Neither of us is a spring chicken, hmm?"

I heard him start snoring not long after, the only night in our marriage that he snored. I wonder now if he was faking it. I feel a pang all over again that he's not here for me to ask him, like missing a breath.

*

I moved into his apartment and every night we shared a bed. Three times in all the years we were together, I counted, we were together as man and wife, and it was fine; perfunctory and surprisingly not intimate. But mostly Ainslie would kiss me on the forehead, cheek, or lips, sometimes put his arms around me. In the two months it took us to get ready to go to the islands, there were three nights when Ainslie didn't come home. As an intelligence employee, I knew better than to ask him where he'd been. Plus, he'd enter the apartment in a state of abject despair, clothes disheveled, smelling of alcohol and sweat. His color was off and he stumbled straight into the shower, where he would stay for thirty minutes. Then he'd come out, shaved and dressed, his old cheerful self, asking if the coffee was ready. He invariably brought me flowers afterward, as if instructed by men's magazines.

Still, I couldn't complain. I was an old maid. I had never been the pretty one, and age had not been kind to me. It was not surprising that he didn't want me. I should be grateful that I had a husband at all. Ainslie was kind and pleasant to be around. He made me laugh. He paid attention to me in a way that no one ever had. And it was wonderful to come home and have someone to talk to in the evenings, someone with whom to listen to the radio. I wasn't worried that we'd lack for things to talk about on the islands. I was looking a tad forward to getting away from the bars that called to Ainslie like sirens. Maybe far from San Francisco he would become my true husband.

*

We met daily with Childress (who, after my censorious glances the day after our wedding, was sheepish around me), studying the files that weren't to leave the secret meeting room. That meant long days in a windowless room that consisted of just a standard-issue table and mismatched chairs, an old projector, and a screen with a rope tied to the ring to pull it down.

Not long after our union, a commander whose name I no longer remember came to the office to brief us. He had recently been promoted and was unhappy to be stuck with this duty, unenthusiastic about our mission. He spoke in a monotone, barely concealing his contempt. "Look, I don't go in for shadow tactics. It's a dirty business," he said. "Gentlemen do not spy."

It was all I could do to hold my tongue and not mention the fact that I was not a gentleman. Perhaps the commander thought it was more honorable to shoot each other? It seemed to me that intelligence gathering was a cleaner way to go about it.

Here was the current situation as the commander described it: The American government was interested in establishing a base in the Pacific. Strategically, the Galápagos were a jewel—in fact, it's said they helped turn the tide in the War of 1812. The archipelago consisted of thirty-odd islands, some of which were mere rocks jutting out of the seabed. There were ten major islands and only four were inhabited. Floreana was currently home to at least nine Germans (we were later to find out this number was a bit inflated), a curious coincidence considering the aggression Germany was showing in Europe at the time. Were they as interested in the Galápagos as we were?

Germany had agents all over South America; they had signed a pact with Japan; they were probably going to invade Poland after annexing Austria. Yes, they were in talks with Chamberlain, but no one actually believed that Herr Hitler would join with the country that so roundly beat his nation during the Great War and sent it into a depression that was only now lifting. Hitler was planning something; we just weren't sure what it was.

America's weakest line of defense was the Panama Canal. Destroy that, and you've crippled America by crippling her supply lines. But it was a long trip from Japan to the canal, and the opportunity to get fresh water, muster forces, and organize troops on, say, an uninhabited archipelago just under a thousand miles from the canal, would make the Galápagos an attractive landing spot. Ecuador was distracted by its war with Peru. The Germans or their allies could organize a naval invasion.

We were to go and keep an eye on the Germans and on the ocean. We would radio in once a week to Guayaquil where our message would be relayed, eventually, to the United States. The commander expected that the message would be "all clear" and that it was a waste of military money to send us all the way to the Galápagos. We were also to see if Floreana might be suitable for an American air corps or navy base.

Were we sure the Germans were spies? No. Did it seem likely that Germans or Japanese would target the Panama Canal? No. Would the radio signal even reach across the ocean? Yes.

Our mission was given the code name Pomegranate for no reason that anyone has ever been able to ascertain. We have never even come up with a working theory.

I'm afraid I agreed with the commander. I wondered if we weren't being sent there only to give a message to the Germans that we were watching them. I imagined all of us on the side of a hill, binoculars trained at each other, watching each other watch each other through the lenses. Still, orders are orders. Ours were for Ainslie to depart in six weeks for training at the Office of Naval Intelligence camp in Carmel. There he would receive survival and combat retraining, and I was to join him four weeks later, for basic intelligence training.

*

In the following weeks, Rosalie and I spent a good deal of time together, or at least as much time as she could spare. She was incredibly busy—she was on the board of the light opera, she helped out at the children's school, and she and Clarence had an active social life. Yes, life was not fair; this had been apparent again and again, but still it was a cruel irony that I who had the education and training to appreciate the arts had no time or money to attend, while Rosalie, who could not have cared less, who never finished high school, considered evenings spent at arts and theater galas a burden she had to undertake for her family's sake.

She was the old Rosalie, vivacious, fun-loving. She poured all of her drama into her conversation and loved my sardonic wit. Making her laugh felt like winning at a game. She paid for everything. When I protested, she silenced me. "This was the deal, back then. It was my turn. Now it's yours. Plus, it's barely even money to Clarence."

I wasn't sure if she loved him or not. She never complained about him, was never reluctant to spend time with him, and if it was a marriage of convenience they both appeared to want nothing more. It was possible that Rosalie had a lover; no one could keep tabs on her socializing—she flitted from luncheon to meeting to social call to tennis practice, and any of those could have been a lie. But I had taken to heart a piece of advice that Ainslie offered: Don't ask a question you don't want to know the answer to.

Since quitting my teaching job, I had spent little time around children. I began to like to spend time with Rosalie's brood. Barbara and Sylvie were pretty, like their mother, while Dan took after his father, talking a lot and growing red in the face when expounding on a topic he particularly enjoyed discussing, namely baseball and airplanes.

Barbara was very curious about her mother's childhood. When she pressed me for information, I gave her some general observations, told about how we met, and about the time Rosalie passed a note to a boy telling him I liked him. Now, I saw how cruel that was, to the boy, who was not well-liked, but then I thought it an excellent prank. I talked about weekends I used to spend with Rosalie at her house, about how good the food was, how tastefully decorated the house was.

I also told her, with Rosalie's approval, a highly edited story of our move to Chicago. Now it was after we had finished high school and with the approval of our parents. I sanitized the hotel we stayed in, but told the story of our trip to the Young Ladies' Aid Society meeting pretty much as it happened. And then, I said, I went to university and we lost touch.

Sylvie liked for me to describe my childhood apartment, with its crowded laundry dampness. She could not believe that so many people would have lived together in that small space. She also liked us to braid our hair in the old style, and describe our long skirts and ruffled blouses. She laughed at how old-fashioned it was. And then I told stories of what it was like before telephones and airplanes, when even automobiles were a novelty, and she stared at me saucer-eyed with wonder.

When I took them to lunch, the library, or simply out for a walk to look at the ships, I found myself sorry, for the first time, that I did not have any children of my own. But this regret, as Mrs. Keane the suffragette would have said, was like closing the barn door after the horse is already out.

*

During those six weeks, I kept Rosalie and Ainslie far apart. This was due partly to instinct, partly to necessity. As I read my clearance manuals, it was emphasized again and again that it was preferable for agents to have few close friends or family. Ainslie never mentioned any of his friends, and I suspected he kept everyone at arm's length with his charm. So while I was breaking the rules by "consorting" with Rosalie, I simply never mentioned it to Ainslie in a tacit agreement that what we didn't know couldn't hurt us.

Also, I hadn't mentioned to Ainslie that I was Jewish. It just hadn't come up. Since Chicago I had called myself Frances Frank. It had become my reflex, starting with my residency in Nebraska, not to mention my religion. One was never sure in those days (nor in these) what people thought about Jews. There was growing anti-Semitism in Europe, which either riled up people's sense of unfairness or their agreement that Jews needed to be restricted. It was ever thus, and probably will always be.

Ainslie never spoke of religion. I wasn't even sure what religion he was. There were so many things I didn't know about him, and so few that had revealed themselves to me. I didn't know his attitude toward Jews. Or his opinion on whether the toilet paper should roll over or under. Or whether he liked Brussels sprouts. So I just never said anything about my being Jewish. I was sure he must have suspected. But if I introduced him to Rosalie and Clarence he would know immediately; Clarence covered his head with a yarmulke. So it was easier to keep them apart, though Rosalie pushed constantly for the four of us to get together. I had to use all my imagination to keep her from insisting.

*

I dreaded telling Rosalie that I was going to the Galápagos. I knew she wouldn't understand. Our cover story didn't make much sense, it was true. There was nothing about my life that suggested I'd be interested in going to an island to try to subsist on nature's bounty, or that Ainslie needed the warm climate to cure tuberculosis. I would have been surprised too, which is why when I finally did tell her, one week before Ainslie was to leave for training, she thought I was joking.

"Oh, the famous Frances Frankowski sense of humor!" she said. We were at the pool of her country club, sipping something frothy and sweet and watching Sylvie play in the water. It was one of those warm spring days that make you love California, especially if you're from Minnesota.

"I'm serious," I said. "We're really going. Ainslie has medical leave from the navy."

Rosalie pulled her glasses down her nose. She looked at me intensely as if to stare inside and see if I were lying.

"I've never even heard of those islands," she said.

"Yes, you have," I insisted. I was getting a bit sunburned and I scooted my chair farther under the umbrella. "They're where Darwin discovered evolution."

"Where in the heck are they?" Her eyes scanned the pool for Sylvie. There were three lifeguards on duty, and Sylvie had been swimming for years, but Rosalie was a nervous parent.

"The Pacific Ocean, near the equator. You take a boat to Panama and then to Guayaquil."

"This makes absolutely no sense, Frances. Why on earth would you go to a desert island, at your age?"

"Our age," I corrected. The children yelling and squealing in the background were percussion accompaniment to our conversation.

"So is it a vacation? How long will you be gone?"

"About a year," I said. The sun chased me even farther under the umbrella.

"A year? I absolutely forbid it!" Rosalie was joking, but there was an undercurrent to her voice that she used when her children misbehaved.

"I'm afraid you don't have a say," I said. "I'll be back, don't worry."

"But what will you eat? How will you live?" She had completely turned away from the pool and pushed her glasses up onto her head. She did look remarkably young, I had to admit.

"Well, you take provisions with you and then you construct a house from materials on the islands. It's always warm there, so you plant a garden. It's very fertile."

Rosalie was struck dumb. "You're just going to up and leave?"

"Well, not tomorrow," I said. I sensed that this was about more than my yearlong adventure.

To my surprise, Rosalie started to cry. "You can't," she said. "I just found you, you can't leave again." There was an anguish to her crying that really touched me. Perhaps Rosalie had been as lonely as I had. I considered how a few months ago I'd had no one and now I had two people in my life, important people, who wanted my company. My cup ranneth over.

I held Rosalie while she wept, and when Sylvie got out of the pool and came over, questioningly, I said her mother was sad. I would cheer her up, and Sylvie should go get a sandwich at the clubhouse.

Eventually, Rosalie calmed. She wiped her eyes and smiled, embarrassed. "Crying makes you look older," she said. "But Frances, really, you have to explain this to me. Otherwise it seems like your husband is kidnapping you. This is his idea, isn't it? This can't have come from you."

I could lie to many people, but I still found it difficult to lie to Rosalie. I had to turn my head to the cement beneath the chairs so I didn't have to meet her gaze. "It's Ainslie's drinking," I said. "It's a real problem, and he can't stop. He's going to a sanatorium for a month to dry out and then I think if we go somewhere where there's no possibility . . ."

Rosalie's mouth opened into an O. She patted me on the shoulder, consolingly, as though I were the one who had been weeping. I realized as I said this that it was true, that I wanted Ainslie away from the bars and the distractions. I wanted him to myself.

Rosalie leaned over to her purse and took out her compact, powdering her face and reapplying her lipstick.

"I'll let you go on two conditions."

"What?" I chuckled.

"First, you have to promise me not to die and to write me constantly."

"That's two already."

"And second," she said, ignoring me, "I'm meeting this Ainslie before he whisks you away to the ends of the earth."

*

I tried to make it sound like a casual invitation: *Oh, Ainslie, by the way, we're invited for dinner at my friend's on Friday*. I must have pulled it off, because he amiably agreed.

I could not have been more nervous that night than if I were about to take center stage at the Lyric Opera. When we arrived at Rosalie's house, Ainslie's wide eyes betrayed his surprise at its grandeur. I had told him very little about Rosalie and her family, only that she was an old friend. I should have warned him so he would have been prepared for the prayers before dinner, so he would have been prepared to discover that I was Jewish. I had accepted Rosalie's invitation in part because it would force me to tell him, giving myself an ultimatum. But each time I began I found a convenient excuse not to do it. So now we were here at her front door, Ainslie in perfect ignorance. A good phrase—perfect ignorance, in contrast to flawed enlightenment.

The maid showed us to the parlor and Ainslie kissed Rosalie's hand. I saw him stare for a second at the yarmulke on Clarence's head as confusion and then worry crossed his face before he composed himself. We sat down. Clarence and Ainslie smoked cigars before we ate. We made small talk; Ainslie and Clarence compared service in the Great War, which was always the topic Ainslie discussed when he met men of his age, but Clarence had served at a desk in Washington, while Ainslie was in Morocco and France. Rosalie had honed her gift for hostessing, so while our conversation wasn't fluid, neither was it filled with awkward silences.

Soon we moved into the dining room. Clarence said the blessing over the bread and wine and Ainslie shifted uncomfortably.

What did we talk about? I'm not sure. I'm not certain I said two words. What would Ainslie say when we were alone? Would he be more angry at the lie of omission or the awkwardness? What was his attitude toward Jews? What if I had married an anti-Semite?

The main course was a large steak, bone in. At least I knew that Ainslie would appreciate this part of the meal. He loved to eat meat; it wasn't a meal unless an animal died. There was a side of pasta with tomato sauce and some carrots and we all ate heartily until Ainslie said, "Do you possibly have some cheese for the pasta?"

"I'm sorry?" Rosalie said.

"Some parmesan or something. It's very good on pasta; Italians always use it when they eat noodles."

"These are the meat dishes," Clarence said, confused, as though Ainslie had suggested using them as pillows.

"The what?"

"Jewish dietary laws," Rosalie said.

Ainslie's face showed plainly his confusion. "Hebrews don't eat cheese?"

"We don't mix milk and meat," Rosalie said, speaking slowly as if stating the obvious.

"I'll explain later," I said.

"*You'll* explain later?" I saw his mouth turn down as he took in the meaning of this phrase. It was dawning on him that if I understood these laws, I must be Jewish as well. Had he really not guessed? He was a consummate professional, I'll give him that; he recovered instantly. The only betrayal of surprise was his napkin crushed tight in his fist.

The children came in to share dessert with us, and Ainslie entertained them with his amateur magic, which was entirely too young for Barbara and Dan, though they played along sportingly. Sylvie was delighted. "Magic is okay, right? Not against rules?" he asked.

Rosalie smiled her old strained smile, the white teeth stacked in a wall. "It's fine," she said. "Oh, Frances, I have a dress I want your opinion on. Do you mind coming to my dressing room?"

This was thinly veiled—no one on earth had ever asked my sartorial opinion. When we got upstairs Rosalie sat at her vanity and I sat on the bench at the end of the bed. I looked at her reflection in the mirror while she powdered her nose.

"Ainslie seems so outgoing," she said.

"Yes. He's the social one. Drinking a bit too much as usual."

"Hmm." Rosalie always wore the same shade of bright red lipstick; her lips were chrysanthemums constantly in bloom. "You met at work, right?"

I nodded. I could see Rosalie trying to formulate a question. She didn't look at me but at herself in the mirror we were sitting in front of.

"He seems . . . tall."

"He is tall," I said. "And *goyishe*, I knew you were going to say that."

"Actually, I wasn't," she said. "I was going to say sensitive. He seems sensitive."

I actually found Ainslie to be thick-skinned, able to take a lot of ribbing, which was one of the things I liked about him, but I didn't want to contradict her. "He's very kind."

Rosalie took my hand. "Don't let him cut you off from me, from us," she said. She leaned over and painted my lips with her lipstick. In the mirror, my mouth looked bloody, like a cat after a kill.

*

In the taxi on the way home, Ainslie lit a cigarette, breathing in deeply. The pleasure and relief he took from smoking made me smile. "Your friends are nice," he said, but his tone was devoid of sentiment. "Had a nice chat with Clarence about real estate."

"That was kind of you to come to dinner. I should have said something about . . . how they live."

"Well, yes, you should have, Frances. Not that I'd care." He continued to look out the window, not at me. "But it does put me in a bit of a spot. *I* don't care," he said again. "It's just one more thing that people could find out about you, about us. The more secrets we have to hide, the more insecure our cover. It's leverage against you."

"It's hardly a big deal," I said. "It's not like I keep kosher."

Ainslie looked at me and furled his brow.

"It's not like I have separate milk and meat dishes."

"Why on earth would you? Why would anyone choose to be so . . . different?"

This rubbed me wrong. "I think to them you're different," I said.

"Maybe," Ainslie said. "Although, I have to say, I'm surprised a bit."

"At?" The taxi swung left and I leaned into Ainslie. Did I feel him flinch?

"I didn't know you were religious."

He was hinting at something, and I was not going to help him. "I'm not."

"I didn't know you were a Hebrew, all right?"

"I'm *Jewish*. I was born Frances Frankowski."

"Polish? I thought you were German."

"Would it have made a difference?"

Ainslie tossed his cigarette out the window and lit another one. It was cold in the taxi and I wished he'd close the window. He didn't answer me.

"Well, I've been friends with Rosalie since we were kids. You know how it is. Old friends are just like family. You simply accept them, no matter how they change."

"Actually, I don't," Ainslie said. He never talked about his family. His parents were deceased, and though he had two brothers, they never spoke.

"Rosalie wasn't like that as a kid. My family was a lot more religious than hers. They were American. Mine were the immigrants. It's Clarence who's made her so devout."

Ainslie took a long drag.

"We don't have to spend too much time with them," I said.

"We can spend as much time with them as you like," Ainslie said, exhaling smoke.

*

I lay in bed that night, ashamed. Rosalie and her husband were too Jewish for me and my husband. I hated myself for not calling Ainslie to task. I hated myself for hating myself. Germany's Nuremberg Laws had shown that no matter how much you think you're part of a society, when you're Jewish you're always that first, no matter how you act, what you look like, or what you eat. I was a horrible person, I thought. But I had so many secrets, so much of a desire to please my stranger of a husband, that it was easier to blame everything on Clarence and his devotion. Why did they have to be so different? Why couldn't they eat in restaurants and go bareheaded like everyone else? Why couldn't they be more like Ainslie? Why couldn't I be more like someone Ainslie would love?

On Monday, Ainslie departed for Carmel. We would be apart a month until I joined him. I walked him down to the car and he kissed me quickly on the lips before getting in and pulling a screeching U-turn. When I went back into the apartment, it was at once devastatingly empty and wonderfully large.

CHAPTER EIGHT

I was jolted out of sleep one night by a pounding on the door. At first I thought it was the wind; spring in San Francisco was not kind, and it had been raining for what felt like years. I got up and put on a dressing gown. It was full, deep night. I was too asleep even to wonder who it might be.

"Aunt Fanny, please open up." Rosalie's older daughter, Barbara, stood at my door, her hair flat, her eyes red. "I'm sorry," she said.

"What are you doing here? Come in." I ushered her inside. "What on earth?"

She burst into tears. "It's Momma. We had an enormous fight. You know how she can be."

I did, but I said nothing, handing her a tissue. "A fight about what?"

Barbara looked at the tissue, folding and unfolding it. "A boy," she said.

"Oh." I was relieved. For a moment I'd worried that something was really wrong. I do have a tendency to expect the worst. "I'll make tea," I said. I set the kettle on to boil. I've always disliked tea, but I kept a few bags around for guests.

"She found me with a boy. And I know it's wrong, that we shouldn't have been together without someone else around, but we were only kissing. And she went just crazy. She hit him with her pocketbook and screamed things at me . . . I don't even know what some of them mean." Barbara was crying quietly now. "And Pat left and now he'll never talk to me again. And I love him."

I resisted the urge to roll my eyes. The kettle began to rattle and I stood up to turn it off before it whistled.

While I made the tea, Barbara told me a long, dramatic story. Some afternoons she took Sylvie to the playground, and she and this boy would arrange to meet to talk. Then they began to hold hands. Then they would sneak off to kiss behind the gazebo. On this day, Rosalie stopped by the park. Sylvie, though sworn to secrecy, easily gave Barbara up when pressed and Rosalie found them.

I held my cup between my hands, letting it warm them. "What do you think she was most angry about?" I asked.

"I don't know." Barbara looked at her teacup. "I'm almost sixteen."

"Practically halfway to the grave," I said.

"Don't poke fun, Aunt Fanny."

"Sorry," I said. "Seriously, what do you think? Was it that you left Sylvie alone? That the boy isn't Jewish? That you were sneaking around?" I took a small sip of the tea and encountered uninspiring flower water. I put the cup down.

"It seemed to be . . ." Barbara paused. "Like she was angry at Pat. But it wasn't his fault. I wanted him to do it."

I thought I knew, though I had no training in psychology, what Rosalie was angry at. We had never spoken of what I saw at her house, what happened to her. But how could it not have affected her? It had affected me, and it hadn't even happened to me.

"Your mother had a difficult time growing up," I said carefully. "I think she wants to spare you that."

"She just wants to make sure I never have a beau, that I never grow up."

"Maybe that's part of it. I'm just saying, it's complicated."

Barbara began to cry anew. "I can't live without him. I love him."

"I seriously doubt that you won't live without him," I couldn't help but say.

She picked up her teacup; liquid sloshed over the side onto the table. We both watched it spread. I put the kitchen towel on top of the wet.

"Why are you taking her side? You know how she is. She's selfish. She doesn't care about anybody but herself," Barbara said.

It was true that Rosalie was selfish. But I had enough sense not to tell her daughter that. "She loves you."

"Hah," Barbara scoffed.

"You know that's true," I said.

Barbara looked down, admitting I was right. "I'm sorry I spilled the tea. I hate tea."

"I hate tea too," I said. I smiled. "I have always hated tea."

"Me too!" Barbara said. "It's like someone put grass in water."

"How about some milk and honey?" I asked. "That always makes me feel better. And I tell you what, because you're almost sixteen, I'll put a bit of brandy in it too. You can sleep here. Does anyone know where you are?"

Barbara shook her head.

"Do you want me to call or do you want to?"

"You, please," Barbara said. "Thank you, Aunt Fanny."

Later, I watched her as she slept in my bed. She still slept like a child, face slack and innocent. When I crawled in beside her, she stirred and moaned but did not wake. I lay there for a while, watching the street-lights make shadows on the ceiling until I fell asleep.

*

A week after he left, I received the following letter from Ainslie:

Dear Mrs. Elmer Ainslie Conway,

Greetings from this golf resort, where I am forced to hit the links day in and day out. You may say to yourself, oh, poor Ainslie, stuck on a golf course, but I tell you, madam, it's maddening here.

Instruction began with an introduction to the concept of hitting a ball with a club. Having mastered that complicated task, complete with a question-and-answer period, we were taught how to tell one club from the other, but since the manufacturers were kind enough to print their number on the side, it doesn't exactly take a surgeon's skill.

Now, I'm no Gene Sarazen, but this is not my first time around the links. I'm better than your uncle George. Speaking of Uncle George, how goes it at the homestead? Hope you're keeping busy; don't knit me too many sweaters. How is Rosalie? I hope you two aren't plotting to take over the universe. I wouldn't put it past you!

I'm getting my three squares, but you can hardly call this living. Your dinnertime conversation will be most welcome next month, for I have fallen into a pit of humorless garden snakes at the pro table. Apparently reading while you eat is considered rude, you were right. I have had to resort to my most low-down, dirty tricks: telling moron jokes.

Why did the moron cut off his fingers? So he could write shorthand.

Why did the moron panic when he swallowed the thermometer? He thought he would die by degrees.

Have I told you these? If not, it is a testament to my affection for you. Do you see what I'm reduced to? Hurry by, April, and bring my Frances to me! One note: When you see me, please don't say, "I forgot how tall you are." Everyone always feels the need to remark upon my height after a separation, and I'm never sure how to answer. "I forgot how short you are"?

Honest to Frances, I'm bored out of my mind here. Ah, the exciting life of a ▉▉▉▉▉▉▉

[Here the censor had left his mark]

Please hurry, and bring diversions.

Well, here's my tee time. I must shoulder once again the burden of my bag of clubs and seek to avoid sand traps and water hazards.

Yours in abject misery, awaiting with impatience the arrival of my bride,

Ainslie

I had no idea what the metaphors meant, but the subtext was unmistakable. This was a waste of his time, teaching him things he already knew. I would have been better served taking his place; I knew nothing of intelligence other than what I read in spy novels. I took a slew of them out of the library to study up, but they were of little help. His letter made me miss him, his ability to find the humor in any situation.

When it was time to join Ainslie, I put the apartment in order and took the train down, saying goodbye to Rosalie before I left. Embarrassingly, I had never been to Carmel, though I'd lived nearby for nearly thirty years. I stepped off the train to a fragrant breeze. No wonder people came here for vacation—it smelled of frangipani and bougainvillea and salty sea air, unlike San Francisco, which always smelled vaguely of mold and fish.

The porter took my suitcases off the train and I stood there for five minutes until Ainslie came careening to a halt in front of the station.

He called a cheerful hello and left the car running while he came over to me and picked up my suitcases one in each hand. Then he remembered himself and put them down to give me a peck on the lips and a hug.

"*Willkommen*, Fräulein. Okay, that's the only German I've learned. That language is terrible. Like people clearing their throats at each other. Tired? Hungry?"

I was learning that Ainslie went through periods of excitability. On some level, it was a welcome contrast to my plodding personality, a characteristic that had only grown more marked the older and more set in my ways I got.

"Always tired, never hungry," I said.

"We're a pair. I'm always hungry and never tired."

"And so between the two of us we'll lick the platter clean?"

Ainslie laughed. He took me on a tour of downtown Carmel. The main street was out of a storybook—the fairy village of an eight-year-old girl's dreams, all undulating shingled roofs and swaying Dutch doors. Chimneys stacked haphazardly, stucco walls, and half-timbering added to the effect, along with perfectly pruned azaleas and shrubbery; the signs announced the houses' names in druid script. Comstock houses, Ainslie said these were called, after the gnome who built them. Outside the town center, mission architecture took over with its putty-smooth walls and red roofs. We drove a bit up the coast and inland to an old golf resort. There was a man at the entrance inside a small guard booth. He came out to check his clipboard, but then saw that he knew Ainslie.

"This the missus then?" he asked.

"Frances," I leaned over Ainslie to give him my hand to shake.

"My mother's name was Frances. Welcome to Clifton."

We drove up the long driveway. It was shaded by palm trees and topped by a grand clubhouse in the neoclassic style. "That's HQ," Ainslie said. "Headquarters, that means."

"That much spy lingo I know," I said.

"You've been reading Maugham?" Ainslie joked.

"Let's just say my library card has been spending a lot of time with Ashenden."

We drove past the first tee and down a hill. There was a chain stretched across the road here, and two guards with pistols in their holsters. They waved Ainslie through, unhooking the chain so we could pass.

On what used to be the third fairway (I knew because the sign announcing it as a par five was still visible) there were a series of prefabricated huts. "Here's ours." Ainslie pulled up to one that was indistinguishable from its neighbor. He got my bags out of the car while I went inside.

It was small but serviceable, a kitchenette, a two-person table, and a sofa, with a bathroom to the left and a bedroom to the right. True to his nature, Ainslie hadn't decorated, except, I noticed, for a portrait of me on the nightstand table, which touched me.

"Home sweet home," Ainslie said behind me, and I shuddered with the chill of what we'd jumped into. It hadn't seemed real when we were in San Francisco, but now I saw that I had joined my lot to this man I barely knew.

Ainslie looked at his watch. "Perfect timing," he said. "We can make the first seating for dinner."

That night Ainslie announced, "I don't want to wake you with my snoring. I'll sleep on the sofa."

I wanted, indeed, I expected us to continue to occupy one bed, even though we weren't together in that sense, and his announcing that he was going to sleep on the couch stung. I told myself that he was under stress, that now that we were with people who understood the circumstances under which we got married he didn't have to pretend. Ainslie was fond of me, found me amusing, but wanted to make it clear that while we were married, we were not man and wife.

*

My basic-intelligence instructor was named Mr. Fox. This was not his real name. He could have told us his name; we were not actually under-cover at this point, but he wanted us to get used to answering to names not our own, if need be. We changed our names weekly. I chose Beatrice Dante for my first week. No one noticed the reference.

My other classmates were young recruits. Two of the women worked as secretaries like me and there was another woman whose qualifica-tions seemed to consist merely of her beauty. I don't love meeting new people, so avoiding intimacies with them was not a hardship. But I could see how some of the more extroverted participants were surprised to come up against a wall of loneliness.

That first week, we went over basic intelligence training. Most of it was common sense, but there were several matters of standard trade-craft that intelligence officers had to follow, most of which involved the amount and methods of communication, basic signal encoding, and strategies to get people to trust us. I learned how to recruit an asset—find their weakness (usually a woman or a child) and either exploit it or offer to help it.

I won't deny that some of it was useful and interesting (though I never had much use for disguising my appearance), but the majority was deadly dull and not applicable to my situation. I would presumably never have to shed a tail in a city or create and execute a drop.

The second week we moved on to communications, where I learned Morse code, various military acronyms that I promptly forgot, and basic radio technology. As it turned out, I was completely useless with all things electronic. I could never diagnose or repair a radio, no matter how often I was shown its basic circuitry. I just fundamentally didn't understand how electricity could transport sound. I also had to be shown how to turn on and operate each new radio I encountered, the logic of the knobs and buttons opaque to me. But once I was familiar with them, I was very quick at sending the Morse code messages. "Well done, Miss Austen," Mr. Wolf said at the end of the second week.

"Do they have any idea you're taking your code names from litera-ture?" Ainslie asked when I arrived back at our bungalow.

"None," I said. I set my notebook on our kitchen counter. "You could come in and call yourself Bill Shakespeare and no one would bat an eye. It's like the perfect cover."

"Was it Shakespeare who said, 'You'll never go broke underestimating the ignorance of intelligence trainees'?" Ainslie said, lighting one cigarette off the remnant of the other.

Week three was physical training. I, now called Mrs. Shelley, had to laugh. I was fifty-five years old. My fellow participants refused to spar with me (thank goodness). Instead, I learned how to make a knife out of bone, how to target the solar plexus, how to drive the nose into the brain, how to put out eyes, and how to disable a man (take a guess).

Week four was survival training. Here was where Mrs. Alcott really shone, according to Mr. Buck. I learned how to shoot (though not how to aim), how to determine which berries could be eaten, how to make and tie ropes and create shelter. I knew from my time on the farm how to turn a rabbit from a living creature into a meal. I wasn't bad with snares, and I won my colleagues' admiration with my squirrel-skinning abilities. I am uncommonly quick at it. It's funny when you find an aptitude where you don't expect it.

*

It was the closest thing to a honeymoon Ainslie and I had. On Saturday nights we would go with the other officers and their wives to the Pines, get tight, and dance until midnight. There was always a passable band, and oh, how Ainslie could dance! No matter his partner, he made her look as graceful as Ginger Rogers, his footwork effortless, his carriage erect.

We laughed and laughed, and I fell a little in love with him on those nights. Or in love with the image of him: dashing, popular, carefree. I knew they whispered behind our backs, wondering about the age difference, the personality difference. I tried not to let that bother me.

In the evenings, we played cribbage, or spite and malice, or worked on our cover stories. The trick was to get them close enough to the real thing so as to be able to remember them, to tell stories about childhood. That's what tripped people up. They were unwilling (unable) to recount past exploits, and that made people suspicious of them. I was a farm girl from Nebraska, he a veteran of the western front.

A couple of times, I heard him sneak out the door. I wondered whom he was going to meet—girls from down the road, who sold themselves to officers, or some more permanent girlfriend who had followed us down here. I never found lipstick or cologne on his clothes, but I knew he had to be somewhere at night. I wasn't jealous, or rather not too jealous. He should be allowed to carry on with his former life.

It was at the officers' mess that I ate pork on purpose for the first time. My mother never served it and Mrs. Keane never served it. It wasn't a conscious avoidance on my part and not a religious conviction. It just didn't seem like food, the way you wouldn't eat horse (though people do—French people, I think).

But Ainslie had noticed my eating around the ham at supper, and that night he came into the bedroom where I was studying German grammar.

"Franny-Lou," he said. I don't know where he got this nickname from, but sometimes he called me endearments. "You have to eat the meat that's on your plate."

"I don't eat pork," I said.

"You mean Frances Frank does not eat pork; Frances Conway certainly does."

My chest opened up wide. "I don't think I can do it," I said.

He sat on the edge of the bed, leaning on one arm on the other side of my outstretched legs. "Franny, you've signed up to be an actress. Think of yourself as playing a role."

I opened my mouth to protest.

"It makes no sense, dear, for me to have married you, as . . . different as we are. We need to be as unassuming as possible, and that means blending in with the crowd. So jettison this preference and embrace your life as Frances Conway." He kissed my forehead, stood up, and then paused, thinking about saying something.

"There are things we keep to ourselves, Frances, things that are embarrassing or compromising. If people were to find out, they would have leverage over us. We want to avoid being leveraged at all costs. I've found the best way to do that is to not think about what you're giving up. Pretend it was never part of you. It's like a rebirth that way."

I had the feeling he was convincing himself of something, but before I could say anything else, he left the room.

*

Ainslie took up pipe smoking at that juncture as well as his cigarettes. I didn't mind it. It actually smelled rather good, and it was comforting to enter an empty room and know that Ainslie had been there not so long ago. He took to it avidly, though, and I worried he would miss the tobacco once we got to the islands. Surely it would be hard to find.

In keeping with our cover story, we were allotted $500 to buy items to take with us. Supposedly Ainslie had been sick with tuberculosis, hence our stay in Carmel and subsequent desire to partake of the salubrious air of the islands to further heal him. I was a schoolteacher, but had left for the term to take care of my husband. Our savings had dwindled, and so, in the spirit of our pioneer forefathers, we decided to pull a Swiss Family Robinson and civilize the jungle.

But what to get for $500? To last a year? We would need everything from pots and pans to roofing materials, pounds of provisions, shovels, axes, a shotgun, cups and plates, silverware, clothing . . . Plus we had to pay for our passage.

We began to make lists, an activity in which both Ainslie and I liked to engage, and then switched and began to cross out frivolous items. Even so, the lists stretched on and on. We cut tents, camp beds, timber, fencing, but still we had more than our meager budget would manage. Plus we were restricted by weight, and the radio we had to bring was a brick. "Can't the government say you're an heir to the Rockefeller fortune or something?" I asked.

Ainslie laughed. "If only."

Try as I might, I couldn't make the budget stretch. I took money out of my savings account and bought a few of the things I considered essential: makeup (why?), a mirror, muslin, two different sizes of frying pans, sandals, and a few of the things Ainslie couldn't live without, such as lifeboat matches (for lighting pipes, not fires), a carpenter's square, fishhooks. We needed precisely none of this, as it turned out.

Since we did not know when we would be deployed, we waited in Carmel. "Don't learn too much German," Ainslie said. "We can't know too much when we get there."

"Don't worry," I said. "It's a beast of a language, and even if I do learn it, I can always pretend to understand less than I do."

"Try Spanish," he said. "After all, it is a Spanish-speaking country."

"You could learn it," I said. "Divide and conquer?"

Ainslie shook his head. "I'm hopeless with languages. Was in France for three years, couldn't even say 'please.'"

"Doesn't seem to be a word you're too familiar with in English either," I teased him.

*

And then suddenly, we had our orders. We were to ship out in one week from San Francisco, stop at Panama, and end in Guayaquil, where we would have to catch the sometimes-boat (our later name for it) that toured the islands whenever the mood struck its captain.

When Ainslie told me this, though I'd been calmly awaiting the news for weeks, my throat began to close up and my vision narrowed. I fought to breathe.

Ainslie came close. "Put your head between your legs." He forced me over and held me there, stroking my back until my breathing calmed, though there were still bright spots behind my eyes. "I think I had a heart attack," I said.

"That was a panic attack," Ainslie said.

"I thought I was going to die."

"Just your body's response to stress. Lads had them all the time in the trenches."

"But I'm not a lad. And I'm not in the trenches."

"No, it's worse than the trenches, it's the middle of the ocean. If you weren't a bit scared I'd be worried about you."

"You don't seem nervous," I said.

Ainslie took his pipe out of his mouth. I could see that the mouth-piece was chewed almost through. "Why do you think I took up this habit?" he asked.

"What if we die?" I whispered.

"Has to happen sometime."

"What if we die of thirst?"

"Well now"—Ainslie sat back—"that would be unfortunate."

"And painful," I said, thinking of parched cows on the farm too dehy-drated to low.

"We'll just have to make sure that doesn't happen, Franny-Lou. Come on, trust me, have I let you down yet?"

"We've only been married three months," I said. And thought: And still haven't consummated it. And now we're going off to a desert island where we'll be the only two people around for miles, in contact with the world only through intermittent radio transmissions. There will be plenty of opportunities to be let down, I thought. Some have already happened.

Part Three

Only Childress came to see us off from San Francisco harbor. I couldn't tell Rosalie about our departure; we were "catching a ride" on an aircraft carrier, the USS *Erie*, to Panama. Our cabin was right at the waterline; we were lobsters in a tank, waiting to be plucked to serve as dinner.

The three days passed slowly. Ainslie spent most of his time on deck, contemplating the horizon and chewing his pipe. I spent most of my time trying to keep my lunch down.

We were accompanied as far as Panama by a navy captain whose name I don't recall. He and Ainslie discussed the mission, which we faithfully referred to as Pomegranate, over poker every night. They played in the captain's stateroom, so as not to keep me awake. And sometimes they would get so drunk that Ainslie would stay there, returning in the morning with a headache and a scowl, crawling into his bed and sleeping until lunch.

Ainslie and the captain had an easy familiarity about them. They'd both served in France where the captain was a commanding officer on the USS *Fanning*. And so their looks, their small intimacies, the brush of a hand when lighting a cigarette, the clap on the back that lingered just a little too long, were understandable.

You'll wonder how I could have been so blind. But in my defense I say that such a thing as you must now suspect had never occurred to me. Yes, I lived in San Francisco, but my little world of female boardinghouses, schoolteachers, and clandestine military offices did not permit more than a passing knowledge of those men. I imagined them to be as obvious as dwarfs, their differences plastered on their faces and bodies. It did not occur to me that they could be as Ainslie was—robust, manly.

I knew so little about men. If he were overly fond of his fellow officers, well, he'd been through a war, the Great War. It made sense that he should find comfort with those who had similar experiences. Plus we all drank so much then . . . Now that we were sailing to the ends of the earth, what difference would it make?

*

We put ashore at Panama and checked into the Metropole. Ainslie disappeared—he had a briefing to attend with an attaché who had served in Rio.

I wandered around Panama City. I paid my five cents to marvel at the genius accomplishment of the best of our engineers—the canal—and took a walk down the Avenida Central. I went to the officers' club for lunch, where I had my last salad for a while, savoring the lettuce and tomatoes. The salad had pieces of bacon in it, and I ate them without a second thought, playing the role of Mrs. Conway effortlessly. Bacon was delicious. Why had I avoided it all these years? As I ate, I looked around. It was a fine day, and the windows were open. You could hear the songs of birds and industry invading the dining room, and men and women sat together, drinking and laughing. In the afternoon, I went shopping, but I was shocked at how high the prices were. In comparison, San Francisco was a bargain!

I thought about how my life had become such a secret. There was no one in whom I could confide—it was a matter of national security. And a matter of privacy, impossible to violate.

When Ainslie came back to the hotel that evening to shave and change, he expressed interest in my day, asking me questions about the canal and my lunch. But he volunteered no information in return. I asked him to take me dancing.

"I would be honored to dance with you," he said. "We'll have an intimate dinner you and me, *manducemus*."

"That's Latin," I said. "Have you been studying Spanish at all?"

"*Sí,*" he said, winningly. Then he kissed me on the forehead and closed the bathroom door to keep the steam in.

I got dressed in the only nice dress I'd brought. It was dowdy and passé, more suitable for 1918 than 1938, but no one was looking at an old lady anyway. We took a bicycle taxi to a cabaret Ainslie had heard about. The concierge had reserved us a floor-side table where we could watch the bands and the acts while we ate. I'll always remember that meal. It comes back to me sometimes, especially these days as I choke down the watery paste that passes for food at the Chelonia. I had chateaubriand, and it came in the most beautiful swan-shaped crust, with berries for eyes and braided wings.

Ainslie had a steak. He took big greedy bites. I made my bites daintier as if to make up for it, using my silverware the Continental way as Mrs. Keane had taught me, placing them down after every bite to take small sips of wine. In this way, Ainslie finished long before I did, and sat back with a satisfied grunt to watch the seventeen-piece orchestra. They played the classics: "Begin the Beguine," "Ain't Misbehavin'," "Heart and Soul."

And then the most beautiful foreign woman came to the mic. I suppose we were the foreigners, but her skin was a lovely mocha color I'd never seen before. Her hair was pulled back so tightly that I couldn't tell if it was curly or straight, and her dress was cut out everywhere it was seemly (and some places it wasn't). The fabric that was left was shiny as if painted with diamond dust, and the restaurant fell silent as we waited to hear her sing. She exerted a palpable pull on the audience, and as she cleared her throat, a lone fork clanked to a plate.

She sang a rumba, a sultry piece that had everyone hanging on each phrase. I envied her, oh how I envied her! I'd lived a life where no one noticed me. Here was an example of raw femininity, magnetic power over both sexes. The singer demanded attention and received it, just like that.

She had a high breathy voice that hit each note with the exactitude of an Indian's arrow. The music wound around the room. Even those in the far back stopped talking. And she swayed between verses, dancing without moving. When she reached the end of the song, there was wild applause, and she bowed, slightly. I saw that the cutout parts of her

dress were covered with a flesh-colored mesh, the skin smooth underneath. The orchestra began again, and she went around the dance floor
asking men to dance. The first turned bright red and hid in his napkin.
The second was prevented by a very stern wife. Then Ainslie stood up,
his napkin folded neatly as though by its own volition.

"You'll be all right, here?"

I nodded. "Go ahead."

Ainslie glided over to the woman, taking her outstretched hand. I
have said that he was a gifted dancer, but tonight, with a worthy partner,
he took my breath away. His hair may have been thinning and his waist
a bit too tiny, but I could see every woman falling for Ainslie. Together,
they danced like they'd been practicing for years, and I could see the
delight in the singer's eyes that she'd finally found her equal on the
dance floor. He spun her, swung her hips, ending with a dip.

The room applauded noisily. Some of the men whistled, putting their
fingers in their mouths to amplify the noise. When Ainslie bowed and
made toward our table, the crowd booed. They wanted more. More of
the beautiful couple floating above the floor. More of the cinema stars
come to life.

I gulped down the last of my wine and slid Ainslie's glass over toward
me. I was learning to drink. He liked gin martinis and the taste was
acerbic but warming. He caught my eye over an up-tempo waltz and
shrugged as if to say: I'm sorry, but what can I do?

I waved him on with my free hand. And I was fine. Because as much
as I wanted to be that woman, that dancer who merged so effortlessly
with my husband, I knew that eventually he would sit back down at our
table. I would never really know him, I saw now, but I would know him
more than these people, and his confidence, our shared secret, grew at
the bottom of my chest in a way that I could only describe as love.

*

The next morning we caught the ship for Guayaquil, the capital of the
Ecuadorian nation. It was to be the last vestiges of civilization as I knew
it, and I waved goodbye to land with real tears in my eyes.

"Cheer up, Mrs. Conway," Ainslie said. "It's not so bad."

"At least it's not raining," I completed the sentence. It was our little refrain, said in sarcasm when things were grim, and often when it was raining as if to console ourselves that things could not get any worse and would therefore have to get better. He put his arm around me and squeezed, briefly.

Though the commercial ship we were on was large and carried freight as well as passengers, the crossing was rocky and I felt green the entire way. Why do they say a crossing is "rocky"? I would have given my left arm for some rocks to cast ashore on, even if the ship were smashed to pieces. I could have at least been on land then, something stable that didn't pitch beneath my feet like dice tumbling across the gaming table.

I was unable to keep anything down, and even Ainslie, solid, iron stomach though he possessed, was a bit puce around the gills. He liked the wind on his face, watching the horizon for signs of land. I, on the other hand, was in the cabin, too weak even to stand, sipping lemon water and eating the occasional cracker for strength. I don't think we exchanged three words.

Finally, on the fourth day at sea, the water calmed, and I felt well enough to at least sit on deck and try to let the sun heal some of my weakness. Ainslie joined me with his book, a copy of *The Swiss Family Robinson*. "Since we're supposedly inspired by it, I should at least read it," he said. "Plus, it's said to be a book one can read multiple times, so it will come in handy when we've read everything we've brought to the point where we can recite to each other, while juggling, in our sleep."

A stronger self would have replied, "I can't juggle," whereas the weak reality of Frances merely smiled.

"Oh poor Franny-Lou," he said. "You're not much of a mariner, are you?"

And I tipped my head over the chair and retched into the bin I'd brought for that purpose; a more emphatic reply I could not have planned.

*

The port in Guayaquil was everything one expects from a busy port in a third world country. I was surprised, though, at the quantity of Indians in charge. I had been led to believe that there were few Indians left in the cities. The books I'd read said that they lived up in the hills, or had so intermingled with Europeans that it was difficult to tell which was which. But now I heard the strains of Quechua, which sounds nothing like Spanish, and from captains and *gerentes* alike.

Ainslie supervised the unloading of our boxes of provisions, while I sat up by the road with our steamer trunk and three suitcases. I saw the vagrant dogs one hears about nosing around for food, their taut ribs showing, and a little varmint that may have been a mouse or rat or some sort of chipmunk scurrying across the stones. All around there was bustle, freight being loaded or unloaded, people yelling, greeting each other, hurrying to their next order of business. The ships all looked run-down, purchased third-hand long ago and then handed down again. I scanned the docks for the one boat that traveled to the Galápagos, but the *San Cristóbal* was not in port. Or, rather, I would learn, it *was* in port, but had no immediate plans to travel. We were to stop by every couple of days to see when the mood might strike Capitán Oswaldo to leave. While I waited for Ainslie, I read my guidebook. It recommended the Tivoly Hotel, which had rooms from fifteen sucres. I marked the page.

After several hours, when my stomach was telling me it was finally on land and wanted sustenance to make up for the last few days of privation, Ainslie came up from the docks. He walked wearily, one of the few times I'd seen him with anything less than a completely enthusiastic countenance. I was struck by how little I knew of my husband, how much time we'd spent pretending, even to each other.

He recovered his smile by the time he reached me and set his pipe in his mouth, which always lifted his spirits. He picked up his case and whistled to one of the boys who sat waiting for jobs there. "Ask him to get us a taxi."

"Where are we going?"

"A hotel that's been recommended," Ainslie said.

"By whom? The guidebook says—"

"Ask him," he urged.

I asked him in my pidgin Spanish, which the boy understood, taking up two suitcases that were almost as big as he was. He yelled for two of his friends, who grabbed the trunk between them and hauled it to the road. They looked so small, their skin brown and leathery from the sun.

The ride they hailed us was not exactly a taxi but rather another friend of theirs who drove what used to be a car and was now four wheels with a rusted hood held together by sailor's rope. Still, we piled our luggage and ourselves in, and Ainslie handed the boys a few coins. "Did you give them American money?" I asked, for we'd been unable to change currencies before our trip.

"No, I exchanged some money down at the port."

"On the black market?" I was shocked, and worried. We were expected to conduct ourselves with propriety when it came to local law.

"We're south of the border now, dear," he said. "And the rates are better. Hang on for the ride!"

After we got settled in at the hotel, which could best be described as "adequate," we were expected to check in at the consulate. The consul had a reputation as an egotistical man, who would take our intelligence presence as evidence that he wasn't trusted enough to keep tabs on the islands. So we maintained our cover as American civilians who wanted to "get away from it all." Also, the fewer people who knew about Operation Pomegranate, the easier it would be to keep it secret. Secrets have a tendency to spread in unpredictable ways, like ink on a page.

Ainslie went to meet with him, but he kept Ainslie waiting an hour and then insisted that he return—he didn't have the right papers, and then those didn't contain the right stamp. He was merely exercising his meager power. Ainslie had little else to do, or he would have ignored this pompous man entirely.

"He reminded me that should we have to be rescued, we'd be leaching resources from the United States, which we must love, of course, less than he does. I had to bite my tongue to remind him that I'd been in France during the Great War and lost more for this country than he could ever hope to gain."

"His current opinion of the German situation on Floreana?"

"A colony of utopianists who have fled civilization to prove themselves modern-day Swiss Family Robinsons. He may have something there. Germans do seem particularly susceptible to ideas, do they not?"

Certainly Hitler's rise would indicate that this was true. "They're antagonizing Poland again, like an older sibling teases the younger one."

I nodded. Despite having Polish parents, I knew very little about the old country, not even the name of the village my parents had come from. My father had never spoken of his life—actually, he rarely spoke at all, which is why Ainslie's talkativeness was both a surprise and a delight.

The *San Cristóbal* showed no sign of hurrying to the islands, and we were captive to its whims; there was no other transportation. When I asked when it might leave, I was met with shrugs. Could be days, could be weeks. But an estimate? Ecuadorians don't estimate, it turns out. So we made ourselves as comfortable as possible for a wait of unknown duration, victims of *mañana*.

I would walk down to the embassy every day to see if a telegram or package had come for us. There was usually something weekly from Childress, transmitted in a simple code that I was in charge of transcribing. One of our frustrations was having our orders countermanded constantly. If Childress would tell us to jump, Rear Admiral Holmes would tell us to squat, and then he would get a directive from CNO Admiral Leahy, saying that we should crawl on our bellies like reptiles. As a result, our reaction when receiving most orders was to simply wait until the next week's came.

So we busied ourselves readying supplies. In addition to everything we would need for an indefinite stay, we also had to conceal a radio, flares, flags, and weapons. A hunting rifle was easy enough to hide, but it was a serious calculation to decide how much flour to sacrifice in exchange for ammunition. Our stomachs or our lives, which would occasionally amount to the same thing.

By force of having nothing else to do, my study of German was coming along. The only problem was that I had no one to practice with and therefore my knowledge was theoretical and literary rather than fluent. Would I understand an actual person when he or she spoke?

It was hot in Guayaquil, and foreign, and after two weeks my spirits were low. Ainslie tried to cheer me up, but the fact that we were nearly strangers merely increased my despondency.

"So tell me, bride," he'd say. "What's your favorite ice-cream flavor?"

"Oh, I don't know," I said. "Vanilla maybe?"

Another time: "Do you like turkey?"

Me: "What does it matter? There won't be a delicatessen on Floreana."

Ainslie: "True, true, but just humor me."

Me: "I've actually grown fond of bacon."

Ainslie raised his eyebrows at this one. "Well," he said. "You always want what's forbidden to you. Yes, the forbidden fruit, that might be my favorite food."

Ainslie walked the streets by himself after dinner. I think he would go down to the wharf to watch the ships. One night he came home with a chocolate bar. It was Ecuadorian chocolate, rough and bitter, and I have an aversion to chocolate, but I thanked him anyway. I recognized that he was trying to be a good husband.

It was during this time that we consummated our relationship. We went out for dinner one night and imbibed what was becoming our usual excess of alcohol (my liver would be glad to get to a place where there was no booze). We completed our evening ablutions, and I climbed into my bed to read. Ainslie came out of the bathroom and instead of going to his bed, he wordlessly climbed into mine. And it was . . . nice. There are secrets a lady must keep to herself, even in her intimate memoirs, and so I will say no more except that we were truly married at last.

During those weeks, he acted more like my husband. He was always home for dinner and rarely went out afterward, content to sit and read and smoke his pipe. He was also fond of taking apart and putting back together the radio in our hotel room. When he was done, there were invariably parts left over, small screws and wires, washers, and bits of solder.

Our room had a small balcony, and Ainslie spent many hours out on it, practicing knots and snares, and smoking his pipe, lost in thought. We spoke as married couples do, about meals and errands, about funny anecdotes from our days, about the idiosyncrasies of the Spanish language. We played cards and read books. If it weren't for my anxiety about our mission, and my constant worry of contracting stomach viruses, I would have considered it a pleasant vacation.

*

Came the day to sail, and I sobered to discover that our ship had already consumed eight of its nine cat lives. There was even a bracket for a gun mount on the deck, dating from the motor schooner's use as a fighting ship in the Great War. Needless to say, I was not anxious to make the crossing, having finally again filled out the trousers that hung off me when we arrived on the mainland. It was a five-day sail, five miserable, tempest-toss't, stomach-churning days, our skin frying in the hot equatorial sun, until we put into port at Chatham, the regional capital.

I was shocked at the landscape of the first island. It was like a desert, with white-hot sand and rough rocks. Here and there gnarled branches of shrubbery stuck out like pimples on a young person's face, equally as angry. I later found them to be prickly to the touch and often full of pink-red berries that were veined inside with darker red and which the islanders told me not to eat, though I wasn't planning to. Higher up there were a few trees, also gnarled, like the hands of farmers, and thickset like the indigenous people.

"Welcome to Las Islas Encantadas," I said to Ainslie.

He looked at me quizzically.

"Las Islas Encantadas, the Enchanted Isles, the old name for Galápagos. Did you not read the brief at all?"

"Of course I did," Ainslie said. "I just didn't understand your Spanish accent."

I gave him my best disapproving look.

"Wait, they're enchanted?" Ainslie said. "Turn the ship around!"

Our fellow passengers looked at us like we'd gone mad, two sunburned gringos yelling in English.

We anchored and took a dinghy to the dock, which was the center of a little town. Shacks had been thrown up haphazardly, in between what passed for trees. There were women waiting for us on shore, squatting on their haunches as though birthing a baby. I tried it later and fell over backward. Hips must be trained from childhood if they want to hold you up like that later in life.

Ainslie paced the dock nervously smoking, using up precious cigarettes, making sure no one stole our cargo. When he was satisfied, we went into the "town" to buy seedlings and seeds for the garden (pine-apple, yucca, *camote* vines, bananas), a few chickens for eggs, lard, coffee, and tobacco, and possibly a donkey. Also, we wanted to find out what we could about Floreana and its residents.

One small hut served as a sort of general store, and we found that the proprietor spoke English, of a sort. He had been sent to the islands to serve out a prison sentence (for what, we did not ask). It was not lost on me that I was volunteering to go to a place where people were sent for punishment. Ainslie and he negotiated prices then sat down for a smoke.

I helped his wife shuck corn, and while doing so I found out the fol-lowing: The most current count of souls on Floreana was nine. One German couple and their son, who had come for the salubrious salt air (the child had a congenital lung disorder). Another elderly couple had come to study with Dr. Ritter and were devastated to discover that he had died and they had crossed paths with his widow somewhere in the ocean. They stayed, however, and took over the garden at Friedo, Dore and Ritter's home, continuing their idiosyncratic Nietzschean isola-tionism. Another couple had lived on the island for a year or so, young, attractive, outgoing. They seemed an odd pair to be survivalists, accord-ing to this woman, but then all people who wanted to come to this god-forsaken place were odd, no offense.

None taken.

There was also the governmental representative and his wife, a cousin of the woman in whose "kitchen" I was standing. My hostess apparently did not like this cousin; she spit on the ground as she said her name, which I didn't catch. All this was communicated to me in rapid-fire Spanish. The woman did not care that I spoke very little; she continued her narrative apace. I repeated back to her what I thought she said, and she nodded vigorously.

This I reported to Ainslie once we were back on the *San Cristóbal*. We stood near the motor to "sound mask." The fumes were overwhelming but no one could hear us above the din. Ainslie had to lean down so he could hear what I was saying. I put my lips right to his ear and we took turns offering the sides of our heads.

"You are apparently a better spy than I," he said.

"Speaking the language helps."

"Don't rub it in. So it seems the newest residents are our most likely bet for German government representatives. The others have been here too long."

"What if they're just people?" I asked. "How do we even know they're here for any other reason than to get away from it all?" The wind kept whipping my hair into my eyes and mouth, and I kept brushing it back.

"Are you doubting the intelligence of the United States Navy?" he asked in mock indignation. "I don't even know where this intelligence came from. We'll just live out our year, keep our eyes and ears open, and we'll have served Uncle Sam plenty. Just be Frances Conway. That's all you have to do."

*

Luckily, Floreana was the next stop on the *San Cristóbal*'s tour, for I was anxious to get off the ship. I craned my neck to make out the barest hint of land, and then—was that a cloud? No, it was a mountain with a rounded top, and a few minutes later it was joined by its cousins. Then it took on a green tint, and as we got closer I got a first look at our island. Cliffs, covered in birds and their "souvenirs," fell down to the water. Here and there a little greenery would tentatively make a stab at growth, while up above scrub brush tangled with its neighbor.

We dropped anchor at Post Office Bay, a small strip of sand that rose sharply to the wall of thornbushes that guarded the bay. Hardly a warm welcome.

Floreana is shaped like a sphere, about eight miles wide, but it is impossible to cross without a team of Indios machete-ing the way for you. There is only one beach on the east side, and so it and the south side are underexplored. It has seven hills, or *cerros*. The landscape is desert from the beach up about two miles to higher ground, called *arriba*, where it becomes abruptly green, thanks to the *garúa*, the mist that lingers even in the dry season from May to December.

When the dinghy arrived ashore, I experienced such a wave of regret that I nearly burst into tears. I had expected it to be desolate, but now, faced with the utter absence of any sign of human habitation, I was nervous. An army of land and marine iguanas stood sentry, their ancient jowls seemingly salivating at our approach (they are vegetarians). The two or three sea lions who had accompanied us hoisted themselves onto the rocks and gave heavy sighs as they lay down in the sun. I asked our skipper how they could possibly be comfortable on the sharp points of lava.

Misunderstanding me, he answered, "Oh señora, you must never eat these. They are so few."

Ainslie smiled at me and raised his eyebrows as if to say, I told you so.

He began to drag our belongings up the beach so that when the tide came in it wouldn't sweep them to sea. I went with Capitán Oswaldo to look at the post barrel, which was actually a barrel; Floreana residents used it as an official post office. They put their letters inside and the next passing ship would take them to post. The captain emptied the box; later we saw him reading the contents.

Returning to Ainslie, I said, "Miraculous thing, mail. How does a little piece of paper find the right person?"

Ainslie smiled. "It's a big world, but it's a small one too." He was taking a break, leaning against the oil drum. He was wearing a shirt, which would be an uncommon occurrence in subsequent days, and its white fabric contrasted with his deep tan. His arms were sinewy with muscle. He really was a very good-looking man, my husband.

There is nothing quite like getting off a boat on an island without knowing where you will be spending the night, or rather, knowing you'll be spending it on the shore, fending off insects and curious animals. Add to this the anxiety of getting off a boat on a spy mission on an island of possibly hostile Germans, and you are bound to suffer indigestion at least. It must have registered on my face.

"Could be worse, pet," he said.

"Could be *not* raining," I replied. Of course, it wasn't raining. It never rained that time of year and we had heard that drought was a real worry.

"Cheer up," Ainslie said. "We'll have lots to do and new friends to make."

We had not even finished carrying our belongings up the beach when we had our first visitors. Of course, they spotted the boat when we entered the harbor, and began their one- or two-hour journey to the beach to see what the boat had brought, and probably to get and send some letters. I turned to see a graying blonde of about forty, cheekbones like golf balls in her expressive face. Even though she was very thin, she still had enormous breasts that were pendulously threatening to leave her threadbare blouse. She smiled; her teeth were bucked, and yet she looked at me with the confidence of someone used to finding people daunted by her beauty. A few steps behind her was a short young man, compactly built, with blond hair, cheeks red from re-burning every day.

"'Alo. You are coming to live on the island?" she said in Spanish, her strong German accent discernible even to me. Her face was concerned, and I didn't blame her. Any new person on a nearly deserted island would be suspicious and likely unwelcome, spy or not.

"Frances," I said, knowing that Ainslie probably didn't understand even this much Spanish. The woman stuck out her hand. It was heavily callused. "Genevieve," she said. She pointed to the man. "Victor."

"Ainslie," I pointed at Ainslie. *"Encantada."* That much Spanish I knew. Yes, the old name of the Galápagos is also the word you use when you meet someone. We stood around looking at one another, not sure which language to speak nor what to talk about, taking each other's measure. Finally, as one unit, we went to sit under the meager shade of a small tree. Simultaneously, we offered each other water.

Ainslie pulled out his pipe. Victor's eyes lit up and so Ainslie, though I knew how much it cost him to share, handed it to him once it was lit. The two puffed together. It was seemingly all the conversation they needed. Genevieve and I tried to talk in a mixture of hand signs and broken Spanish, as I could not reveal I knew any German.

She said something in Spanish that I didn't understand. I shook my head.

"No casas," she said.

"Ja," I said, and then realized this was German. I pantomimed building one.

"Dónde dormir?" she asked. We had no plans for where we'd sleep that night, and her question reminded me of this.

I shrugged to show that we didn't know. *"Playa,"* I said. I wouldn't have minded sleeping under a roof tonight. I hated the exposure of the beach.

Genevieve muttered something to the extent of "suit yourself." She fingered the fabric of my blouse, now faded from the sun and salt water. "*Bonito,*" she said, clearly meaning the opposite. Our first encounter was not going well.

Just then the brush behind them began to rustle and from it emerged a pair of young cholo Indians with a donkey held loosely by a rope. They were the only plump people I'd yet seen on the islands, and it must have been a congenital situation, for I would come to see that while we didn't starve, there was not a surplus of calories. They introduced themselves as the Jiménezes, Gonzalo and his wife, Gansa, which means goose. I never learned why they called her that.

Gonzalo told us he was the Ecuadorian representative on the island. I'm not sure if he was self-appointed or actually sanctioned in an official capacity. They had lived on Floreana for almost a year and were about to celebrate their first anniversary. He kissed her and she blushed. As the government official, he informed us, he was able to marry people, if there were any people who wanted to be married. He was in charge of all large-game hunting, and he reminded us of the law that we could only kill male pigs and steers. We would come to see that he frequently ignored his own directives, as the sows and heifers were much tastier. He also felt entitled to the lion's share of anything a passing boat might gift to the island and its residents. Still, he was such a friendly person, and his wife so generous (and a good cook to boot), that we forgave him his idiosyncrasies. He had learned his governance style from Ecuadorians, after all, and he knew no better.

The other two families lived on the other side of the sierra, and would not have seen the boat. The captain left some provisions for them, and the Jiménezes promised to pass them along. Then the *San Cristóbal* pulled out of the bay, and any possibility of returning to civilization went with it. I swallowed the lump in my throat and stared after the old bucket of bolts like she was my lover going off to war.

The sun slipped down behind us; darkness fell quickly in the islands.

Genevieve, Victor, Gonzalo, and Gansa had been watching us unpack. They now reluctantly took their leave, carrying some of our bounty of fruit and seedlings from Chatham we had offered. Genevieve patted me on the head in leave-taking, condescendingly, I thought, and Victor bowed deeply. Gonzalo shook my hand and Gansa kissed me on the cheek. Then Victor stepped in front of Genevieve and pulled aside a branch for her, letting it slap back afterward, almost hitting the Jiménezes. When they had disappeared into the brush, Ainslie came up behind me and whispered softly, "Don't say anything yet."

So I unpacked our few necessary belongings in silence. Could Genevieve and Victor be our German equivalents? What if the only spying we were doing was on each other? I imagined a *College Humor* cartoon where spies trained field glasses on each other while real sabotage goes on behind them. These were the lofty ideas I was contemplating as I laid out our dinner—beef jerky, biscuits, fruit, a boiled egg.

In front of me the Pacific Ocean slumbered, placid, and a light breeze was cooling the air and keeping the bugs at bay. To my right, the trail shone with golden dust in the dying light, illuminating the hills up high with a red-violet glow.

When it grew too dark to see, Ainslie finally spoke to me. "We'll have to see tomorrow about a place to settle." He was stating the obvious. I could hear the weariness in his voice. In the meager light of the new moon, I could see the angles of his face. "And a place for our other belongings," he said, hinting at the radio. I nodded. I could hear the rhythm of the island—the waves on the shore, the birds calling to each other and the wind answering. Far off, I heard a bull bellowing and a donkey braying and the hum of a thousand predatory insects.

Everyone was trying to stake a claim on this island, fauna and humans alike.

*

The water was so calm the night we first went in. I remember that Ainslie took off his clothes and jumped in as free as a bird. I was more modest, tiptoeing to the edge of the water, afraid of the rocks underneath the thin coating of sand. I was seduced by Ainslie's yelping and hooting (the water was cold). And we were alone, really alone. Alone in a way humans rarely are on this earth. So I took off my culottes and waded in, self-conscious and chilly.

Ainslie swam toward me and peeled my hands away from my torso. The water reflected the moonlight onto his face, chiseled and pointed, the inherited genes of the Anglo-Saxons, who, Darwin-like, took on the phenotype of the craggy bluffs of Dover. He led me farther into the water, and then, once I was floating, took off swimming parallel to the shore, leaving me to tread water and contemplate what monsters of the deep might be nibbling on my toes.

I later learned there were sharks off this bay. We never swam out past the break again.

*

The following morning Ainslie said he was going to look for a site for our homestead. I stayed behind and organized our belongings, making sure nothing ate the seedlings we'd purchased in Chatham and that they remained watered. There was a sort of path up from the beach, and Ainslie disappeared quickly into the brush. His plan was to find a place close to the natural spring up near Asilo de la Paz so we wouldn't have to walk too far for water. He would go up high and then follow a game trail to a likely place. We wanted to be *arriba* because there was more water and therefore an environment more hospitable for growing plants. The Jiménezes were up there as well, though they made it clear they didn't want us too near them, and the feeling was mutual. Genevieve and Victor were lower down, not far from Black Beach (not far by Galápagos standards, about an hour's walk). They had taken over the ruins of a Norwegian fishing camp and were living off provisions they'd brought as well as fruit from the trees that someone had fortuitously planted years ago.

Ainslie came back to the beach just as the sun was getting ready to disappear. "I found us a lovely place, bride-o'-mine. Flat, lush, got the shade of a couple of trees for the house and a nice place for the garden. Tomorrow we can make our way up there."

I had started a fire with three of our precious matches. Training had taught me the saying "one match, one fire" but not how to achieve it. The beans were almost done, cooked with salt water and the rest of the beef jerky shredded. Ainslie paced the fire as though activity would make dinner cook faster. We ate, and then, exhausted, fell into "bed."

The next morning, Ainslie took a load up to the site and then went to borrow the Jiménezes' burro. It was as stubborn as its cousin the mule and wore an expression of bemused displeasure constantly. "He stares at me like I owe him money," Ainslie said.

We loaded him up (Chuclu was his name, I remember now) with the most necessary items in our camp—the oil drum with the radio, the seedlings, our bedroll ponchos. We walked for about an hour on the only road, the Camino de la Muerte (Highway of Death), the sun beating down on us. The land was so dry it was desert, the bushes not much more than sticks. And then it appeared someone had drawn a demarcation line; it began to get more lush until after about another half hour we were walking in the tropics. The ground was spongy, tangled with brambles, bushes, leaves, and shrubbery all vying for light under the canopy, growing on top of their fallen comrades. I had to pick my way carefully as their thorny grip threatened to trip me. The occasional lava boulders were now covered in a blanket of pale blue moss and overhead the sky was green with leaves. The air smelled of peaty decay, wet grass, and our own sweat. I was amazed that the landscape could change that quickly, and I later learned that this kind of variation is typical of the Galápagos Islands: If you don't like the scenery, walk three miles.

Ainslie's scouting skills were developed from childhood, and he left the main trail at a place only he would recognize. After another half hour uphill, I was completely winded. Never particularly hardy, I had atrophied during the weeks at sea.

"Just a bit more," Ainslie said. "It'll be worth it."

I had no choice but to forge ahead. Ainslie had indeed picked a lovely spot, verdant and well located. We could see just a hint of sea, enough to spot an approaching ship, and we were equidistant to both Black Beach and Post Office Bay.

"Why don't you wait here?" Ainslie said. "I'll make another trip." I took him up on the offer, gratefully.

It was so quiet. Far from the sea, the noise of crashing waves didn't drown out all that surrounded it. Instead I could hear birds chatting with each other, the wind brushing the hair of the tall grass. There were other noises too, benign animal noise, or noises that the land makes, in much the same way a house will clear its throat and sigh at night.

That night we slept beneath our new stars. It was a promising start.

*

One of our first tasks was to get the radio up and running. Ainslie spent two days scouting sites, then was gone an entire day machete-ing his way up and back to his chosen hiding spot.

"Why don't you tell me where it is?" I said. "That way, if I ever need to use it, I'll know."

"That's not protocol," Ainslie said. "That makes you vulnerable, as you well know. And you don't know how to use it." He sat down and began to take off his shoes, groaning when he had to bend over.

"Yes, but aren't these circumstances in which it might be wise to eschew protocol?" I knelt, pushing his hands away, and untied his shoes for him, slipping them off his hot feet.

"Oh thank you. I'm career military. You're asking me to not follow protocol?" Ainslie took a long drink from the jug on the table. "Not going to happen, pet."

"I'm worried," I said. "What if something happens to you?"

"First of all, nothing is going to happen to me. And second, if it does, then everyone will take care of you and the next ship will take you back to the mainland. Go to the embassy there and they'll get you home."

"I don't like it," I said.

"It's the navy," Ainslie said. "You're not supposed to *like* it." He stood up, signaling the end of the conversation. When he was done talking, he was done talking. I was fuming, and I took it out on our one poor pot.

CHAPTER TEN

Once we settled in, it was easy to forget for days at a time our reasons for being in the Galápagos. Each day brought its chores; each evening the wonderful exhaustion of a day of manual labor overtook us. We slept like babies.

The first few weeks we spent constructing a house. We salvaged some timber from the beach (illegally, since any building materials belonged to the "governor's representative," as Gonzalo would later inform us) and used the corrugated tin we brought from the mainland as our roof. Employing the straightest, longest trees we could find, we made ourselves two chairs and two platforms for beds. At the same time, we had to clear the ground for a garden. The undergrowth was thick, and we only had one machete between us, so that I went around pulling what I could and then Ainslie came behind me to get the larger plants. Then we would both dig with our fingers until we got at the root of the offending weed. Our hands ended up bloody, our fingernails torn.

Once our garden was established, Ainslie and I rarely worked together. His main duties—fetching water, hunting animals—took him away from our home. However great his virtues, Ainslie had equally infuriating personality quirks, one of which was his obsession with neatness. Neatness should not be confused with cleanliness, which is grounded in health and one of my obsessions. Ainslie would eat off of filthy dishes, wear soiled clothing, forget to bathe for days if it weren't for my reminders (and I did wonder how he managed in the forty-odd years before he met me). But he insisted on objects being lined up by size and shape, their corners perfectly parallel. His shirts, stained, were folded military style, and he would frequently stop to adjust something completely innocuous in nature—a flower whose bloom he believed should have been farther to the right, or a leaf blocking his way.

He was engaged, therefore, when not out hunting, with improving Floreana's "roads," namely the Camino de la Muerte that ran from the beach to our home. A road, in his opinion, needed to be wide enough for a loaded horse. It was a perfectly worthless and insane endeavor, as there were no travelers but ourselves, and there would likely never be any. But I suppose men must spend their time doing something, and God forbid that something should be helping women.

It wasn't uncommon for him to be gone all day on an improvement project. And the projects improved his moods too; I've never seen anyone grumpier in the morning. He left with a scowl and came back whistling.

"Want to show me your progress?" I asked one day, mistakenly in the morning. Before he'd had his coffee even!

"Not until I'm done. You don't ask me to taste the batter, do you?" he growled. I let it drop.

My days were spent on the garden and the house and most of all on making food. First, I had to roast coffee, for this was more important to us even than water. Then every grain of rice or cup of flour had to be inspected for weevils or other *bichos*. After that, I milled the grain, and since I had forgotten this essential instrument, I had to construct a cavewoman's mortar and pestle. The garden needed weeding and watering and the fire needed stoking and the clothes needed washing and the house needed sweeping and the chickens needed tending and . . . well, the point is I was busy.

The islands were frustrating. No one tells you that. Every task takes twice as long, and often must be repeated after the first attempt fails. And a chore like getting cooking water can take up to two or three hours. Cooking water came from the sea (our only abundant natural resource was salt), but I had to take my jug down to the ocean and wet my feet collecting it. Fresh water had to be fetched from the stream.

In dry periods, like the one we suffered through when we first landed, "sweet water," as it was called in Spanish, was hard to come by.

Despite their monotony, the chores were satisfying in a way that the mind-numbing filing and typing in the Office of Naval Intelligence were not. Everything I did had a direct application to my quality of life. It was all necessary. There would be no bread without milled flour. It was easy to see the connections between actions and their dividends, and I understood why this kind of a life might be attractive to people (Germans) who were put off by the past consumerism of (Weimar) society or the current rise of fascism (Nazism) in Europe.

But you'll never know the satisfaction like that of a completed task on a nearly uninhabited island. Every triumph is yours, and you walk with your chin high, proud of your resourcefulness. Independence was the ultimate compliment that nature could pay you.

Gradually things got easier, though, and I found myself in mid-June with an afternoon free and decided to hike down to the hacienda, the abandoned site of the baroness's homestead, which had looked so homey in the file photos. Foliage waited for no man's return here; the structure was overrun by vines and weeds. The garden had gone to seed, and high palo santos and vines had crowded out the vegetables, or else the animals had eaten them. Except for the poles and the roof, there was little sign that humans had ever improved this land. There was nothing left of the shelves of the "kitchen." Someone had removed all the cups and plates and then the shelves themselves. Nothing went to waste here in the Galápagos. There were two broken plates and I put them in my satchel—I was sure I could find a use for them as bird-deterrents or drainage for the garden. I sat for a moment on the fireplace. It might have been the end of the world and I the only person left on the planet to negotiate civilization's ruins. I was filled with that feeling of uselessness that pervades our psyches in difficult times. And the feeling spiraled so that I wondered why we were even bothering with any of this in the first place. Why we were working for the government, why government even existed at all . . . Island living can do this to you. It took a good hour before I snapped out of it and walked briskly back home.

*

Though our island was not deserted, we rarely saw our neighbors unless we wanted to. But there was a steady stream of strangers at our "door." Boats, ships, and yachts arrived with relative frequency, both to gawk at the settlers and to get some shore time. This was positive, as it brought us items we couldn't manufacture on Floreana, as well as food, conversation, mail, and news, but it also meant that our daily routines were frequently interrupted. When a boat arrived, announcing itself with a foghorn or a whistle, Gonzalo came to inform us, though we could clearly see the ocean. We had taught each other the English and Spanish for "There's a ship in the harbor." Gonzalo would say it over and over. I thought about teaching him a second sentence, just to double the power of his tongue, but he was always in such a hurry to get down to the beach that I never bothered.

A quick trip to the beach was a two-hour hike. So by the time we got down there and returned the day was over. The worst was when we headed down to Black Beach and it turned out the ship had sent a launch to Post Office Bay. Then we had to wait in the hope that they'd figure out their mistake and come back for us. Otherwise, they'd do their socializing with whoever came down to the correct beach and leave our portion of the spoils, which were never quite as evenly divided as they should have been.

Visitors came in many flavors. Researchers, following in the footsteps of Darwin, were inevitably pale, burning rather than tanning. Government officials (Ecuadorian, Brazilian, American . . .) would come inspect the island. What they were looking for, I do not know. In the spring, Norwegian or Canadian fishermen assayed our waters. Summer brought the rich with their luxury yachts (gifting chocolate; why always chocolate?). The publication of various articles about the death of Dr. Ritter and the "disappearance" of the baroness only fueled the fire of morbid curiosity. The rumors of buried treasure, which to my knowledge were invented whole hog, didn't help. People also came in search of the giant tortoises, which had been extinct on Floreana for years thanks to the pigs, goats, and human hunters. They left disappointed on both counts. Winter, though not cold in the Minnesota or Nebraska sense, brought rain and discouraged travelers.

Thus, our days were frequently punctuated by disappointed and uninvited visitors. Then we would be put on display for the amusement of any ladies present, who told me I was so "innovative" and that they loved how I "made do" with so little. They even indulged in a bit of role-playing, tending to my fire while all the time I'm sure thinking of going back to the yacht and having a real shower and a cocktail. Sometimes they asked us to take them on hikes, and then we had to drop what we were doing and spend the day traipsing about. When a storm came through, or it got late, we had overnight visitors, which meant a woman in my bed as I lay sleepless on the dirt floor, trying not to toss and turn and disturb our "guest."

*

Ainslie could be melancholy. It was not until we had been on the island awhile, and the newness had worn off, and we bickered sometimes over chores or out of tiredness or boredom, that I realized how much he was like Rosalie in that respect. I walked on eggshells around him, waiting to see what kind of humor he was in before I spoke to him. Mostly he was his usual cheerful self, but sometimes I'd come in from the garden to find him pacing our small shelter and then I'd know the crabs had got him, as we said.

We wrote down the movements of ships, but they did nothing to arouse suspicion. To communicate with "home" we would have to rely on the Galápagos post, which meant waiting until a passing ship anchored and then handing them a letter to post when they arrived on a continent. I wrote frequently to Rosalie though I knew that the letters would go unposted for months. It was possible we would die in the Galápagos, either from an injury or from being discovered, and it struck me as horribly sad that I would never see Rosalie again. She was the person I thought of most on the island, usually while doing something totally unrelated to "regular life." For instance, I found myself missing her most acutely when I sat peeling skin off a goat that Ainslie had only perfunctorily butchered. Rosalie would have been horrified. I laughed and imagined her laughing with me. I felt a sweet longing for her company. Any company really, but hers in particular.

It would be summer in San Francisco, such as it was, the sky gray and misty. I would calculate the time of day and try to imagine what Rosalie might be doing. She'd be helping Sylvie with her homework, or tying Clarence's bow tie, or planning a menu with her cook. It amused me to think of the contrast between her daily activities and mine.

I began to talk to her during the day to hear the sound of my own voice, when Ainslie was out hunting or exploring or "improving our circumstances," as he called his busywork. I asked her opinion on my cooking. Was the fire too hot? Was there enough pepper? I told her about the garden I was growing and my mortal enemies the magpies. I talked about my irrational fear of male animals, donkeys and bulls and billy goats, their snorting aggression giving me the all-overs (as Mrs. Keane used to say). Sometimes I cried to her, out of frustration, when I could not get the fire lit, or the misty fog socked me in for the seventeenth straight day and even my tears were soggy.

I spoke to a young Rosalie, as though we were both still girls. I relived our good times, a visit to a municipal swimming pool, a birthday celebration. And experiences that grew amusing now that they had receded: the terrifying train ride, the time we tried on Mrs. Klein's face powder and it turned out I was terribly allergic. Our lives were all in front of us.

Once, I forgot that Ainslie was around, and I began to tell an imaginary Rosalie about my trip to collect rocks for the fireplace. "Who are you talking to?" he asked me.

I must have blushed as crimson as the day we were sunburned on the ship's deck. "The cat," I answered. We had "adopted" one of the feral cats to help us with our rat problem.

Ainslie seemed not to think this odd. "Which one is it?"

"You've scared her away," I said, "but I'll point her out next time."

This satisfied him. He himself had some peculiarities, and one of his virtues was that he didn't often point out those in others.

Living on a deserted island is not for the claustrophobic. It may seem ironic, but even in this place with no walls, the steps I took each day were few. I did a lot of gardening and chopping of wood, and I was lean like one of the wild dogs, but I rarely left our compound. On days when work was light—clothes and linens were washed, meals were prepared in advance—I liked to take my time exploring, especially at the beach.

There, hundreds of iguanas stared at me placidly, like men having coffee at a train station. I was the most interesting thing happening, but I was not very interesting. Floreana's fascinating fauna, which make the Galápagos such a traveler's delight, could mostly be seen only at the beach (with the exception of flamingos in the lagoon): blue- and red-footed boobies (a cartoon of a bird with brightly colored feet), frigates with their red pouches, penguins and dolphins, Sally Lightfoot crabs.

I liked to squint and try to see land. Though I understood intellectually how one can travel so far as to not be able to see where one has come from, it still struck me as odd that I used to be there but was no longer. What was Rosalie doing? Was she planning a meal? Wiping a tear from Sylvie's face? Out in Union Square "stirring the pot," as she used to call shopping?

I was not opposed to solitude—I was mostly by myself when I was not working back in San Francisco, but then at least there was a city around me, with its spicy noise and its fervency. Now, when I was not with Ainslie, I was alone. When he was gone, I had the uncanny sense that I was being watched. Indeed I was being watched carefully by several animals to see if I'd be so careless as to leave the top off the sugar or drop a bit of meat. I was vulnerable in our house without walls, like I was in a fishbowl. At the beach, however, I had a sense that there was a whole world around me, and it gave me comfort.

I began to keep a diary, under cover as Mrs. Conway, intrepid explorer, to reinforce my story and assuage my loneliness. It turned into my first book, *The Enchanted Islands*, which you can find a copy of, if you search diligently. By the end, I was so adept at writing fiction that my second book, *Return to the Island*, is a near-complete work of imagination (except, of course, for the banal events, which happened with great regularity throughout our island stay). It's a misconception that island life is always hopping. Rather, it is full of routine and hoping for weather other than what you have. When it's hot, you wish it were cooler, and then the cool weather arrives and you wish the sun would shine with greater enthusiasm. During the rainy season, you'd pay a great deal of money for one dry day, and then the drought comes and you dream of rainstorms. It is a flaw of the human spirit that we always want what we don't have, and the achievement of one goal merely sparks the setting of another, at least in those of us who strive to better ourselves.

*

We celebrated two months of residence, and our garden was finally starting to bear its first edibles. I was finding new ways to eliminate pests and discourage foragers. Our house, such as it was, was complete. It was time for some reconnaissance. We still had not met our other neighbors who lived over the sierra, so Ainslie said he'd hike around and say hello. His secondary motive was to fill in the details of the rudimentary maps of the islands we had been provided with. He would also look for other sources of water, always a concern and essential to any future military usage. He forewarned me he might be spending the night away, either "on the road" or with the couple who lived on the other side of the sierra, the Weisses. He set off with a bundle of dried meat and some cornmeal cakes. Night fell and he wasn't back.

It had been a rainy day, odd for this time of year, and I spent it running from receptacle to receptacle, pouring what little water I collected into a jug so as to save it from evaporation and to stop the birds from fouling it. The ground, which so often rejected the meager rainwater, pushing it away in little clumps, finally gave in and absorbed it, and the result was miraculous mud! I scooped some and plugged the holes in the roof as best I could, then tried to make our dirt floor a bit less dusty, as I'd read they do in Africa. If that's true, then I needed some African guidance, because I merely succeeded in making our floor deeply rutted.

I spent the night huddling under my thin sheet, simultaneously hoping for and dreading the rats' arrival. Sure enough they came, their familiar presence comforting in its regularity, but of course, rats are no friends and no substitute for a husband. As they ran over our tin roof, I imagined the worst. What would happen if I were to fall—would Ainslie find me? Would I be eaten before then? What if I were bitten by some poisonous spider? Ate something rotten and vomited out my insides organ by organ like what felled poor Dr. Ritter? What if Ainslie never came back and I was left to fend for myself until the next boat came by? The thought of Ainslie's demise struck me with a coldness and panic I didn't know I was capable of feeling.

As if the moon couldn't decide if I needed light or dark, it shone half. Not enough to see by but enough to cast shadows. And shadows I saw, as I alternated between keeping my eyes open and shutting them tight like a child willing ghosts away. Every paw- or hoof-fall was a murderess coming to ply her trade. Every snapping twig a cocked gun. Even the wind blew louder.

I must have fallen asleep because something woke me during the night. A boar? A goat? A murderous German? I sat shivering until dawn. At first light, the rats retreated and noises outside returned to their non-scary incarnations: branches, birds, wind. I was all right.

Until I went out front. There were brush marks in the front area, striations in the wet dirt like something had tried to cover its footsteps.

Could an animal have done this, dragging a branch? It was rather unlikely. A sense of dread lodged within me and stayed for the day. But there was nothing to be done, and there was bread to bake and a garden to clear and no end of other chores.

As a second dusk began to fall, I scanned the horizon nervously, a Penelope waiting for her wandering Odysseus. For a spy, Ainslie walked with a heavy step. I could tell they were his footfalls for long minutes before he arrived; he took large strides and often paused at the top of his gait. There would be a long silence and then the crash of a crush of underbrush, sometimes accompanied by the whoosh of branches being swept out of the way to make room for him.

With a simultaneous sense of relief and also of joy, I called, "What ho!"

"Friend or foe?" he replied.

"That's what I'm supposed to say!" I laughed and took his pack off his shoulders.

Ainslie gave me a hug, lingering and squeezing in a way that reassured me he was happy to be back. He looked rested but troubled. I didn't dare ask him what was wrong, though, for I knew he would just make a joke and pull away even further. The only way to get information from him was to allow him to divulge it in his own time.

Our worry for each other's safety was mutual, and I was thrilled to think I occupied his thoughts when he was gone.

"Of course you do! You're my wife—who else am I supposed to think about?" He sat down and wiped his face with the kerchief he always wore around his neck. After he rested a while he said, "The Weiss kid looks terrible, odd pale tint to his skin. They've lived here five years, so I'm marking them down as harmless. But might as well radio it in tomorrow. Tomorrow is Thursday, right?" We had a standard Thursday-afternoon radio appointment. Communications were so limited that both receivers had to be on at the same time and same frequency for Guayaquil to copy us.

I had prepared a homecoming meal of fried ham and cornmeal biscuits, assuming he'd be hungry after his journey, and I was not wrong. He drank his customary black coffee and strode around the house, examining it like I'd done some damage that needed to be inspected, which made me feel self-conscious about the mud plugs in the roof.

"What's this, then?" he asked, looking at the branch marks near the path.

"I don't know," I said. "They were there when I woke up. Do you think it's an animal?"

Ainslie squatted down to look more closely. "Did anything else . . . happen?" he asked.

"I'm not sure if this counts as happening," I said, "but no, it was utterly quiet here. Scarily quiet, in fact. A rat got into the sugar again, even though I put a rock on top. Those things are much cleverer than we give them credit for."

I had set Ainslie up for a joke here, but he didn't rise to the bait. Instead, he looked concerned, which tamped the feeling of joy at his return.

"You don't think it's . . ." I trailed off. I couldn't imagine what it might have been.

"I'm sure it's nothing, pet," he said. "Your imagination gets active when you're by yourself. I brought some papayas from upcountry. They're not particularly good. Picked too early. Give one a try. Maybe you can turn them into something more interesting." I smiled. So much was confusing about Ainslie. He flirted, professed affection for me, which I really believed he felt, but he shared so little with me, and we hadn't repeated our night in Guayaquil. At night he pecked my cheek and retired to his own bed. It's true that it was easier to keep bugs at bay with separate nets, but it was an obvious rebuke.

And then, like any other husband come home from a day of work, Ainslie lit his pipe with *muyuyo* grass and contemplated the rapidly setting sun, turning in as soon as it fell into the water, another day.

*

A week passed, and Ainslie prepared to pay a visit to the other German couple we had yet to meet, the Muellers. I asked Ainslie if I could accompany him. I didn't want to spend another night alone if he somehow found himself unable to return before dark. So we hiked the hour and a half to Friedo, as Dr. Ritter and Dore had christened their home in a combination of their names. He strode ahead of me as though he'd trod the path many times. His legs were so long, I had to hurry to keep up and eventually I asked him to slow down. He was apologetic—he hadn't realized he was rushing. It was an old habit from the service.

He let me rest until I'd caught my breath, and then had me hike on before him. But his presence just behind me, looming, made me more cross than hurrying to follow him had done. "Just go," I snapped.

Ainslie was patient. He sat on the path and said, "Let's have lunch."

I did feel better after eating and drinking, and I had changed my attitude by the time we got to Friedo's front gate, which had its own name like the entrance to the Forbidden City in China: Elephant Gate. Ainslie said to me, "Tell them hello in German."

"'Allo!" I yelled, a trilingual mix of *hallo*, *hello,* and *hola*.

I had been told that the Muellers were old, but Ingrid was about my age, though browned and leathered by the sun. I was shocked, if only because that meant that I was old too. My age occasionally snuck up on me like this, a startled look in the mirror, a twinge in the mornings.

Tasks that required viewing of small details, like threading a needle, were hard (all right, impossible).

Though she had a reputation for being unpleasant, Ingrid was as warm as her Teutonic heritage could let her be. She shook our hands—I was impressed with the strong grip—and then called to her husband that the American couple had finally arrived, as if we had been expected and were tardy.

We sat down with her and Alexandre and drank an odd tea that may have been just twigs. Their English was excellent; Alexandre had learned it at university. He had a long gray beard, Santa Claus style, which made him seem friendly. He spoke very slowly, and put great thought into each word. He had been a professor, he said, of philosophy at Stuttgart. I was curious as to what would make someone cross an ocean to study with a two-bit philosopher like Ritter. Of course, I didn't raise the question in quite that way. To answer me, he thought he had better begin way in the past, and we sat for an hour or so while he related his entire life story. By the time he explained the effect that Ritter's philosophy had on him, my bottom hurt from sitting so long. It was the longest I had sat since leaving the boat more than two months ago. Ainslie was growing increasingly restless next to me. He was not built for holding still, and first his knee began to jostle, then he started tapping his fingers together. I could feel our mutual annoyance building, but I was powerless to stop Alexandre's tirade. His wife sat placidly by his side; from her expression I believe she had left her body and was imagining herself somewhere very different. She would have to be. How could she stand to listen to him drone on and on? Occasionally he would ask her for a word in English, which she could usually provide, but other than that she said nothing.

Finally, Ainslie stood. "I have to go finish that project before dark. You stay, Franny, and help plant those seedlings you wanted to give Frau Mueller." He smirked at me. He was teasing me even as he was throwing me to the wolves.

"Please come to the garden, *ja*?" Ingrid was obviously desperate for company. She grabbed my arm and practically pulled me away.

"You want to see my papers?" Alexandre asked Ainslie.

"Next time, I'm afraid. Have to make tracks."

We needed some cucumber seedlings and mature sugarcane, and they were obviously growing in abundance in the Muellers' garden, but I would rather have gone without sugar forever than spend another minute with these bores. "How will I get home? You know I'm hopeless with directions."

"You'll make it. It's easy, you can't miss it. Be home before dark!" And Ainslie took off out the gate and down the path on his long legs before I could gather my belongings. I reluctantly let Ingrid take me to the garden, where I got my sugarcane and a long explanation of the life cycle of garden beetles, and how much we can learn from them about our own society. Then I received a lecture on the lettuce seeds that I had brought her. I also got to see Alexandre's papers, which were luckily in German, or I'm sure he would have had me read them in their entirety. They had created a little shrine to the departed Ritters, with the doctor's rusting typewriter and a moldy notebook that Dore had left behind when she returned to Germany.

I did have to admire the house though, and their luck in finding such a dwelling place already built. There were wood plank floors, with lumber obviously purchased off-island, and their veranda was large and completely covered by a tarp. They also had tarp walls, and on the windward side a wall made of corrugated metal of which I was very jealous. The long, straight poles that held up their house made it airy and spacious, with copious shelves for the many books and papers that Ritter and Dore had collected in their ten years on the islands. Now, though, they were mostly empty.

Still, their house made me feel uneasy; the deceased's belongings haunted the place. I didn't think it was the Muellers who created the brush marks in front of our house, but they were obviously a bit off their nuts. I find unpredictability in humans very off-putting, and so I breathed a sigh of relief as I finally extricated myself from their clutches.

I did find my way back because I spent the entire journey thinking about the Muellers, and whether they could possibly be German government employees. Therefore my feet had free rein to find their own way without interference from my intellect, and they did splendidly.

It was easy for me to imagine the Muellers getting sent away just so the continent of Europe would have some breathing room, but as far as strategies go, sending a myopic drip to look for ships or a place to moor a fleet could not have been the wisest course of action. The famed German efficiency wouldn't have tolerated such sluggishness. These were not government agents.

*

I was near home when my body went into high alert. What was wrong? I heard voices laughing. Voices. Plural. A strange sound for the islands. Ainslie was sitting at our table drinking lemonade with Genevieve and Victor.

"Hello, what's this?" I said.

Ainslie said, "I ran into them on the way home and they came by for a drink, such as it is."

"Oh," I said. I was tired, and not excited about having guests, especially these. I'd had enough trying Germans for a day, nay, a week. "Can you help me with this?" I held out the sugarcane.

"Of course." Ainslie stood to take the package from me. He set it next to the stove. "Have a seat. We were talking about . . . I'm not sure."

Genevieve came toward me and kissed my cheek. I must have smelled terrible. "You the eyes of the nice person, yes?" she said in Spanish.

I have always been a sucker for a compliment, and Genevieve delivered this one with such sincerity that I was forced to examine her for once in return. She must indeed have been striking when she was younger and less disheveled. She still held herself regally. She could see me soften. She gestured around our house. "I come to say hello to friend."

"How nice," I said in Spanish.

She sat ceremoniously on our bench, legs crossed at the knees. Her shorts were frayed at the ends, and she picked at a thread. I noticed her extreme thinness. Her collarbones were protruding and her rib cage was poking through the gap in her blouse. My pity won out over my wariness, and I invited them to stay for dinner.

It was a bit in retaliation for Ainslie leaving me at the Muellers', though it would mean more work for me, preparing dinner, than for him. I stoked the fire and cooked a double portion of the cow we'd butchered recently.

We sat down to eat, smiling, nodding, and pantomiming, but mostly eating. Our guests seemed untroubled that they had contributed nothing to the meal and were consuming the lion's share of it.

Genevieve was flirty with Ainslie, smiling with her oversize teeth showing. The grin crinkled the skin around her eyes, which made me suspect her more. I didn't like the way both Ainslie and Victor paid so much attention to her. I didn't like the way she demanded it, laughing too loudly, using her hands to gesture so that everyone became protective of their glass lest she knock it over.

Whenever I tried to contribute to the conversation, either by translating or adding my own thoughts, Genevieve laughed, too high, humoring me. She began to sing, and her voice was solid, if not beautiful. She sang something melancholy and when she stopped, both men applauded her roundly. She gestured with her hand to say, Your turn, but my voice is so bad that when I was teaching they asked me not to sing at my school's seasonal concert. I shook my head. I found myself exhausted by the effort to entertain as well as the activity of the day. Once you're out of the habit, interacting with others is a trial. All right, I'll say it: I was jealous. She was younger and charismatic in a way that I never was. A way that Rosalie was able to master effortlessly. An old insecurity rearing its ugly head again. It always made me feel my plainness and my age acutely. I stood up and began to scrub the dishes with sand and salt water. Genevieve did not help me, which annoyed me further. Where I came from, the women helped to serve and clear the meal.

The three of them shared a cigarette while I banged our tin plates together to signal my displeasure. But either no one heard me or no one cared. Finally Genevieve said she was ready to go home. We said our goodbyes. Genevieve tried to hug me, and I let her put her arms around me. Oddly, she smelled like flowers. I was so used to Ainslie's and my stink, it was a shock to smell something on a person other than body odor.

Ainslie walked them to the Camino de la Muerte so they could find their way back, and also to make sure that they were safely out of ear-shot when he returned.

"That's who has been lurking around, I'd bet my life on it," Ainslie said.

"Hopefully you don't have to," I said.

"Run into them my foot." Ainslie paced our small home. "I caught them poking around."

"In the house?" I looked around, to see if anything was out of place, not that there was anything I particularly cared about in it. My diary was harmless enough, and there were no letters to "Ainslie's sister," even in code.

Ainslie said, "Let's just keep our eyes open."

"And look for what?" I asked.

"You'll know it when you see it."

"Elmer Ainslie Conway, I have never in my life known it when I saw it."

*

For two weeks I saw no human being other than Ainslie. No ships came in, no neighbors visited. I liked it like this. Ainslie reported seeing Genevieve and Victor on his daily outings to improve his roads or to hunt or to visit the radio, but I was always at home. We played our cover so convincingly that there were occasions when I forgot it wasn't true. We were homesteaders, Swiss Family Robinsons, newlyweds. Ainslie was affectionate, even when it was clear that we weren't being watched. Though living on the island was difficult, physically, I felt freer there than I had ever in my life. I wanted to keep the real world on the other side of the ocean. I wanted to keep away a looming war, an inevitable return to civilization.

Ainslie's mood began to improve. I wasn't sure what the change was, but I could hear him whistling as he came down the path for dinner. Even in the morning he was less like a beast of the jungle and more his best self. I thought it was perhaps that he was finally getting to be the spy we came here for. When a man lacks a vocation (even if he's busy), he is less of a man. Ainslie's purpose gave him strength.

Three weeks to the day, which made me think they planned it on purpose, our neighbors came to visit again. They sat down to my famous "sandcakes" (a sort of flatbread/pancake) and strong coffee. At least this time they brought oranges, though our grove overproduced them anyway.

Genevieve was dressed in the same outfit as the last time I'd seen her (then again, so was I). There was a new hole in her shirt, under her arm. Victor's hair had grown longer and his beard had come in full, red on his chin, patchy toward his ears. He looked a bit like a wild dog.

Ainslie treated Genevieve as royalty. He greeted her by kissing her hand. He pulled out our bench so that she could sit down, and poured her more coffee each time she took a sip. He was convincingly enthralled—could he actually be fooled by her fake solicitousness? He leaned forward across the table and rested his chin on his hands, really listening. He laughed when she did, so loudly that I could see the gold of his fillings. I got angrier and angrier, gripping my fists tightly. I even thought of flirting with Victor, but I was so out of practice, I wouldn't even know what to do.

Once they left, I planned to tell Ainslie exactly what I thought of his attitude toward Genevieve. To see him desiring another woman made me furious. Why? I wondered as I scrubbed the plates. What did I care if he found someone attractive? Why wouldn't he? And though I thought Genevieve ugly, she *was* a decade or so younger than I.

"What is wrong with you?" I hissed.

"What do you mean?"

"You were practically fondling her."

"It's our job." Ainslie laughed, which made me angrier. "I only have eyes for you, Mrs. Conway," he said.

"I don't believe that," I said. "You don't have eyes for me."

The tenor of the conversation changed. "Franny, I don't really have eyes for anyone." He sat on the bench and rested his elbows on his knees, which made him look smaller.

There had been so many of these men in my life, men who wanted a sister rather than a lover, men who would rather live alone in their own thoughts. Was I one of them? One of those people who ultimately wanted to be alone? Maybe that was why I never married. What did that say about me?

"I'm not sure I even understand what that means," I said. I remained on the other side of our house. I didn't want to be near him so he could kiss me on the head or pat my knee.

"This has worked out better than I'd hoped," he said, waving his hand back and forth, indicating us. "Sure as hell beats Verdun as assignments go, but you have to remember why we entered into this."

I was stung, as though slapped. I'd begun to believe the lie of our marriage. But I looked at Ainslie now, and I was sure, as I stared at his brows, unknit and wrinkleless, that he had been pretending. Was any of his affection for me real? Or was it all another job, like clearing the spring of brush or radioing Guayaquil? My heart began to beat rapidly. Ainslie was so good at deceiving, I felt a chill.

He must have seen my dejection. He leaped to his feet and put his arms around me. "Oh Franny, I didn't mean it like that. I'm thrilled to be saddled with you, but we need to remember to put Pomegranate first."

"What will happen to us," I whispered, "when it's over?" It was so good to be held that I relaxed into his embrace.

"Oh I don't know," Ainslie said breezily. "A mission's over when it's over, and until then, can't we enjoy how well it's working out?"

I willed a tear not to fall.

"I mean," he continued, "it could have been awful, and it's rather nice."

"Do you think so?" I asked.

He pushed me back so that he could see my face. "Of course." He looked stricken. "Don't you?"

"Yes," I said. "It is rather nice, I suppose."

His face relaxed. "I'm sorry, I'm not used to working with women. I probably say all the wrong things. I'm very fond of you, you have to know that."

"I'm just . . . I have island fever, I think."

"Happens to the best of them," he said. "You're doing a great job. We'll keep an eye on them. I'll stick close to home."

It is an interesting quality in humans (or in my incarnation of humanity) that this promise gave me hope, or kept hope alive. He kissed the top of my head and hugged me, and I could hear his heart beating. I willed mine to beat in time and we stood that way a long while, letting our blood run through us together, interrupted intimacy.

*

A week or so later, I went down to the ocean to see if I could catch some fish. Usually hunting was Ainslie's job, but he refused to have anything to do with seafood, and I was growing tired of our all-meat diet. I thought perhaps I could find some lobsters, or mussels, or catch a fish with some bait and a line. How naïve I was. Lobsters hide, fish swim far from shore. While I waited for something to bite, sitting on some sharp rocks, the sun beat down on me. I realized I hadn't seen the ocean in a month. I sipped at my water canteen. I felt and wore all the years of my age, the twinges in my knees, the various age spots on my arms, the slight curve of my pre-arthritic fingers. I was struck by the folly of our mission, by my involvement in it, and I retraced the path of my life, wondering how it was that I started the daughter of immigrants in Minnesota and ended up a spy in the Galápagos Islands. At that moment, a curious bug came toward me, its body half stick and half leaf, and I began to think about all the paths Darwin described which brought animals here, and for the first time all day, I was comforted.

I relate these musings not because I imagine that a reader will find them interesting but to explain how an entire day can go by when your only conversation partner is yourself. And how you start to believe in that bifurcated voice as much as you believe in your own, because it *is* your own.

Eventually I gave up the line and waded into the water to get cool, and that's when I saw that the tide had gone out, trapping a couple of fish in the tide pool. I suppose they were young tuna. I don't know very much about fish, but even I could catch these. I grabbed one by the tail and swung it against the rock to put it out of its misery, and repeated the process with a second one.

At home, I started the fire. I had gotten good at this now. I knew what kind and shape of wood made the best kindling, and which was the best for smoking meat. I could tell by looking at its whirled knots, its tender edges, whether it was dry enough to burn or if it would just smoke and peter out like a storm gathering strength out on the water but then deciding not to bother with rain. I could see how heavy it would be, whether or not I could carry it or if it was worth chopping up with the small hand ax.

I had also learned by now how to start a fire without matches, to twist my wrist just so to make the stones spark, where to hold them in relation to the wind so that the smallest wisps would catch, and how to blow on these newborn flames so that their larger siblings would begin to burn.

Ainslie took a while coming back from the radio, but I thought nothing of it. We had dinner; he didn't even complain the way he usually did when I served anything except meat. I took his silence for exhaustion.

After dinner, I knew whether we would need to put the fire out or if it would burn down on its own, not threatening us while we slept. And I thought now of all the things I used to know like this back in my old life. I knew what time the cable car would come. I knew how far in advance to turn the water on so that it would run hot when I got into my bath. And before that, I knew how to stroke a chicken before I wrung its neck so that it would be calm in my arms. I knew how to make my ideas seem like they were Mrs. Keane's. And even before that, I knew how hot the iron was by the sizzle of my spit. I could braid Rosalie's hair into plaits so smooth they might have been corn silk. It seems that with enough practice, we can get to know just about anything.

Chapter Eleven

The next day Ainslie was several hours longer than he'd said he'd be. As dusk fell, I began to worry. My thoughts turned back to my previous jealousy. He was meeting with Genevieve, sleeping with her. A young man has needs, needs that I was certainly not meeting. But I wanted him to sleep with me if he slept with anyone, and certainly not the horse-toothed drama-lover Genevieve.

Maybe he was sleeping with Genevieve to find out her secrets, I reasoned. She did not hide the fact that the way into her confidences was through flattery. I wished he'd have told me, though. But perhaps he didn't want me to act differently around her.

Should I have known or guessed? Probably. But do not forget I was lying to myself about so many things. Lies were my entire life at that point. I had lied about my real name, my religion. I lied about being ready to travel halfway around the world to an island on the edge of nowhere. Ainslie and I lied to everyone we met, and when there was no one to meet, we lied to ourselves.

I knew our relationship was a sham. And I knew that we had only ever shared a bed as man and wife once. But I wanted so badly for that to be just an oddity of our marriage. I had fallen for Ainslie. Who didn't? His charm, his jolliness, which I rarely saw deflated, his humor, his capabilities. Even the way he spent what little leisure time he had improving a road that no one would ever use. I found that all adorable instead of exasperating.

Could he have been helping me instead of building his highway to nowhere? Yes. I was worked to the bone. I had grown so thin my short pants were held up by some rope that we needed for our home, but it was tie them up or walk around in my underthings. The mirror I had brought from the mainland had shattered, but in its fragments, strung up with fishing line in our garden to entertain birds (they were designed to discourage them but merely charmed them), showed partial views of a wan, pale woman with reddened, sunken cheeks. But I found his dedication to the craft as a sign that he was an enlightened being, like those monks who spend years crafting sand paintings only to sweep them away once they've finished. Now I see he was keeping himself busy, keeping the demons at bay. But demons are not dissuaded by oceans or preferences; they stow away like sea lice, unwanted visitors from another place, coming ashore with you wherever you go.

I said nothing to him about needing help. His affection for me felt so tenuous that I didn't want to do anything to jeopardize it. I knew enough of love to know it didn't work this way, but I still fantasized that if I could just catch him at the right moment Ainslie might want me as I wanted him. Did I want to be intimate? Well, yes and no. I wanted to sleep next to him, to breathe in his scent when I awoke. I wanted to be close to him. I felt unloved but only in the sense that Ainslie could not love me, not that I could not be loved, if that makes sense. So I took what love he offered and the two of us pretended that it was enough, that it was all right. We were playacting anyway: A schoolteacher pretending to be a government agent. A Jew pretending to be a Gentile. A man masquerading as a husband. The circles of deception were endless, the spiral of a master hypnotist.

The signs of an affair, which women's magazines love to list, are not applicable on a desert island. There are no collars, let alone lipstick stains. There are no receipts, no late nights at the office, no suspicious business travel. Still, something had changed. Ainslie was lighter, there's no other way to put it. He whistled all the time, signaling his approach like a cat with a bell. He joked more. He was even a bit more physically affectionate toward me. And a woman always knows. I knew. I thought I knew.

So is it coincidence that I neglected to put his sandwich in his bag one day? I think I legitimately forgot, but the subconscious has a funny way of making volition seem like coincidence.

So, armed with a Galápagos sandwich (sandcakes with dried meat), I climbed after Ainslie to his road. It was not a short walk, about an hour each way. But when I reached the end of the improved road, hot and tired, I was surprised to not see him there. Perhaps he had gone another way. Perhaps he had decided to go hunting. By this time I was hungry, and so I ate half the sandwich and drank half the water. On my way back down, I stopped to remove a stone from my shoe, and I saw, oddly, Ainslie's kerchief tied in a knot around an acacia tree. I stopped to untie it before I even thought about what it might be doing there. Silly Ainslie, leaving everything everywhere, as though there were maids to pick up after him.

But tied around a tree? And leaving his poor neck bare to be burned by the sun? It made no sense. The nearby brush had been disturbed by something, animal or human, the branches bent back and slanted, pointing. My feet began to follow the tamped-down undergrowth. I didn't stop to consider what might be waiting for me at the end. I snagged my shirt on a thorn and paused to extricate myself. I had the flash of an image—Ainslie and Genevieve, him kissing her horsey mouth and pawing at her enormous breasts. I gulped down air. I could turn around, I thought. I could just pretend I hadn't seen the handkerchief. But there is no unseeing something once you've seen it.

I was prepared for the tangle of naked limbs, the sweat-soaked sounds of heaving breath, but I was not prepared to see that the second body belonged to Victor. What was most shocking was that they were kissing, passionately.

Of course, I had lived for many years in San Francisco, and I understood the rudiments of homosexual relations. But I never considered that they would do it face-to-face, like they loved each other, and it might have been this realization that hurt most.

They sprang apart at my shocked cry, and I was catapulted back to that moment in Chicago when I saw Rosalie and Zeke together. That discovery changed my life. It was hard to imagine this one wouldn't as well.

I ran madly back to the house, arriving with torn clothes and a skinned knee. I was too upset to cry. I began to breathe heavily. There wasn't enough oxygen in my lungs; my vision was a camera lens that was narrowing rapidly. My heart beat wildly, and I could feel the blood rise to my ears, throbbing. I gasped for air, leaning over. I was sure I was going to die. Can you die from shock? A surge of panic, and the pinhole through which I was seeing the world narrowed to black.

"Shh, shh." I heard Ainslie's voice. He took my wrist, not hard, but firmly. "Shh, calm down. Breathe. Just concentrate on breathing. Here, with me. One, in. Two, out. One, in. Two, out." He urged my head between my knees, like he did the last time this happened, in Carmel.

The air began to return to my lungs, and my brain lost its balloon feeling. I sobbed, covering my face with my hands. I didn't want Ainslie's comfort, but there was no one else. He held me to his chest, where I breathed in the familiar scent of his sweat. Then I remembered what had provoked this panic attack, and I pushed him away.

"I don't know what you think you saw," Ainslie said, "but it's not—"

I held up my hand. I didn't want to speak right now. I didn't want to listen. I just wanted to be away, anywhere but here. But an island is ironically a terrible place to be alone. You are too alone, always, and therefore it offers no respite, no cover. I parted the mosquito netting and lay down on my bed, the first time I'd lain down during daylight since we arrived.

When I awoke, I saw Ainslie struggling with the fire. He was blowing too hard, and the flames were suffocating from too much air. Without speaking, I walked over and pulled him back, blowing softly. The fire recovered. "Thanks," Ainslie said. "I'm not too good at women's work." He was trying to jolly me out of my mood, but this time his jocularity wouldn't suffice. I was numb. Were I to hammer my finger I wouldn't even feel it.

I ate Ainslie's terrible cooking staring off into the middle distance. I know he was worried I was punishing him, and undoubtedly that was a part of the silent treatment, but mostly I felt empty of words, like I was an iguana with a reptilian brain, who could only perform basic bodily functions. Afterward, I left Ainslie to wash up and I lay back down in bed. Mercifully, it got dark quickly. As I was falling asleep, I wondered if I were sick. I had the same separated-from-my-body feeling I had when I ran a fever.

In the middle of the night I awoke and went outside to relieve myself. When I got back to my bed, I could hear from his breathing that Ainslie was not asleep. It was only then that I allowed myself to examine my emotions.

I was hurt. Jealous. Scared. I had cast my lot with Ainslie, and now I realized how little I knew him. I reviewed the history of our relationship. And in the new light of realizing why it was that he didn't want to share a bed with me, I examined every time he came home late, every evening in the company of his navy buddies, every interaction he had with someone of his own sex. And I knew then that everything I had thought had been a lie. I was a useless spy, keeping information even from myself.

I could hear Ainslie breathing. Far away, and yet so close. "Ainslie?" I said. "Was it like this always?"

"Always," I heard him whisper.

I said nothing more.

*

The light came up slowly that morning. Because of the dense vegetation, day usually sprung up on us as soon as the sun crested the trees, but it was overcast and so it was impossible to distinguish dawn from day. Ainslie and I ate breakfast in silence. We spoke only the necessary words to get on with our day. Ainslie told me his plans while I warmed coffee, and then he was gone, so obviously relieved to be away from me that I wanted to throw something at his retreating back. This was not my fault. I was not the one lying to him.

My anger grew along with the heat. By lunchtime I had broken the handle of our only pan. This was actually close to tragedy, as without it, we would have no means of cooking our food, and of course we had no way of fixing it. By midmorning, the anger had blossomed into rage. I cursed the sun, the chickens, the damn mongoose that wouldn't leave us alone, because who brought a mongoose to an island? It's an invasive species, for God's sake. People were always doing that, compounding their problems like a cumulative children's song: the mongoose to eat the rats, the cats to eat the mongoose, the people to kill the cats, the people to spy on the other people . . .

How dare Ainslie start a relationship with the enemy? I turned my personal hurt into righteous indignation. That was the first lesson in Spy 101: no relationships (except the ones they forced you into). Relationships left you vulnerable emotionally, as well as made you a target for blackmail. It gave away for free the leverage Ainslie was always warning against. I had distanced myself from Rosalie for this very reason, and now he had violated one of the basic tenets of our mission and put us in danger as a result.

Ainslie came back for lunch, signaling his approach by his whistle, which completely unhinged me from my supposed sanity.

"How can you whistle?" I screamed in greeting. "How can you just whistle?"

"It's my habit," he said quietly. "It relaxes me."

"Relaxes you." I snapped the cloth I was using to wipe dishes. "You seem to be finding a lot of methods of relaxation."

"If you're ready to talk," he said, "we can talk." He took out his pipe and began to chew on it.

"How long has this been going on?" I asked.

"Oh I've smoked all my life." I glared at him. I was not amused. "A week or two." Ainslie sat in his chair. He traced patterns on the dirt floor with his feet. "I didn't mean for it to, Franny, it just did, somehow."

"And there have been others?"

"Not on Floreana." He grimaced. "Ever since I can remember, it's been . . . I tried the military, but there were as many people like me in there as there were out. Then I tried intelligence, but that just taught me how to lie even better. I've never been caught. Until now."

I opened my mouth to speak, but no sound came out. My anger was gone, replaced with a sadness so heavy I might have ingested glue. I sat down next to him on the bench.

"But Franny, and I mean this." He took my hand. His was cool though it was hot out. So much larger than mine, he encompassed it wholly.

"I've never felt . . . It's never been this way with anybody like it is with you."

I harrumphed. I didn't believe him. How could I ever believe him now?

"I'm serious, Franny. I love you. Not the way a husband should love his wife, but the way that I can love you. There's no one else I could live with like this. Like this." He spread his free hand out to indicate the house. "We've gone to the ends of the earth together. You're not just anyone to me."

The words were good to hear, and I was mortified to find myself crying. Ainslie took me into his arms and I wept against his bony shoulder for a while until I calmed down. I blew my nose into the towel I was still holding.

"I feel the same," I said. "I've never been as close to anyone as I feel to you. I suppose I knew, have known all along. I was just wishing it would be different."

"Well, it *is* different," Ainslie said. I smiled.

I would have thought I'd be disgusted by Ainslie, by his perverse preference. That I wouldn't want to touch him. But it didn't feel like that. It felt calming, like it explained the answers to questions I hadn't been able to ask myself. I also wanted to talk more, to know more. But I wasn't sure how to ask. I wasn't sure what answers I was looking for.

"Nothing has changed. Between us." When he said this, something snapped inside me, a ruler rapping on my desk calling for my attention when I'd been sleeping.

"This is dangerous, Ainslie. Victor is the enemy."

"Exactly. How else does one extract secrets? Pillow talk. So to speak."

"What if he's doing the same to you?" My hand had begun to feel heavy in Ainslie's. I twisted it so he'd drop it.

"He's not. I'm better than he is."

"How do I know you're not working with them?" I asked, cruelly.

Ainslie looked appropriately wounded. I felt a small burst of satisfaction. "I'm not even going to give that question the respect of an answer," he said. "How could you ask me that?"

"There's apparently a lot I don't know about you," I said.

Ainslie sighed heavily. "He's not a problem. He's a fairly simple-minded man. If anyone is a spy, it's Genevieve."

"This is dangerous," I repeated. "What if someone found out? You'd be kicked out of the navy."

"No one will find out."

"We're exposed."

"It won't be a problem," Ainslie repeated.

*

It was only a day or two later that Gonzalo came running to our house. Breathless, he repeated the English I'd taught him: "There is a ship in the harbor." Then he repeated "ship, ship," which sound like "sheep" so that I thought he was telling us that he had found a wild flock somewhere that we could butcher for food. My first thoughts in the Galápagos were always of food.

When I finally understood he meant a boat, which most likely also meant food, I quickly put on my best and only skirt on top of my shorts. On the way down, I heard the foghorn announcing its arrival, and by the time I got down to the beach, the launch from the ship had made it to shore and all the Floreanans except the Muellers and the Weisses were crowded around its occupants.

This was the first time I had seen Victor or Genevieve since I discovered Ainslie, and a lump grew in my throat. I had an unbidden flash of memory of Victor and Ainslie together, which I tried to snuff out. I think I even shook my head to clear it. Victor could not meet my gaze. He looked smaller than the last time I saw him, and he cowered by Genevieve, picking at the ground with a walking stick. It was just as well; I had nothing to say to him.

The crowd of excited onlookers parted to reveal a man about my age, with a white mustache. I recognized him not only from the newspapers but also from his photo in the navy's files on the Galápagos.

"Mrs. Conway," I heard a voice. "I'm Allan Hancock."

He stepped forward to shake my hand, and I automatically smoothed my hair behind my ears. There are some customs you can never unlearn.

"So very pleased to meet you," he said. "I've heard so much about 'the

Americans of Floreana.' I hope you and your husband will be my guests later. I have some specimens I'd like you to see."

I have sometimes been accused of being none too swift, but I caught his drift right away. He had obviously been sent to meet with us. It was a peculiarity of our post on the Galápagos that the usual methods of contacting operatives were unavailable. There could be no prearranged meeting points, no exchanging of briefcases in crowded squares, no drops in empty phone booths. I was excited to hear what Hancock had to tell us.

Hancock had brought with him in the dinghy two other men. They were handing out packs of cigarettes and cartons of sugar to Gonzalo and Victor, who were eagerly holding out their hands.

"Don't forget the Conways," Hancock called. "Where is Mr. Conway?" he asked me.

"He's *arriba*," I said, automatically, forgetting that Hancock did not speak our patois. "I mean, he's clearing a path up above. He'll have heard the horn, don't worry."

Hancock smiled. "How are you holding up out here?" There was a note of pity in his voice for our ridiculous posting. I wanted to defend our island. In the short months we had been there, I realized, it had become our island.

"Actually," I said, "it's rather . . . lovely."

Hancock lifted an eyebrow in surprise.

We all sat down on the beach to a meal provided by Hancock's chef, which included luxuries I hadn't tasted in weeks: butter, peanut butter, jam, milk, fresh bread made with white flour. The purpose and nationality of the visitor didn't matter. When a boat showed up, we all got to partake of its bounty. Ainslie arrived just as we were about to dig in to dessert. He merely nodded his head at the other guests, giving no special attention to Victor, who sat apart from the group. If I hadn't known of their relationship, I would not have suspected anything. Ainslie was good.

He said to Hancock, "Hope I didn't miss anything. Hello, old chap!"

"You know each other?" I asked.

"We've never actually met." Ainslie pumped Hancock's hand. "I'm just happy to see a fellow American, who comes bringing, what's this? Jelly? Oh praises be!"

Ainslie forwent the lunch to skip straight to the dessert—peaches in syrup and crackers with jelly. "It's just that it tastes so good," he said by way of excusing himself. "You don't know how much you'll miss something as stupid as jelly until it's gone. And then, it's delicious, even though it's Ecuadorian jelly."

"We ran out of American preserves on the way down," Hancock said. "If I had known this was a favorite, I would have purchased more."

I had eaten so much my stomach hurt, though I was not letting that stop me from shoving large pieces of bread and honey into my mouth.

"No need," I said. "It's not roughing it if you're not roughing it."

"That reminds me, I have your mail," Hancock said. "Joey, can you get it?" One of the sailors stood and went to the waxed dock bag.

Ainslie helped himself to another scoop of jam and another cracker. "Might as well," he said. "Once they're opened they won't keep." And we all laughed, for it's funny to see such a skinny man eat so prodigiously.

Gonzalo asked about the tensions between Ecuador and Peru, and I translated. I had completely forgotten their border skirmish; we were living in a country and yet knew nothing of what was happening within it. I could tell you who was arguing with whom over fishing territories on San Cristóbal, for that news reached us with every crew on every schooner, but as to what was happening in Quito, I knew nothing.

Now Hancock looked around the beach. "Say, is that Camino de la Muerte? Wow! Did Roosevelt start New Dealing on Floreana too?"

"I'm improving local roads," Ainslie said with pride. He would object to the denigration of Roosevelt, who was, after all, Ainslie's commander in chief.

Hancock failed to notice Ainslie's tone. "That's a damn fool thing to spend your time on!"

"I beg your pardon," Ainslie began. My heart sank. Of all the things to say to Ainslie, insulting his road might have been the cruelest. "Not all of us get to sail around on yachts. Some of us work to build what we need."

"Okay, boys," I said, before they turned to pistols at dawn. "Let's finish up the crackers before the rats get at them."

"*Ratones,*" Gonzalo said loudly, as though cursing, which made everyone laugh, including him.

As we ate the last of the lunch, Hancock asked, "Will you come with me, Mr. and Mrs. Conway, for a tour?" Though he and Ainslie glared at each other with undisguised loathing, we got into the launch and were rowed out to the yacht.

"So," I said, but Hancock shook his head, indicating that we shouldn't speak.

I was so rarely out on the water, which must sound strange for someone who lives on a tiny island. But we really rarely had reason to go, and frankly the water scared me. First of all, there were sharks. And though I couldn't see far into the brush, at least I could see my feet. Swimming, who knew what was under there? And the thought of something going on without my knowledge terrified me. I held on to the gunwales with both hands.

"You can relax, Frances. May I call you Frances?" Hancock asked. I nodded, afraid to speak.

"We won't tip. Can't you swim?" he asked. I nodded again.

"I'm afraid Franny's not much of a sailor, are you?" Ainslie said. I smiled, gratefully. "Tell us about your research." Ainslie extended the olive branch. And Hancock, being baited with this juicy morsel, proceeded to tell us in great detail about his research until we reached the boat.

The *Velero III* was a fine yacht, white and teak, with just a bit of weathering to prove she was a real boat. There were three cabins and a bunk room, as well as several specimen rooms that Hancock showed us. There was one devoted to reptiles, with many of our saurian friends suspended in preserving liquid to be taken far from their natal land. They were in various states of undress: some lacked skin and some were reduced to skeletons. Hancock said, "I'm sorry, this must be very repulsive to you, Frances." He didn't look very sorry.

Now he had offended me. I tried to make a joke. "Who do you think does our butchering? You don't live on an island unless you're comfortable with death, or grow comfortable with it. Nature is the cruelest mistress."

Hancock replied, "True. But humans don't do nature any favors." Beneath his antagonism, he was a scientist through and through, you could tell by the excitement with which he showed us his work. He was obviously uncomfortable with the position he had been put in. How had he been recruited? Enticed by the carrot or threatened with the stick?

He continued to give us the tour. Perhaps I had misread the situation, and he really was simply showing off his yacht. We repaired to his study for coffee, brought to us by a member of his staff. Though the cabin was hot, and the trade winds were blowing nicely across through the open portholes, he closed the windows one by one.

"I was told to give you this," Hancock said, handing Ainslie an envelope. "I don't like it. I'm not in the army—"

"Neither am I," said Ainslie.

"I mean I'm not in the armed forces. I'm a scientist. I'm told where to go by the science, not by some bureaucrat. I'm not used to following orders like a lemming."

"Interesting," Ainslie said. "I follow orders so that scientists can be free to pursue their investigations, not because I enjoy spending my time on a deserted island full of Krauts."

I was stung by his comment, though I knew he was just trying to get back at Hancock, who, it was true, was not my favorite person at the moment.

Ainslie took the proffered envelope, broke its classified seal, and read its contents in silence. I looked at Hancock. "What's the mood at home?" I asked.

"I don't know anything in particular," he said.

"I mean," I clarified, "just your personal opinion."

"No one wants a war." Hancock sank into his leather chair. I could see now that he was stressed at having to deliver this letter. Having foisted it off on its recipient, he looked relieved, like he'd been carrying explosives in the hold. "Especially so soon after the Great War. So I don't think we'll enter, even though Roosevelt . . . But people are concerned. There are rumors . . ." He trailed off.

"Rumors about . . ." I prompted him.

"That the Nazis are running work camps for Jews and Gypsies and . . . others."

"That's terrible," I said.

"Yes, and the Polish threat. I wouldn't be surprised if there was an invasion."

"But surely the United States won't try to protect Poland." I felt bad for the people who were being sent to work camps just because they were Jewish. There but for the grace of God . . .

"No." Hancock rubbed his forehead. My own was slick with sweat. Couldn't we open the windows now that our topic was not confidential? "It's just that nobody believes that Hitler will stop there. He's completely insane."

"But some people like him."

"People like Stalin," Hancock said.

Ainslie abruptly folded the letter and stood up. "A match, please?"

"Are you kidding me?" Hancock said. "On a ship?"

Ainslie gave him a look that chilled my skin, even in the damp heat. "You smoke, don't you?"

Hancock handed him a fussy-looking antique lighter, in distressed and carved silver. Ainslie set fire to the letter, holding it by its corner until it burned into ash. Then he dropped it on the table, and Hancock quickly smothered it, cursing.

"Thank you," Ainslie said. "The United States Navy appreciates your service."

"Frances," Hancock said. "Your husband and I have a few things to discuss. It was lovely to meet you. I'll have you rowed back to shore with some extra provisions. I hope we meet again."

I said nothing. I was being exiled. Ainslie did nothing to stop this indignity, looking down at his shabby shoes. Whatever came next was above my clearance level. I was so angry I wanted to stamp my foot, steal the lighter, and burn down Hancock's damn pleasure yacht.

What choice did I have? I was rowed back to shore in silence, a cloth full of canned goods, tied into a knot like a hobo's bundle, on my lap. I didn't care what Ainslie thought of Hancock, I was accepting his canned goods. Some green beans and sugared peaches would do us good.

*

Whatever had transpired between the men on the ship, it was clear Ainslie didn't want to talk about it. He looked pale, didn't whistle. He ate little (well, for Ainslie he ate little). And he spent the better part of one afternoon claiming to help me weed the garden and instead looking off at the sea while chewing his pipe. I decided to ask him what was in the letter Hancock gave him. I tried to phrase it casually, like it had just occurred to me, and so I mentioned it as I was putting our dinner on the table: canned beans and pork. "Oh, is there anything I need to know about that letter from Hancock?"

Ainslie put down his pipe. He looked at me funny, as though he didn't know what I was talking about. "Oh that, no."

"No?" I asked.

He shook his head.

"Look," I sat down. "We are in this together. I know my clearance is not as high as yours, but the circumstances are such that I need to know what you do, so I can help, or at least not hinder, and most of all so I don't get into danger."

Ainslie appeared to consider this statement.

"You've done things," I continued, "that put us at risk. Us. So I want to know what's going on." Ainslie knew what I was referring to. He blushed and looked away, helping himself to more beans. He put a large spoonful in his mouth and added some pork. His manners had really gotten atrocious. I'd have to remind him before he ate like that in company. Ainslie did everything full throttle. He ate greedily, drank too much, was constantly busy, indulged in sweets whenever possible and, now I knew, also in strange love. He could never control his appetites.

He swallowed. "I know," he said.

I scraped the bottom of the pot to scoop the last bit of beans onto

Ainslie's plate. "What did Hancock do, do you think, that he was conscripted for this? They must have something on him, right?"

Ainslie finished his plate and put down his fork. "You know how you never ask a lady her age? You never ask for a spy's motivation. Never."

I bristled. I didn't like Ainslie's tone.

In the past, I'd wished for home's conveniences to be here on the island, but now I wished I were back in San Francisco, or back in Nebraska or even Duluth. And though I am not one for looking back, I permitted myself a brief wonder at what my life would have been like without Ainslie. I would have stayed in San Francisco, continued in my secretarial job, seeing movies on Sunday afternoons, spending time with Rosalie's family. Both scenarios, the imagined and the real, were so terribly sad that uncharacteristically my eyes welled up. I looked away.

"I'm tired," I said. "I think I'll go to bed."

"Sleep tight," Ainslie called. Why did I continue to expect him to read between the lines, even though he'd not once shown himself interested or capable of doing so? I turned away from the table.

*

I never saw Genevieve or Victor again. I gradually became aware that they were no longer on the island with us. Presence is noticed suddenly—a misplaced rock cairn, a stolen piece of jerky. But absence is stealthy; one day you realize that it's been a while since there has been any disturbance and then you look more closely and notice nothing.

I never found out what happened to them. When I asked Ainslie, his face darkened and he shook his head. To the others, he said that Victor had come to tell Ainslie that they were sick of the island and that they were catching a ride to Chatham on a fishing boat.

"What day?" Gonzalo asked. "Did I see a fishing boat?"

I translated from the Spanish. "I don't know." Ainslie shrugged. "I was *arriba*. He found me there, so I didn't look." He was a fantastic dissimulator. Liar, I supposed, was the better word.

Perhaps they were picked up by a passing ship I didn't see. Perhaps Ainslie arranged for their transportation off the island. Could Ainslie have . . . ? I couldn't ask him. I couldn't ask him because I didn't have clearance to know the answer, because I didn't want to know the answer. The similarity between his story and that of the disappearance of the baroness did not escape my notice.

Our relations became cold. Often many hours would go by without us conversing at all. It's so easy not to speak, so hard to really talk. Ainslie chewed his pipe. I wrote in my journal. How I wanted to write what was on my mind, but it was too dangerous. All codes are breakable. And I was trying to hide most of all from my husband, and the depth of his training and commitment to military intelligence was perhaps more profound than I had thought.

Throughout this time, our mission had been a bit murky to me. I accepted my confusion because things were moving so quickly, I didn't have the security clearance, I was preoccupied with surviving. But now I had nothing but time to examine the predicament I had placed myself in.

I began to avoid Ainslie. I even went to visit the Muellers once or twice, submitting to Herr Mueller's endless lectures on German philosophy and cringing while Frau Mueller waited on him hand and foot.

Finally, Ainslie broke the silence. "Look, I know you're upset with me, but . . ." He trailed off. "I'm sorry, really. I wish so much it could be otherwise. I meant what I said. I wish I could feel about you that way, but I'm just not made like that. I know you don't believe me, but I do love you."

It felt good to hear. "I guess it's just that no one ever has." It was not easy to say, this secret I'd held so long. Shameful, because I was sure it was my looks, and possibly my personality, that kept men away.

I sighed. He stepped forward, warily, and I accepted his embrace. It was so nice just to lean. He kissed my hair and rocked me back and forth.

"Oh, Franny," he said. "We don't get what we deserve."

CHAPTER TWELVE

It didn't seem possible, but there she was, the *San Cristóbal*! I found it miraculous that she could survive another trip (though she was to survive many more, chugging along like the proverbial little engine that could). Capitán Oswaldo put in at Post Office Bay, and we rushed down to say hello and retrieve our mail and news.

The first panga was coming toward us, and it contained, along with Oswaldo and the mate who rowed, two Caucasians, a man and a woman. The woman stepped out of the boat wearing a full skirt, which I thought very impractical. Like Genevieve, she was in her early forties, sturdy. Her hair had a defiant shock of white at the crown. Her husband was dressed more for a garden party than a remote island—linen pants (how had he kept them creased?) and a collared shirt. After El Capitán kissed us like we were old friends (though last time we parted I heard him mutter *"me tocan los cojones"*—a benign translation of which would be "pain in the butt" but more colorful), he introduced us to the new couple. Unsurprisingly, they were German: Elke and Heinrich. They were coming to stay; we were getting new neighbors.

Was it coincidence that just two months after Genevieve and Victor left, a new German couple came? I knew she was most likely the enemy; still, something about her was . . . friendly. She smiled with her entire face, eyebrows up and lips wide. I realized how starved I'd been for friendship, and there is nothing quite like female companionship. We could not have been more different—I lanky and slight, she squat; I

American and Jewish, she German—but still I recognized something of a kindred spirit in her.

The men were likewise hitting it off splendidly. Heinrich had gratefully accepted Ainslie's offer of tobacco and both were now smoking, stretched out in the shade like cats. Neither had a scrap of the other's language, but they managed to communicate through gestures, diagrams in the sand, and a few cognates, that they had both fought in France in the Great War (though on opposite sides, of course) but shared a hatred of the French that transcended that now-defunct animosity (though I didn't understand at the time how much hostilities were ramping up between our two nations as we spoke). Ainslie towered over him, as if they were different species, and Heinrich's full head of hair put Ainslie's straw fluff to shame. They took turns imitating French soldiers, much to the other's delight. I looked over and sighed. Boys will still be boys, even when they are men and most likely employed at cross-purposes. Elke saw my expression and laughed, which reminded me pleasantly of the sound of rice being poured into a bowl.

Elke's English was decent; she had been educated in her home country. She also spoke competent Spanish, as they had been living on San Cristóbal for about six months. They found it too commercial, she said. There were always boats in port, fishermen haggling, tourists. They wanted a quieter island, otherwise why bother coming halfway around the world? She had two children, she said, but their father (who was apparently not Heinrich) insisted they attend boarding school in Switzerland, so they moved from Europe in part to ease the pain of missing them. I told her that we had been living in California and wanted to try our hand at self-sufficiency.

At this she brightened. "California? Do you know Marlene Dietrich?"

I laughed. "That's Hollywood, Los Angeles," I said. "We lived in San Francisco. But I did have a friend who once was in a film where she served Greta Garbo coffee."

This did not impress Elke. She uttered a sort of "harrumph" noise that I would come to learn indicated dissatisfaction. She folded her small hands together at her belly like a schoolmarm.

The panga kept making trips to and from the boat. How much had they brought? There were boxes and boxes and crates and crates. I was impressed they'd convinced El Capitán to transport all that. He was very strict about the number and weight of boxes we'd brought aboard. I was surprised to discover that they brought a dog, a mix of German shepherd and what looked like wolf, who was very serious. She sniffed my crotch carefully, sized me up, and went to sit near Ainslie. They also had a nanny goat with them for milk. I thought greedily of all the delicious food I could make with access to dairy, even goat dairy. (Though there were goats and cows on the island, they were impossible to domesticate.)

I studied Ainslie, nervous of a repeat of his previous relationship, but I found no sign of attraction on either end. I believed him when he said he regretted the relationship with Victor. We had a lovely picnic with Elke and Heinrich, El Capitán, and a Canadian named Joe we'd met previously who was hitching a ride to Santa Cruz.

Ainslie helped Heinrich move the boxes up the beach, and we showed them to the remains of our beach camp. By now the Jiménezes had arrived at the beach in their official capacity as regional representatives to greet the newcomers and promise Chuclu for their labors. I even offered to play hooky from my duties the following day and show them where Genevieve and Victor had lived, so they wouldn't have to start from scratch in homemaking, regretting it even as I said it. I had things to do and this would take all day. Thankfully, they declined.

Walking back home with Ainslie, he teased me about volunteering my time. "Will you make their beds every day, Franny? Do their taxes?" He had improved the road such that we could walk abreast. It might have been a "damn fool" thing to waste his time on, but the new road was nicer than the game trail that used to be our Main Street.

"Very funny," I said. "As it happens, I like her."

"Yes," Ainslie said, "were they not our enemies, they would most likely be our friends."

"Isn't *enemy* a strong word?" I tripped on a root and Ainslie caught my arm automatically.

"Hitler is dangerous. More dangerous even than Franco or Mussolini.

And if the Three Stooges form an alliance, or join with the Japanese, it's not good news."

"But are they necessarily representatives of their government? I hardly want to be blamed for Warren Harding."

"I'm just saying be friendly but not too friendly."

"And you and Victor weren't too friendly?" I meant this lightheartedly, as least I thought I did. I thought we were teasing each other, but Ainslie took offense. Instead of saying anything, he strode on ahead of me, leaving me to negotiate my own way in the growing dark.

*

I let a couple of weeks go by, and then I paid a visit to Elke. The dog heard me approach and came to greet me, sniffing at my hands and rooting around my pockets looking for treats. Elke greeted me with a warm pumping handshake and invited me in. She had settled in much more quickly than Ainslie and I had, but to what end? Did she need drapes, and did they need to match the tablecloth? Did she need a tablecloth?

The ostensible reason for my visit was to borrow her scissors for a haircut. I actually did need one. My bangs were low over my eyes and were driving me crazy. *"Reinkommen,"* she said, swinging the makeshift door wide. She looked genuinely pleased to see me.

I pantomimed scissors with my fingers while I asked to borrow them. This became our habit, an invented simultaneous sign-language translation of our speech.

Elke plucked a slightly rusty pair of scissors off a nail hook. "Here," she said in English. "I do it."

I sat down in the chair and she brought over some water. She wet my hair carefully. Inside her house it was somehow quieter than it was outside, or in mine; the birds chirped mutedly and the rustle of the breeze stilled.

Her hands were not gentle but rather matter-of-fact. She combed through my mess, holding the hair at the root to prevent it from pulling as she eased out the tangles. I could smell her—we all smelled on Floreana, but Elke had a tinge of sweetness about her, as though she had daubed her skin in maple syrup. I closed my eyes and relaxed into her ministrations.

When she had wet the hair, she took a line of it between her fingers and cut straight with the other hand. I could see my reflection in the small mirror above the basin used as a sink. I looked old, freckled.

I had thought I wouldn't miss female friendship; the girls I lived with at the boardinghouse had mostly annoyed me. Rosalie is really the only woman I've ever been close to. I've never had time for fussing with my hair or trying on different frocks. But I did miss it. Elke's hand reminded me of Rosalie smoothing my hair behind my ear and I felt a cloud of homesickness.

When Elke was done my hair looked serviceable at best, but what did I care? We sat and ground wheat for a while, gossiping in two languages about how silly our husbands were. Elke did an uncanny Heinrich imitation—his pipe-chewing, small-man swagger. And she laughed kindly as I dramatized Ainslie's obsessive straightening of anything not perfectly lined up.

"What made you want to come to the Galápagos?" I asked. She had told me the basics of her story at the beach, but I was wondering if there was a more complicated narrative. I reminded myself to watch her face as she answered to see if she was lying.

"Heinrich is a journalist," she said. "The magazine pay that we come here and write about living without . . . *Zivilisation.*"

"Civilization." I supplied the word.

Elke went back to her mending while she talked. "Also," she said, "Heinrich *y yo tenemos problemas.* My husband very *enfadado* that I am with Heinrich. He send the *Kinder* to boarding school, make problems for me." She wiped away a furtive tear that I pretended not to see. So she and Heinrich weren't married. I tried to muster disapproval for this "sin" but it was weak, vestigial, like the wings on a flightless cormorant. The islands were changing me; I no longer cared what others did. Society's rules no longer applied; there was no society.

I knew she had answered me with emotional honestly, even if she was not exactly factually forthcoming.

"You?" Elke asked.

"Me?"

"Why do you come to Galápagos, Franzi?" Her nickname for me stuck.

I gave her our cover story, that we were here to help cure Ainslie's tuberculosis while getting away from civilization and trying our hand at survivalism. The story, as it came out of my mouth, sounded implausible. Elke said nothing, but I continued, unprompted. "Also, this is the only place Ainslie will stop drinking. And stop . . . wandering."

I was being honest as well, though of course the island hadn't stopped his wandering. She betrayed no reaction, and for her lack of judgment I would forever respect her and be grateful.

*

Elke came to my house the following week in search of a rolling pin. I happened to have seen one in her house the previous week, so I knew right away that she had arrived to chat with me or to suss me out. I made coffee and we talked for a while.

She said, "I see *camotes* not happy, *ja?*"

The plants were wilting, it was true, though I watered and weeded them religiously.

"You mind I help?" She stood up and walked out to the garden. "Here," she switched to Spanish, *"hay que ponerlos en una montaña, así,"* she pulled one out halfway, building up the soil around it like a volcano. "They like it much more better if they are *arriba.*"

"Thanks," I said. "I've been having trouble with them since we arrived. In fact, I'd never eaten one until this year, and now I don't care if I never eat another again!"

Elke laughed. "I help, Franzi." And so together we created little hills for my *camotes*.

I said, "Your English is excellent. How did you learn it?"

"We study in the school," she said. "But it is no good."

"It's better than my German." I laughed. "I can only say '*Ich habe hunger.*'"

"It is a phrase we say much on Floreana, no?" We had reached the end of the row. We started on the next row and worked our way back to the house. "Yes. In Germany I go to one special school where the children are learning English. Not French. And now I learn Spanish."

I smiled. "I'm studying Spanish here, but it's not going very well."

"Es difícil," Elke said.

"All languages are difficult," I said. "Even English I struggle with."

"But is hardest to say what is in the heart," Elke said. She sounded like she was quoting something.

Her eyes were squinted from the sun, and I saw she had a small scar near her temple. How could she be a spy? How could I? We had more in common than we even knew, and I decided that if she was keeping tabs on us, she was doing it in the same way I was, which was to say, ineptly and incidentally. I decided she was my friend.

*

Elke and I began to spend more time together. My days had been lonely, I realized, without Ainslie or anyone, really, except for a cat to talk to. We didn't see each other every day; it was, after all, a two-hour walk for a visit, but we saw each other often enough. Elke and I tried to speak in Spanish, to practice, but when neither person speaks a language as a native, it is difficult to know if one is getting better or not. So we spoke a lot of English.

What did we do together? We combined some of our household chores, and it made it easier on both of us. I'd mill the flour while she sorted the beans. And that way less was wasted and the entire activity went faster, both for the efficiency and the company. Elke knew to prune the melons before they overgrew and lost their taste or exploded. I knew you could remove weevils from grain by spreading it out in the sun. My house was better for drying plants: husks and grain and corn and fruit. And hers was better equipped for cooking, baking, rolling out dough, pounding meat, chopping. Either home was fine for mending clothes (clothes on Floreana needed constant mending) while we chatted. So it came to pass that I heard about her life in Germany before she was with Heinrich.

Her family suffered much after the Great War, and she came of age right when morale and money were at their lowest. She had wanted to go to university, but her parents insisted that she go to work instead.

"Me too!" I grabbed her arm in excitement. "What did you do?"

"I marry," she said. "But the school is impossible. I want, how you say? *Ingenieurin?*"

I could only imagine how difficult it would be to become an engineer as a woman in postwar Germany. It was hard enough for me to study literature in America, and my heart went out to her. For as different as we were, we had lived mirrored lives. She chose one path and ended up here, and I chose another and ended up here as well. It made me consider the existence of fate.

For my part, I told her about my family in Duluth (leaving out the Jewish part). Maybe this was why I was so comfortable around Elke. She had the same habits that Rosalie's mother had. She and Heinrich shared a bed, but they each had separate coverlets. Both Elke's and Rosalie's mothers crimped the edges of their loaves with the same pinching motion. Elke even occasionally braided her hair like Rosalie's mother had, in a wall of hair high up over her forehead.

Around this time I began to dream of Rosalie. She came to me in my sleep and asked about things on Floreana. In one dream, she arrived on the *Velero III* with Hancock, sitting in his stuffy bunk and looking for a piece of ice for her whiskey. I had to tell her that I hadn't seen ice in months. In another, she was helping me hunt crabs on the beach, but we beat them too hard and the bodies were too mangled to eat. In yet another, I found her in bed with Ainslie.

*

Ainslie insisted we throw a dinner party. There was no particular occasion for this fiesta, but I think he was hoping that someone would bring real tobacco and he could stop smoking the cured banana leaves that were a poor substitute.

Our dinner party bore only a rudimentary resemblance to its citified cousin. First of all, I couldn't consult a recipe book for the dish. It was Floreana boar pork roast with potatoes and gravy. I took some of our precious factory-made sugar and prepared a sort of papaya tart. It actually looked appetizing. Second, it was bring your own dishes, for Ainslie and I had only three plates and forks.

I bustled around that day, sweeping and re-sweeping the floor. "For goodness' sake, Frances," said Ainslie, finally, exasperated. "It's not like we're trying to keep up with the Joneses here. We all have the same dirt floor."

"I know," I said, putting down my broom. "I'm nervous. We haven't socialized in so long."

"It's like riding a bike," Ainslie said. "Wobbly and possibly injurious."

"Very funny," I said. "All you have to do is make a bench. I am in charge of all the food. I haven't cooked for more than two people . . ." I thought about it for a minute. "Ever."

"This is only my second bench," Ainslie said. "And cooking for two is more than I've ever done. But, if you want to switch . . ."

I swiped at his feet with the broom and he laughed.

His bench was an interesting affair. He ran a palo santo branch into the notched crotch made of two crossing branches lashed with a *muyuyo* vine. He made three of these braces and produced a bench fit for only the smallest of bottoms. We then ran into trouble. There were no large trees on the island. Instead, Ainslie cut a series of palos in half with the ax and lashed them to the structure. It would not be a seat fit for a king, but our Galápagos bottoms were accustomed to much worse. Ainslie spent several hours leveling it out in his perfectionist manner.

Our guests were the Jiménezes and Elke and Heinrich. Of course we had extended invitations to the Weiss family and the Muellers, but they both declined, the older couple saying that they preferred their solitude and that it was hard for them to travel at night, and the Weisses said their child was too fragile. Therefore, we would have a crowd of six, including us.

We had called the party for three hours before sunset. A bit early for dinner, perhaps, but no one wanted to make their way home in the dark. Elke and Heinrich were the first to arrive, of course, being German. Elke had made cheese from milk from her goat, and paired it with a sort of flatbread. It made an excellent appetizer. She also baked a batch of her famous yucca cookies. Heinrich brought a bottle of aquavit he said had been given to him the last time Count von Luckner had been through the islands. He had been saving it for a special occasion. I suppose he must have deemed this adequate, and perhaps he had started celebrating the occasion a bit early, as the bottle had obviously been sampled from. It was impossible to be an alcoholic on the islands, but I have no doubt that both Heinrich and Ainslie would have walked miles to get to the pub, were there one.

The Jiménezes were fashionably late, in the Ecuadorian manner. They arrived with a cucumber, radish, and tomato salad. Gansa also brought an avocado-and-banana pudding (it's better than it sounds). Together with Elke's cheese and my pork roast, potatoes, and tart, we would have a real meal tonight.

It is difficult to reproduce our conversations because no real sentences were spoken, and yet they seemed to flow as naturally (or nearly so) as a conversation that included people who spoke the same language. Gansa pointed out an improvement to our hearth that made it burn much hotter while consuming less fuel. Elke told a story about the disastrous results the first time she cooked for Heinrich, soon after they met.

Once the aquavit had made its way around the table, the trilingual conversation got more lively. Ainslie loved an audience. He recounted his war experience, how he found himself in the Philippines, then got promoted by accident and sent to France. He told it in English, and I translated into Spanish. The story trickled down into German as well, as Heinrich's English was not as good as Elke's. But mostly Ainslie acted it out, his long limbs adding to the buffoonishness of it. Then he and Heinrich acted out their various experiences fighting the French, Heinrich pantomiming his unfortunate arm injury. He showed us how he tried to light his pipe one-handed, which had him following it around the room like a bird trapped indoors. We all laughed.

"I hope the Germans can work things out," Gansa said in Spanish. "Lord knows we don't want another world war."

There was a silence while each of us decided how to respond to her statement. Elke looked at her hands, Heinrich at his pipe. Gonzalo

looked at his wife and I looked at Ainslie. The tension rose, spongy like
wet moss.

Ainslie saved the day. "Why is politics never discussed during the
meat course?"

No one spoke.

"Because one gives you indigestion and the other needs steak sauce."

Elke began to laugh first. She translated for Heinrich and then into
Spanish for Gansa and Gonzalo, who also giggled.

"Is the coffee ready, do you think?" Ainslie asked.

As I was cleaning up later that evening, belly full as there was no
refrigeration for the cheese or bread box for the bread and therefore
both had to be eaten that evening (we would never allow a full stomach
to let us waste food), Ainslie came up behind me and put his hands on
my shoulders. He sighed. "That was fun. Didn't feel like work."

"You like people," I said. "This is hard for you, this living here." It was
easier to talk in the dark when I didn't have to see his face, just feel his
warm body behind me while I scrubbed dishes.

"I'm just glad you're here with me," he said. "It would be infinitely
harder alone."

*

Soon after, it was Christmas, and Heinrich and Elke invited us to their
casita for dinner. We spent a pleasant evening singing Christmas carols
by their fire. The Jiménezes came as well, and I finally met the Weiss
family, and I agreed with Ainslie that their child did not look well. I
made a note to myself that when the next luxury yacht with a doctor
stopped, I would insist that he attend to the child. The Muellers had
visited earlier in the day with a gift of many lemons, which was nice
enough of them.

There was *chicha* (a rice and corn beer) and a rum made from sugarcane, but Ainslie only had a sip. Lest you think he was being abstemious,
it tastes rather like curdled milk. Elke had decorated with a small artificial tree that looked oddly out of place where nothing else had been
machine-produced. On the table lay her good tablecloth dotted with
hibiscus blossoms. She had sliced all varieties of fruits and vegetables:

four kinds of bananas, pineapples, tomatoes, avocados, guavas. But the pièce de résistance was her *Weihnachtskuchen*, several kinds of traditional German Christmas cakes and cookies. She must have saved up the refined sugar, white flour, and baking powder for months.

When we sang "Silent Night" in our respective languages, Ainslie took my hand. I let myself believe for a moment that he and I experienced such a moment of peace as I would assume most Christians feel on the holiest of days. His warmth spread, though I had not known that I was cold.

*

The new year in the Galápagos means the end of the rainy season and the return of abundant sunshine. It was wonderful to see the sun again, until the heat wave hit. Even with a hat my brain turned to mush under its rays. Everyone was lethargic; all activity had to cease midday for a siesta in the shade, and fanning ourselves was not worth the effort. I have never anywhere experienced heat like this. When it was this hot, my body began to shut down all nonessential functions. I moved little; I spoke little; I ate little. I was reduced to my reptilian brain—breathing, sleeping, blinking.

Then finally it rained and the heat broke and I resumed functioning again, albeit slowly, to reap the fruits of our labor in the garden. The year anniversary of our arrival on the islands was fast approaching, the end of our period of service. Ainslie waited until April and asked about the plans for our removal in his weekly radio check-in. It must have taken a while to trickle up to HQ, as we heard nothing back. We could not leave until we had our orders, and though we could have caught a ride back to Guayaquil with one of the passing boats, until we had an actual piece of paper, we risked being charged with going AWOL. Why we had not thought of this before we left, I don't know. But we would have to wait.

It was not a hardship. I found myself extremely at peace. Ainslie and Elke were tremendously good company, and there was so much satisfaction in eating only what we grew with our own hands. I slept like a puppy at night, exhausted from my labors, and felt younger than I had in years. My hands grew tough with calluses, and I ceased to wear shoes most of the time. I was proud of myself and what I was doing. And a little bit of Ainslie's "improvement syndrome" must have hit me, for I started enlarging the garden, though I knew we might have to abandon it at any time.

By the time Ainslie heard back from HQ, I was happily planting another row of each vegetable, and even some flowers for sheer decoration. They wanted us to stay another year. And could Ainslie write a feasibility study for a potential military outpost on the island (water, place for an airstrip, etc.)? I told Ainslie I'd like to, blasé, without thinking, and he agreed and so there was no reason to discuss it any further.

*

In May, Ainslie happened to be up high on the pampa and could therefore spot the incoming boat from very far. So it was that we were down on the beach waiting when it dropped anchor. It was the *Seeteufel*, whose captain was Count von Luckner, provider of the aquavit that had so enhanced our dinner party. By then I had heard all sorts of stories about Luckner, from nearly everyone who came to the islands and from Elke and Heinrich, who considered him a good friend. There was no way he could live up to his reputation. Supposedly, he was the strongest man anyone had ever seen. He could bend nails with one hand, lift large rocks without aid. He was a trained opera baritone and spoke six languages as a native. During the Great War he had been a feared pirate who managed to commandeer ships without bloodshed, and he escaped from a prison in New Zealand. He was also an accomplished magician. Really, he was the stuff of legend.

So imagine my excitement when I knew I would finally get to meet this modern-day Hercules. The dinghy approached. I suppose he was handsome. Even if his hair was thinning, he had typical chiseled German features. As to his physique, I suppose he was muscular, and even a bit large, unlike all the other Europeans I knew in the Galápagos, who were thin and wiry. One thing I did notice was how pale he was, even after thirty years on the sea.

He stepped daintily out of the boat before it beached, and made his way to land where he took my hand and kissed it passionately. I couldn't help it; I giggled. "Felix Graf von Luckner, *a votre service*." He bowed low.

"I'm Frances Conway, and this is my husband, Ainslie."

"Of course I know," he said. His English was fluent, yes, but he would be hard-pressed to convince any native speaker that it was his mother tongue. "The reports of your beauty did not do you justice." Now I knew he was merely slinging sunshine; I'd been called a lot of things in my life, but beautiful was not one. Handsome, perhaps, or winsome. Beautiful, not likely. He extended his hand to Ainslie to shake. "Sir," he said.

Ainslie shook briefly then pulled his hand back and rubbed it.

While we'd been talking, Elke and Heinrich had arrived on the beach. The count kissed Elke's hand and shook Heinrich's. All this time his companions had been unloading crates from the panga. Elke, Heinrich, and the count exchanged pleasantries in German. I could understand them, but it was hardly the stuff of spying. Gossip about people they knew in common, who had given birth, how so-and-so's rheumatism was. They knew Elke's cousin in common, and the count told her a story about running into him at the cinema in Berlin, and also something about a small dog which I didn't quite get.

Elke and Heinrich's hound had accompanied them, and she knew the count as well. He must have given her treats when he last saw her, for she turned in circles in excitement, sniffing at his pockets and crotch. The count bent over and wrestled her head playfully, then fed her something out of his pocket. As ludicrous as I found this man, I had to admire his ability to charm every living thing.

He parceled out his gifts—for me a new frying pan (how did he know?) and for Ainslie some real tobacco from the West Indies. For Elke he brought a stack of magazines and mail. Heinrich actually was a journalist; his byline appeared and was translated into magazines all over the globe. Perhaps Elke had told me the literal truth—they were a journalist and his lover escaping her husband. The two pieces in English talked about our life on the island. One was a humorous struggle to make their house a home, and the other talked about the food they grew and shot.

Of the Norwegian version we could make neither head nor tails, but the count assured us it was a faithful translation.

In one of the magazines there was a picture of me and Ainslie along with Elke and Heinrich. Ainslie was a giant, and I was laughing about something with my mouth open. My hair was in disarray, and I was holding one of our larger chickens. Ainslie's gaze was outside the photo, toward something distant; he had a humoring smile on his face. Elke and Heinrich were holding hands. We looked, to all unsuspecting eyes, like a pair of neighbors having a drink in the summertime. We looked like we were having fun.

It bothered me that I couldn't remember having had that picture taken. Everyone who visited Floreana wanted to take pictures of us, the zoo animals. We generally obliged. The picture was indistinguishable from the others—I was wearing the same thing in all of them, of course, as was everyone. A moment captured on film forever and forgotten by me.

The count had our mail. I was hoping for a letter from Rosalie. I had received one per month, though they arrived in clumps of two or three via the consulate in Guayaquil where I'm sure someone read them. Though they were deadly dull, full of news about people I didn't remember meeting or the exploits of her children, I savored them. But today there was nothing for me except the magazine subscriptions, held for me at the American Express office in Guayaquil. I was excited to get to read *Life* and *The Saturday Evening Post*. There were a good six issues of each.

And then the count invited everyone back to his ship for supper. The *Seeteufel* was large and well-appointed, even if it was showing its age a bit. It had been outfitted as a goodwill touring yacht, so it had comfortable staterooms and a large gathering salon. We ate fish, canned vegetables, and even cow cheese (what a luxury!). Most of all, we drank wine, a good German Riesling, which was deliciously cold. I might have had more than my share.

The talk at dinner turned to politics, and I could feel Ainslie's ears perk up. The count held forth in both languages about how wonderful Germany was again since Hitler came to power. Ainslie's distrust of

Hitler had infected me and the mention of his name made me nervous, even then, even before we knew what horrors he'd unleash. But the count spoke so fluently and gave such beautiful examples that I had to shake my head to clear the reverie.

Ainslie sat very still during the dinner, smoking one cigarette after another. I could see his knee twitch with the influx of the chemical. Afterward he switched to a pipe, puffing on it like a diver on oxygen. He said very little. I wasn't sure if this was a tactic or just due to his incomprehension of the parts of the conversation in German. Elke said, "It's nice to know that the *Mutterland* is in good hands."

Heinrich nodded vigorously.

The count motioned to the person who was serving us. The man went out and came back with a flat wrapped object about a foot square. "I bring you this for you, Elke and Heinrich, but also for all of Floreana, with compliments from the Führer."

Elke unwrapped it to show a portrait of Adolf Hitler. "*Danke*, Graf Luckner," she said. "I will make sure it has a place of honor in my home."

I was abruptly nervous, as though infused with caffeine. I knew Hitler's view on people like me, that is to say, Jewish people, and also his views on homosexuals. Jews were not welcome in Germany, and by extension now Austria and Czechoslovakia. If he continued on his rise, and on his mission to annex Europe, and if this hatred infected others, we were at risk. I will also admit that I was not pleased to be lumped with Gypsies and homosexuals. Being Jewish was something I was born into; that Ainslie chose to be with other men I thought at that time was a lack of willpower.

My Judaism was not something I thought about often. Sometimes, when talking with Elke, I had to censor a certain memory, but religion didn't seem to have a place on the island. We all worshipped at the altar of the weather gods, nature, our own self-reliance. Religious faith was incompatible.

Luckner handed us each a printed pamphlet. It was in Spanish and extolled the virtues of a unified and Germanized Europe, with beautiful mountain aeries and buxom fair serving wenches carrying multiple steins of *Bier*. I scanned the text quickly. What on earth was this supposed to convince people of? And which people were supposed to be convinced? Count von Luckner was too important to be dismissed as a clown, but how was I to read his actions as anything but buffoonish?

The tension in the small room was palpable, the breeze barely blowing. Then Heinrich asked if the count wouldn't like to perform some tricks, and the count's mustachioed mouth smiled and he called for something, which arrived in the form of a large black box.

He opened it and rummaged around for a while until he removed a black hat and a white-tipped wand. "Please, someone, give me your watch." Of course, no one here carried a watch, so no one volunteered. "Very well," said the count, "I provide my own." He removed a pocket watch. "This was from my grandfather, *ja*? The fourth Count of Luckner. It is precious to me, so I will not lose it in the land of magic."

I giggled, but Elke shot me a severe look so I stifled it. Out of the corner of my eye I saw Ainslie do the same, holding up his pipe so that his hand blocked his mouth. The count put the watch into the hat and waved his wand over it, incanting what was most likely *abracadabra* in German. Then he flipped the hat high into the air and caught it on his head. The watch was gone. The flipping trick was perhaps the greater feat, but still I applauded. He was not a bad amateur magician.

Afterward he did two card tricks, making the ace of hearts appear under Ainslie's charger plate, and then pulling out of the deck the card that Elke had picked and sealed in an envelope. Then he lamented that he had no rabbit, but made a Darwin finch appear from the hat. Where had he been keeping the bird all this time?

We were so starved for entertainment that I began to relax and simply enjoy myself. I knew that the count was no mere magician, and this was likely no mere goodwill visit; still, it was a good show. The alcohol slowly took effect. The room was hot and shimmery as if in a dream. The mahogany gleamed; there was carpet on the floor. Carpet! On a ship! I hadn't seen carpeting in forever. The glasses all matched, and none were chipped. We had eaten vegetables grown outside the islands, food that had been spiced, ice cream even. I saw how someone could be lulled by this excess, by this comfort.

It was reluctantly that we went ashore and made the long trek back to our house. So many of these episodes end, here in the Galápagos, with Ainslie and me trudging home in the dark. Make of that metaphor what you will.

*

The next morning Ainslie asked, "Ready to be a real spy?"

"You mean our super-top-secret feasibility study for a base for a war we probably won't fight?"

Ainslie ignored my sarcasm. "The portrait of Die Führer." He exaggerated the German pronunciation. "See if you can get access to its lining. Since you and Frau Elke are such dear friends." There was some menace behind his statement, but I chose to ignore it.

"Launching Operation Pomegranate," I said.

I had my opportunity not two days later when I went to Elke's. She had flowers on a makeshift vase on the table. I was struck again by the civilization of her home. I had made no such improvements to our shack, and even though I thought it was a bit of a waste, to come all the way around the world and then cave to the convention of matching bedspreads, I wondered if Ainslie wouldn't have preferred me if I were a better homemaker. I still had these thoughts that if I were just a different person, maybe then Ainslie would want me. They came unbidden before I chased them out of my mind.

We batted our gums over tea with goat milk, two terrible-tasting substances that did nothing for each other. Heinrich was working in the garden and called for a hand, and Elke excused herself.

Now was my chance. I took the portrait off the wall. The back was covered with brown paper, already peeling along the edges where the humidity was working its charm. This would be a good hiding place. In fact, it was one of the ones recommended to me during Spy 101.

I was about to tear it farther when I paused. What if this was a trap, to see if I was spying on her? What if she'd rigged up a way to tell if something was disturbed? Another lesson from Spy 101. In fact, I'd already probably disturbed it (a hair, a line of dust). Perhaps she was wondering what this mismatched pair of middle-aged Americans was doing on the islands. I could see things from her point of view, which was startlingly similar to my own. Were we spies? I smiled at the likelihood of Heinrich and Elke having the exact same conversations that Ainslie and I did.

I smoothed my hand over the paper. There was definitely something underneath. But what could it be? It was about the same size as a passport, but also could have been a small book, a manual, or even just a certificate of authenticity for the portrait. I couldn't tell.

I held the portrait up to the light, but of course I couldn't see through it. The only way I would know would be to peel back the paper, but no matter how carefully I did it Elke was bound to know that someone had tampered with it, and that the someone was me. Was leaving me here in her house a trap or a test? She was probably looking in on me right now. But no, the dog was sleeping peacefully, which she would never do if her masters were nearby.

If I were to open it and find fake passports, or illicit documents, or . . . my mind searched for other possibilities and found none plausible, then my friendship with Elke would be over. Not that it was a real friendship—but if I knew for certain that she was here in the same capacity I was, then our afternoons together would be over. It would be too hard to keep up the charade.

And I treasured those afternoons. I genuinely liked her. In another world, we would be friends. And I couldn't afford to lose the only friend I had, even if it meant that I was a bad spy. I put the portrait back on the wall and told Ainslie I found nothing.

The next time I came to visit, the portrait was gone.

CHAPTER THIRTEEN

News reached us piecemeal of Hitler's invasion of Poland. First we heard a rumor from an Ecuadorian fishing schooner. It was corroborated by a Norwegian skiff, which was touring the islands looking for possible fishery grounds. Governor Puente stopped by the islands (we hadn't seen him in a year—governorships were simultaneously a reward and a punishment, and the occupants of the office did not pain themselves trying to fulfill the duties of office) to tell us that members of the Ecuadorian military would be scouting for a place to construct a possible landing strip and a military enclave. That sent our little island into a tizzy. An entire army base? I spent many nights awake worrying that it would come to pass. Ainslie pooh-poohed my worrying in advance. It was Ecuador, remember, where plans were worth less than sucres on the black market. Puente would change his mind a thousand times and then abscond with the money. And that was pretty much what came to pass.

Elke and I avoided the subject of Europe, though she did say she was worried about her children at boarding school in Switzerland if—or when—war broke out. The Great War taught us that wars are started by a few men, and the women and children suffer the consequences. Everyone remembered the shortages during the Greats—War and Depression—and no one wanted to relive that nor wish it on our worst enemies. Elke had a sister, she told me, a bit younger than herself, who had four children. She was married to a local policeman in their small Bavarian town. What would become of them if he got conscripted? Or if England and France decided to retaliate?

Our radio signal was strengthened—we now had access to Guayaquil and Quito without an appointment. Ainslie started going to the radio twice a week for updates. One day he came home with some interesting news. "Elke's uncle was sent to jail for writing against the Nazis."

"What does that mean?"

"Not sure," Ainslie said. "Maybe she's spying in exchange for his release? Or to prove that her whole family is not that way? Or maybe it's fabricated?"

This was so like the government, giving intelligence without interpretation so all you could do was file it away under your hat.

"Why would it be fabricated?"

"The Germans love their propaganda. Remember Luckner's pamphlet? They've been feeding misinformation throughout South America for years, have agents in all the major cities."

"How do you know?" I asked. Ainslie tilted his head in disappointment at me. "I suppose I'm trying to ask what that means for our relationship with Elke and Heinrich. Do we suspect them more or less?"

"Equally," Ainslie said. "Can we eat?"

*

I had brought along Darwin's *Origin of Species*, which I had not read since college. Rereading it gave me solace. It's the same sort of cold comfort when we look up into a clear sky and see that we are mere specks in the enormous universe. Our actions here on earth contribute, no doubt, to the evolution of civilization, but in such a minor and minuscule way that there is freedom in knowing that what you do doesn't really matter, can't matter, in the scheme of things.

Around this time I began to develop ulcers on my legs. I had slipped while hiking in the dark and the scabs never really healed, remaining red and weepy, then turning yellow. They hurt when I walked, then even when I wasn't walking.

Ainslie frowned at the sores, examining them closely. We poured warm water over my legs, then tried keeping them dry. We treated them with the only alcohol we could find, high-proof German schnapps, but the wounds continued to fester. Soon I was spending most of my time in bed, lying as still as possible.

"When the next ship comes in, Franny, you're seeing the doctor."

I wanted to be the brave soul who argued, but I did seem to need medical attention. I started feeling feverish. Throughout our stay, we'd both been free of colds, of course, since we had so little contact with the outside world. We were plagued by minor injuries—sprains, bruises, aches, bites from bugs, and also fungus. Always fungus. But there had never been anything serious. No gunshot wounds or life-threatening illnesses. Until now. I remember feeling very dizzy and then slipping in and out of consciousness.

Ainslie built a large brushfire on the beach as the international signal for "come help us," and sure enough a tuna boat weighed anchor. Ainslie asked them to go to Chatham and request that a boat with a medical officer stop by. Then I woke up and my arms were tied while Elke poked around with a knife to try to cut out the necrotic tissue. I have never experienced so much pain in my life, searing, fiery agony. Before I passed out, Elke said she thought she saw bone.

As it turns out, a yacht was nearby and a physician was on it. The fishing boat passed on Ainslie's worry and it quickly motored to Black Bay. This was all told to me afterward, of course, as I was unconscious the whole time.

And what yacht was it, traipsing about our island home? President Roosevelt's no less, the USS *Nourmahal*. He was vacationing in the Galápagos and was planning to visit the Americans, so he was headed toward Floreana. Ainslie and Heinrich carried me to the beach and the physician treated my wounds with Dakin's solution. I'm told I howled; Ainslie said it sounded like a drove of dying donkeys. The doctor wanted me to stay on board with them for a day or two, and so I spent two days luxuriating in a first-class cabin, with electricity for the first time in more than a year, not to mention running water and real bedding. I wish I had been awake to enjoy it.

Ainslie said he met with Roosevelt during this time. I was not allowed to know what was said, or even if Roosevelt was aware of our presence in the Galápagos as intelligence agents before his trip, but Ainslie and I joked later that I had gotten sick on purpose so that he could powwow with the president. I never set eyes on the man, but Ainslie says that he was kind, asking after me.

The president!

*

A month later I was almost healed, back to my regular tasks. Ainslie was *arriba* and I was at home shelling beans when I heard the honk of a donkey. They really do say "hee-haw." I wiped my hands quickly on my shorts. It was either a dray belonging to a visitor or a wild donkey raiding my garden. Either way, it would require my immediate attention.

The donkey was indeed foraging through the plants and I could tell by the way it left the lesser melons for the choicer ones that it was one of the island's domesticated donkeys. It might have been Chuclu; I found donkeys oddly difficult to differentiate. I could tell specific birds from each other, and even the squirrels had personalities, but my hatred of donkeys made them interchangeable.

"Shoo," I yelled, waving my arms. Occasionally, the donkeys could get mean. I'd seen one turn on its owner on Chatham, bucking and rearing and then pawing him down. The donkey was subdued before it did him harm, and the man merely slapped it on the rump good-naturedly as though it was all in good fun and the donkey had simply won this round. I was not going to be so happy about a charging donkey. This one looked at me with pure condescension in its eyes. It knew an easy mark when it saw one. It dropped the half-eaten melon from its mouth and took a large bite out of a second one, just to spite me. It made sure to twitch its tail at me too, so I knew exactly how much esteem it held for me.

I got braver in the face of this insolence. "Get on out of here!" I said. I was not a total rube; after all, I lived for six years on Mrs. Keane's farm, where the horses and cows were occasionally intractable, but a wild ass was another thing. I picked up a tin cup and threw it at the donkey. Of course, I missed (I have terrible aim), and it rolled away. The donkey raised an eyebrow at me. So I took a step or two closer and pushed its flank. I was worried it would kick me.

The donkey pushed back at me, forcing me to retreat. I got a pan and a pot, thinking that a loud noise might scare it away, and while my back was turned the donkey trotted over to the table and shoved its nose into my bean pile, eating several hours of work. The rage crashed inside of me. I'm afraid I cursed a blue streak. I'm glad no one heard me.

This indelicacy finally roused the donkey and he walked back toward whence he came. He paused at our clothesline, though, and sniffed around, finally pulling down a pair of my unmentionables with his teeth. Only now did he begin to hurry, running down a game trail.

In other times, other places, I would have let that donkey go with my underthings. But I only had one spare pair, so I could wear one while the other pair was drying. These were extremely important textiles, and I couldn't let the donkey just run off with them. I took off after him. If he dropped them, I needed to be there to pick them up.

He ran uphill. I recognized the game trail as one leading to Elke and Heinrich's house; it was the trail their dog took when she bounded ahead. I was able to keep up for a while. And then the donkey turned abruptly down a path that I was not aware of before this moment. The path was less trod, but the marks of pigs' hooves led me to guess that it, too, was a game trail. The donkey was slowing but still hadn't dropped my panties. I hoped it would stop at a stream at some point and loosen its jaw to relinquish what was mine. Instead, I followed it deeper and deeper to a place only it knew.

We continued on this way for some time. Thorns tore at my skin and clothing, and I realized how stupid I was being, risking injury, and probably losing what clothing I had left in this bizarre chase. Just then the donkey stopped and I lurched forward to grab my underwear from its mouth. He feinted and bounded onward, and I, committed to my leap, fell over. There was an immediate searing pain in my elbow, and I cursed how idiotic I'd been. I lay on my side for a while as the pain throbbed, trying to catch my breath.

Gingerly, I raised my head and looked at the injury. There was a large thorn embedded half an inch inside the soft part just above my elbow. I removed it, and blood began to emerge. I quickly clamped my hand over it, and now wished that I had the underwear to use as a tourniquet.

Instead, I took the handkerchief I often wore around my neck to protect me from sunburn and used it to tie off the bleeding. My arm was beginning to swell.

A glint caught my eye, a reflective surface like a flashlight. I blinked. Yes, definitely something shiny, which was strange. Had I dropped something? I stood up, woozily, to examine it. It was a metal corner covered in flakey green paint, hidden by undergrowth. I pulled at a branch and a few of them lifted off like a cover to expose a radio, older but in good condition.

What had I found? Was this ours? I brushed it off and saw its brand: Siemens. This was not a potential false passport. This was real evidence that they were spies, and my heart sank. I couldn't ignore this. I would have to tell Ainslie and it would change everything. I found myself beginning to tear up, sad that my friendship with Elke was over. Though if we were both spies, then it was never really a friendship to begin with.

I placed the brush cover back over the radio as best I could and made it look like no one had been there. There was blood on the ground, but I dug a bit and resettled the dirt so that it covered it. Then I spread a few leaves around to camouflage my tracks.

Gingerly, I made my way back, pushing aside the brush with my good arm, trying to keep the other one elevated to stop the bleeding. Now that I was looking for them, I noticed a few cairns to mark the path. I tried to fix these in my mind as I followed the game trail back home.

I emerged from the forest *arriba* in a different place than I'd entered, and I had to backtrack an hour to get home. When I finally did arrive, the handkerchief was soaked with blood, though my arm was no longer bleeding. I lay down, elevating my arm on a pot.

The first thing Ainslie said when he walked into the house was, "Where's dinner?"

"I fell," I said. "I was bleeding."

"You're okay," Ainslie said, giving me an order.

"Yes, I'm okay," I said. "But I'm hurt. I didn't do dinner."

Ainslie sighed heavily. He came over and took my arm in his hands. I winced. "A bit swollen. Is that a thorn?"

"It was," I said. "But listen." I told Ainslie about my discovery.

"Nicely done, Mrs. Conway," he said in admiration. "Tomorrow you'll show me where it is."

"I'll try," I said. "I might have a time finding it. And I also have to find my knickers."

*

We never found the knickers, but Ainslie was suitably impressed by my discovery. He promised that he'd inform our higher-ups that I was the one who found it. I told him not to bother.

Elke and I continued our afternoon soirees but something was different, strained. I'm sure she felt it too, and they just tapered off. Still, Ainslie was encouraging me to befriend her, so occasionally I'd show up with some little cakes (we had plenty of sugarcane now since ours had come in; they had almost none) and we'd sit and gossip for a while. Her dog had puppies with one of the wild dogs on the island and we took one, but after a month he went on his daily adventure and didn't come home. That's how it was in the Galápagos. Nature is brutal.

The elbow healed, but with a permanent scar that still aches. Another lesson.

*

War broke out. It was a surprise to no one. A military ship came by with a copy of *The New York Times*, now a week old. Its banner headline, above the name of the newspaper, read CHAMBERLAIN ANNOUNCES BRITAIN IS AT WAR WITH GERMANY. I saw Elke at the beach. I wasn't sure what to say, and I could tell she was also at a loss for words. "It's so far away," I said. "It's like it's not even happening."

She burst into tears and without thinking about it, I pulled her to my chest. "There there," I said. Why we always say that in times of trouble I'll never know, as they seem the least sympathetic words in the English language.

"My children," she said.

"Aren't they in Switzerland?"

"Also I carry worry for my sister." She wiped her eyes. "In Dresden. And my cousin, he is twenty years old."

"I'm sorry," I said. War seemed completely absurd to me then. If the United States ended up getting involved (which Ainslie swore would not happen), then Elke and I would be actual enemies, not merely employed at cross-purposes. The gulf between us would widen. I silently cursed governments. Nothing was different. Everything was different.

*

That night, Ainslie and I ate a gloomy solitary dinner, canned carrots (thank you, USS *Charleston*), canned meat, and canned peaches for dessert. I tried to explain to him how I felt, how I understood Elke better than before. Ainslie put down his fork.

"You do know, Franny, that Elke is our enemy no matter whether America enters the war or not."

"I know," I said.

"I mean, we can be friendly with them. We have to be friendly with them, but that's all, that's as far as it goes. Don't develop real feelings, Franny-Lou."

"I can't help it," I said. We were talking about more than just Elke and Heinrich. "I feel things."

"They won't ever feel that way about you," he said. "And if push comes to shove they'll sacrifice you. They have their duty."

"Duty," I repeated, like a dirty word.

"It's bigger than just a person or two."

"Duty," I sputtered again. "Everything is for duty."

Ainslie stood up and carried our dishes to the "sink," then sat back down, chewing his pipe. "I was so worried, when you were sick. I can't imagine what I'd do without you."

"If we enter the war, we go home," I whispered. My voice cracked.

"Probably, that's right, but we're not going to war."

"And when we go home, we don't have to pretend to be married anymore."

Ainslie took his pipe out of his mouth. To my surprise, he looked hurt. "I'm really married to you, Frances. Maybe I wasn't at first, but I am now. You don't feel married to me?"

There was an opening. I wanted to say so much. "I do," I said. "And I don't."

I hadn't been letting myself wonder what would happen when we returned to the States. Every time the thought arose I repressed it. Mostly because I assumed we'd go our separate ways. But maybe I'd been assuming wrong. Did I want to stay with Ainslie? Was it enough?

*

Another rainy season, the *garúa*, and then the hot, hot bake of summer. And then another cycle, and another with the rhythm of the tides, imperceptibly cresting and waning. Before I knew it, we had been living on Floreana for more than three years. It was my home. Others came to the island to live for shorter periods; the Weisses' child died and they went back to the mainland, but Elke and Heinrich and the Jiménezes were permanent neighbors.

As the war in Europe occupied more of the international stage, U.S. warships came frequently to the islands. They would offload a hundred or so bored sailors, who started bonfires on the beach and shot at goats for sport. We could hear their whooping long into the night. The USS *Lapwing* stayed for a month while their experts photographed and charted our island. We began to dread the sound of a ship's whistle. They did little more than loiter—awkward youngsters at a dance. We began to wish there'd been an Ecuadorian base constructed after all; then at least we wouldn't have to deal with American ships.

Even if outwardly the United States proclaimed its isolationism, its military was in full exercise. Few were the days when we looked out into Black Bay or Post Office Bay and did not see a warship mustering for exercises. Of course it is in every military's best interest to anticipate all potential threats and have a plan of action; the navy saw the inevitability of American involvement in the Pacific front. The Japanese were in a tight space, having all their access to natural resources frozen. It was logical that they might target our shipping mechanisms, which is to say the Panama Canal. And the closest islands to the canal were our own Enchanteds.

So we had a vague threat on sea, and a near-constant stream of servicemen. As the only Americans, we were always invited down to the beach, or called upon to give tours of the island or host people for dinner with our meager supplies. Some of these guests ended up being good company, but most were tiresome, annoying, and distracting.

It was starting to get to me. After three straight days of making small talk with sailors, juicing lemons, and using most of our sugar, I snapped at Ainslie, and he looked at me queerly. "You're not cracking, are you, Franny?"

"Why are there so many? Is the entire armada here?"

"Really, Franny? You haven't figured it out?"

I sat down. "What? That we're going to war?"

"The whole reason we're here is so that we don't go to war." My face must have given my ignorance and confusion away. "It amazes me how you can live here in complete denial of what's happening around us."

He was right. I was a smart, educated woman. Why did it not occur to me to question, to wonder? In my defense, it may have been war in Europe, but here in the Galápagos we were fighting our own wars against the damp, the animals, the niguas, the mosquitoes, our own solitude, and it was easy to forget for weeks at a time that tensions were mounting internationally.

Ainslie began to whisper, sound-masking by drumming his hands on the table. "Since you found the radio, it's clear that our actions are being reported back to the Germans. If we mass here, the ships will be reported, and it looks like we have a strong naval presence."

"But we do have a strong naval presence," I said.

"Of course we do, but flexing our muscles when they don't think we're looking makes us seem even stronger. It's worth sending a few ships down here, especially since they'll be deployed and trained should their presence be necessary. The larger the fleet looks, the less likely it is that Japan will retaliate against the sanctions."

I thought about this for a moment. "That can't possibly be the strategy. *We* can't possibly be the strategy."

"No, not the *only* strategy."

"Oh," I said. "I thought us being here was . . . was—"

"This is not some game, Franny. This is not just playacting." Ainslie raised his voice. He had stopped pounding on the table. I was scared; he was so rarely angry. "You just skip around blithely braiding Elke's hair." (For the record, I had never done this.) "Do you understand what's at stake here? Thousands, hundreds of thousands, millions of lives. This is real. This is serious. Hitler is killing people every day, *your* people, and you're more interested in whether the bread rises or if we'll stay together after it's all over. It hasn't even begun."

My nerves were frayed; I was exhausted. That is the only explanation I can think of for why this rare display of anger from Ainslie triggered a giggle. A single burst emerged before I could quell it.

"Don't cry. I'm sorry I was short with you. Please don't." I was very far from crying but there didn't seem to be any upside to admitting it. I just found it so absurd that we were influencing history. It seemed utterly preposterous, farcical.

*

You could always tell who hadn't been accustomed to undergrowth. They walked with heavy feet, in boots. Our shoes were long worn down: I only bothered with them when I knew I would have to walk on lava. These boots came in the form of a sailor who must have lied about his age to get into the navy. He was years from his first shave.

"Ma'am," he said, wiping his brow with his dirty hand, leaving a gray patch, "I'm sent . . . to . . ."

"Catch your breath, sailor," I said. "We're on island time here, nothing is that urgent." I led him to our bench. He sat and drank the proffered glass of water quickly, drops falling off his chin.

"We're having a bonfire tonight," he said. "The captain hopes you'll join us."

"Which ship are you on?" I didn't want to trek down to the beach and pretend to have a good time with under-stimulated adolescents and whatever alcohol the captain could spare. Only if the captain was someone I knew and admired would I bother.

"The USS *Georgia*," he said. "We're—"

"I know who you are," I interrupted. The battleship was commanded by Thompson. He was an honorable fellow and a personal friend of Ainslie's. Most likely he had some communiqué for Ainslie. I accepted the invitation and sent the child on his way.

It was nearing dusk, so I collected my gardening tools and put them away. I washed my face and tried to pin my hair up, looking at myself in the scrap of mirror that Ainslie used for shaving. I was unfamiliar with the leathered old woman who stared out at me from it.

Pulling on my skirt, I waited for Ainslie, who came down from his daily pilgrimage soon enough. He readied himself more slowly, so that it was getting dark when we set out. We knew the path by then; there was little danger of losing our way.

Though the smoke drifted up above the trees and created a hazy mist of the night sky, we could hear the men at the bonfire before smelling or seeing it. When we came around the last bend, it looked like a real party. Where the wood came from is anybody's guess, but it was piled high and blazing. The ship's band was playing loudly: a guitar, saxophone, and drums improvised from various buckets and barrels. I hadn't heard the songs before, but then again, I had been on a desert island for more than three years. Elke and Heinrich were already there, their dog as always at their heels, sitting with the officers upwind from the smoke. I was not surprised to see them there, despite the hostilities between our two nations. If there were cigarettes to be had, you could expect Heinrich and Ainslie, even if the devil himself were handing them out.

On the beach the young men were dancing, some with each other, and there was a pig roasting on a spit on a smaller fire just to the right. As we trudged down the beach one of the young men grabbed my hand and spun me around a few times until I slipped, dizzy, and he laughed and let me go. I plopped down next to Ainslie and said hello to Thompson and the other assembled officers. There were several empty bottles of rum, and each enlisted man had had his ration, hence the dancing. And now another was opened. Ainslie poured himself a generous glass and gave another, smaller portion to me.

"To America!" the first officer toasted, and we all looked at Elke and

Heinrich, uncomfortable. They did not raise their glasses, but neither did they say anything.

I brought mine to my lips. The unfamiliar liquid burned on its way down my throat, and I poured the rest into Ainslie's glass. Everyone else refilled theirs and toasted again, this time to Darwin, who was a cause everyone could get behind, and all quaffed heartily. There were a few more toasts, the officers getting sillier, and I sat back, amused, and watched as the evening began to get sloppy. At one point, Ainslie and Heinrich joined elbows and sang a French drinking song, and then everyone joined in on the chorus, which was the repetition of "ooh la la" several times. I watched my husband clown with our friend. We could have been any couple enjoying a night on the beach. I dug my toes into the sand. The fire grew too hot, then began to wane.

Some of the junior men decided to put on a variety show. One with a prominent brow tied a shirt around his waist and pretended to be a Guayaquil prostitute, sashaying seductively and yelling out in mangled English. I was so starved for amusement that I found even these drunken talentless antics entertaining. Then three seamen improvised drums on a mop bucket and beat a tune while two others high-stepped. They quickly grew tired in the soft sand. There were two Negroes, and they sang a song together in tight harmony.

Ainslie put his hand on my back, which was cold, and rubbed a bit. I relaxed into him. He was thin and wiry from his work on the island, but there was a crook between his shoulder and neck that fit my head precisely.

One seaman took a piece of charcoal and penciled on a mustache that was clearly Hitler's. He ordered the other men around in pretend German that was actually fairly convincing (it does sound like sea lion bull barking), marching in circles. Another pulled his eyes in a slant and pranced like a monkey. I laughed, in spite of myself, but Ainslie's face was grim. I remembered that Elke and Heinrich were there too, watching, and shame stole my smile.

They should have gone home after that. They would have, had they not been intelligence officers. Anyone else would have known they were no longer wanted. And then none of what follows would have happened.

An ensign picked up a torch like the Statue of Liberty and said clearly, "We're sending the Rainbow after you, Kraut. Watch out for yellow, you yellow cowards! Take that!" He kicked sand at the two playactors.

Everyone stiffened. Perhaps if they had been less drunk they might have been able to disguise their reaction, but their fear was obvious. What had been flushed with drink and fire was now pale, blue in the firelight. I didn't understand what was wrong, but Ainslie quickly changed the subject, launching into a Cole Porter song that everyone knew the words to. He watched Elke and Heinrich, whose eyes were narrower, discerning. Elke missed nothing. She could not have missed the frisson that passed over the crowd. It was not just that he was threatening the supposed enemy—people had been doing that all night. This was something else. When the song ended, Ainslie nudged me. "The ball and chain is tired," he said. "We'll trek on back."

"Nonsense," said Thompson. "You can sleep on the ship. It's much more comfortable. Clean sheets, beds, a fan."

"Oh I don't think so," Ainslie said. "We should get back."

"I bet the missus would like to, wouldn't you, Frances?"

I would, actually, but I could feel Ainslie's anxiety, and though I didn't know its cause, I said, "We have to feed the chickens or they won't come home to roost and I'll never find tomorrow's eggs." Thinking that didn't sound serious enough, I added, "And who knows what will eat them if we're not there."

Elke must have known this was nonsense. Usually I jumped at the chance to spend the night in a semblance of a real bed. I watched as her eyes twitched slightly, moving from Ainslie to me and back to the officers, who were straightening their ties and fixing their belts. The awkwardness was palpable.

"Thank you for a lovely time," Ainslie said. "And for sharing your liquor. Does a body good sometimes, though tomorrow morning will be no picnic, ha!" He laughed. I could hear the tension in his voice.

We shook everyone's hand, and then Ainslie and I set off leisurely down the beach. He grabbed my hand, and I could feel his was moist. He clutched mine until it ached, but still he set a strolling pace, inviting me up the path before him with a chivalric flourish.

The second we were out of sight Ainslie spun around. "That fucking cretin just announced our strategy to the whole Third Reich. Hell, the entire Axis."

"But it doesn't mean anything," I said. "The Rainbow plan? It's like Pomegranate. It's just a nonsense word."

"If they know what it's called, they can start looking for references to it in Intel," Ainslie said. "I don't have time to explain. I'm going up to radio it in. Hopefully Thompson will too. You have to destroy their radio. Can you do that?"

He didn't wait for my answer. "Fuck. I'm going to court-martial that son of a bitch. I'm . . . Franny, run. Do it." He took off up the path. I tried to keep up but his legs were so much longer that by the time I reached the place where our trails diverged he was far ahead of me, out of sight.

I ran as quickly as my old legs would take me. I hoped I could find the radio again. I had only been there twice, and what if they had moved it? I don't know if it was the running or my nerves, but I felt light-headed. The path narrowed before me. And then it petered out altogether.

I stood for a second, hearing the pounding of my heart. The foliage was dense, denser than I remembered, which made sense as it had rained so much in the last month. The leaves took on menacing shapes, as they could do sometimes at night, casting pale amalgamated shadows that formed themselves into beasts that my brain told me did not live on the islands but that my heart worried about: tigers, ghosts, wolves. And a few things that did live on the islands: Germans.

I calmed my breath and thought about the day I followed the donkey. And then I let the more animal part of my brain take over. It remembered. The same mechanism that reminds a squirrel where it left its nuts, the same one that tells dogs that to the right is the veterinarian and to the left is the park. I could remember. I let my feet take me upward. Did I recognize that oddly shaped *lechoso* tree, the one whose branches formed an almost perfect sphere? Was that the flower that was more purple than any I'd seen on Floreana? I went around a tree and came up short. The radio was here the last time, I was sure of it. At least, I thought I was sure of it. But now it was night. I spun around several times, hoping that it would magically appear, but though there was a place where the underbrush was perhaps tamped down a bit more than the parts around it, there was no evidence of any radio, anywhere.

The clouds parted and the wan moon came out, illuminating the small clearing where I stood. I saw the glint of an animal track, hardly surprising, except that this was a dog's three-fingered paw mark. There was a patch of mud so the prints were rendered clearly. These paw prints went around in circles. The dog was waiting for someone, excited. Why would there be paw prints and not footprints? They stopped abruptly when the mud turned back into undergrowth. I pushed my way through a fence of bushes there and glimpsed another opening to my right. Struggling through, I saw the green box of the radio's case clearly. I had found it.

I breathed a sigh of relief until I remembered that my mission was only half done.

It's true that when faced with danger, adrenaline pumping, you can hear the blood rushing in your ears. I examined the box, wondering if a rock would do the trick of smashing it, or if I should attempt to open it and pull out some wires. But that would be obvious sabotage. Maybe there was a way to make it look like a natural malfunction, or enough of one to create a plausible doubt. In my rucksack I had a canteen. If I poured it in the right spot, it would certainly short the battery. I had the canteen out and poised to pour through the metal casing when I heard the crash of footsteps coming quickly, not bothering to be stealthy or quiet. I let the water splash onto the metal, waited for the hiss or spark of a short that never came, and then I turned around as the bushes parted and Elke emerged, breathless and red. She carried a shotgun.

I was still holding the canteen, the last few drops dripping guiltily from its lip. There was no talking my way out of this one. We paused and looked at each other. I saw no surprise on her face, and realized that she was as certain of our role on Floreana as we were of hers. There was nothing to say and no language to say it in. With the muzzle of the gun she motioned me up against a tree. I considered running, but then she would shoot me and perhaps go after Ainslie. If she were a career spy, and not just a Johnny-come-lately like me, she'd have training, both physical and mental. I had no doubt her aim would be true. I slowly stood up and inched backward to the tree.

Though she was still breathing heavily, the blood had drained from her face. Elke put one hand on the radio, as if to check if it was still breathing. She considered, then pulled a length of cord from her belt and tossed it at me.

I might have tied the trick knot I learned in Spy 101, but this was not a film or a radio play. I did as I was told and wrapped the cord around the tree, then around my ankles, knotting it and tugging so that Elke could see that I had really tied it. She set the gun down well out of reach and came behind me to tie my hands around the back of the trunk. I could smell her there, sweat mixed with fire smoke, and the maple-syrup scent. She was still panting. My breaths fell in with hers, both quickened with the rabbit-thumping of our hearts.

Finished, she went back and picked up the gun. She leaned over the radio, feeling around it, and then she pushed a latch underneath and the front folded down to reveal its controls. I could see that the water had pooled at the bottom. Had it done its job on the way down? Elke turned a knob. Nothing happened. No lit dials, no crack of static. The radio was indeed dead, though she gave it the traditional thump up its side as corporal punishment or encouragement. She wheeled more dials but there was nothing.

Elke grunted in anger. I had succeeded. I would have been happy about this, but it lessened my chances of survival. I recognized that I might have just given my life for my country, if it even helped my country. I didn't want Elke dead, just as I suspected she didn't want me dead. Our friendship might not have been real but the affection was. I didn't doubt that.

Instead of frightened or anxious, I felt sad, a dull sting in my chest. We were pawns of our governments, dying over rumors and plans with our silly little radios. We had struggled so much. For this?

I wonder if Elke was thinking the same thing. She stood and pointed the gun at me, far enough away that we didn't share the same air, and so that the bullet had a greater chance of lodging in me instead of passing through, but also near enough that her target was unmissable. She was aiming for my heart, I saw. My head would have been a more obvious death, but the heart was a more gentlemanly choice. She was granting me dignity even as she ended my time on earth. I was surprised to find that my thoughts were so logical. I was outside my body, a dove in a tree, observing these two strange creatures with their odd customs.

She pulled back the safety and I could see that her hands were trembling. I might have been able to talk her out of shooting me, maybe even pulling out the German I'd been steadily studying, but my mouth refused to obey my brain's suggestion. Perhaps I knew it would be for naught. It was difficult to swallow. I shrugged my shoulders to pull my head down into my torso as though I had a tortoiseshell that might protect me. I looked up at her eyes, which were red now, and wide, and then I looked at my feet. Next to my worn shoes a small bug crawled over a leaf I'd stepped on. He made his way down its main vein and then disappeared underneath it. I imagined it traveling upside down, its insect legs defying gravity, and I wondered when the shot would come. I shut my eyes tight, concentrating on screwing up my face, waiting for the report. After a moment, I looked up.

Elke had lowered the gun. Her free hand clenched. She met my eye for a brief moment, then turned and ran back through the brush in the direction of her house.

I slid down to the ground, exhausted. The tree I was tied to was uncomfortable; its trunk was knobby and bent. If I crossed my legs I could sit, though Elke had tied my hands too tightly and I had to move my wrists around to keep the circulation going. It was hard not to speculate what was going to happen. Was she leaving me here to die? If so, I should make some attempt to signal someone, though I had no idea how. Was she going to get Heinrich? I had no doubt that he would not suffer qualms about killing me. He had been through a war, after all. If that was the case, then I had maybe an hour before he returned. Perhaps Ainslie would find me in that time. But I doubted it. He wouldn't think to worry for a couple of hours, and by then it would be too late.

I considered that these were likely my last hours on earth, and a peculiar calm came over me. I didn't do anything maudlin, like review the choices I'd made in my life, or lament the things I hadn't accomplished, or regret those I did. Instead I thought about my parents, which I hadn't done in years. I could even conjure the smell of the apartment, the wet leaves surrounding me not unlike the wet laundry hanging from the beams. This naturally led me to think about Rosalie. I wondered where she was at that moment. Was she thinking about me too? She could go on for years, never knowing that I died.

A Darwin finch landed near me and sang once to his brethren. One finch. The finch that launched a thousand evolutionists. The specific finch that sparked the theory was lost to history, but that bird gave Darwin a theory which changed everything the world knew about science and God. I was that finch, trapped in a snare, lost to history. I hissed at it, and took pleasure in the fact that it flew away, startled. There. Let it fear humans in the future. We are a terrifying and awful species.

I don't know how much time passed. I began to grow very thirsty. The full moon started to sink and the bush around me grew quiet as the nocturnal animals retreated. Shadows grew longer and then night fell in earnest. I waited, still, a condemned man in the gallows. My wrists were aching and my feet were asleep. I considered trying to stand back up.

Something was approaching. As it got louder, I could tell it was human, moving with a regularity and purpose that no other mammal possessed. Here, then, was my executioner.

I expected Heinrich, sent by Elke to dispatch me, but she appeared again, her hair disheveled. Instead of a gun, she held a buck knife, already unsheathed. Had she steeled herself to the task, then? Had Heinrich insisted that she do the deed, or perhaps she didn't tell him she hadn't done it? Maybe, after consideration, she didn't want the troops to hear the sound of the shot, or I wasn't worth the bullet. I'd had time to resign myself to death, but the prospect of a knife terrified me. I went cold; I began to shake. Behind the tree I fingered my wedding ring, rubbing it. What would it feel like, the serrated blade on my throat?

Elke came closer; she smelled sour now. I trembled. Despite myself, tears began to stream down my face and I coughed. Elke stood behind me, and I hoped her slash across my throat would be deep and strong.

Instead she grabbed the cord around my wrists and began to saw at it. It dropped to the ground and the relief of being set free temporarily overwhelmed any question I might have as to why she was untying me. I rubbed the feeling back in, shrugged my shoulders and elbows. Then Elke stood in front and cut the cord around my ankles. I was still seated awkwardly, and she extended a hand to help me up. My feet were asleep and I stumbled. She held out her arm and I leaned on her.

I was still crying, with relief now at my reprieve. I wasn't even trying to figure out why I'd been set free. I was just glad I had been. "Thank you," I said. "Thank you so much. I don't know how—"

Elke shook her head. "*Nein*. This is never happen. This we are never talking about, Franzi."

"Never," I said. And until this day I haven't.

*

Ainslie was pacing the front of the house when I returned, just as the rosy fingers of dawn were creeping into our island. "Frances, oh thank God. What happened?" He grabbed me and hugged me. Then he held me at arm's length and hugged me again, so tightly it hurt my already abused shoulders.

"I did it," I said. "The radio is dead."

"What took so long?" he asked. "I was terrified for you."

"I—" I knew that Elke had said nothing to Heinrich. He would have insisted on my death. So I would say nothing to Ainslie. It was the least I could do. Secrets shared by women are sacred. They transcend the duties of country or marriage. I struggled to think of a lie. "I got lost on the way back." There, the simplest lie is always the most plausible, thank you, Spy 101. I had used more of my training in the past twelve hours than I had in the three years I'd been stationed here.

"We've only bought ourselves a few days, but that might just be enough," Ainslie said. "Frances, you might have saved thousands, hundreds of thousands of lives."

"Just glad I saved my own," I said.

*

A few days was all we needed. Word reached us two days later of the Japanese attack on Pearl Harbor. We moved to our old camp on the shore where we would have military protection. Boats were coming all the time now, and the beach looked like a busy port town with all the bustle. Ainslie was as excited as I've ever seen him.

My life immediately got a lot easier. There were plentiful canned goods, for one, and bread. My food-preparation time dwindled. I mostly just popped open some cans, or we invited ourselves to a mess on a ship.

I went up to check on the garden every day, as much to have something to do and to get out of the hullabaloo as by necessity. I couldn't let it go to seed just yet, not when I had spent so much time improving it, though I knew we were not likely to stay on Floreana. It was on one of these walks up that I ran into Elke. My face got hot with a surge of fear, as if she were still carrying the gun and I was still tied to the tree. She must have felt it too, because she looked at her shoes. The trail was narrow enough that our sleeves touched as we passed by. It affected me so much that once she was out of earshot I began to sob, not with sorrow but simply overwhelmed by emotion.

*

We had been living at the beach only a few days, when Ainslie followed me up to the house. "I want us to talk, and we can't do it down on the beach." He sat in the chair he'd carved and woven, and lit his pipe. His lighter had fluid and the pipe finally had tobacco. It reminded me of home, and I moved a bit more downwind so as to be able to absorb it fully, the sweet, civilized smell.

"I've my orders. They've decided to build the base on Baltra, you know, next to Santa Cruz."

I breathed a sigh of relief that we wouldn't have to endure construction. "Floreana not flat enough?" I asked.

"They want me in charge of intelligence on the base."

"That's terrific," I said. I had hoped this might happen, that we would get to stay on the islands. Though I didn't relish living on a base, I didn't want to go back to the States where I would have to get another boring office job. I was so used to living in the outdoors, how could I possibly adapt to city life, or even suburban life? I hadn't been in any kind of motorcar for several years. I was hyper-attuned to sounds, smells. I couldn't sleep without a breeze. And the things that seemed so onerous when I first arrived—keeping an airtight seal on anything I wanted to consume, growing whatever I wanted to eat—were now an elemental way to live.

Furthermore, I didn't want to get a job. I was done with teaching and fed up with being a secretary. Maybe I could get a higher job in the navy, but I doubted a desk job would suit me. I was spoiled for regular life, I realized.

"So when will we be going?" I asked.

"I leave on Wednesday," Ainslie said. He stared at his pipe, studying it intently to see what was wrong with it.

"What's today?"

"Friday."

"And when do I come?" I tried to catch his eye, but he was looking everywhere except at me.

"That's the thing . . . No civilians."

For a second I couldn't breathe. He was leaving me behind? "I can't stay here by myself."

"No," Ainslie agreed. Finally he looked at me, and I could see the squint in his eye that meant he was not enjoying what he had to tell me. "They'll take you back."

"What?" I asked. "What do you mean? Back to Guayaquil? That armpit?"

"Back to the States," Ainslie said. "There's a war on. You need to be at home."

"No." I stood up and shook my head. "I'm not going back there to sit the war out like a good little girl. You can't do that to me."

"If you're here you're a liability, you're a foreign national. Ecuador doesn't want you here. You're trouble to them."

"I'm the least amount of trouble of anyone on this island!" My argument wasn't making sense. "I can't go back there."

Ainslie put down his pipe, a sign that he took this seriously. He took my hands in his. "I don't want you to go, but we have orders. A base is no place for a woman."

"The kitchen will need supervision."

"And the messmen will do that. There'll be hundreds of men."

I hung my head. I knew that he was right, and that arguing further was futile. Instead I began to fling our kitchenware to the ground, all the pots and silverware and cups and plates. I threw the sliver of mirror angrily, and tried to turn over the table but wasn't strong enough. I tried again, but it was still stuck so I sat on the bed, spent.

Ainslie watched me from his chair.

"I don't want to leave. I love it here. I don't want to go back to the world and get a job and take the cable car and eat sandwiches and complain about the weather." Ainslie laughed. We'd long since ceased complaining about the weather. "And I don't want to leave you," I said softly.

He sat beside me on the bed, brushing my overlong bangs out of my face. "I don't want you to go."

He kissed me, and I stirred. But that's as far as it went. He pulled away. "But that's the way it is. This was never forever."

"I know," I said. But sometimes forever feels further away than other times.

It is amazing how long it takes to assemble a life, and how short a time it takes to dismantle it. What little I didn't break wasn't worth bringing back to the mainland, and Ainslie was going straight to Baltra to eat his three squares courtesy of Uncle Sam.

I took the pan that Elke had always admired, as well as a few other kitchen things (even castoffs were indispensable in the Galápagos) and walked the path to her house. The dog recognized me and came to smell my privates. Elke was waiting at the door.

"You heard I'm leaving," I said, by way of greeting.

"Yes," Elke said. "War is same as losing." She sounded more sad than bitter.

"Thank you," I said. "I never said thank you."

Elke waved at me in dismissal, and then held up her hand as if to say, Stop. She looked at the corner of the room. "You will like coffee?"

"I can't stay," I said. "I brought you these; better they go to use."

Elke took the pots and the bundle of kitchen knickknacks from my hands. She put them on her table.

"Will you go to Germany?" I asked.

She made a noise that was neither assent nor its opposite. There was more to her story. But I couldn't ask her, and she couldn't tell me. The chasm between us grew greater; the wisps of our friendship curled up into the air like cinders.

"Well," I said. "Goodbye. *Auf Wiedersehen.*"

"I do not think we meet again," she said. "It is a large world."

"Even large worlds have small islands," I responded. "I prefer to say 'See you.' You never know."

Elke reached for me and took me into her arms, hugging me tightly. It was a passionate hug, but brief. "We do not know," she said, dabbing her eyes. "*Auf Wiedersehen*, then. See you on other islands."

And I left my only friend on Floreana, who doubled as my worst enemy.

Part Four

CHAPTER FOURTEEN

How to describe the utter disconnect from my previous life? Every morning I toasted my store-bought bread, caught the cable car downtown, pressed together uncomfortably with strangers, took an elevator, also full of strange bodies, and punched a time clock, concerned if I arrived a minute or two late. I put the coffee on (the beans were already roasted and ground) and then I spent my day seated, answering the telephone and typing. When the intercom buzzed, I had to do whatever Childress asked me to do. And so I remembered wistfully my time in the Galápagos.

Living on my own, I rarely bothered to prepare a meal, but I still developed a bit of a paunch. I missed Ainslie. I missed Elke. At night I read books, mostly nineteenth-century adventure novels, and I dreamed, when I did manage to sleep amid all the city noise, of being on Black Beach. It was half a life.

But we were at war, and so many of us were living half-lives with husbands and sons away. San Francisco was full of sailors on leave or getting ready to ship out, and it was not a surprise to see someone with only one arm or crutching around on a stub. Still, San Francisco didn't feel the war privations as acutely as other places—our food was grown locally and there were lots of jobs building, riveting. If you stayed away from the military areas, and most of us had little business there, then it was life as usual, minus stockings, which were never that popular in San Francisco anyway.

Some weekends I would go for a walk in the hills near Mill Valley or Sausalito, taking the bus early Sunday morning and returning in time to get a good night's sleep before work the next day. I slept better those nights, exhausted from the exertion but also pacified by communing with nature. We were all biding our time until the war ended, and in that way I was no worse off than anyone else. At least I was no longer living in a rooming house.

I present for edification one of Ainslie's letters to me:

Dear Mrs. Elmer Ainslie Conway,

I am stuck on the rock. Literally, we are calling the island of Baltra "The Rock." Its resemblance to Alcatraz is intentional, for it is a jail. I suppose we should be grateful that we are not seeing any action (other than a misfired gun on the rifle range and a stepped-on toe). But believe me when I tell you that we are not seeing any action. It's a struggle to keep the boys from chewing off their own fingers in boredom.

About a week ago the boys caught a goat and wanted to raise it in camp as our own live navy mascot. That's against regulations, obviously, but I thought, what's the harm? And at the same time, I got a note from Supply saying the requisition of boots had gone way up and could I investigate what the boys were doing to them. So I do, and wouldn't you know they were leaving them outside the barracks to air out and pairs were disappearing. The boys all assumed it was a prank, but I put two on watch one night and sure enough the goat would escape its corral and grab a boot to munch on as an hors d'oeuvre. I have no idea how they digest a rubber sole or the metal eyelets. Scientists should study that. I feel like that information would be useful, from a scientific perspective. So I had to smooth the waters between the goat, the boys, and the brass.

There is a persistent rumor that iguanas grow back their tails immediately if they are cut off. No amount of education will dispel this rumor; every man must see it for himself. So we outlawed iguana-maiming. I am now known as the great iguana avenger.

This is the kind of thing I spend my time doing. That and missing you

and our beloved Floreana. I've heard no news from there—but if anything
exciting had happened, I would have heard, so rest easy.

I hope you dream in your favorite color,

Ainslie

So Ainslie was the dorm monitor in a fraternity. I worried that on an
island full of young men, he would surely get to know some of them well.
And perhaps even very well. I knew that he could never pursue that as
a lifestyle, though there were certainly bachelors who roomed together
to save money in San Francisco and no one was stupid enough to think
that frugality was the only reason. But Ainslie could not keep his security clearance if he was caught with another man, and I knew that it was
important to him. But what if he found a companion better suited to
him? What if he shared with this person his hopes and dreams, revealed
himself in a way he never did to me? I knew that I could live without
physical intimacy, but the idea of someone else having the emotional
connection to Ainslie that I so longed for made my elbows ache with
fear. I still hoped—no, *hope* is not the right word because it implies the
hoped-for thing is a possibility, and I knew it would never come to pass.
Hofen un haren machen klugeh far naren, my mother used to say, which
means something like "only idiots hope." Hope I did not have. But I
wished that Ainslie would come to me.

At night I dreamed he sailed down the runway in a prop plane, forgetting about me. I dreamed he was at the canteen and didn't recognize
me. I dreamed he died and I didn't know anyone at his funeral.

Ainslie came home on leave only once in those four years and I was
disappointed that he didn't have more time to spend with me. He was
home for six nights (after such a long journey!) and had to go to Carmel to brief the rear admiral on landing protocols or some such. He
brought a pressed passion flower with him that was sadly decollated by
the time it got to me, but I was still grateful he thought of it. The first
night we went to dinner and Ainslie drank quite a bit. I supposed he had

gone without for so long that I didn't begrudge him tying one on. That night, he kissed me good night and moved on top of me, making love to me quickly and soundlessly before dropping off into his characteristic drunken deep sleep. This left me confused, unsure what he was trying to communicate. That he hadn't been with other men? That he missed me? Did he consider this a duty he had to fulfill while on leave? Was he merely drunk? I was up most of the night, the bed spinning from alcohol, trying to parse his actions. But I couldn't ask him about it; there were things about which we never spoke, and I was too scared to destroy that equilibrium, especially when he was going away again so soon.

We spent the next day together in Golden Gate Park with a picnic and a walk through the Japanese Tea Garden, rechristened the Oriental Tea Garden. It had fallen into sad disrepair: empty pedestals for missing sculptures, holes where plants used to be, broken fences . . . That night, he said he wanted to go see some friends, and it was clear I wasn't invited. I had never met any of Ainslie's friends, did not even know their names. When he stumbled in at first light, I pretended to be asleep. In the morning, I decided not to be angry. We had so little time together. We ate breakfast at a small diner near our apartment, and Ainslie ordered everything he couldn't get on the Galápagos—sausage, gravy, pancakes—and we made small talk.

On the weekend, we went to Napa. It was lovely; the weather cooperated perfectly, and we returned home in good moods. Emptying his pockets before packing his affairs, I found a receipt for a hotel. He had arrived one night earlier than he told me and stayed at the Huntington. My heart sank with the surprise of a sudden fall. Who had he been with? Did he meet with someone in particular, or did he pick someone up off the street? I worried about the possibility of disease. Could men communicate disease to other men? I dismissed that line of thinking. What was there to do? I merely kissed him goodbye and shoved the knowledge down in my stomach where it hardened into a ball of doubt and frustration. I was relieved when he left. I was starting to get used to my bachelorettehood.

I was burning to talk about my feelings with someone, but there was no one in whom I could confide. Every time I saw Rosalie, the secret was like a belch threatening to erupt, yet I held my tongue. As for marriage troubles, I was certain she would be sympathetic, for she definitely had her own, if only I could share mine with her. And until I made that overture, she kept her feelings about Clarence from me.

Apart from this necessary distancing, Rosalie and I continued to spend time together, when she wasn't volunteering or lunching, which she did a great deal of. After Ainslie's visit she held a party to raise money for the Eastern European Jewish Refugee Association. The extent of the Nazi perfidy was finally becoming clear, and people were outraged. She insisted that I come, though I complained that I would be out of place among her synagogue friends. Nonsense, she replied, you have a husband in the war. In fact, she would make a special toast in my and Ainslie's honor. I had to beg her not to, the price of which was agreeing to attend.

I protested that I had nothing to wear, which is how I came to be wearing a dress of Barbara's (which was too big on me in the bust) at a party where I knew no one.

In the corner, a small man caught my eye. He was bearded and peering closely at the books on Rosalie's shelf. I happened to know that she had purchased them by the yard. He was studying the titles, pretending to look for a specific volume, like a professor at the library. In fact, he looked a little like a plump Sigmund Freud. Perhaps it was the glasses, which he wore in an antique style, perched on the end of his nose.

As I also had no one to talk to, I approached him. But then I didn't know what to say, so I stood beside him and pretended to look at the titles. He smelled of aftershave, though he had a full beard. He seemed unperturbed by my presence, and we stood there in silence.

Finally, I spoke. "Have you read much Hardy? I found *Jude* slow going, but then I grew to enjoy it."

"I'm not a supporter of Hardy," he said, with the hint of an accent. He still didn't look at me. "He's overly dramatic."

"Oh," I said, rebuked. There was a longer silence, and I tried to think of a way to excuse myself.

"But," he said finally, "I do like James, and he does not avoid emotion."

"I do too," I said. "But I never truly understand his characters. They are American, but in a way that seems foreign to me. I've never been to the East Coast."

Finally, he turned to me. Behind his spectacles, one eye was milky, the other a solid clear blue. "You should see New York."

"I've been elsewhere. I've been to Panama and the Galápagos Islands. I lived there, in fact." I'm not sure why I wanted to impress him.

He betrayed no reaction. I continued, babbling now. "I lived there before the war. They're islands off the coast of—"

"Ecuador," we said at the same time. "I know. Darwin's *Origin of Species*. There are many Germans there now, yes? It is in the papers."

"Oh that's just gossip. Mostly, it was solitary." I felt the need to defend the islands.

"That is the way of most places we live," he said. And finally there was the hint of a smile. It was warmer for having been reluctantly granted.

"Are you from Europe?" I asked.

"Czechoslovakia," he said. "Not especially a popular place right now for communists. Or Jews."

"Is anywhere?"

He shook his head. "I was fortunate. I have a connection to the university here. Berkeley. Many of my colleagues don't have that luxury."

"I'm sorry," I said. There was nothing else to say. I could have inquired about how many family members he lost, or how he snuck in around the quota, but it was a rude question for a party, and I didn't really want to know the answer.

"I've been friends with Rosalie since childhood," I said.

He said nothing. We had turned now to look at the party, jolly around us with finally released energy. We were so separate we were not in the room; we were watching it happen on a movie screen. His elbow brushed my sleeve.

Rosalie saw us standing there and came over, taking my hands. "You have to come help me over here," she said, flimsily. "Can I steal her away from you, Mr. Hradistsky?"

When we were safely out of earshot, Rosalie said, "Ugh, he's like a puddle of something sticky. He's the colleague of a friend from the synagogue, so I invite him to things, but he's so morose. You don't think it's a language problem, do you? Can I introduce you to someone?"

When I looked around the room again, Mr. Hradistsky was gone, and I thought no more about him.

*

Now that the base on Baltra was up and running, I expected Ainslie home soon. The Office of Naval Intelligence was folded into the centralized Office of the Coordinator of Information, but my job changed very little. It appeared, though, that there was more to do on "The Rock." I received a letter from Ainslie saying that they wanted him to stay and help run it. He even got a promotion to commander. I was green with envy when I read his letter, which was completely devoid of any sympathy for me alone at home and expressed the most generic sentiments of missing me. I crumpled the letter up, then, embarrassed, smoothed it out. I put it with Ainslie's other letters in the desk drawer and stood at the kitchen window, looking out over the tops of buildings at the tiny sliver of the bay that was visible from my apartment. It was my apartment, I thought. Not Ainslie's at all. He'd been there a handful of nights.

Why did I even still live in San Francisco? What was here for me? What was there for me anywhere? I had no roots, no children, no family, and my husband was not really my husband. Thus encloaked in self-pity, I decided to go for a walk.

When I returned the mail had arrived and there was an invitation from Rosalie to dinner that Friday. She already knew I would accept; I would have no other plans. I reflected on how lonely I'd be if I hadn't run into Rosalie. What role chance plays in our lives, I mused. And then I ate a peanut butter sandwich for dinner and read a book until I fell asleep.

*

At dinner on Friday, Mr. Hradistsky was there, along with four couples. "Sorry," Rosalie whispered. "Clarence's friend wanted to bring him, and the numbers were off anyway. I put you on my right so you don't have to talk to him all night."

If he recognized me, he gave no sign, extending his hand for me to shake and telling me to call him Joseph. He was kind enough to pull my chair back for me. "Miss Conway," he said.

"Mrs. Conway," Rosalie corrected him.

As it turned out, we had much to talk about, and Rosalie was engaged in conversation to her left, where she was adamantly arguing that the American Jewish Congress's moderate approach would do nothing.

"Rabbi Silver was right," she said. "Palestine is historically ours. We need to take it back, not wait for some committee to vote about it." I was surprised that she had such a vehement and informed opinion.

"I want to move to Palestine," Mr. Hradistsky said. I could see his eyes alight; finally a subject about which he showed passion. "But I'm troubled. What if our utopia is not all we hope it will be?"

"Utopias are better in theory than in practice, I've found," I said. "But this has been a Zionist dream for so long."

"I don't like it here," he said. "I'm sorry." He took a sip of wine. "I don't mean to insult you. This country took me in, and I am alive and for that I give thanks. But I can't feel at home here, do you understand?"

"I think I do," I said. I watched him drain his glass. He had surprisingly small, feminine hands. "Well? Will you go, to Palestine? After the war?"

"Perhaps." He shrugged.

He looked so sad. I wanted to comfort him somehow. So I put my hand on his and gave a small squeeze.

*

About a month later, I was sitting in a luncheonette waiting for Rosalie. She had maintained her childhood habit of never being anywhere on time. I had only one hour to eat, which she knew. After about fifteen minutes, I ordered a chicken salad sandwich and a cup of coffee. The bread wasn't toasted. I sent it back and at that moment, I saw Mr. Hradistsky sit down at the counter.

I debated whether or not I should get his attention. I knew Rosalie disliked him, but I felt warmly toward him. On the other hand, he was a bit of a wet smack. If I wanted to return to work without having my good humor dashed against the rocks, I would do well to keep my nose in my book. Did I really want to discuss Zionism before one in the afternoon?

I reread the page I'd just finished, and I became aware of a presence next to me.

"Mrs. Conway."

"Mr. Hradistsky, how nice to see you!" I might have overcompensated, sounding too happy. He was wearing the same tweed suit I'd seen him in the previous times I'd met him, and his glasses were smudged. The milky eye stared at me unfocused.

"I came downtown," he said. "I have a visa matter to attend to."

"Oh," I said. "Won't you join me?" I cursed myself. I'd uttered this statement without thinking. Rosalie was bound to show up soon, and what would she think? And then I thought to myself, Who cares what she thinks?

He considered, sighed, and sat down heavily as though he'd been carrying a bushel of rice up a long hill. "Have you ordered?" he asked. I nodded. He motioned to the waitress. "I will have whatever she is eating."

"That's a lot of trust," I said. "I don't keep kosher."

"Obviously," he said.

"I mean, I might have ordered pork. Or bacon and cheese on a burger."

"But you probably did not."

"I didn't." I smiled. He did too. His teeth were very straight.

He set his hat down on the empty chair and there was a silence. Had we already run out of things to talk about?

He began to speak about his work, which had to do with the process of how governments can affect and effect the recovery from economic slumps. He spoke to me as to a fellow economist, using terms I didn't understand and referring to philosophies whose authors I was not familiar with. In the middle, our sandwiches arrived. He made no move to eat his. I was hungry, and my lunch hour was escaping, so I added a bit of mustard and took a bite. Undaunted, he continued with bond purchasing, interest rate adjustment, federal reserves . . . before long I had finished, and he had yet to take a bite. When he finally finished expounding his own theory about how the United States might avoid another depression, he stopped talking and attacked his food. Three bites later and both halves of the sandwich were consumed.

He sucked his teeth and reached for a toothpick from the dispenser. I expected him to start picking right there, at the table, but he shielded his mouth and only spelunked for one particularly offensive particle. "Well?" he asked.

I smiled politely.

"What do you think?"

"About . . . ?" I asked.

"Hradistsky's theory."

"I don't know enough about economic theory to say anything other than it sounds fully formed."

"And you?"

"Me?" I checked my watch. I had ten more minutes before I had to leave.

"What is your passion?"

"I—" No one had ever asked me that before. "Well, my husband and I are—"

"Not his passion. Yours." He leaned forward. The collar on his shirt was threadbare. He had a university appointment, so it must have been neglect and not poverty that made him use his clothing so hard.

"I loved living off the land, the solitary tilling of the garden, making do only with what there was."

"What else?" he asked.

I saw Rosalie approaching. She was carrying a shopping bag, out of breath and a bit sweaty from hurrying. "Fanny, I'm so sorry, I got—oh, hello, Mr. Hradistsky."

He stood and picked up his hat. "Hello, Mrs. Fischer. I was just leaving. Mrs. Conway and I ran into each other. Two souls having lonely lunches. I'm sure we'll see each other soon. Goodbye, both of you."

"If he is not the queerest man I've ever met, I don't know who is." Rosalie sat down. His question was still resonating within me, even as I agreed with Rosalie that they came no queerer.

"I'm starving," Rosalie said. "What did you eat?"

"Chicken salad, but Rosie, I have to go."

"No!" Rosalie protested. "We were to have lunch!"

"I only have an hour," I said. "I'm sorry."

Rosalie sighed. "It's my fault. I just lost track of time. Why are mornings so short and afternoons so long?"

I debated informing her that when you work an eight-hour day with an hour for lunch, the mornings and afternoons are of equal length.

Rosalie's spoiledness was still a bone of contention in our relationship, but part of her brattiness was affected. These were the roles we played. She was flighty and irresponsible; I was irascible and serious. She was forever late to everything; I was always five minutes early. But Rosalie was more my sister than my actual siblings, and we don't get to choose our sisters. We can't even let their personality differences annoy us too much—they are a part of us. And so Rosalie's behavior, which I would not have tolerated in anyone else, I simply accepted. I believe she felt the same way. I know that my routines, my inflexibility, my refusal to pay attention to my clothes and hair infuriated her, and yet she accepted this in me. I found this very comforting. There was nothing I could do that would ever make her hate me.

I got up to pay the tab at the cashier. "Here," Rosalie said, handing me money, "you don't have to pay for Hradistsky. It's my fault you know him. And I stood you up, so take this."

I ignored her proffered cash and bent to kiss her on the cheek. "We'll meet next week for lunch," I said.

When I got to the cashier I was informed that Hradistsky had already paid both of our checks.

*

I was unused to the phone ringing, and it startled me. I was so shocked to hear the voice on the other end of the line that it took me a moment to figure out what Mr. Hradistsky was asking. Would I meet him for coffee?

"Why?" I asked.

"I don't know many people here. I sense that you do not either. We can practice human company together."

I had to laugh. His request would have been insulting if it weren't so earnest. I was about to decline, but I remembered that he had bought me lunch. I owed him at least a listen. And he was right; I could use the practice with human company. Besides my colleagues, I only ever saw Rosalie. "I have to work," I said.

"How about on your lunch break, at the same diner?" he pressed.

I could think of no excuse not to meet him. "All right."

We settled on the following day. I was surprised to find myself trying on various outfits that morning. Usually I threw on any old thing; the Galápagos had done away with whatever vanity I might have possessed. I didn't actually tie my sudden interest in things sartorial to my lunch appointment until I got on the bus and found that my shoes were pinching. And then I scolded myself, promised I would think no more of it, and spent the morning busy with work, pushing out any thoughts of lunch until the hour approached.

First, I want to make it clear that I wasn't looking for anything. I was married, and though my husband was absent, many husbands were, and it didn't give wives leave to go about in search of a replacement. And I didn't want anything. An affair seemed so complicated. Yes, Ainslie did have . . . assignations, but it was merely physical. I didn't have the same physical needs as he did, and if I felt lonely, it was because of the war. We all felt lonely.

Second, I was not attracted to Hradistsky. He was short, as I've said, and his clothes needed a good wash. His beard was unkempt and old-fashioned. No one wore facial hair anymore. He walked with a bit of a hunch, like life had beaten him down, which it probably had. In comparison to Ainslie . . . well, there was no comparing them. Apples and oranges. Plantains and guavas. Hradistsky merited no emotion other than pity.

When I arrived at the diner, exactly on time, he was already seated. He stood up when I came over and helped me scoot in my chair.

"Thank you for meeting me," he said. I opened the menu, though I knew it by heart.

Neither of us spoke. I pretended to read the menu until the waitress came over. I was here often enough that she knew me and nodded in recognition. "What can I get you?"

"I'll have coffee," I said.

"Not lunch?" Mr. Hradistsky said.

"Oh, are you ready to order?" I asked.

He nodded and showed his palm as if to say, You first.

"The usual?" the waitress asked.

"Tell them to toast the bread."

"I'll have the same," he said.

The waitress took our menus. "Be right back with coffee," she said. "Want some too?"

"I will have tea," Mr. Hradistsky said. A wave of superiority washed over me.

There was more silence. Finally, I said, "So, Mr. Hradistsky—"

"Joseph," he said, making the first letter sound like a Y. "Please call me Joseph."

"All right, Joseph," I mimicked his pronunciation. "What would you like to talk about?"

"Umm," he said. "Perhaps you could tell me about what it is like living on a desert island."

That I was glad to do. Sometimes the Galápagos seemed a dream, I wanted to speak of it, but there was no one to listen.

"Well," I said, "it's more like a tropical island. Deserted, not quite, and desert, yes, but not like sand. More like thick, tangled bramble." I spent a few minutes describing the *muyuyo* and palo santo trees and how difficult it was to cut through them. I also described Ainslie's struggles with the machete. "If I ever go back, I will be sure to bring a quality machete, and a whetstone."

"Will you? Go back?" he asked.

Our beverages arrived.

"I can't imagine so," I said. "But I would never have imagined we'd go there in the first place, so I wouldn't put any money on my imagination's abilities."

"You would like to return?"

I thought about it for a minute. It seemed so unlikely, I hadn't even entertained the concept. "Yes and no," I said. "But isn't that how most things are? How about you? Do you want to go back to Czechoslovakia?"

"Today we are talking about you."

"You do understand that's not how conversation works?" I said. "Usually humans ask each other questions in turns. It's what separates us from the lower species."

"I thought that was opposable thumbs."

He had made a joke, a feat of which I had thought him incapable. I laughed.

The coffee cup shook on its saucer, and the silverware began to jump around on the table. The salt and pepper shakers knocked together, and before I could wrap my mind around what was happening, I had been pulled onto the dirty floor under the table.

I had lived in San Francisco long enough that a small earthquake didn't scare me, especially after the big one of 1906, and it was likely that I would have stayed seated waiting for it to pass. Of course, Joseph was right to get under the table, but if one did that for every small tremor, we'd be living under tables.

I could hear his breathing and he reached for and clutched my hand tightly, though the tremor passed quickly. I felt a shock of electricity. He looked at me, his eyes searching, vulnerable. So this is how it starts, I thought. A heightened shared experience, a significant look.

I could choose now. And I thrilled to think I had a choice. I could make this happen, easily, this affair with this stilted man. Certainly Ainslie had done so. I didn't think he would begrudge me the same freedoms he enjoyed. Joseph belonged to my Rosalie life, a separate plane of existence, almost a different planet. Rosalie was San Francisco, was history, was the alternate story where I married within the faith and raised children.

The noise of the diner resumed, the nervous laughs of relief, the banging of dishes put back on the shelf or rattling as they were swept up from the floor. I heard the waitress yell, "Over easy!"

I couldn't think. I couldn't speak. Of their own accord my legs got me up out from under the table and I grabbed my purse and coat, running outside. If Joseph called my name, I didn't hear him.

Throughout that afternoon I had cotton in my ears. I could hear people, but only from far away. I told everyone I was rattled by the earthquake, which I'm sure no one believed. Finally Childress told me to go home a bit early and not to worry about the personal hours.

"That bad?" I asked.

"No, not at all," he said. "I just don't need you. No reason for you to sit here and push papers."

That bad.

I decided to walk home, to lose myself in the bustle of immigrant Chinatown, through my old neighborhood, the Fillmore, which had become the jazz district. I had thought all the nonsense of sex was behind me. And now someone wanted me, an experience I had rarely enjoyed. I wasn't sure how deep his interests lay, whether he was simply lonely and I was available, or if he really saw something in me that he wanted to be closer to.

I wanted to do this, I realized. I wanted to do this for myself. I had sacrificed so much, deprived myself of so many things for my country, for Ainslie. Now I wanted something for me. I wasn't particularly attracted to Joseph, but I was attracted to his attraction to me. Even on Ainslie's most attentive days, his mind was always racing elsewhere. And, if I had been honest with myself, I wanted Ainslie to know that I was capable of having an affair as well.

But was Joseph a good choice? First, I barely knew him, but I could see that all was not peaceful within him. Then there was the clear complication that Rosalie knew both of us. How could I explain to her that my marriage was not what it seemed?

And then there was the same argument that I'd used with Ainslie when I caught him with Victor. Infidelity meant that someone could blackmail you, someone had that dreaded leverage. Worse, you could volunteer your secrets. Better to stay distant.

I went back and forth. I'm sure no one ever agonized so rationally over an affair. And then I asked for a sign from above from a God I

didn't think I believed in. If that streetlight changed before I entered
the intersection, if that dog turned around three times . . .

I got home to find a letter from Ainslie, full of his jolly anecdotes that
would pass the censor. He closed with love and missing me, and while
I'm not sure if I believed that or not, I knew he meant it in his own way,
and I was comforted.

*

I avoided Rosalie's Shabbat dinners; I was worried I'd see Joseph there.
Instead, I went to the library and took out the classics that had comforted me in the past. I reread all of Austen, of Defoe, of Thackeray.
Then I read Tolstoy (that took a while). And then something curious
overtook me. I brought out my Galápagos diary and pen and paper and
began to set down our adventures as a book. I doubted that the government would let even a sanitized account be published, but it gave me
pleasure to pretend we were still there, to listen to sirens and imagine
braying donkeys, to hear horns and imagine birds, to be interrupted
by shouts and imagine sea lion bulls. It ended up being a rather funny
account, and in this way many weeks passed without me realizing that
they had. It was the best sort of distraction.

Rosalie continued to invite me out; she wouldn't take no for an
answer. She said I wasn't allowed to "wallow in the soup of sadness." But
I turned down luncheons, lectures, outings, lessons. Then it was Clarence's fiftieth birthday. Rosalie was planning quite a to-do, and would
not be put off by my excuses that I was working on a book. It was ridiculous to her that I would bother to write in my off-hours. I assumed
Joseph would be there. But who cared? We hid under the table during an
earthquake. Hardly news. I should have known by the way I overreacted
that I was indeed reacting to something.

I put on a dress that I knew Rosalie would dislike, a little act of rebellion. It was plum and waistless, more of a 1920s style than 1940s. The
1920s had been kinder to those built like me. I pinned my hair up mess-
ily, wore only lipstick as makeup. There was no buying new stockings, so
I went bare-legged.

It was a large party, noisy in Rosalie's high-ceilinged rooms. Waiters were passing Tom Collinses and so I took one. I knew various people vaguely, but they knew me to be a bit of a challenged conversationalist, and so they merely greeted me instead of coming over. I took a second Tom Collins.

Rosalie had a proprietary hand on Clarence's back. She was steering him around the party, pulling him away from the bores and making sure his glass was full. Did Rosalie love Clarence? She was unable to tease apart what he gave her—security, children, a nice life, servants—with how she might have felt about him. So she was content. And, like I had been our entire childhood, up to our abrupt rupture, I was jealous. Rosalie was beautiful; Rosalie was rich. She'd had a hard life, yes, but she was a fur seal: Water slid off her back as she glided through it, at home in sea and on land.

I stood apart as I tend to do at social events, a scientist observing the finches chattering at one another, flitting off to alight on other branches. I was the lone human observer. I felt this separation keenly, tragically. My glass empty, I plopped onto the sofa. And then here, of course, was Joseph.

"Are you all right?"

I bit my lips to avoid the tears that were welling.

He must have seen my distress. "Come," he said. "I'll take you home."

I could not have afforded a taxi, and I doubt that he had budgeted for one either, but we found one dropping off another couple and I mumbled my address. He saw me into the apartment and put on water for coffee. And then I took off my coat. I unzipped my dress and let it fall to the ground. He stood watching me. I pulled my slip over my head, unhooked my bra. I stepped out of my panties. All the while he stood at the sink. His expression was impossible to read. I steeled myself for rejection. For a moment I thought I'd had it all wrong, that I'd completely misread the cues. He turned around and I wanted to disappear off the planet, so intense was my humiliation.

He turned off the kettle and walked toward me, appraising me. He took my hands and brought them to his mouth, kissing them, and we fell into each other.

*

We continued to see each other in the weeks that followed. I was free of guilt. Joseph proved to be a skilled lover, attentive in a way he was not during conversations. He would come over, we had sexual relations, and he left. So different from Ainslie's chattering. He rarely spent the night, and when he did our conversations in the morning were like an old married couple's—the weather, the strength of the coffee, who should go down and get the newspaper.

The landlord lived on the bottom floor, and one day his wife knocked on my door just after I'd gotten home from work. She must have been waiting for me to arrive. I invited her in; she claimed she couldn't stay but a moment and stood in the hallway.

"This is delicate," she said. "I've seen a man, coming over, several times."

I wasn't going to help her out. I smiled.

"And sometimes I see him leaving. In the morning."

I continued to offer her nothing.

"It's just that, for the sake of the other tenants, families, you know . . . I thought you were married. Your husband was helping the war effort?"

"That's right," I said. "Ainslie's in the Pacific."

"Well, we appreciate his service, of course. So brave, but I'm just wondering who your visitor is, then."

I was taking a grim pleasure in her suffering, like a dog toying with a chicken he's caught. "You must be referring to my cousin Joseph. He was recently widowed, so he comes over and I make him dinner, the poor dear, and sometimes it gets late and he stays on the sofa. Not that it's any of your beeswax."

"Of course not," she said quickly. "I'm just making sure you're safe."

"I believe I'm safe enough with my cousin."

Red-faced, stammering, she left.

I laughed about this with Joseph. He was smoking in bed, a habit he shared with Ainslie that I abhorred.

"Well, cousin," he said. "Thank you for consoling me. And all the meals."

"Were you ever married, cousin?" We had never spoken about our lives. He knew I was married, saw the picture of Ainslie and me on the entry table, but he never asked about it. He never asked me about any-thing after that day at the luncheonette.

"I might still be," he said, "though I doubt it."

I looked at him.

"When I came here, I offered for her to come, but she said she didn't want to until I was settled. So I got settled, and then she said she needed a year. And then she said she didn't want to leave home. I was preparing to return when the war broke out."

"And . . . what happened to her?"

Joseph looked up at the ceiling as he shrugged. "Who knows?" he said. "There is no communication there." He rolled over to stub out his cigarette.

"How can you be so . . ." I trailed off.

"So?" he asked.

"Callous? Cavalier?"

"What is my choice? We were estranged before I left. At least we had no children. I hope for her sake she is alive and married elsewhere. More likely she is dead. But I do not expect to see her again in this life."

I lay back against the pillow, aghast. I pulled the covers up over me with a shiver. With whom was I sharing my bed?

*

"You're strange," Rosalie said, as we were getting our hair done on Satur-day afternoon. I was reading *The Woman in White* and Rosalie was read-ing *Woman's World* magazine while we sat under the silent dryers, waiting for our set hair to cool enough to remove the curlers.

"I don't know what you mean," I said.

"You're queer, somehow, cagey."

"And you're paranoid," I said.

"You know," she turned to me from the bubble of her dryer, "you never said what you do all day at work."

"You've never asked."

"Okay, fine, what do you do all day?"

"Mostly I answer phones, type letters, fill in budget reports."

"But for whom?"

"I told you, navy intelligence, which is not an oxymoron, despite the name." I looked across the salon at the clock, whose hands were moving slowly. Another ten minutes to dry.

"As in, spying?"

"Ha." I threw my head back, overselling it, perhaps, as the curlers bumped the dryer. "More like observations. Cargo ships, aircraft carriers, cruisers, what they see."

"And do you get any information from the Pacific?"

"Well, yes," I answered truthfully. My boring job had gotten even more boring, now that all the real intelligence was done in the central OSS office. "But mostly it's just in the form of data, so it's not particularly interesting. It's not like I'm decoding messages from the Japs or arranging prisoner-of-war exchanges."

Rosalie nodded. "Why is life never as glamorous as we imagine it?"

"So that there is a market for fantasy." I pointed at her magazine.

Rosalie returned to the page. I could tell something was brewing, though.

"Fanny?" she asked. "The magazine says that there are five signs that your man is straying, and, well, Clarence has some of those."

"Do you think?" I asked. Her eyes were wide and glistening.

"I don't know what to think. He goes down to Los Angeles every other week. He could be doing anything."

"What are the signs?" I asked.

She read: "'He's secretive about his plans, and he often comes home late.' True, but that was always the case. And he's not secretive, he's just not . . . communicative."

"That doesn't seem damning," I said. "What else?"

"'He seems distracted.' He does. I commented on it a couple of days ago at dinner. It's like he's physically present but his mind is somewhere else entirely."

"What did he say?" I was still unconcerned. One of the great advantages of living on the Galápagos was freedom from the women's rags, which were invented to make women feel incompetent and inferior, not to mention fearful and insecure.

"He said work was stressful."

"Hmm," I said.

"'There is an increase in presents, bought for no reason.' He brought home this brooch just last week saying it made him think of me!"

"Well, it is a rose," I said, "so it probably did make him think of you."

"But why was he in a jewelry store? Fan, this is bad."

"It's a women's magazine," I said. "It's not like it's for real."

"It's real enough for"—Rosalie searched for the byline—"Dr. Ellsworth Mercer."

"We both know that's a bunch of malarkey."

Rosalie continued reading. "'He's become more particular about the way he dresses.'"

"Well, that's not true," I said. "See?"

Rosalie continued. "'He's no longer intimate with you as before.'"

I looked at her. She looked down at her hands. The manicure was chipping—her standing appointment was for Monday morning. "It's been a while," she said. "You know how it is. I . . . I'm changing. I don't feel so much like . . . Wait, have I driven him away? Have I not given him what he needs so he has to go elsewhere?"

"I'm sure not," I said. Rosalie was breathing hard now, her eyes bright. "I'm sure that's just a stupid article and you're overreacting. What proof do you have that he's with someone else? He adores you!"

Rosalie let a few tears run down her cheeks. "It just feels like . . . something's changed."

"Of course something's changed," I said. "I mean, I haven't been married as long as you, but our relationship changes all the time. Of course it does. We grow, we change."

Rosalie began to weep softly into her handkerchief. I hadn't seen her cry in ages, not since I told her I was leaving for the Galápagos, and the sight upset me. I put out my hand to pat hers. I couldn't quite reach with the dryer's arms in the way.

"And, really, even if he is . . . going elsewhere . . . does it matter? Isn't it a bit of a relief?"

Rosalie jerked her head up, her eyes sharp. She opened her mouth to say something, but the hairdresser swooped in and the moment was lost.

*

"Why do men cheat?" I asked Joseph. We had settled into a routine, Tuesday and Thursday nights. Sometimes a matinee on Sunday.

"Why are you always asking me questions about all men?" he asked. "I'm not all men. I don't understand how they think. How they spend money, maybe—"

"But I mean, do you know married men who cheat?" I was married to a man who cheated and was cheating on him with a man who was married. But our circumstances were exceptional.

"Of course."

"You do?" I sat up on one elbow.

"Yes." He reached for a cigarette and lit it.

"Do you cheat?" I was worried.

"On you?" He blew out a ring of smoke. "You are the cheat, cousin."

"Right."

"Where is this coming from?"

"Rosalie and I were reading this women's magazine. I know, it's dreck, but it was talking about—"

"Oh, Clarence has a mistress."

The wind was knocked out of me. "What?"

"He has had this one in particular for a while. Usually they are less durable."

"I don't believe you," I said. I got out of bed to put on my robe.

"Believe me or don't, it doesn't change the fact. It makes very little economic sense." He reached down for his pants.

"Where? Who?"

"Some coat check girl. What does it matter? The Italians have a great word for it, what is it? . . . It means, how do you say, a side dish. You know, nothing serious. But it costs so much money. To keep her happy. To keep the wife happy. Pfft."

"I wish you hadn't told me," I said. "Now I have to keep it a secret from Rosalie." My stomach turned. I cinched the robe's belt tighter.

"You asked!" he said. "I don't understand you."

I was angry with him. "You don't even try!"

"And now you're mad at me. And now we're fighting?"

"I'm just tired," I said.

"Yes, well, you go to sleep and I'm going home." He finished dressing and left without kissing me good night.

I poured myself a small drink. I felt like I had when I found out about Ainslie, like the foundation of my life had crumbled without warning. Rosalie would be so hurt when she found out. Would she find out? Did I have to tell her?

I thought about it for a while. I had a second drink. No, I didn't have to tell her, I decided. I heard about it secondhand. Plus, I couldn't tell her how I found out. When she found out, and, because she was Rosalie I had no doubt she would, I would simply console her. I would hold her and tell her it was all right, and I would help her decide whether to leave or to stay.

She would stay. I understood. I stayed too.

Chapter Fifteen

It was easier to keep this secret from Rosalie than I thought it would be because finally, just as it seemed it would never do so, the war ended. The day Japan surrendered everyone took to the streets, shedding tears of gratitude, throwing confetti. I tried to leave a message for Joseph at his university housing, but those messages often got lost. I got a telegram from Ainslie that he was being sent home. He'd arrive in a week, more or less. This sent me into a flurry of activity without there being anything to do. I went to the market and got his favorite foods, which I knew he'd be missing after his long absence, and his favorite fancy cigarettes, but beyond that, there was little else that needed tending to. I took the day off of work on Thursday, waited for him.

I cooked what he had always said was my "best" dish: lasagna. I debated whether or not to light candles. It was not a romantic homecoming, but candles did make the apartment look better. It dulled the assault of the blue flowered wallpaper in the kitchen. I was expecting him around dinnertime, but he was coming in on a ship, and it was hard to predict when he'd arrive. It was late, almost nine thirty, and I was rereading the same page of my book when I heard footsteps on the stairs, the heavy, hurried tread that could only be Ainslie.

He rang the doorbell. Of course he did; he had no key. I opened the door and there he was, my tall, handsome husband. Hair a little thinner, eyes still bright, smirk still on his mouth. He grabbed me and swung me around, kissing me on the cheek.

"Frances Conway, a sight for sore eyes," he said. "You look wonderful!"

His hug was welcome, tight and fond. Though I'd been intimate with another man for months, there was affection missing in Joseph's embrace. Ainslie was impulsive but genuine. Joseph was calculating, hidden.

He set me down and walked into the kitchen. "Smells terrific, wife of mine. Sorry I'm later than I thought. Spend a week with the boys at sea and then when it comes time to leave you want to have some pints!"

So he'd stopped off at a bar. I could tell by his walk that he wasn't drunk, so he had, in his hyper-social way, come straight home.

"Are you hungry?" I asked.

"Famished. Especially if you made lasagna." He sat down and poured himself some wine. "Ooh, candles, fancy."

"I did make lasagna."

"You know how to welcome a man home!" he said. And he ate my lasagna as though he hadn't eaten in days. "The food on the ship," he said. "It's like it's cooked by people who hate to eat!"

He asked what I'd been doing since he last saw me. I had so much to report, and yet nothing I could tell him. I mentioned Rosalie, but didn't say how much time I'd been spending with her, and I could not say Joseph's name. So I told a story about some people he knew at work, and we talked about them for a while.

"But that's so dull," I said. "Tell me about Baltra."

"I was stuck on a base in the middle of the ocean with a bunch of goon recruits. Once that place was built it was as boring as watching vines grow."

"Vines can grow quickly." I picked up our plates and brought them to the sink.

"What gives, Franny?" he asked. "You've hardly said two words since I'm back."

I didn't know how to answer him. Instead, to my humiliation and surprise, I burst into tears.

"What's wrong? Franny? What is it?" Ainslie's concern was real.

"I'm not sure, I'm sorry." I wiped my eyes with my apron. "I'm just, I guess I missed you, and now having you back is—"

"Overwhelming, I know. We'll have to get to know each other again.

Or know each other in the real world. It's like getting married all over again."

I smiled. It was nice to know he was nervous too.

"Are we still married?"

"This is a conversation we should have with a drink," he said. "Multiple drinks."

He brought the dishes to the counter and I washed them while Ainslie made us whiskeys. I had restocked the liquor cabinet when Joseph finished the bottle of whiskey.

Ainslie held it up. "Acquired the habit too then?" he asked. I didn't answer him. But I did take the glass and join him on our love seat.

"I didn't want to bring this up on my first night back, but . . . we have the opportunity to go back to the islands. Would you want to . . . do you . . . ?"

"But for what?"

Ainslie smirked, uncomfortable. "There's a rumor that Hitler escaped and has gone to live there. It's ridiculous, I know. But you've obviously heard about the Central Intelligence Agency. Well, it's creating some redundancies here at home, and they've asked me to take a post elsewhere."

"Elsewhere than San Francisco? Why didn't Childress mention this to me?"

Ainslie drained his glass. He was pouring another and not looking at me. "Clearance."

"Why am I always the last to know?" I drained my glass too, letting the liquor be the fire instead of my temper. I held it out to Ainslie and he obediently refilled it. I could hear the whining in my own voice. *I have a lover*, I wanted to shout. *I make decisions too. I have secrets. Someone wants me!*

"That's the government for you," Ainslie said. "I am obligated to go. I hope you'll come with me, Frances. I want you with me. I need you. I've been so lonely without you."

"Have you?" I asked. My voice was sharper than I meant it to be. "Have you been so lonely?"

Ainslie turned red and swirled the ice around in his glass. "You know how much I care about you, how much I enjoy your company. How much I love you. Even if I don't show it in certain ways." He downed his drink and came to kneel in front of me. He held my face, kissed me, and then let his hands slide lower to my breasts. Now that I'd been with Joseph, I could feel the lack of passion in his touch. He was doing his husbandly duty, nothing more.

"Let's not," I said. "Let's just not."

Ainslie sat back on his heels, below me, looking up.

"Can I think about it?" I asked. "Can we just live for a month or so and think about it?"

"Sure." Ainslie nodded. "Sure we can."

*

Over the next two weeks, Ainslie and I were the picture of domesticity. We went to our separate offices—Ainslie was reporting to the Federal Building, working for the Office of Strategic Services. I told Rosalie they'd given him a desk job.

He was home every night for supper. On weekends, we went for a sail around the bay, had seafood at a nice restaurant, hiked along the coast. We had fun, and there was even a night when the fog cleared enough to actually see the fireworks. The end of the war had brought a vitality to the population. All over, people were reuniting, falling back in love, celebrating the end of a four-year winter. And probably, many were as awkward as we were, having gotten used to living apart, trying now to build lives together. I imagined people as bubbles, the way sometimes two can stick together, then either become one or grow too big and pop.

Joseph knew that Ainslie was coming home. I knew he wasn't like that, but I had hoped he'd be a bit jealous. Not Joseph Hradistsky. He didn't even try to call me or see me. Finally, after two weeks, the longest we'd been apart since we'd started together, I called him. When he came to the extension I asked him to meet me for lunch.

We met at our usual diner, and I got there early. It was a cold day, and I was wrapping my hands around a cup of coffee when he walked in. He had trimmed his beard and he looked somehow simultaneously thinner and more robust. I was struck with desire for him and kissed him recklessly.

"What's this about?" he asked.

"Can we go to your apartment?" I asked. I'd never been there, never even asked to go. "I want to talk to you."

"All right," he said. He motioned to the waitress for the check. I called the office on the pay phone and said I had a headache and was taking the afternoon off. I had never done that before. The receptionist was worried rather than suspicious and said she hoped I'd feel better.

We hailed a taxi and rode over the Bay Bridge not speaking. Joseph lived in faculty housing, a row of identical buildings. His apartment was a tiny efficiency with a nice view of Berkeley Hills. I took it in for just a second before I stripped my clothes off, and we made love with a hurry that we hadn't felt before.

"So I don't have to ask you about how it is now that your husband's home," he said, afterward.

I turned my head. "I was going to tell you we couldn't see each other anymore," I said. "I didn't mean for this to happen."

"This, now? Or this any of this?" I had meant the two of us in bed now, but now that he said it, I might have meant much more.

"I'm actually happy with Ainslie," I said. "Except . . ." I searched Joseph's face for some sign of hurt or disappointment. If he felt any, he concealed it well. "How do you feel about it?"

Joseph shrugged. "I am not so good with how I feel. I will miss you, certainly. But you are married, and it was known from the beginning."

"So you won't fight to keep me."

"Fight? With whom? You are not mine to keep."

"And if I were?"

"If you were what? Unmarried? You're not."

"I could be," I said. "I could get a divorce. He would give me one."

Joseph sat up to light a cigarette. He said nothing.

"Joseph?"

"If you want to get a divorce, then get a divorce. It's none of my business."

"But it is your business," I said. I put my hand on his shoulder.

"I am telling you that it is not my business," he said. He spoke slowly and carefully. His back went rigid. My heart contracted as though a hand were squeezing it, and the edges of the room went blurry. I blinked rapidly.

"Okay," I said. I wanted to say something more. Something more elegant, a fine closing line, *Frankly, my dear, I don't give a damn*. But all that I produced was "Okay."

Joseph stood up and ran the shower and I understood that it was my cue to leave. I felt used. And cheap. And sorry for myself that no one loved me the way a woman deserves to be loved.

I waited for the Key train, weeping openly. A few people looked my way pityingly. I berated myself the entire way home. I had known it would end eventually, and I was the one who was married. And Joseph had told me countless times not to fall in love, that he found love a bad investment from an economic point of view. I knew that he had been hurt by his wife and then devastated by the war. I was aware that there were things I didn't know, things he didn't want to speak of. He had stories he wasn't telling me; he had hardened. I couldn't help but feel, though, that a different kind of woman, a different woman, might have cracked that exterior.

By the time I got home, Ainslie was making fried eggs for dinner and singing along to the radio. When he saw me he said only, "Poor puppy." He put the egg on my plate with a piece of toast and I stared at it, numb.

Then he led me to the bed, pulled back the covers, and sat me down. He removed my shoes and tucked me in.

*

I could have gotten a divorce. I could have refused to return to the Galápagos. But the same arguments that existed before I went the first time still applied. My job was boring; I had no friends except Rosalie. And her life was so different from mine. I was nothing like her other friends; we had a good time together, but it was impossible to imagine that we would be together except for our shared origins.

She invited Ainslie and me to Shabbat dinner each week, but there was no way we could go. I didn't even tell Ainslie. His off-color jokes, his merciless humor, were not right for a Sabbath dinner just after the war. Plus, what if Joseph were there? I didn't want to face him, and I especially did not want Joseph and Ainslie to see each other. Rosalie's world could not have accommodated Ainslie. He would have stuck out like a sore thumb. I couldn't ask him into this world. Nor would Rosalie's cohorts admit him. It was better just to keep them separate.

Seeing Rosalie reminded me too much of Joseph. I was shocked at how easy it was to distance myself. First, work was busy and I couldn't meet her for lunch. Then, Ainslie and I had plans for the cinema, to go to Muir Woods, to play tennis on the municipal courts. If she noticed anything, she said nothing. My knowledge of her husband's affairs made it hard to look at her. By keeping his secret, I was helping him betray her.

If it seems I was excusing the same behavior in myself that I was condemning in Clarence, that's because I was. I considered our situations so different. I honestly thought that Ainslie wouldn't care if I sought companionship outside our marriage. He had hinted so throughout our relationship. It wasn't as though I had fallen in love; it wasn't as though I would leave him.

Sometimes, though, in the darkest hour of the night, I knew my feelings for Joseph were more than affection, and sometimes I would let myself feel them. And would it have been different if he had wanted to be with me? Probably. I had two incomplete men, and only one wanted me. It would have to be enough.

*

Ainslie and I set November 1 as our day of departure. We had a little over a month to dismantle lives and prepare ourselves for the islands. This time, we knew what we were getting into. I bought us proper clothing, extra sneakers, quality hats, airtight containers, sheets and pillowcases, iron roofing, wire, a good shovel, the machete I dreamed about . . . When I gave Childress notice, he told me he'd already heard of our posting.

"Got the queer exile," he said, nodding. "I'd heard."

"I suppose it is a bit queer," I said. "But we've lived down there before. And the Germans are still there."

"Right," my boss said. "Got to keep an eye on those Germans. We'll miss you, Mrs. C."

*

Ainslie was out all night again. I willed myself to sleep, tried to tell myself not to worry. But worry wasn't what I felt. It was jealousy, that green-eyed monster. I scolded myself. I'd had my fun while he was gone. And now he could have his.

He must have gone straight to work, or maybe he skipped the day, because he arrived home around dinnertime the next evening, in good spirits, with marzipan, which he knew I liked. It was in the shapes of tropical fruits, glistening grapes, cherries, and bananas.

"Thanks," I said, as he pecked me on the cheek.

"Won't be much of this in the islands. Eat up. You got too thin the last time."

I had a flash of Elke's face as she turned to leave me tied up to the tree, the drawn veins across her forehead. I pushed the memory away. "Are they still there?" I asked.

"Who?" I spent so much time alone that sometimes I forgot that I needed to speak out loud if I wanted someone to hear me.

"Elke and Heinrich."

"Not sure. They were when I left, but they were making noises about going home. I think it was hard for them to be away."

"What would happen to them if they go home? What's it like in Germany?"

"Who knows, who cares," Ainslie said. "Why worry about them?"

"I worry about everything," I said. I paused. Was I really going to say this? "I worried about you last night."

"You needn't have," Ainslie said.

"Where were you?"

Ainslie sat down on our love seat and crossed his arms. "Franny, you don't want to do this."

"I do, actually," I said. "If we're going back to the islands I don't want us to have secrets. I'd rather know."

Ainslie spoke quietly. "I went to a bar."

"A bar where there are . . . people like you?" I asked.

He nodded.

"And did you meet someone?" I asked.

He nodded again.

"Someone in particular, or just someone?"

"Just someone. It's always just a someone."

I couldn't look at him. "And where did you go?"

"There are rooms upstairs from the bar."

"Oh," I said. Outside, the sky was the same gray color as the building across the street. I could see a woman at her sink, washing dishes. I could feel my rib cage expanding with the naked conversation, breaking open. I sat on my hands to hold myself together.

"I had a lover, while you were gone," I said, trying to wound him.

"Do you want to be with him?" he asked. "It's a him, I assume."

"Yes!" I said too quickly. "No, I don't want to be with him. And he doesn't want to be with me, so it's over, obviously."

Ainslie reached over and pulled my hand from under my leg. I let him hold it. "So it's us," he said.

I knew what he was asking. "It's us."

"You don't have to come to the Galápagos," he said. "I understand if you don't want to."

"I want to," I said. "I haven't had a moment of peace since I left."

*

I couldn't put Rosalie off forever. "Thank you, Melanie," she said when the maid had brought us coffee. "How is it now that Ainslie's home?"

"Fine," I said. "Good."

"Uh-huh . . . And what about Joseph?"

"I don't know what you—" I started.

Rosalie gave me the same censorious look she'd been giving me for more than forty years, nostrils wide, eyes narrowed.

"How did you know?"

Rosalie continued to give me that look. "Anyone who knows you, Fanny, would have known. It's like you came alive, like suddenly your skin looked glowy."

"Glowy?" I said.

"I wouldn't have thought it would be Joseph, but then, to each her own."

I couldn't speak. Tears sprang to my eyes.

"Oh, I'm so sorry," Rosalie said. "I didn't think it would hurt to speak about it. I thought it was just for fun, until Ainslie got back."

"It was," I said, shaking my head vigorously to dislodge the melancholy that had settled there. "And now it's over."

"Well, I won't invite him anymore if it makes you uncomfortable."

"That's okay," I said, dabbing my eyes. One of the good things about eschewing makeup is that it never runs during times of emotional indulgence. "We won't be around that much anyway. I think we're going back to the islands."

"No!" Rosalie said. "No, Frances, you can't!"

"We are," I said. "Ainslie got posted there again."

"Hasn't he aged out of the navy yet? The war just ended. Tell him to resign. Clarence will get him a job."

"I want to go too," I said. "I miss it. It was hard there but everything just felt much more . . . purposeful. What am I doing here?"

"The same thing we all are, Frances. Living."

I said nothing.

"I can't change your mind? Invite you to come live here with me?"

I shook my head.

"The children will miss you so much," she said. I doubted this was true. "You have to spend all your free time here before you leave. And you have to tell them. I refuse to be the bearer of this bad news." The lamps lit the room only dimly. Rosalie poured me some more coffee.

"That's plenty," I said.

"So," Rosalie said. The silences between us had grown long, full of all the things I couldn't say to her.

"Sew buttons," I said, which made her laugh.

"Frances, I want to talk to you about something," she said.

"Uh-oh, this sounds serious," I said.

Rosalie grimaced. "Well, there's no way to say it but to say it. Ainslie has been frequenting bars of . . . ill repute."

"Ill repute? Are you in a Western movie?"

"I don't know how else to say it. Bars that only serve men, but not gentlemen's clubs, do you know what I mean?"

Of course I did, but I didn't want to admit it. I shook my head.

"Bars that men go to in order to meet other men. For sex. There, I said it."

Because I am such a bad liar, I tried not to look at her. Instead, I stared into her fireplace, which needed sweeping. So much for all that household help. "It's not true. Who told you this?"

"Clarence's firm needs to hire detectives sometimes, and he wanted to try one out so we . . . we hired him."

"To follow Ainslie?" I said. I didn't believe her story.

"I wanted to know who he was, married to my best friend. I got the sense when we met that he was hiding something. And as it turns out, I'm right."

"You don't know that," I said. "That's a terrible accusation."

"I do, Fanny. It's not that hard to believe. But you knew. You had to know. I knew when I met him."

I had known. I had known and not known at the same time. I wanted not to know. How angry must Adam have been at Eve for destroying his ignorance. I was angry at myself, at my stupid blindness, at all my years of pining. But I took out that anger on the person in front of me.

"Clarence has a girlfriend," I said. "He's cheating on you too."

Rosalie didn't flinch. This was not news to her.

"It's filthy," I said. "How can you live with him?" But I knew. I knew how one could live with someone's dirty secret.

Now Rosalie was angry. Little bits of spittle stuck to the sides of her mouth. "I didn't judge you when you were with Hradistsky. I don't judge you now. But how dare you tell me what's acceptable and what's not in my own marriage!"

I wanted to tell her so badly. I wanted to explain that Ainslie and I got married so we could do a job and protect this country. "Your marriage was for money. You got married so you could eat. You're a whore dressed up in fancy clothes." I didn't know what had come over me. I had never in my life spewed so much vitriol.

"At least Clarence doesn't fuck men." I had never heard a woman use that word. It was coarse like sandpaper as it came through my ears and the shock made my jaw drop.

Rosalie recoiled, slapped out of her anger by an unseen hand, and she clamped a hand over her mouth like it didn't belong to her. "Frances, I'm so sorry." Rosalie stood up and grabbed my shoulders.

Half of me wanted to throw off her arms and half wanted to embrace her. I was angry, but I knew she was right. Plus, I had said something so hurtful. The old Frances would have stormed out of the house, nursed the grudge until I was in the grave. But I had grown brave in the Galápagos; I knew the braver thing would be to repair this relationship.

We spoke at the same time.

"I don't know—"

"I shouldn't—"

"I'm so sorry."

"I didn't mean it."

We hugged. I forgave her. For her betrayal forty years ago, for saying that about Ainslie, for her wealth and success.

We fell onto the sofa, still hugging and crying. I finished sobbing first, and we parted, both rubbing our eyes with handkerchiefs. Rosalie said, "I must look terrible."

She did have gobs of mascara leaving dirty footprints down her cheeks. "It'll wash," I said.

She stroked my hair. "I know about Clarence's girls. I've known since that day at the hairdresser, but I knew even before that. We have an agreement. He keeps it mostly quiet. Did Hradistsky tell you? I thought so."

"I didn't know about Ainslie when we got married, but I found out. I suppose we have an arrangement too. It's all right."

"But you'd want it differently?"

Fresh tears sprouted. "There's no use wanting."

"I'd had a hard life, and Clarence offered me a chance to rest. That's all I wanted. Just to relax."

"I understand, I do," I said.

"Ainslie doesn't like us," Rosalie said.

"Not really," I admitted.

"We're too Jewish?"

"Something like that."

Rosalie sighed. "Well, we'll just have to have girl time without him. Without them. Those stupid men. But why is he taking you back to the Galápagos now? Why are you going?"

"We liked it there."

"But the war's over."

"There's the base, and some other things that need taking care of."

Rosalie looked skeptical. "I don't think I'll ever forgive him for taking you away."

"He's not taking me anywhere, Rosie. I want to go."

"All right. I don't understand it, but all right. Go to your desert island. But we are *not* to be separated again. The second you move from the Galápagos or get back to the United States you must tell me immediately where you are. I will be here, so it's on you."

"I promise," I said.

"And if you need anything, you'll let me know somehow."

"I'll send smoke signals."

"Tell me it all. Tell me everything. I feel like there's been this distance."

So I told her all that didn't require intelligence clearance. I tried to explain how Ainslie and I loved each other, and that it was a love that was profound and binding, even if it wasn't typical. I told her I didn't understand his proclivities, but they were too strong a force to ignore. I described him dancing the tango in Panama and how beautiful I found him, how beautiful everyone found him. And then I told her of his kindness, how he worked on roads in Floreana knowing that we would probably never set foot on them again, how he believed in the perfection of things, or of trying to attain that perfection. And I told her I was happy with him, because I was, even if sometimes I felt rejected. Rosalie was a good listener.

Then she took her turn and told me about how poor she was in Los Angeles, how she would go out with men to get a good meal and if she spent the night they'd give her breakfast and cab fare. Clarence was one of these men, but different. He treated her like an equal, saw that she would be a good person to partner with, if that was the right word. And so she'd gone along with his religious "hooey." It wasn't so hard once you got in the rhythm of it. And she genuinely liked going to synagogue, to watch the heads turn to see her in her finery. She was so happy to have the children, even Sylvie, who was a mistake, it was true. Was I sad I never had any?

I thought about it. I was both sad and not sad. It never seemed to be a choice and so it was hard to regret.

Wasn't she worried about diseases? I asked, thinking of myself as well.

"He only goes with clean girls, and only when he's in L.A.," Rosalie said. "I asked him to make sure of that. Have you ever been with Ainslie?"

"A few times," I said. I hadn't spoken with anyone so frankly possibly ever. And it was so pleasant that I forgot about my life outside of Rosalie's house until the maid came in and said it was time for dinner.

I hadn't prepared anything for Ainslie and me, and the shops would be closed by the time I got home. Rosalie invited me to dine with them, and I called the apartment to tell Ainslie he should make himself an egg sandwich, but there was no answer. Let him worry, I thought. I worried often enough about him. Let the tables be turned for once.

We sat down at the table, minus Clarence, who was in Los Angeles. I broke the news to the children, who were no longer children. As I suspected, they were not exactly upset, though their faces did fall in disappointment.

"Can I come visit on vacation?" Sylvie asked.

"It's way too far," Barbara chided her. She was halfway through college at this point, going steady with a young man from the synagogue. Dan would be applying to Stanford in the fall.

Barbara said, "You'd hate it there. There's no ice cream because there's no refrigeration."

"Then it's not a vacation," Sylvie said. "Not without ice cream." She had inherited Clarence's sweet tooth and was getting a bit plump.

"You'll have to write us postcards," Dan said. "And we'll write you back and I'll tell you that I got into Stanford because my dad built a library or something."

"Or you could just do the work and get in on merit," Rosalie told him.

"I'll write," I said.

Barbara said, "Please be careful, Aunt Fanny."

"Of course," I said.

I lowered my head for the blessings over the wine and bread. I was back home in my parents' apartment, with its wet laundry and the sounds of children at once soothing and saddening. Yet I knew I was only borrowing this feeling, and that soon enough I was going back to the life I'd made, on an island far away.

*

I saw Joseph only one other time in my life, at a garden party in Berkeley in 1949. He looked the same. So he had not moved to Israel. I had imagined seeing him a thousand times, and now that it was happening I felt only fondness. I nodded and smiled; he did as well. Then I turned away to excuse myself from a conversation to go and speak to him, but he had disappeared. He is surely gone now, as is most everyone else I knew and loved. Yes, I loved him. I was able to deny it back then, but I see now that I was just protecting myself. I thought then that he was not in love with me, but now I wonder if he was making it easier for me to make a choice. There is a nobility in that. But maybe I'm just telling myself that to get over the wound that still festers.

After our confessions, Rosalie and I began to have fun again, giggling like schoolgirls at matinees or at a particularly bad exhibition at a local gallery. In contrast, Ainslie and I began to bicker. What I used to find charming and mildly exasperating I now found irritating. His habit of whistling constantly, his need to always have something in his mouth (a cigarette, a pipe). His responding to everything with a joke, which I used to find so jollying, now struck me as juvenile. I don't know what had come over me.

As I was packing up my desk, Childress asked if he could take me to lunch to say goodbye.

We went to the local steak house. This is where he took people he wanted to impress. I'd never eaten there before, though I'd been in to deliver messages and once to pick up steaks for some VIP who either didn't want to be seen in public or else just preferred eating in our windowless office. The restaurant was made dark by mahogany wood wainscoting and maroon velveteen wallpaper. The tables were lit with lamps masquerading as gaslights.

Childress had gotten even bigger with successive years, though I would have sworn that it wasn't possible. His shirts strained at the buttons; the banquette looked dwarfed in comparison to his shoulders. He ordered a scotch, so I had a martini, though I was not used to drinking during the day. It would be my last for a while, I reasoned. I ordered the prime rib with a baked potato. We made small talk while we waited for the food, and when it arrived we were occupied with the business of eating.

Childress's bites were as large as his person. I worried for a minute that he wouldn't be able to fit a particularly large piece into his mouth, and then, when he did, that he wouldn't be able to chew and swallow it, and I almost applauded when he managed.

"So, back to the old island, huh?" Childress asked me when his plate was clean.

"I liked it there," I said. "It was quiet. Don't underestimate the pleasure of no telephones."

"No." He laughed. "I would never underestimate that."

We made small talk for the rest of the meal. He ordered another scotch and I ordered a coffee.

"It's a shame," he said, then hid behind his drink.

"I'm sorry?" I asked. "A shame about what?"

"That whole business with Ainslie."

My toes went cold. "What do you mean?"

"Just that being forced out . . . I did what I could for you, because I like you."

My mouth went dry; it was wide open. I wasn't exactly sure what Childress meant, but I knew that we should not discuss it further.

"That's very kind of you," I said. "We appreciate everything you've done for us."

The rest of that afternoon I was in a state of unparalleled anxiety. The other receptionists in the office gave me a cake as a send-off, and the sugar coursed through my veins. I thought I might be having a heart attack, that's how quickly my heart was beating. I was tempted to telephone Ainslie, but there was nowhere private to talk, and what could be said over the phone? Finally it was five o'clock, and I stood in the bus the entire way home, willing it to go faster.

When I arrived home, Ainslie was out. I poured myself a drink to calm my nerves. And then I poured another. I looked at the level of the bottle. Throughout his entire four-year absence I had nursed three bottles with Joseph's help. Since Ainslie came home, I had purchased six bottles. And he was not solely to blame.

When Ainslie came in the door, his hands full of packages, I was more than tipsy.

"You have a lot to tell me," I said.

"I do?" He set down his packages. He moved with his typical grace.

"I had lunch with Childress today."

"How is the old so-and-so?" Ainslie said. He opened the refrigerator and took out some water. He liked his water cold, another preference to be altered on the islands. "He make you pick up the check?"

"He said he pulled strings to get us to the Galápagos. What did he mean by 'get us to the Galápagos'? I thought they were asking us to go."

Ainslie downed his water and washed the glass, placing it upside down next to the sink. He didn't look at me. "Ah, yes, well, there was some talk of me not being in the navy anymore."

"Civilian life? Were you going to discuss this with me?"

"It was, shall we say, not exactly voluntary, this potential retirement."

"Ainslie, stop being coy!" I raised my voice. I could hear its note of hysteria. "Just tell me."

"I was caught, all right? They set me up—it was like Newport all over again, sending in someone to make advances while I was on the Rock. And I got caught. I was due for a court-martial, dishonorable discharge at the minimum. I didn't know it was Childress who pulled the strings. I'm grateful. I would hate prison. Though Alcatraz wouldn't be much different from Baltra, I suppose."

"It would be a military prison," I said. "It wouldn't be Alcatraz."

"See, now, Frances, this is why I love you." Ainslie came over to me and put his arm around me. "Because that's what you choose to comment on, when you hear I almost ruined our lives. That I used a bad metaphor."

"You should have told me," I said. "You should have told me straight-away. Take your arm off me; I'm angry." I shrugged out of his embrace.

Ainslie stepped back. He noticed the empty glass on the table and went to the sideboard to begin to catch up. He poured me a good stiff one, then one for himself. And he got two ice cubes out of the icebox and dropped them in our drinks with a satisfying splash.

"I know," he said.

"You keep claiming we're a team, but you don't tell me anything."

Ainslie slumped down into a chair. "It's hard."

"I do a lot of hard things, Ainslie."

"I'm ashamed. I want to stop. I try to, but then I have a few drinks and I forget that I'm trying to stop. Or, I don't forget, but I just don't care that I'm trying." He was looking at his feet. His voice cracked. "Why is it like this?"

I sighed. "I don't know. But you have to try harder. And you have to tell me everything."

"I promise, Franny," he said. "I want to go back. I was happy they sent us. I think, when I'm there, there's no temptation. I can just be with you."

"I want to go back too," I said. "But I need to understand the circumstances."

"It's a punishment."

"It sounds like a lifeline. A dishonorable discharge? You'd be unemployable."

"That's what you're worried about?"

"Someone has to think of these things, because it's patently obvious that you never do. You only think about your—" I gestured at his crotch.

I could see a change come over Ainslie's face. His features hardened. "I'm the reason we went to the islands in the first place. You'd never have gone if it weren't for me. You'd still be pushing papers for Childress in the vault."

Always, I'd been afraid if I confronted someone they would leave me—end a friendship, a business relationship, a marriage. Now I had the upper hand, the leverage. I could decide to walk away. "How dare you!" I said. "You have lied to me from the beginning!" It felt good to scream.

"I didn't lie—" Ainslie replied.

"You did, by omission. You didn't tell me the truth."

"You lied to me too. I know what you think about people like me. You wouldn't have gone through with it."

"You tricked me. What else haven't you told me? What other secrets are you keeping 'for my own good'?"

"You really want to know? Don't ask, Franny, unless you're prepared to handle the answer." Ainslie marched to the liquor cabinet, angrily guzzled his drink, and poured another.

"I want to know," I said. I took the drink from his hand and drank it like he did, the sandpaper slide of it soothing. He refilled the glass.

"You don't want to know. You want to live on some enchanted island where German spies are your bosom buddies and the war is thousands of miles away." He gestured with the hand holding the drink and it sloshed over. "You want to know the secrets? You do?" He was challenging me now.

"I want to know it all."

Ainslie grew steely, his voice even and measured. "You never asked me what happened to Victor and Genevieve." He looked into my eyes, his face sharp like a lava rock. "He heard me, talking with Hancock. It was something . . . important. I saw him on the ship's ladder as I left. And then I had no choice."

My chest hollowed out. Ainslie was right. I said I wanted to know, but I didn't. If I thought about it, there was only one thing that could have logically happened to Genevieve and Victor. But because it was too painful to recognize, too scary, I had put it out of my little head.

But now I had to know the whole story. "How?"

"Knife. Lava pit."

I fell onto the sofa and looked at the stain on the carpet intently. Ainslie poured himself another drink, then brought me one. This time I sipped it, still staring vacantly.

"Did you love him?" I asked.

Ainslie laughed mirthlessly, a single honk of a syllable. He shook his head slowly. "For someone so smart, Franny—"

"You scare me," I whispered.

Ainslie shrugged.

*

I spent the night walking the city. It wasn't terribly safe, I suppose, but I had protection in my age and my scowl. First I wandered through Lafayette Park, so as to wind myself and drive any thoughts from my head, but that succeeded only in sobering me up, so I walked downhill. I was tempted to stop in at a bar, but I got as far as the doorway before I decided I didn't want more liquor. I didn't want to numb and obfuscate the way Ainslie did.

So now I knew: Ainslie was a murderer. He had killed during the Great War, but a soldier killing a soldier was a far different thing than murdering someone you knew. Someone you'd been intimate with.

I had wandered down to the docks, and there were soldiers all around me, in navy blues and army greens. I wanted to see one of the bars that Ainslie frequented, but I wasn't sure how to find it. I walked out on the pier and threw a large rock into the bay. It disappeared in the night but made a satisfying plunk as it splashed, hurrying down to the bottom.

I made my way back. As I passed an alley, I heard a noise and turned to look. Two men against a wall, pants pulled down, both facing the bricks. Like penguins, one pinning down the other, grunting. I looked away. I no longer found this disgusting. It was animal, nothing more, animal desire, and I could no more condemn Ainslie for it than I could condemn the burro for desiring a burro.

I searched myself for fear and found that it had gone now that I had the leverage over Ainslie that he was always talking about. I imagined him stabbing Victor, pushing him into a lava tube, and watching as the water swallowed him up, to be eaten by sharks or swept out to sea. I never heard Genevieve scream. Perhaps she went first. Duty. Desire. These abstract concepts that dictate our lives.

Later, after the sun rose, I would go back to the apartment and climb into bed next to Ainslie, who would sleepily put his arm around me. We would make our preparations, buy our supplies, book our passage. I would make him promise to never again let me learn things secondhand. We would live our dutiful, desiring lives.

Now, though, I was relieved; I'd been holding my breath and was finally able to exhale. It wasn't just leverage I had over Ainslie; it was understanding. Ainslie and I were laid bare. And beyond that, he had chosen me. I loved him. I knew him better than any other being, and he me. This was intimacy, the like of which I'd never known except with Rosalie, and even that relationship was fraught with secrets. We can know each other deeper than mere facts. We can love each other deeper than our actions.

Part Five

꙳

We spent two months on Baltra, Ainslie overseeing the dismantling of the base, giving away the building supplies. It made no sense to me—build a base and then allow residents to come cart away the supplies just when the war had ended. We'd had two world wars in thirty years; didn't anyone think we'd need the base? A lot of military decisions were made like this, I came to see. They made sense in the short term, were politically expedient and curried favor, but disregarded any long-term good or savings.

Ainslie carried a clipboard everywhere he went, and I have to say he looked handsome in his uniform. He created a list of raw materials and a priority list ranked by need of locals who wanted the wood and furniture. The distribution, though, was as chaotic as all things Ecuadorian. Even the best strategies falter under native execution.

The whole process was remarkably quick. There was a fully functional (albeit almost empty) base one day, and the next the buildings were reduced to mere foundations, the locals having carted everything off like ants at a picnic. I took a walk among the ruins—that's what they looked like, ruins. I've never been to Europe, but I assume this is what the remnants of Greek civilization look like, a blueprint of what once was. Nature, too, had already started to encroach on the site, with grass and small shrubs poking up through any slit in the concrete. Iguanas had reclaimed their territory. A dozen of them were crowding onto one cement block, each refusing to cede his perch to another. I took a long walk down the runway. This would be the flattest walk I'd take for as

long as we were on the islands. And the only one where I could walk
upright without fear of a branch or a thorn catching me.

The sun beat down, the heat shimmering in the distance. "I'm sorry,"
I whispered to no one, to myself. I think I meant it both ways: apology
and regret.

*

Floreana gossip had reached us on Baltra. When our acquaintance Leif
Jurgensen came to Baltra to collect building materials, he told us that
the Muellers had caught a ride on his fishing boat to Chatham. Apparently they thought that Alexandre's philosophy would help the German
war recovery. So that left only Elke and Heinrich and the Jiménezes.

Only the latter came to greet us at Post Office Bay. Gonzalo was effu-
sive in his handshake, Gansa squeezed me tightly, tearing up. She had
worried about me in the United States, a country at war. It was useless
explaining to her that although our country was very involved in the
war, the closest actual fighting was several thousand miles off the coast.
I think she imagined hand-to-hand combat in Philadelphia.

Gansa had given birth to two children in our absence, but both she
and her husband looked unchanged in the four years we'd been gone.
The children were perched placidly in baskets on Chuclu, who was still
trodding his stubborn path. He didn't look happy about having two
papooses strapped to his side, but then he never looked happy about
anything. I gave Gansa my congratulations, and told her I was sure I had
something for the children in my boxes, once I unpacked.

"How long are you staying?" Gonzalo asked.

I looked at Ainslie, but of course he hadn't understood the Spanish.
"Oh, a while," I answered breezily.

They apologized for not having their burro available to help us. We
assured them it was no problem—we had brought our own from Chatham, who liked us scarcely better than Chuclu. But he didn't have a
name.

Gonzalo waited patiently until the crew had loaded the burro into
the panga, much against its will, then stared it in the eyes once it had

arrived gratefully on land. The donkey stared back at him and let out noisy flatulence that made Gonzalo laugh like it had told him a hilarious joke. "His name is Pedo," he said. I looked it up later. Translation: fart.

I asked after Elke and Heinrich. I was nervous to see them. Their not appearing on the beach was not a good sign. But Gonzalo said that they had tired of boats and visitors during the war and now didn't come to the beach. I tried to imagine what they must be feeling, and failed.

We trekked up to our home and found it largely intact. Someone had obviously made use of the platforms and stuffed mattresses, and then the birds and rats had torn them apart. There were empty cans on what was left of the beds.

We gave up on the mattresses and slept on the floor in our bedrolls the first night. When we woke up the next morning, sipping our cold coffee from the flask I'd brought, Ainslie strategized bringing our belongings up from the beach. He would go down straightaway and check on poor Pedo, whom we had tied up to a tree for the evening. I was anxious, for what exactly, I didn't know, until Ainslie said, "Go see her."

"What?"

"You're obviously not going to be able to do anything else until you do, so go ahead."

"Who, Elke?"

Ainslie gave me a look that said, I'm no dummy.

"I'll go later. We'll get settled first."

"Go now, Frances."

I packed up a bit of water and some fruit leather and set off on the path toward Elke and Heinrich's house. My anxiety grew as I traveled. What was I worried about? That she would be cold? That she would be warm? That it would be awkward?

The dog greeted me first, wary, but then sniffing my crotch she recognized me and bounded back to the house to let Elke know that someone known was arriving.

Elke's hair had gone grayer in the time we'd been away, but otherwise she was her usual no-nonsense self. She was genuinely shocked to see me. Her jaw actually dropped, the way it does in cartoons, and she ran over, still holding the spoon she was stirring the pot on the stove with, hugging me and dripping liquid down my back.

"Franzi!" She kept saying my nickname and she alternately hugged me, drew back to look at me, and hugged me again.

From behind the house came a young woman in her late teens. "This is Brigitta," Elke said in Spanish. "Gitta. Her father sent her here for the war, *Gott sei Dank.*"

She had Elke's ruddy coloring, the same concentration of features in the middle of her face, the same open gaze. *"Wie geht es Ihnen?"*

"Es geht mir sehr gut," I said.

"I knew you understood German!" Elke said in triumph in her native language.

"A bit," I said. I considered telling her that I grew up speaking a version of it in my parents' house, and decided not to. Perhaps not all confidences needed to be shared.

Any worries I'd had about awkwardness were immediately banished. Heinrich greeted me warmly as well and asked after Ainslie. I said he was very well. They were anxious to show me the improvements they'd made in the house since I'd left—a new hearth, a bigger table, a second room for Gitta, a pipe that led the stream directly into their kitchen.

"Oh, das ist deiner!" Elke said, handing me a pot I'd given her.

"Keep it," I said. "It was a gift." I answered her in English, and this, then, was how we began to communicate, each in our own language, which seemed somehow fairer and more honest. I was committed to honesty now. It was my religion.

"And your brother?" I said to Gitta. Elke's eyes welled up and she walked out of the back of the house to the garden.

Gitta's eyes turned to the floor. "He was fighting on the Russian front and he didn't come home."

"Entschuldigung," I said. I had wanted to say "My condolences," but instead I had apologized as though it were my fault that he was dead. There was a silence.

Elke came back into the house with some lemons. She was sunny again. "I will make lemonade."

*

We settled back into life on Floreana, no spying necessary. "How are they justifying our pay?" I asked Ainslie.

"Dunno," he said. "That's the wonderful thing about government, no justification necessary. We're integral to maintaining postwar peace."

"Peace with blue-footed boobies?"

"Well, that quest for peace is what's keeping you in the style to which you are accustomed."

"Oh, what style!" I spread my arms out to indicate our hut. "The luxury."

"You wouldn't have it any other way."

"I would have it a bit differently, if I had my druthers. Plumbing would be nice, for instance. Perhaps some mail service."

"People can't even imagine what our life is like here, can they?" Ainslie asked.

It was around then that I went back to turning my diary into a book. Usually the entries were boring: "Garden, lunch of *camotes* and beans, cut wood, fed goat." "Hiked to lava flow, Ainslie trapped a boar." But I discovered that with a little embellishment, they were amusing. More amusing in the telling than in the living. There was interest in living like we did, and maybe we could earn a little money from publicity. We would need money. Even if we had escaped a discharge, Ainslie would be asked to retire at the first opportunity, of that I was sure.

So I busied myself in writing down all the things that happened (few though they were). I had always been told I had a flair for writing, and I was surprised at how much I enjoyed it. We had come prepared this time, so I had more leisure time, and I used it well.

Every few days I would go to Elke's or she would come over and we resumed our habit of dividing our grudge work. She was kind enough to give us plants to replenish our garden (they had been using it to grow manioc and roquette in our absence and let the other plants go to seed— she said it grew better with less shade than their garden had), so it was in decent shape.

We had agreed, tacitly, to wipe the slate clean. We had only one conversation about what happened, and it was full of metaphor, conducted in our new German-English habit. We were talking about our childhoods and I told her about a time, which actually happened, when a chicken had bitten me at Mrs. Keane's farm in Nebraska. I had never seen a live chicken before, and this one was beautiful, with multicolored feathers and a fluffy head that looked made for making pillows. It pecked its way near to me, and I held still so that I wouldn't scare it away. The underside of its beak was blue like a morning sky and before I thought about what I was doing, I put my hand out to touch it. The chicken struck first, pecking my hand two or three times before I could pull it away. Bright spots of blood appeared on my palm, and a searing pain caused me to cry out and jump up. When the housekeeper asked me what happened, I said I had been attacked, which provided no end of amusement. For months afterward the words "Attacked by a chicken!" could send the whole household into fits of hysteria.

Elke laughed, then turned serious. "Sometimes chickens attack," she said, "when they feel threat." We were no longer talking about chickens.

"I know," I said, forgiving her. "Chickens are just being chickens. I should not have stuck my hand near its beak."

"And still you love chicken."

I smiled. "I do," I said.

*

One day Ainslie came back to the house in a pitch of excitement.

"Franny, he's here. He might be here!"

"Who?"

"Guess! Wait, don't bother, you'll never get it."

"Okay," I said. "I won't guess."

"Hitler."

"You're right," I said, "I wouldn't have guessed that. Because he's dead."

"Ah, but is he?" Ainslie asked.

"Ainslie, that's completely ridiculous."

"Of course it is," he said. "But how much fun will we have while we look for him?"

Indeed, it was a total flurry of activity by the Ecuadorian military, the coast guard, and the U.S. Air Force. For three days I cooked nonstop for the fifty-odd men who were on our island, no small feat considering that it was all done on a one-fire hearth. The best I can say is that no one died from my cooking.

While looking for Hitler, who was obviously not on the island, the search party came across some human remains, bones bleached white from years in the sun. Who knows whose they were or how long they'd been in repose. A mutineer exiled on the island. An intrepid, doomed survivalist. I thought it might even be the famous baroness, but the bones belonged to a man. They buried them in a grave near Black Beach, but before they did I caught a glimpse of the bones, white and straight like pieces of a ruined picket fence.

It made me think again about dying on the island, being buried there and having no one know it. This kind of morbid thinking cheered me up, ironically. If life meant so little, then nothing I could do would have that much of an effect. That's why I've been able to stay silent about the war for so long. If I hadn't destroyed the radio, then perhaps the war would have turned out another way, but the world would still have continued in its inexorable path around the sun.

I think Ainslie made a friend among these soldiers, for he was out all night and I only saw him the next morning at breakfast. We didn't need the charade now of him pretending to have been searching through the night for a dictator who was not there. I knew what he was doing. I accepted it.

The soldiers were eventually satisfied that their wild-goose chase was going to produce no geese, and they left us to ourselves again. The quiet of the island was blissful after the assault of the army. We spent several days picking up after them—cigarette butts and pieces of paper, small parts of things in plastic and metal and wood that had come off of something or another that civilization had deemed necessary. We found handkerchiefs, socks, lighters, two dolls' heads, a belt buckle, a mayonnaise jar, a coat hanger. It took the island a year to recover from the boots and machete damage. But recover it did, for man is but a momentary annoyance, a fly on nature's back.

*

We spent two glorious years on Floreana, perhaps the best years of my life. I felt strong, secure. I was busy with activities that were central to life—growing food, cooking. I had good friends in Ainslie and Elke and Gitta. I missed Rosalie and her children, yes, but we wrote each other often. And I worked on my books.

I will give the navy this: They sent someone in person to tell us it was time to retire. The lieutenant wore his uniform on the long hike to our house, informed us briefly of his news, and left immediately. All intelligence agencies were to be incorporated into the new Central Intelligence Agency, eliminating Ainslie's position. According to the navy, Ainslie had developed a cough, and it was best if he was removed from active duty. (His supposed cough was part of our cover story before the war as well. Not much imagination in the navy.) It was the first and only time I ever saw Ainslie cry. He waited until the officer left, and then he got into bed and wept. There was no consoling him, though I tried, rubbing his back. Finally I got in his bed with him and held him until he stopped shaking. We spent the night like that, and the next morning we began to pack.

*

When I think about the time that came after, the time that is most recent, I find that it is just outside the grasp of my memory, like in the morning before sleep fully leaves your eyes. Could we have stayed without the navy's support? I suppose so. We had everything we needed to survive. But we were getting older, and if there's one thing the islands do not tolerate, it is the weakness of old age. Animals routinely leave their wounded and aged to die. Perhaps it was time to give up our Swiss Family Robinson existence and try to make a bit of money before we became too old to work.

I'll spare you the goodbye story. Everyone hugged. Everyone knew this time we would never see each other again. There were tears and promises, and a fond farewell look as the island receded into the horizon.

When I'm asked when I was happiest, as these group therapy sessions are always harping on (we old folks are prone to depression—no wonder, we're about to die, it's depressing), I always answer, "On Floreana." There is a strange serenity that comes with only having to worry about your basic needs. It makes me think that primitive man might have been better off than we are today. But that's a different discussion.

I became a teacher again and served a few more years. I was not the most inspirational educator, but I suppose there were worse. Ainslie found a job as a lecturer at the University of California, and we moved to the East Bay. It was nice being around students, all those young minds.

I saw Rosalie often. Ainslie and Clarence joined us occasionally and were generally on good behavior. I wouldn't say they ever got to be friends, but they were happy acquaintances. As we got older, Ainslie spent less time away from home. We avoided boats, beaches, and camping, as well as all islands. When we wanted to celebrate, we went into San Francisco. The joy of having someone else cook your meals never wears off. Never until the Chelonia Manor, that is.

Clarence had a heart attack in 1950. Ainslie walked Barbara down the aisle at her wedding the following year, and her daughter calls me Granny (Rosalie is Nana). Ainslie actually did develop a cough (is the navy psychic?) and got imperceptibly weaker and weaker each month until Rosalie finally asked if I needed help caring for him.

The question shocked me. Help caring for whom? But then I saw that he could no longer leave the house, that he had trouble bathing without my help, that he was winded just walking down the hall. I had been wearing glasses that had the landscape I wanted printed on the inside, and now someone had wiped them clear again.

Though we had our navy pensions and my teacher savings, full-time in-home nursing care was expensive. The day after I mentioned this to Rosalie a man appeared, a man who was like Ainslie in that way, saying he'd been hired to help out during the day. I called Rosalie to tell her she shouldn't have done that.

"It's not for you, Fanny, it's for me. I'm so sick of you telling me you can't go anywhere."

I didn't believe her and told her so.

"What else am I supposed to do with the money?" She sighed. "It's not really mine anyway. I just married it."

When Ainslie died, Rosalie moved me into her house, and I finally got a taste of the finer life. I would like to say that I enjoyed having a staff, but actually it just felt like someone was always hovering. By then I had my own mobility problems and my own nurse.

It had never occurred to me that I would outlive Ainslie, as he was so much younger. I suppose that for a bit of time I felt untethered to the earth, like I might be blown back into the ocean by a stiff breeze. But Rosalie buoyed me. She drove me crazy; we bickered constantly, but the way sisters do, harmlessly.

When she fell and broke her hip, her son, Dan, moved us both into the Hebrew Home for the Aged. "Is it 'aged' or 'age-*ed*'?" she asked the intake nurse.

The nurse smiled as though Rosalie were a babbling baby.

Maybe I do need an ear trumpet, I can't hear anything over the sounds of the ladies lunching, their shrill voices competing with each other, the clatter of silverware on plates. Rosalie is wheeled onstage to accept her award, and everyone stands up to applaud her.

"What did you do during the war, Frances?" Susie asks. It takes me a minute to understand what she's saying.

"Oh, I was a secretary."

"It must have been a fascinating time."

"That's one word for it," I say.

Susie laughs. "You and Rosalie have obviously been friends for a long time. You share the same emanations."

A long time. "Since we were eight years old."

Susie looks at me with admiration. "I bet you've got some stories to tell."

"You have no idea," I say.

*

Rosalie gets the front seat on the way home but wastes the experience by falling asleep immediately—I can tell by her head loll. I feel bad for the things I called Susie in my head. She's been incredibly nice to two old ladies. We drive through the wooded roads, the windows open for a cool breeze. "You'll tell me if you're cold, Frances?" Susie calls back.

"It feels lovely."

The air smells of pine and eucalyptus here, of mushrooms and sponge bark. I breathe in deeply.

We stop at the top of the circular driveway and Susie puts her hearse into park. "Nice ceremony," Susie says. "I wish Rosalie's children could have been there."

"Israel is a long way to come for a luncheon. And Dan is so busy with work."

"Hmm," Susie says companionably. She reminds me of Elke, tolerant of silence, even with a near stranger. She could be Elke's granddaughter, I think, if Gitta had moved to America and married. But even as I think it, I know it isn't possible.

They're all gone: Ainslie, Elke, Joseph, all the people I've loved who've loved me back in their own ways. Except for Rosalie, my sister, my albatross. And we will soon be gone too, bleached bones, grains of sand swept to sea as the tide goes out, carried by the Humboldt current to a cold country where everything is unfamiliar.

"Rosalie," I call. "Rosalie, wake up! Rosie!"

Rosalie opens her eyes. "Are we there, Frances?"

Frances and Ainslie Conway were real people who lived on the Galápagos Islands: Santiago (1937–1938), Floreana (1938–1941), and again on Santiago (1946–1950). Frances wrote two memoirs about their time there, *The Enchanted Islands* and *Return to the Island*, published in 1948 and 1952, respectively.

Frances's memoirs reveal little beyond her daily tribulations living on the islands and say nothing about any espionage activities, though the idea that they were spies has been suggested by others before me. I based the characters on Frances's and Ainslie's birth and death dates, and Frances's memoirs, which are dedicated to Rosaline Fisher. Everything else is pure invention.

Throughout, I tried to stay generally true to historical events (though I may have moved a sea voyage or two) except when they conflicted with the narrative (I am a novelist first, and a mediocre historian). President Roosevelt really did visit the Galápagos, and there was indeed a military base there during World War II.

The Galápagos Islands are an enchanted place, and their human history is fascinating. As Darwin put it, "this archipelago . . . seems to be a little world within itself."

The author wishes to thank the usual suspects:
Sheila and Jim Amend
Anthony Amend and Nicole Hynson
Adelman Cousins
Terra Chalberg
Ronit Wagman
Nan A. Talese
Dan Meyer
Carolyn Hessel
Margot Grover and Mark Bailie
Lynn and Steven Perkins
Francesca Segal
Irina Reyn
Nora Gomringer
The Delta Schmeltas: Sheri Joseph, Dika Lam, Lara JK Wilson, and Margo Rabb

The following Galapágueños (and honorary citizens) provided lodging and advice:
Kerrie Littlejohn
Magno Bennett
Ros Cameron
Claudio Cruz
Aura Cruz
Erika Wittmer
Linda Cayot
Dayna Goldfine

The following organizations provided support:

Hawthornden Castle International Retreat for Writers

Writers Omi at Ledig House

Paragraph Workspace for Writers

The Sami Rohr Prize for Jewish Literature

The Jewish Book Council

The Professional Staff Congress and the City University of
New York

Lynn Perkins, Jamie Chatel, and Vice Admiral Jim Perkins, USN
(Ret) provided expertise and research help.

Valuable information was obtained from John Woram's wonderful
website: www.galapagos.to as well as his fascinating book *Charles
Darwin Slept Here*, which I recommend highly to those who
want more information about the human history of the
Galápagos.

William Baehr of the Franklin D. Roosevelt Presidential Library
in Hyde Park, New York, and Melinda Hayes of the Hancock
Foundation Archive at the University of Southern California in
Los Angeles were very helpful, as were the resources at the New
York Public Library.

Other sources consulted include:

The Enchanted Islands by Ainslie and Frances Conway

Return to the Island by Ainslie and Frances Conway

Satan Came to Eden: A Survivor's Account of the "Galapagos Affair" by
Dore Stauch

Floreana: A Woman's Pilgrimage to the Galapagos by Margret Wittmer

The Galapagos Affair: Satan Came to Eden (film)

The private letters of Marilyn Hynson (1928–2015)

And thank you, Frances, for living and recording your remarkable experience.

A PLUME BOOK

WHY MANNERS MATTER

LUCINDA HOLDFORTH lives in Sydney, Australia, and is a speechwriter. Her first book, *True Pleasures: A Memoir of Women in Paris*, was published in 2004.

Praise for *Why Manners Matter*

"Lucinda Holdforth's delightful book is the best I have seen on this subject in many years. She sets herself the Herculean task of arguing for manners in a world that deems them unimportant. She is equally at ease with Rousseau and Rosa Parks, with the Bloomsbury Group and the Bible, with nineteenth-century etiquette books and second-century Hollywood. (She also makes reference to Castiglione's sixteenth-century *Book of the Courtier*, among my favorites in my own college days.) Rejecting the cant that good manners are some sort of right-wing conspiracy, Holdforth persuasively links good manners not only to good character but to the stability and the progress of the society itself. Not to pay attention to a book this thoughtful might even be considered unmannerly."
—Stephen L. Carter

"Ms. Holdforth came to praise manners—too hastily buried by self-absorbed baby boomers—and does so with both intellectual pull and zest. My hope is that legions of parents and teachers will ponder her lucid pages with an open mind and rediscover what is

really good about good manners. Don't miss this small but compelling book."

—P. M. Forni, author of
The Civility Solution: What to Do When People Are Rude

"Lucinda Holdforth offers a breezy and concise—yet also a seriously thoughtful—take on the perennial crisis of contemporary manners. Her refreshing down-under approach to the subject offers a new dimension, with its canny Australian's reappraisal of the tradition-driven approach many of us associate with British etiquette and the unnerving free-for-all that Americans often perceive when we look at the state of our own civil relations."

—Mark Caldwell, author of *A Short History of Rudeness* and
New York Night: The Mystique and Its History

"From the communal activities of ancient Greeks on the Acropolis, to Thomas Jefferson's view of the importance of manners on a young republic, to people who take calls on their cell phones while in a movie theater, Lucinda Holdforth holds forth on the true meaning of civilized conduct. *Why Manners Matter* will make you reconsider the etiquette of human behavior in fresh and revelatory ways. (Did you know that men originally shook hands to prove they had no weapons?) This is a smart, thoughtful book, filled with observations both unexpected and unforgettable."

—Joan Caraganis Jakobson, author of *And One More Thing . . .*
A Mother's Advice on Life, Love, and Lipstick

ALSO BY LUCINDA HOLDFORTH

True Pleasures:
A Memoir of Women in Paris

Why Manners Matter

What Confucius, Jefferson, and Jackie O Knew and You Should Too

Lucinda Holdforth

A PLUME BOOK

PLUME
Published by the Penguin Group
Penguin Group (USA) Inc., 375 Hudson Street, New York, New York 10014, USA • Penguin
Group (Canada), 90 Eglinton Avenue East, Suite 700, Toronto, Ontario M4P 2Y3, Canada
(a division of Pearson Canada Inc.) • Penguin Books Ltd., 80 Strand, London WC2R 0RL,
England • Penguin Ireland, 25 St. Stephen's Green, Dublin 2, Ireland (a division of Penguin
Books Ltd.) • Penguin Group (Australia), 250 Camberwell Road, Camberwell, Victoria 3124,
Australia (a division of Pearson Australia Group Pty. Ltd.) • Penguin Books India Pvt. Ltd.,
11 Community Centre, Panchsheel Park, New Delhi – 110 017, India • Penguin Group (NZ),
67 Apollo Drive, Rosedale, North Shore 0632, New Zealand (a division of Pearson New Zealand
Ltd.) • Penguin Books (South Africa) (Pty.) Ltd., 24 Sturdee Avenue, Rosebank, Johannesburg
2196, South Africa

Penguin Books Ltd, Registered Offices: 80 Strand, London WC2R 0RL, England

Published by Plume, a member of Penguin Group (USA) Inc. Previously published in Australia by
Random House Australia, and in the United States by Amy Einhorn Books.

First Plume Printing, March 2010
10 9 8 7 6 5 4 3 2 1

 REGISTERED TRADEMARK—MARCA REGISTRADA

The Library of Congress has catalogued the Amy Einhorn Books edition as follows:

Holdforth, Lucinda.
    Why manners matter : the case for civilized behavior in a barbarous world / Lucinda Holdforth.
        p.   cm.
    ISBN 978-0-399-15532-1 (hc.)
    ISBN 978-0-452-29586-5 (pbk.)
    1. Etiquette. I. Title.
    BJ1853.H67   2009   2008026142
    395—dc22

Printed in the United States of America
Original hardcover design by Michelle McMilian

To Syd Hickman

CONTENTS

Zilu asked what makes a gentleman. The Master said: Through self-cultivation, he achieves dignity.

Is that all?

Through self-cultivation he spreads his peace to his neighbours.

Is that all?

Through self-cultivation he spreads his peace to all the people.

Through self-cultivation to spread one's peace to all the people: even Yao and Shun could not have aimed for more.

—CONFUCIUS, *The Analects*

(from the translation by Simon Leys, 1997)

Why Manners Matter

INTRODUCTION

Perhaps it's wise to begin with a disclaimer.

When I told my mother that I was writing an essay on the subject of manners, I heard a long and intense silence down the phone followed by, "You. *You?* We sent you to that expensive school and all you learned was how to swear."

I then rang my friend Rachel, told her my plan and, in anticipation of indignant sympathy, mentioned my mother's dispiriting response. There was another long pause before Rachel's reply: "Well, you do say 'fuck' a lot."

As word got around, friends and acquaintances appeared at my apartment proffering etiquette books. At first I was flattered by their interest, but then it occurred to me that this might be a very polite way indeed to send a message.

This was all rather unnerving.

Arguing the case for manners——when not famous for possessing them——may seem like the literary equivalent of moving into a glass house and setting neat piles of stones outside with a sign inviting passersby to help themselves.

And that's just the start of the challenge.

"Good manners," observed the American author and philosopher Ralph Waldo Emerson, "are made up of petty sacrifices." This quaint notion no doubt appealed to his nineteenth-century audience; can you think of many aphorisms less likely to appeal to the modern mind?

We live in an era that is profoundly antithetical to the idea of sacrifice. Oh, in theory, in principle, in *public*, we are all in favor of manners, and agree wholeheartedly that there should be more of them——especially among other people.

But manners require a range of attributes that are deeply unfashionable today. Patience. Self control. Awareness of others. Deferral of self-gratification. A readiness to make those small Emersonian sacrifices. A preparedness to comply with rules that are less than ideal or may, in truth, seem rather silly.

And while we may appreciate that rare young fellow who holds out his elbow to little old ladies, queues placidly at the bank, turns off his phone in restaurants, abides uncomplainingly by the road rules and waits patiently for his colleagues to finish their sentences; while we may even admire him, as one delights at a glimpse of a shy rare bird, we are unlikely to

whisper in awe to ourselves: *There's a man whose destiny lies at the top!* An amplitude of manners, far from being to our young man's advantage, may well suggest to us that he lacks the ego-istic aggression necessary to win the Darwinian contest of modern life.

The irony is that once—not so very long ago—such fine behavior would have communicated to observers an aura of obvious strength. For a thousand years, good manners in Western civilization were regarded as the very emblem of so-cial and political authority. Etymology draws the link: the word *courtesy* takes its origins from the European court system, just as *chivalry* relates to the officer class that rode horses into battle. Indeed, manners were not only inculcated as a virtue, they were an active means to demonstrate superiority. That's why *noblesse* was rather inclined to *oblige.*

And, now that I think of it, there's still another problem.

This is a time of big and important words. Globalization and terrorism and fundamentalism and climate change. As Emerson reminds us, manners are just so, well, so petty. It's hard not to feel that there is something meager about arguing the case for cell phone etiquette when the planet is hotting up, the Middle East is imploding, terrorists plot our demise and much of Africa is starving. It's hard not to wonder if, among the grand and awe-inspiring issues of our day, manners must come a long way down the list.

And perhaps it's partly for this exact reason that I am interested in the humble and concrete topic of everyday civility. Manners are one of the few things each of us has under our own control. No slogans, no outsize goals, no unrealistic ambitions. An arena of life in which we can all effect some tangible if tiny benefit.

And yet, and yet . . .

Surely manners are much more than a minor phenomenon in daily life? After all, they reflect the values of the society from which they spring and they influence the direction that society will take. Manners matter, though not because they are an absolute good in themselves. Of course they are not. But they sit at the nexus of some of our most fundamental challenges.

Daily we wrestle with these human dilemmas: the choice between seizing our moment and waiting our turn; imposing our judgments and accepting the edicts of others; making a noise and holding our tongues; advancing our immediate interests and promoting the broader good. We are constantly making these fine and complex calibrations.

We must each of us discover: what do we owe ourselves and what do we owe the community in which we live and work and make our lives? How do we juggle this conundrum of self and society?

Manners are a civil mode of human interaction. They matter because they represent an optimal means to preserve our

4

own dignity and the dignity of others. So when we give way to others, when we keep our temper, when we help someone old or frail—these individual gestures, seemingly so small, add up to the not inconsiderable achievement of a civil society. Our small sacrifices amount to something big.

There are manners, and then there are *beautiful* manners. These don't merely preserve everyone's dignity; they actively enlarge the social space. Drawing the shy guest into wider conversation. Sending a thank-you note. Going the extra step to help a stranger wearily tugging their heavy bags. Beautiful manners expand the radius of human cooperation and potential. I think that's why witnessing a gracious gesture can unexpectedly fill us with joy.

Much has been said and written about manners in recent times. Lamentations for their decline. Exhortations to improve. Even handbooks on modern manners, many of which gamely attempt to guide us through the myriad new opportunities that the modern office, urban consolidation, sexual freedom, information technology and congested traffic have created for us to be incredibly uncivil to one another.

Such books may have value, but this is not one of them.

This essay explores the case for manners. It stems from a sense that each generation must defend civilized behavior against the human tendency to regress to barbarism. It tries to understand how manners connect us to things we cherish,

such as health, freedom, order, progress, community and authenticity. It seeks to illuminate how manners beneficially shape the ways we nurture our individual humanity, and how we construct and preserve our wider communities. I can't promise, however, that it will have the wit to answer the question posed by a canny four-year-old to her perplexed aunt: "But *why* can't we say 'fuck' at preschool?"

And it is offered with the hope that perhaps, if we were to take a positive interest in manners—if we were in a position to devote our attention to this subject beyond arguing about the basic rules or railing against those who break them—we might even find ourselves concerned with higher things. We might even, who knows, find ourselves engaged in a discussion about the true nature of citizenship and a democratic aesthetics of living.

Because if the idea of civilization matters at all, then so do manners. At least, such is the case I hope to make in the following pages.

I

Because man is an animal

I WAS TWENTY YEARS OLD when I first visited the Renaissance city of Florence. Like so many others before me, I felt an immediate affinity as I walked the streets. After the grandeur of Rome, small-scale Firenze seemed intimate, approachable. *Human.*

And somewhat surprisingly, for I am not a particular fan of sculpture, one moment above all others has stayed with me. One image, one experience, one sense-memory. It was when I visited the Accademia and tilted back my head to take in Michelangelo's statue of David: when my eyes rolled up seventeen marbled feet of perfection.

Completed in 1504, *David* embraces the most moving contradictions: young boy and virile adult; vulnerable nude and godlike figure; flesh-and-blood animal and magnificent

man; private contemplation and heroic action. To gaze at *David* is to apprehend what it means to be human, with all its fragility and soaring possibility.

Which was exactly Michelangelo's point.

Michelangelo and the other leaders of the Renaissance had internalized a big idea. Having rediscovered the glories of the ancient Greeks, they believed that not only were there more things on heaven and earth than the teachings of the all-dominant Catholic Church, but that man was capable of finding them out. Copernicus unveiled the golden revolutions of the sun. Leonardo imagined helicopters whirring through the air. Columbus climbed down from his sailing ship and stumbled onto America. Just as important, Gutenberg with his printing press found a way to disseminate this new learning to ordinary people.

The genius of the Renaissance was to assert that man was not a degraded shadow cowering in the eyes and image of God but an autonomous, questing, dauntless creature. Like Michelangelo's *David*.

So it may come as a surprise to discover that one of the key preoccupations of the Renaissance was farting.

It was in 1530 that Erasmus of Rotterdam, known forever after as Wise Erasmus, published his little book—really a booklet more than a book—called *De Civilitate Morum Puerilium*, or *On Civility Among Boys*. In it, Erasmus addressed his

advice on behavior to the flesh-and-blood equivalents of Michelangelo's marvelous boy. It was an instant and massive best seller. Twelve editions were printed in 1530 alone. For 150 years this handbook spread across Europe—translated into English in 1532 and reprinted in 1534, 1540 and 1554; German in 1536, French and Czech in 1537; Swedish in 1620; Dutch in 1660; and Finnish in 1670. Curious how late the Finns came to modern manners.

And to read this little book is still a pleasure, for it is sane and tolerant and funny and wise. I like to imagine Erasmus during his travels in Italy looking up at Michelangelo's *David*, that delicate and muscular hand, those marble curls, those ripples of thigh and rib and buttock, that tender penis. I like to think of him rubbing his chin and saying to himself, *Mmm, yes, very nice. But none of the lads I know match up to that marbled perfection. My boys are human, all too human.*

That is to say, still animals. For many of Erasmus's injunctions revolved around the management of bodily functions. He issued clear and uncomplicated guidelines for the civil young man:

FARTING: *Don't squeeze your buttocks to prevent the emission as it may injure your health, so if you must in company, cover with a discreet and well-timed cough.*

BAD BREATH: *Rinse your mouth out every morning.*

SNEEZING: *Turn away, and graciously accept a Bless You.*

YAWNING: *Cover your mouth and then make the Sign of the Cross.*

BELCHING: *Some people do it after every third word—this is disgusting.*

NOSE BLOWING: *Best to use a handkerchief, don't trumpet like an elephant, turn away, never wipe your nose on a sleeve, and if you must blow into your fingers resulting in some mucus hitting the dirt, for heaven's sake grind it in with your foot.*

This is a fine example of Renaissance humanism at its best. Civilization wasn't just about raising heroic buildings and making extraordinary scientific discoveries. The emphasis on manners was a way to embrace man's higher aspirations for a civilized life while simultaneously exerting control over his lowest animal functions.

One rarely likes to be reminded that one is an animal. But it must plainly be accepted that while Botox may have eliminated the wrinkle, no one, to my knowledge, has yet eradicated the burp. The tummy rumble. The snotty winter nose. The excruciating squelchy noises that occur during sex. Amazing: we are now capable of cloning our own body parts, but we haven't yet found a way to suppress the uncontrollable urge to cough during the dramatic pause in a play. Or to silence the echoing booms of a diarrhea attack in a thin-walled holiday

cottage shared with new friends you were once hoping to impress—but now hope never to see again.

In our modern world we confront a paradox. In certain circles the human body is increasingly looking like the product of a laboratory experiment conducted by a sexual deviant: ageless and lineless and unmarked and plumped up and thinned down and resculpted. Science is helping us to suppress nature. But even the most exquisite Hollywood specimen can never entirely overcome the bodily realities. As Montaigne, a French admirer of Erasmus, once observed, "Upon the highest throne in the world, we are seated, still, upon our arses . . ."

I thought longingly of Erasmus not long ago as I sat in the back of a cab while the driver hawked and sniffed and comprehensively, indeed luxuriantly, gargled his sputum before spitting a great gelatinous yellow gob sideways out his window onto the street. And I think of him regularly when I see teams of Australian cricketers or American baseball players issuing a seemingly endless stream of expectorant from their lips onto playing fields and ballparks—in front of thousands of admiring fans and a global TV audience.

Someone should inform those sportsmen that social injunctions against spitting are not a capricious imposition on their oral freedoms. They are not a cruel and arbitrary assault on baseball's romantic baccy-chewing traditions. They are a pragmatic issue of germ management.

I was reminded of this in a most alarming way last year when I visited my father in a public hospital. It was one of those brutalist 1950s buildings with long, ominous linoleum corridors. To add to the air of doom, my father's kidney ward was on the same floor as the psychiatric emergency unit. My brother and I emerged from the elevator to be met by a glassy-eyed man dressed in a hospital gown with bandages around his throat and wrists. Our carefully upbeat smiles faltered a little. But this was by no means the worst.

Along the corridors, at the elevator, near the nurses' station, was a series of signs reminding staff to be careful of hygiene and *wash your hands*. Above the sink was a sign with simple pictures showing the staff exactly how to do this. *Don't forget those thumbs!* appeared to be the message. And outside my father's ward was another sign, actively encouraging visitors to remind those forgetful nursing staff of their hygienic obligations. "Jesus," my brother said. We felt it was wise not to mention this apparent ignorance of basic cleanliness to our fragile patient lest it further delay his recovery.

If even professional nursing staff have to be reminded that hygiene is a good thing—and shown on the job how to perform this most basic task—no wonder athletes feel no obligation to swallow their spit.

Whenever we suppress a cough in public, cover our mouths when we sneeze, stay home from work if we are sick,

wash our hands before handling food, wear deodorant, bathe or shower regularly, eat with our mouths closed—when we do these things, we are not simply rehearsing mindless rituals.

We are doing nothing less than contributing to our own survival and that of the species.

. . . a social one

Of course, we are more than just any old animal: man is a social animal.

Human social life is, thankfully, more sophisticated than an ant colony or a beehive. We have progressed beyond assigning permanent, fixed roles to our members. We use our higher faculties to go beyond a mere eating and breeding program. We have learned how to ameliorate weakness and rectify unfairness.

But the simple reality is that each one of us relies upon the cooperation and collaboration of others for our survival. We need each other. Not just the people we know and rely upon for life's necessities, like our forbearing general medical practitioner or the chef at our favorite Thai restaurant. But even people we don't know, and definitely wouldn't like, including the fellow blasting the neighborhood with his leaf blower, or the driver who won't let you into her lane when you need to turn off at the next exit, or the marketing operative who calls to demand your opinion of his company's product just as you are finally sitting down to your first gin and tonic of the day.

Even when we don't want to answer the phone, we are all still connected.

Animals develop instinctive methods to do this. But we humans are forced to use our reason and our sense and our goodwill to figure out what works and what doesn't at each point in our history. There is an innate beauty in the workings of the animal world. We self-conscious creatures have to go a step further to make life beautiful.

Manners are neither authentic nor spontaneous. They are constructed and invented. Artificial. Made up. Like traffic lights. Air-traffic control regulations. Court procedures. Parliamentary rules. Football rules. They may be imperfect, but they are nevertheless a means to direct human traffic in an orderly fashion. They are about making things work.

And when we get it right, we really do make things better.

Not so long ago, I sat at dinner next to a clever man who works with computers. He described to me a future in which our appliances will form a sort of network to look after us— our fridge, phone, car, personal computer, air conditioner, TV and music system will all be in close touch, sorting things out, making things work. No, you can't ask me how.

I immediately began looking forward to the day when I won't have to feel inadequate because I am incapable of utilizing any more than 2 percent of the capacity of any of my appliances: when the future arrives my appliances will have

worked out how to be 100 percent useful to me all by themselves. I was even more amazed to discover that the way this will happen is by a sort of computerized version of manners.

It seems that the terminology of manners has been fully incorporated into all the digital technologies. The Internet is chock-full of *protocols*: standardized sets of rules governing the exchange of data between given devices. Programmers talk about *etiquette*. They even refer to *handshaking*. Alarming to think that our machines might wind up being more polite than our work colleagues. And of course, as systems evolve, so digital manners will evolve, as well. One day soon my car and my fridge will metaphorically bow to each other as they exchange information about the gaps in my food supply, what items should be automatically reordered from the supermarket for home delivery and what fresh items I need to buy on my way home.

Who would ever have thought computer programmers would be at the forefront of civilization? By the end of this conversation I had a delightful vision of a not-very-distant future in which manners might be integrated advantageously into all aspects of our lives.

But then I remembered dismally that overall we seem to be losing our gift for mutually beneficial interaction. Many of us find going out into the world so trying that it seems easier to avoid it altogether. It appears altogether less stressful to the

nervous system to stay at home where one can exert at least partial control over the environment.

And when we do leave home, driven by the overwhelming need to earn a living or go to the January sales or eat good Italian food, our apprehension about what we might encounter in the world proves to be negatively reinforcing. We put on our dark glasses and avoid eye contact. Increasingly we plug in our iPods: less for tuning into the music than tuning out the people around us. We talk or text on our cell phones constantly, on the train or bus, in the shops and cinemas, on the street. It's as if we deprive ourselves of immediate sensory stimulation—shade our eyes, block our ears, stop our mouths—in order to experience the world through a protective mask.

Finally, when with reluctant resignation we do interact with a stranger—with, say, a taxi driver or a coffee barista or a checkout person at the supermarket—we do it all with sign language and half sentences, often still talking on the phone to someone (anyone!) else as if to distract our attention away from the irritations inherent in any physical, material encounter with untested individuals. People we need, and upon whose goodwill we depend.

In our efforts to avoid all the latent rudeness and unpleasantness in the world, we, too, have become harder, and ruder, and less pleasant. Yet the more we distrust each other, the more we are confused and irritated by each other, the greater

the risk that we abandon the task of finding a common language with which to peacefully interact.

In my block of units there's a different but connected problem. We share the same building, we see each other regularly, we pass close by each other in the foyer and on the stairs. But because we don't have manners, we have no formula for successfully relating to each other. Living in the noisy hubbub of the city, each one of us wants to protect our privacy, especially at home. Me, too. I consider myself something of an urban hermit. I don't want to be friends with people purely because we live in close proximity. On the other hand, it's rather strange to pretend you have no knowledge of someone who lives across the hall.

So when we cross paths we all shift our eyes or mumble *Hi*—but it's awkward. No one wants to cross that dreaded threshold into cozy familiarity or, God forbid, mutual obligation. Here is where manners would come in handy. In a more mannered world we'd simply get the introductions over with, have a cup of tea and then return to pleasant but formal distance. *Good morning. Lovely day, isn't it?* we would say. But instead we scuff and shuffle and we're not sure whether to smile or not and the whole process is uncomfortable. The fear of overfamiliarity with our neighbors has led to an inability to relate to each other in any way at all.

Which is weird, because we all live very close together

indeed. The irony of our routine of nonrecognition is brought home to me every Friday night as I lie in bed with the breeze drifting through the window. That's when the circus nearby begins again.

It starts with a male falsetto. *How dare you!* Operatic intake of breath: *How daaaare you!*

And: *Don't you ever, ever say that to me again!*

Then, hoarsely: *Get out, get out, damn you!*

After an interval, sniveling: *Oh no, you're not going, are you? Don't leave me, don't leave me!*

Then later, *Oh, Robert, Robert!* in manly tones.

So much for privacy. If we all knew our manners, we could live with our neighbors more comfortably. We could know just enough about them, but not too much. People might think a mannered world sounds cold and lonely. But when you have no manners at all it becomes almost impossible to relate to people in a functional way. And that can be lonely, too.

We are proud individuals and we are social animals. Manners help us resolve our double identities.

. . . with a habitat to protect

Here's a funny coincidence: declining standards of civility and the looming crisis of global warming. At first glance, no two things could appear to be less connected. But let's tease out this extravagant thought and see where it leads.

As wealth increases and standards of civility decline, we know that more and more people are retreating from society and investing in their own private domains: the forecasters and marketers call this trend *cocooning*.

When the outside world seems difficult and unpleasant, family homes become essential domains for personal autonomy and a sense of *personal space*. In some households, the breakdown in civility extends even to interactions between family members. The parents then build a separate *parents' retreat* to get away from their children. The teenagers get their own private wing. By creating these disparate spaces, intergenerational incivilities can be avoided, except for the occasional gruff encounter at the fridge or, once in a while, the dinner table. Separate bathrooms are a must, to prevent the stresses of forming and managing a queue. And so houses get bigger and bigger for fewer people.

And now the family seeks to replicate privately the pleasures that once would have been sought communally. The private pool replaces the beach or public pool. The wide-screen TV obviates the discomforts of the cinema. Computers and games are installed so that the children can play variations on the cops-and-robbers games that they might once have played out on the streets with the other neighborhood kids. BBQ equipment and outdoor facilities eliminate the need to visit the local public park.

The family is increasingly preserved against society, instead of in concert with it.

To facilitate most of these pleasures the temperature needs to be constant—so air-conditioning is installed. This has the secondary benefit of blocking out the noise from the neighbors. And of course, all family members prefer to travel by car rather than by rail or bus. Preferably separate cars, as a matter of fact. And ideally, enormous fuel-consuming four-wheel-drive vehicles to insulate the occupants as far as possible from the hurly-burly of commuter traffic.

These measures not only contribute to the decline in communal living, they greatly expand each individual's environmental footprint.

Very rich people have additional choices at their disposal. Indeed, one of the great perceived advantages of prosperity in this modern era is the prospect of separating yourself from other people: to flee from the madding crowds with their ugly and importunate ways. Private yachts and planes provide an energy-inefficient bubble of personal comfort to transport the wealthy to exclusive boutique hotels in hard-to-reach hideaways. Remote destinations, away from it all, untouched by human hands. This, too, has environmental implications as large tracts of land are cleared to provide privacy and comfort for a small number of people.

Of course, the behavior of a relatively small group of peo-

ple will have little bearing on the problems of climate change or their solution. Indeed, it may well be that there are aspects of *cocooning*, like online shopping, that actually contribute to energy efficiency rather than its opposite. But it is a statement of fact that when we shrink from society into our private worlds, when the breakdown in civility backs us further and further into our own corners, we each consume more of the planet's scarce resources.

In our heart of hearts, of course, we must know it won't work. There is no escape from the humanity bath. We are all in it: up to our necks in it.

As we embark on our global emergency mission to save the environment, is it too much to ask whether we might also find ourselves incidentally creating a more cooperative and civil world?

Or, to put it another way: Wouldn't it be something if civility helped save the planet?

2

Because manners are more important than laws

I N   O U R   O W N   T I M E , the idea that petty old manners are more important than laws may seem unthinkable, possibly even undemocratic. But in November 1789, the English parliamentarian Edmund Burke received a letter. A young French politician sought his views on recent dramatic developments in Paris. At that time the French Revolution was only a few months old and many of Burke's countrymen regarded the humbling of the French monarch and the humiliation of the Catholic Church as a cause for celebration. *Liberty was on the move!* And surely it would spread like a ray of light across Europe.

Burke himself was a liberal and a modernizer. He believed in tolerance, progress and the vital role of Parliament in good national governance. He'd even gone so far as to criticize the

British king over his stubborn mismanagement of colonial policies in America, India and Ireland.

But Burke was deeply worried about the French Revolution. And once he started writing, he couldn't stop. What began as a simple letter turned into a two-hundred-page polemic. *Reflections on the Revolution in France* deplored the Revolution, predicted its calamitous course and put forward Burke's notions about the ways in which a sane society should protect itself from extremism.

Burke was not a natural ally with the past and conservatism and the old aristocratic values. But he saw that by overthrowing the monarchy and the Catholic Church and by nationalizing church properties, even in the name of Liberty, the Revolution was effectively wiping out the two primary sources of French manners. And he was extremely apprehensive about what might appear in their place.

Burke understood what history later proved—that radical revolutionaries are nearly always authoritarians in disguise:

> ... [T]hese pretended citizens treat France exactly like a country of conquest. . . . The policy of such barbarous victors [is] . . . to destroy all vestiges of the ancient country, in religion, in polity, in laws and in manners; to confound all territorial limits, to produce a general poverty; to put up their properties to auction; to crush their

princes, nobles and pontiffs; to lay low everything which had lifted its head above the level, or which could serve to combine or rally, in their distresses, the disbanded people, under the standard of old opinion.

Throughout the rest of his life, Burke kept returning to the vital connection between culture, society, civilization—and manners. In 1796, in his *Letters on a Regicide Peace*, Burke gave his fullest and most famous statement on the subject:

Manners are of more importance than laws. Upon them, in a great measure, the laws depend. The law touches us but here and there, and now and then. Manners are what vex or soothe, corrupt or purify, exalt or debase, barbarise or refine us, by a constant, steady, uniform, insensible operation, like that of the air we breathe in. They give their whole form and colour to our lives. According to their quality, they aid morals, they supply them, or they totally destroy them.

The logic of Burke's thinking is powerful. Manners are both evidence of a functioning society and an important means to uphold that society. Manners provide a form of social self-limitation, a means by which citizens signal their willingness to live together and to abide by common standards. Legislate all you like, but laws can never have the same socially binding effect as manners, which give their *whole form*

and color to our lives. Destroy manners—sweep aside all of a society's habits, conventions and patterns of behavior—and you may well find you have nothing left but chaos. And because human beings cannot live for long in a state of anarchy, sooner or later some form of oppressive authority will step in to restore order on new, more punitive premises.

Burke's predictions were amazingly accurate. The French revolutionaries quite literally decided to destroy the existing order and start again from scratch. Year Zero. The old aristocracy was thrown out, and property rights, and the church, and French history and all the old ways and manners. In came a new calendar complete with new days and months, new secular gods and goddesses and feast days, new terms of social address—in short, a whole new world was brought into being by edict. And the intoxicating exercise of legislative power didn't end there, because the Jacobin extremists under Robespierre instituted a brief but terrifying orgy of death. The Terror—lasting from 1792 to 1794—would become the first experiment in modern totalitarianism, providing the radical template for tyrants like Stalin in Russia and Mao in China. And still that wasn't the end of the story, because in 1799 Napoleon Bonaparte stepped up to impose a military dictatorship on an exhausted and somewhat relieved France.

The revolutionary zeal to achieve liberty, equality and fraternity had resulted in the sustained triumph of oppression.

In Burke's mind, manners were not a peripheral question. If you cared about civilization, you cared about manners.

Rule of law is a beautiful thing. And legislation has been used to great positive effect, both to reflect changing social attitudes and to accelerate a shift in behaviors. But you simply can't dictate all our human behaviors without enslaving us. The equation is ultimately simple: more laws, more police, more lawyers equals less civilization.

That's why it is alarming to note that there has never in the history of the Western world been as much legislation as there is today. This explosion of laws could legitimately be regarded as a sign of social failure: either the state is attempting overly to restrict its citizens, or we citizens are simply no longer capable of regulating ourselves. This phenomenon is not just a function of new technologies and a more complex world, though that's part of it.

You can be sure it's a problem when even the lawyers—the main beneficiaries of this trend—despair at the infectious spread of legislation. In 2005, the president of the New South Wales Law Society, John McIntyre, gave a speech in which he lamented the proliferation of laws in Australia. McIntyre asked: "Surely human relationships have not undergone such a dramatic change in thirty years that their regulation by

government now demands the attention of numerous Acts of Parliament, including the Family Law Act and Rules which total in excess of a massive 1,000 pages?"

If we look at something as basic as the road traffic laws in any Western country, we can see that they have mushroomed, multiplied, grown wild. Gone from pamphlets to door-stoppers. Expanded and bulged. I guess it's inevitable. Because if you can't achieve driving harmony through manners and good sense, then you try to achieve the same result through laws. More and more and more of them. McIntyre posed the question: "Is driving a motor vehicle in 2005 so different to driving in 1973 that it requires not 20 sections, but 351 road rules?"

But the size of the bits of paper is not the main problem. You only have to walk out onto the street to see people blithely breaking the law every day: jaywalking, littering, running red lights, talking on their cell phones while driving, revving their engines, honking their horns, emitting strident music, tailgating the cars in front of them. All ill-mannered and all illegal. These breaches are rarely enforced and, indeed, are largely unenforceable, unless we were to create a police state.

So we don't have manners. Nor do we have laws that are enforced. We do, however, have road rage. And a generalized sense of despair and apathy because the system doesn't seem to be working.

In 2003, the city of New York mounted a legislative campaign against rudeness. Years of pleading simply hadn't worked with those recalcitrant New Yorkers: it was time to get tough. The mayor, Michael R. Bloomberg, imposed a smoking ban, overhauled the city's noise code and decreed that parents could be ejected from Little League games for unsportsmanlike behavior. Subway riders who rested their feet on a seat were liable to pay a $50 fine. It became illegal for fans to interfere with professional sports events by invading the field or molesting the players. The laws received widespread media coverage and praise.

But here's the catch. When I last checked, the $50 fine on people who used their cell phones during movies, concerts and Broadway shows had never, apparently, been enforced by police.

Some commentators have said that the mere enactment of the law is, of itself, sufficient to revise behavior by signaling broad community attitudes. I have some sympathy with this view. But it risks a more dangerous problem. When too many laws are not enforced, are not *enforceable*, the danger is not only that you diminish the authority of that particular law, but that you diminish the very power and reputation of the law itself.

Of course, in our unmannered era, laws must seem like an appealing shortcut to achieve social harmony. After all, laws

can be rapidly produced: they are simply the product of a conversation in a parliament. Manners take time to catch on. They are delicate and subtle things, relying upon broad agreement and usage, shaped by circumstances, molded by collaborative effort.

And it seems to me there *is* a useful role that civic authorities can play in reflecting and shaping communal standards of manners, but through the employment of charm rather than legal menace. In January 2007, for example, *The New York Times* reported on a campaign by the local transit authority of Paris to improve standards of courtesy. Rather than threaten prosecution, the Parisians decided instead to install humorous posters to persuade commuters to muzzle their pets, refrain from littering, talk softly on cell phones, avoid whacking their neighbors with their backpacks—and to say a pleasant hello and goodbye to their bus drivers.

Such modest education measures seem to me far more useful than the sledgehammer of laws. They give moral reinforcement to the courteous commuters as well as useful correctives to the rude ones.

Imagine how awful life would be if we relied solely upon laws to enforce all decent behavior. In such circumstances, we would be no better than robots. We would be incapable of freely exercising and receiving kindness and courtesy. We would be less than ourselves.

That's why we need the collective endowment, the community collaboration, the unmistakable signs of a coherent, free civilization conferred by the voluntary gift of manners.

. . . less invasive than morals

There's a long tradition that manners are a matter of ethics; that for guidance on manners we should be able to rely upon our shared moral sense and codes. And I agree with this, up to a point.

But there's a problem.

We live in pluralist societies, and they're only getting more diverse. They are multiracial. They are multireligious. We can no longer assume a common Judeo-Christian upbringing to draw us all automatically together. Once, we could confidently agree to do unto others as we would have done unto us because we could roughly agree on what we would—and would not—like done. But today even the differences between the generations are now so significant that advertising agencies have invented different code names for us—gray nomads, baby boomers, Gen X, Gen Y—as if we are separate species of human, which sometimes it appears as though we are.

So it no longer makes sense to exhort us to draw upon our shared moral codes. Because what might seem kind and considerate to you might irritate me. Or what might seem completely inconsequential to me might desperately hurt your

feelings. Indeed, we seem to have brought ourselves to the point where we have few confidently agreed upon rules for social engagement at all. Is it okay if I take this call during our meeting? Will they be offended if I am twenty minutes late? How about if I text-message at the dinner table?

Most of the time, in these uncertain conditions, we rationally conclude in favor of our immediate interests rather than in support of some obscure or uncertain social good. We take the call. We turn up late. We send and receive the text messages. And so the cycle of ill manners continues—leaving many people feeling offended, frustrated, impotent and confused.

While for most of us this is all deeply unpleasant, there are some who sniff an opportunity in social instability. Fundamentalists and ideologues—no matter what their beliefs—favor strict rules, unvaryingly applied, admitting neither flexibility of interpretation nor adaptation to circumstance. Which wouldn't matter a bit except they tend not to limit their views to how they themselves should behave. They have strong opinions about how the rest of us should behave, as well. And they'd like to impose them upon us.

In the twentieth century, fundamentalist idealists like communists and Nazis had a total worldview and were able to impose those views on societies that were simultaneously chaotic and weary enough to embrace them. I lived in the then

communist city of Belgrade for a period and saw for myself that nothing erodes manners like the common ownership of the means of production. Power to the people had produced a society that was sullen, unkind and competitive.

Now we have an upsurge in religious fundamentalism, with evangelists of various kinds admonishing us to model our actions strictly on the guidelines of some or other unhappy Middle Eastern fellow who lived and died a long time ago. But it seems to me these strictures have a very limited utility for the moral or practical conduct of modern life.

It's not, of course, that fundamentalists aren't sincere. On the contrary, it's possible to sincerely hold really horrible thoughts, feelings and values. Racists tend to be sincere. Bigots are sincere. Fundamentalist Muslims and Jews are sincere. And fundamentalist Christians, guided by their comprehensive moral system, are perfectly sincere in trying to impose their vision of God's Kingdom on Earth upon everyone else. But the problem is this: fundamentalists don't just want to tell me what to do when I am out in public. They are unnervingly keen on interfering in my private domain, as well. Coming into my home and telling me how to conduct my romantic life or marriage; poking into my bedroom and pronouncing pruriently on my sex life; even telling me how to dispose of my own body.

Take, for example, death. Surely a personal matter if ever

there was one. It seems to me that while manners are clearly very useful for living, they might come in handy for dying, too. Should I be terminally ill, I like the idea of arranging an orderly departure. One that is well-organized and causes the minimum of physical pain to me and emotional pain to those who care for me. An exit plan that is strictly my choice. And if, by sad fate, I were no longer able to be myself—if I were in a permanent coma, or profoundly demented, or in agonizing pain, or experiencing extreme disability—then I would like my husband to have the right to end my life. (He likes that idea, too, I note with mixed feelings.) In such circumstances, it would seem to me not only cruelly pointless but rather bad manners to go on living, particularly if only by costly artificial means—rather like overstaying my welcome at a dinner party by fifteen or twenty years. And it irritates me that extremists presume bossily to interfere with a process that surely only an extreme optimist would deny was inevitable, and peculiar to me alone.

In short, I would very much prefer not to have anyone use their moral system as an excuse to impose limitations on my personal freedoms, when the exercise of those personal freedoms inflicts no social harm.

Give me manners, by contrast, that ensure the minimum intrusion on my rights and privacy; that adapt flexibly to social evolution; that do not presume; that protect everyone's

rights and dignities; and that contribute ever so gently to the social good.

Indeed, it seems to me that the person who operates in the world on the basis of manners is far less likely to do harm than the God-botherer, fundamentalist, sexist, racist or other morally driven individual.

Manners are a way to render very diverse people acceptable to each other. If we accept that a single arbitrary and sweeping code of morals can no longer bind our varied society together, perhaps manners might pragmatically take its place.

And perhaps, in their low-key way, contribute to a happier society than any perfect ideology could ever achieve.

. . . and better than social confusion

Of course, you are thinking, it's all very well declaring that manners are a terrific idea and more pragmatic than laws or moral systems at shaping a civil society. But how on earth do we establish effective terms and conditions for modern manners?

Excellent question. And you would be perfectly justified in additionally asking whether I would be a person qualified to answer it. I must admit that I find myself writing about manners not because I enjoy mulling over the trivial details of everyday life but precisely because I don't. I dislike it. The truth is, I'd rather not be thoughtful—it requires too much

thought. I don't care to be considerate—that requires too much consideration. And those who know me well would confirm, with unflattering speed, that I'm not thoughtful or considerate, not very.

And yet, like most of us, I hunger for civility. At the very least, I want predictability in my human dealings. I like to know what I am entitled to expect from others and from myself. But often I don't know. Everyday interactions feel more like complicated negotiations. I waste more and more emotional energy simply getting through the minutiae of daily life.

The truth is, I gain no enjoyment from pondering who should send the last email in an email exchange (can we stop now?).

I don't find pleasure in wondering whether I can, with propriety, hang up on someone who puts me on call waiting (is it ruder of them to keep me waiting, or of me to hang up after they've kept me hanging?).

And I experience active irritation weighing up whether I can leave the café if the person I am due to meet hasn't shown up, say, twenty minutes after the agreed upon time (if so, will I be the one required to ring and apologize?).

These situations are infuriating and, worse still, boring. They are matters of negligible import, yet to arrive at the right solution requires weighing up various options and carefully selecting among them.

Does not modern life already have far too many options? Options for how we live, who we have sex with, what we wear, what we believe in? Perhaps some people find this freedom of choice liberating.

Me, I don't like it. I don't like all this choice. I don't want to think about which phone provider will deliver me the best combination of prices for the time of day, longevity and distance of my phone calls. I don't care to fret about which yogurt to select given the choice between biodynamic, low-fat, Greek, acidophilus, vitamin-enriched, without gelatin and with honey.

And there is a high chance that, even after the best efforts at wise deliberation, we'll still get it wrong—whether about phone companies or yogurt, or even on matters of courtesy. After all, some of the most painful situations in modern life occur not because people want to be rude, but because they just aren't sure how to behave.

Suppose, for example, a polite young man stands up for a woman on a crowded train. He does so in an automatic kind of way, but if pressed to explain his motives, he might explain that he's noticed she is carrying a very heavy bag and if she sits down she can rest it on her lap. And anyway, he doesn't mind standing as he is getting off soon and she looks really tired and his mum always encouraged him to be kind to people.

It's possible, just possible, that the subject of our young

man's invitation will thank him and graciously take the proffered seat. It's also possible that she will be offended in any variety of ways, and be tempted to think or express thoughts such as:

So that's it. I'm now an old hag. An. Old. Hag. Hang on. That woman under the Exit sign is clearly older than me. Do I look older than her? No, I do not. You. Utter. Bastard.

Or:

Typical. Forty years of feminism and we're back to this. The patriarchy reigns, even among Generation X. Well, I'm not having a bar of it. Piss off.

Or:

Oh God. Does he think I'm pregnant? He thinks I'm pregnant. I knew I should never have bought an empire line.

And this is where all those etiquette books should now come gloriously into their own. Time to whip out the latest manners instruction manual and turn to page 201: *When to stand up on a bus—and how to react when someone offers you a seat.* But I have noticed these books never seem to have a ready answer to the specific question you have in mind.

As a matter of fact, this is the least of their defects. Oh, they are dull. And *long.* And they date so quickly.

Take *Etiquette for Women: A Book of Modern Modes and Manners* (the author, teasingly, identifies herself merely as *One of the Aristocracy*), which dates from 1902 and tells us in no uncertain terms that after you have been invited to a ball, a dinner

or a reception, whether the invitation has been accepted or not, you should, as a matter of course, pay *a visit of ceremony* to your hostess within a week, ten days at the latest. It also tells us how to cope with that newfangled development, the restaurant, which, it warns us, is here to stay, despite its troubling implications for the decay of hospitality.

Lady Una Troubridge in the 1920s offers the more upbeat *Etiquette and Entertaining: How to Help You on Your Social Way.* In the bright, modern post–World War I era, Lady Troubridge assures us that the new etiquette is informal. That's presumably why she adjures us to "Let Everything Be Simple" when setting the breakfast table.

All we have to do is:

- Use a spirited check-cloth or a coloured one.
- Arrange the dishes on the sideboard.
- At the head of the table place an encampment of cups round the teapot, milk jug, sugar basin and hot water jug or coffee pot and hot-milk jug.
- At each place put a small fork on the left, and two small knives on the right—the extra knife is to spread butter on bread or toast.
- Set a small plate to the left of the larger plate on which bacon and eggs or some other breakfast dish is served.

- And, because it's an informal meal, the loaf can be on the table as well as the toast-rack, butter, honey and marmalade.

Breakfast made easy.

Amy Vanderbilt shows no interest in simplifying things in her masterwork, *New Complete Book of Etiquette: The Guide to Gracious Living*. Obviously gracious living in 1952 took some doing because this book is 740 pages long. It is indeed full of facts. It is certainly comprehensive. It is great for use as a doorstop on a windy day.

It is also practically useless, as Amy's world of manners has, thankfully, all but disappeared. For example, there's a section on how to address your Chinese gardener or the younger son of a duke. What to wear when fox-hunting. How to avoid errors in conversation and terminology ("high class," she explains witheringly, is one of those phrases that seem to indicate social inferiority in the person uttering it). How to address your envelope when your correspondent is a member of the British House of Commons—and also happens to be a lord. What to wear if you are invited to a Hop at the West Point military academy. It's worth reading this book just to feel delighted at how many problems of manners you are never, ever

going to face. At least, you hope not. A couple of sections are timeless, including her advice to parents: "If your children are very young, don't travel with them at all if you can help it."

Etiquette for Australians, revised edition of 1945, is weightily subtitled *Australian Official and Social Life, Government House, The Australian Army, Navy and Air Force and Women's Services. Australian, English and American Titles of Address and Everyday Life.* I rather enjoyed this one for its revelations about the state of Australia in the immediate postwar period. A long section on Farewell Parties suggests that so many of my countrymen were desperate to leave their patch of heaven in the Lucky Country that a whole field of etiquette had to be created to deal with it. (Apparently there are three categories of escapee—those leaving a country district on receipt of a transference or higher appointment to another part of the state or commonwealth; those leaving the commonwealth to take up residence in another country; and those leaving for a trip abroad. No mention is made of the sort of farewell party you should throw for a bankrupt dejectedly quitting town.)

Another section, called Picnic Parties, reiterates, with an air of increasing desperation, the delights of an excursion into the Australian bush: "One of the most delightful features of Australian life! Formalities disappear! A sense of fine comradeship prevails! Happiness and fun!" The end of the section concedes the altogether harsher realities of the great outdoors:

"Don't grumble if the caterpillar from the overhead trees falls into the milk, if the billy tea is smoked, and if the butter melts quickly."

Etiquette for Australians does offer one permanent insight into the Australian psyche. In a long and detailed section, it begs its readers to develop a little sportsmanship. "Don't bawl at the top of your voice or make vulgar gestures at sporting matches," it pleads. "Never rejoice when your opponent makes a bad slip." And it reminds fans and players of a point that still regularly eludes Australian minds: "The decision of the umpire must be accepted."

Today there seem to be more etiquette books than ever on the market. They are variations on the above themes, updated for casual sex and text-messaging. But they remain impossible to scrutinize seriously. Still long. Still dull. Curiously unhelpful. I can't help wondering whether anyone ever reads them. Perhaps they are just given as Christmas gifts to the relatives and friends we consider most likely to need them—who are therefore, it can only be assumed, the very last people who are likely to open and profit from their pages.

I have a different idea. In a gesture combining laziness and pragmatism, I suggest we forget about big books of rules and compromise on a short set of guidelines. There's a precedent

for what I suggest. The lawyers talk about principle-centered law—that is, clear basic rules capable of being readily understood, remembered and flexibly applied to circumstances. The Ten Commandments are a classic example of principle-centered law.

A modern template for manners might have the same memorable simplicity.

How about something like:

1. Keep to the left (or right, depending on jurisdiction).
2. Keep your word, especially about time.
3. Wait your turn.
4. Look after the weak.
5. Obey the laws and regulations, unless you are mounting a campaign of civil disobedience.
6. Watch what you are doing: multitasking is the enemy of manners.
7. Show appreciation for the kind gestures of others; and
8. Most of the time, shut up.

But I'm open to other suggestions. (However, I think you'll find that most public contingencies are covered here, including our young man and his train companion: see points 4 and 7.)

Perhaps "minding one's manners" sounds less civically virtuous than abiding by the letter of the law. "Observing the niceties" certainly lacks the high tone of adhering to the will of the Lord. But manners, so minor, have the unassailable virtue of mitigating subtle yet serious risks to society. Without manners we become vulnerable to the imposition of more legislation. Or we risk having the moral systems of others imposed upon us. The beauty of manners—when everybody knows the accepted rules of behavior—is that we don't have to mean it, or like it, or be moral, or even sincere.

We just have to do it.

3

Because manners nurture
our equality

I N 1776, in their Declaration of Independence, the American Founding Fathers laid out exactly why thirteen United States of America would no longer tolerate the colonial domination of Great Britain. Foremost among their reasons? "We hold these truths to be self-evident," they magnificently declared, "that all men are created equal."

And so a great nation was founded. A democracy based on the exhilarating idea of the equality of man.

A little more than fifty years later, a young Frenchman named Alexis de Tocqueville arrived in the thriving young democracy, ostensibly to study its prison system, but in fact to discover what lessons the new world offered the old. Tocqueville came from an aristocratic French family that had been prominent during the ancien régime and had suffered through

the successive turmoils of the Revolution, Bonapartism and the Restoration. *Democracy in America* is the long and famous product of his study.

And it is a wide-ranging survey. It traverses everything from the American constitution, judicial system and states' rights versus union rights, to the role of religion, the education system, industrial relations and the love of money. Tocqueville is not afraid to say what he thinks: my favorite chapter heading in the book is in part 3, chapter 17: "How American Society Appears Both Agitated and Monotonous."

But it must be said: while Tocqueville admired many aspects of American life, manners was not one of them. Manners in democracies, he thought, were often coarse, rarely dignified, not well disciplined nor very accomplished. In fact, Tocqueville believed, "Nothing does more harm to democracy than its outer forms of behaviour. Many people who would be willing to put up with its defects cannot tolerate its manners." You suspect on reading this that Tocqueville considered himself among them.

One anomaly Tocqueville noticed above all: equality breeds a yearning for inequality.

In democracies where the differences between citizens are never very great and they naturally become so close that at any moment they can merge in the mass of the community, numerous artificial and arbi-

trary distinctions are invented to help individuals in their attempt to remain aloof for fear of being swept along with the crowd . . .

As Tocqueville knew from experience, in aristocracies, for better or for worse, certainty prevails in the social order. From the highest to the lowest, everyone knows their place. Each person understands to whom they must defer, over whom they have power and where their social responsibilities lie. And this social clarity has a calming and dignifying effect upon manners. In democracies, by contrast, there occurs a paradoxical effect: social competition is not eliminated, instead it is amplified: "The personal pride of individuals will always strive to rise above the common level and will hope to achieve some inequality to their own advantage."

Thus follows a potentially ugly striving for superiority as individuals seek to accrue advantage at the expense of one another, and therefore their broader society.

What Tocqueville observed may not have completely surprised America's Founding Fathers—from the start they were genuinely apprehensive about whether America would be capable of supporting a civil society.

When he was just a fifteen-year-old schoolboy, George Washington, America's first president, painstakingly wrote out *110 Rules of Civility and Decent Behavior in Company and Conversation.*

After his death, these guidelines were published and became a best seller.

John Adams, the second president, was optimistic that good Republican government could positively influence American manners: "It is the Form of Government which gives the decisive Colour to the Manners of the People, more than any other Thing," he said. But even stout Adams had such grave doubts about the merits of his compatriots that he wasn't altogether confident of his own assertion: "... there is so much Rascality, so much Venality and Corruption, so much Avarice and Ambition, such a Rage for Profit and Commerce among all Ranks and Degrees of Men even in America, that I sometimes doubt whether there is public Virtue enough to Support a Republic."

Thomas Jefferson, the third president, the man who drafted the most successful founding national statement in world history, was of the view that no matter how strong the laws and constitution of his new country, if manners failed, then his whole society would fail, as well. "It is the manners and spirit of a people which preserve a republic in vigour," he wrote. "A degeneracy in these is a canker which soon eats to the heart of its laws and constitution."

I saw the "manners and spirit" of my own people in action the other day.

I was standing at the end of a movie queue with my husband, waiting to buy our tickets to see *The Queen*. Though the queue was rather long, the patrons were relaxed and there was a pleasant hum along the line. Along came a couple with whom we were slightly acquainted. We went to greet each other when suddenly the wife darted toward the front of the queue and squeezed through the door into the cinema. Her husband gazed sheepishly at us. After a moment she came back out clutching two tickets. With a satisfied air she stage-whispered to us, "You can bypass the queue and get your tickets at the snack bar!" And with this she took her husband by the elbow, led him past the queue and disappeared triumphantly inside. My husband and I did not take advantage of this quick-witted means to evade the system. We stayed in line, bought our tickets, entered the cinema and found ourselves seated three rows in front of this couple.

There were other options available to this woman. She might, for example, have suggested to cinema management that patrons could form three quick lines instead of one slow one. She might have told all the people in the queue about the waiting snack-sellers, instead of just my husband and me. Or she might have simply stayed in line like us. But I could see in her eyes that she gloried in outsmarting the system. She had generated advantage for herself and her husband. She had proved herself superior to the rest of us. Her reward, I noted

without distress, was to watch more advertisements than we did.

And it was ironic that we were all watching *The Queen*, a movie that portrays Queen Elizabeth II of England as a woman almost heroically incapable of taking the easy way out.

All our modern advertising celebrates and indeed encourages this democratic passion for petty social advantage. We are regularly told that if we buy *this* brand of handbag or *that* brand of cell phone we will be just that little bit better than our peers. In fact, that they will no longer be our peers, for we shall have risen a delicious fraction above them.

Consider this advertisement for a Mitsubishi four-wheel drive. A young woman parks the great beast in a tight space between two average-sized cars. But she hasn't room to open her door. Luckily she has the new sunroof feature so she simply climbs out through the top of the 4WD and gaily scrambles down the enormous hood. *Solved!* What the advertisement doesn't do, of course, is solve the problems her action has caused for others—the drivers who return to their cars to discover they can't open their own doors. But this is perhaps the point, for the young lady has not only found a perfect means to advantage herself, she is simultaneously inconveniencing others—a neat way to cap off her automotive and social triumph.

It's a Tuesday midmorning and I am waiting on Plat-

form 9 for the short ride into the city. The train pulls into the station and the doors open. We all stand back as the passengers climb down onto the platform. Or at least, most of us. Because here he is, fidgeting with irritation and stepping from side to side because he wants to get on now. Right now. He can't bear to wait, not even for another second. So he steps forward and up, onto the train, brushing aside a descending mother who is awkwardly maneuvering her stroller with sleeping babe from the train onto the platform, nudging a tired man with a briefcase, dislodging a young bespectacled student. It's not as if he is particularly assertive in his manner. On the contrary, his eyes are averted and his shoulders are angled to minimize his physical impact. He certainly doesn't want to draw attention to himself. But I see him clearly. His silent message to me and to everyone else is abundantly clear. Not for him the ancient courtesy, *after you.* Nor even the cheery and egalitarian, *me, too.* In his case it's definitely, *me first.* And possibly, probably, *and fuck you all.*

Tocqueville's analysis is surely the only plausible explanation for this rudeness—for I assume my traveling companion was bound by various laws of physics to arrive at Town Hall at the same speed as the rest of us. As Tocqueville said of this competitive phenomenon in America: "An American daily refers to the wonderful equality which prevails in the United States. . . . He proclaims out loud his pride on behalf of his

country but secretly on his own behalf he feels considerable distress and aims to show he is an exception to the general rule he is advocating."

I can only imagine that my impolite traveling companion was seeking to allay the considerable distress he felt at being one of the vulgar masses traveling on the public transport system. Yes, so many people, manifestly ordinary, trying desperately via petty means to be an exception to the general rule.

Sometimes this mania for status manifests itself in a different way.

I live in an area that is very popular with actors, who are nearly always out of work. That's why, if they are not sitting in a café, they are serving in it. Actually, usually they are doing both, sitting around looking languid and holding their chin at an interesting angle until finally motivated to wander over and ask you what you'd like to drink, rather in the manner of a favor. Having been brought up to visualize themselves as superstars in waiting, the actors simply will not tolerate being treated as waiters, even when that's exactly what they are and are paid to be. Seemingly anxious to remind me that he is better than this, the actor at one local café likes to serve me my coffee while joining in my private conversations, giving his view of the latest film or book or even my menu choice: *I'd go for the penne!* All of which is rarely a prelude to excellent serv-

ice. Sometimes I feel ashamed of my waiter's shame. I want to tell him about the French professional waiter, who takes such pride in his skill; who abhors overfamiliarity; who feels no nervous compulsion to assert his dignity. I want to say to him: I am not absolutely sure that bad acting would be more honorable than waiting beautifully on tables.

On this matter of social anxiety Tocqueville is particularly insightful when he talks about Americans traveling overseas—and he both prefigures and explains the Ugly American syndrome. As he notes:

> *When a wealthy American lands in Europe . . . he has such a great fear of being taken for the unsophisticated citizen of a democracy. . . . He is all the more fearful at not receiving the respect due to him because he does not know exactly what governs that respect. . . . He questions every look and carefully analyses all your remarks, lest they contain some hidden allusions to affront him.*

American writer Gore Vidal, in his memoir *Point to Point Navigation*, offers us a more contemporary insight into this touchy attitude of mind. As a friend of British Queen Elizabeth's sister Princess Margaret (raffishly referred to by Vidal as PM), Vidal was a guest at a grand party thrown by American businessman Jack Heinz. Vidal and PM were running late, so the queen came over to their pavilion. On being asked by

her sister how the party was going, the queen answered ruefully, "We have shaken many hands," indicating that the many American guests had either ignorantly or willfully ignored the protocol that the sovereign should not be touched. Once again, the Americans had gone overboard in their eagerness to be as good as anyone. Or better.

At the end of this little story, Vidal oh-so-casually reminds his readers that he knew exactly the right form: "PM presented me, I did the nod." It seems that even the most patrician American still feels an uneasy compulsion to prove his superiority over his compatriots.

Perhaps Vidal should have taken a leaf from the woman with whom he shared a stepfather: America's extraordinary first lady, Jacqueline Bouvier Kennedy Onassis. Jackie O understood the force of courtesy and the merits of refined reticence. When battling for privacy after the assassination of her husband, she declared her strategem for dealing with the press: Minimum information, given with maximum politness . . .

. . . modify self-esteem

But, I regret to advise, there's more. The desire of individuals to rise above the herd was not the only trend that Tocqueville identified as a strong and largely negative feature of democratic society.

He also noted that, as social equality spreads and more

people acquire the wealth to satisfy their needs, they progressively retreat from the broader community. Pleased to owe nothing to anyone, they come to expect nothing from anyone, either. This trend toward individualism Tocqueville defined as ". . . a calm and considered feeling which persuades each citizen to cut himself off from his fellows and to withdraw into the circle of his family and friends in such a way that he thus creates a small group of his own and willingly abandons society at large to its own devices."

In order to show that individualism was not necessarily pernicious, Tocqueville contrasted it with egoism, which, he said, was an "ardent and excessive love of oneself that caused people to relate everything to themselves and to prefer themselves above everything."

When I read this section of Tocqueville I did a sort of literary double take. Because at first I couldn't see the real-world difference between citizens cutting themselves off from their fellows and people preferring themselves above everything. Then I realized that I couldn't see the difference between individualism and egoism because in modern life there isn't any. If Tocqueville were to turn up today, I expect he would observe that these formerly separate qualities have now morphed into a single syndrome, whereby people not only embrace utter selfishness but even consider it socially acceptable, if not an active social good. And because we live in an age of misleading euphemisms, we've given this syndrome a palatable and therapeutic label: self-esteem.

Self-esteem is not, of course, a new term. It gained currency in the late nineteenth century as part of the emerging practice of psychology. A body of work emerged suggesting that low self-esteem contributed to individual unhappiness and broader antisocial behavior. I have no doubt the original goals of the self-esteem movement were noble. And I am sure it was once a valuable tool of therapy for the troubled and unhappy.

But where once self-esteem referred to a healthy and unassuming self-confidence, it has now come to represent uncritical self-regard. A campaign that idealizes narcissism. A crusade that encourages people who dislike aspects of themselves to celebrate their shortcomings, rather than to correct them. Self-esteem has become less a neutral descriptor than an active cause.

I looked up *self-esteem* under Amazon books and found 85,962 books devoted to this topic. Among the titles: *The Self-Esteem Workbook. How to Raise Your Self-Esteem: The Proven Action-Oriented Approach to Greater Self-Respect and Self-Confidence. The Self-Esteem Companion. Six Pillars of Self-Esteem. Breaking the Chain of Low Self-Esteem.* And the fast-track version: *Ten Days to Self-Esteem.*

You would think that we were all morally obliged to regard ourselves not only equal by creation but equal in virtue, talent and achievement. How often have I heard someone simpering about their low self-esteem and longed to turn to them and say, "Yes, but perhaps in compensation you have very sound judgment."

Here's an astonishing thing: the self-esteem epidemic breaks the basic rule of civilization—the need to preserve what's best for the group. Self-esteem demands that I am just as important, no, I must regard myself as more important than you. And I must be accommodated no matter how great the inconvenience. And following this cruel logic means that individuals not only demand that others make exceptions for them, but they show no appreciation in return. They feel absolutely no need to connect to their society—it's all and always, just about them. Self-esteem has become the catch-all excuse for putting oneself first all the time.

The consequences are not always minor ones. We, the group, are increasingly at the mercy of:

- The woman who answers her cell phone during a movie and ruins the experience for thirty other people, some of whom no longer feel refreshed by the entertainment but instead emerge from the cinema irritable and take it out on the next-door café waitress, who goes home and cries because her life is so pointless and people are so cruel.

- The parents who insist on allowing their four-year-old to run around the restaurant after 9 P.M., destroying the experience for all the other diners, and especially the tired couple who pulled out their wallets for a babysitter so they could have a rare evening away from their children, and who are now so rattled they don't make love when they get home, which further tests the straining bonds of their marriage.

- The pedestrian who refuses to wait at the lights but insists on walking straight out into the middle of the road, not only risking his own life, but also startling the drivers, holding up the cars and setting in motion a chain reaction of traffic snarls and, three kilometers away, an accident.

- The man who casually drops his cigarette butt on the footpath so it drifts into the great flood tide of rubbish that poisons our waterways, killing off small organisms that are the main food source for a fish that may have certain rare and scientifically valuable enzymes.

- The young man in the elevator who turns to the mirror and spends the journey from the foyer to level 35 grooming himself and treating the public space so egoistically that one of his copassengers, distressed by this annihilating disregard, turns still

further in upon herself, and later fails to recognize the unmistakable signs that a work colleague fancies her and loses a chance at happiness.

- The neighbor who thinks it is his perfect right to listen to techno music between 3 A.M. and 6 A.M. after he gets home all hyped-up from a nightclub while around the neighborhood people toss and turn and beat their pillows and finally stagger bleary-eyed and under-slept to their offices the next day where one of them makes a poor decision that loses the company a fortune.

The acid of egoistic individualism has burned deep into our moral and social structures. When *you* behave badly, you are an ill-mannered boor; when I do so, I have good reasons and am completely justified. When *you* jaywalk, you are a selfish fool; when I do it, it's because the lights have taken too long to change and I'm in a hurry. When *you* take that call, you are an antisocial pig; when I do, it's because it is bound to be very important.

And just as individuals with *self-esteem* never say thank you when you make a courteous concession to them—for, after all, it is their perfect right to do exactly as they please—they get very touchy indeed if you dare to criticize them for any wrongdoing.

True story: in Texas, in 2005, one foolish idealist actually

tapped a woman on the shoulder and asked her to stop talking on the phone because she was disturbing the other cinema patrons in the middle of watching a film. The woman immediately had her up on assault charges and the defender of manners was convicted and fined for the crime.

True story: during a Thanksgiving dinner in 2004, two revelers reprimanded another guest for picking at the turkey with his fingers instead of slicing off pieces with a knife. The man responded by taking hold of the carving knife and stabbing them.

This is all, of course, very disheartening. And there's another angle. The flip side of this culture of relentless self-esteem is that to step back, to defer, to make way, is a warning signal of that worst ailment of modern times: *low self-esteem*. Even a simple gesture of courtesy can be misconstrued as a symptom of this sad psychological dysfunction. I've seen parents push their child aggressively forward for fear of what might be said of their parenting techniques if their child is true to his nature and hangs shyly back.

And indeed, it seems to me that parenting is where the worst of the self-esteem epidemic has manifested itself.

The role of children in society has changed. They were once regarded quite literally as the property of their parents and therefore had no rights. Then in a more liberal age, children obtained rights and their parents suddenly had responsibilities.

Now it's not so clear. Some parents seem to regard their children as personal investments, to be nurtured and groomed to offer big dividends in terms of parental pride and vicarious achievement. Others seem to have given birth to their new best friends, so their children are alternately placated, indulged and ignored.

But whenever I see parents excessively, duplicitously lavishing praise upon their five-year-old's finger paintings—rather as if the *Mona Lisa* had just emerged magically from those stained and chubby fingertips—I see not another genius-in-waiting but yet another self-esteem monster rising to self-assuredly torment us all in twenty years with an inferior PowerPoint diagram in a marketing meeting.

True story: in January 2007, the American airline AirTran Airways asked a family to leave an aircraft before takeoff when the three-year-old daughter threw a tantrum so severe she could not be persuaded to get into her seat and put on a seat belt. While the parents tried to settle the child, the flight was considerably delayed. But the child absolutely refused to comply, alternately climbing under the seat and emerging to hit her parents. Finally, in accordance with aviation safety rules and in fairness to the other 112 passengers, the crew made an operational decision to remove the family from the aircraft. The mother was utterly dismayed and complained: "We weren't given an opportunity to hold her, console her or anything!"

The family assured the media they would never fly AirTran again, a promise of retribution I am fairly certain AirTran contemplated with relief.

I suppose the parents consoled themselves with the knowledge that at least they hadn't wounded the child's developing self-esteem by compulsorily strapping her in like all the other ordinary mortals.

On any Tuesday somewhere near you, you'll find a Rotary Club meeting. Here, accompanied by tepid tea and stewed coffee (if it's a breakfast meeting) or rubber chicken and overcooked spinach (if it's dinner), a strange and well-honed ritual will be played out.

And this ritual will bear a remarkable resemblance to the gatherings of hundreds and thousands of similar groups in countries all around the world. In Australia, we have the St. John Ambulance Brigade and Lions Clubs and Zonta and Probus and Returned Servicemen's Leagues and many more. These private associations serve the interests of their members and, as important, contribute to the common good. The widespread readiness of Americans to participate in such groups (alongside their religion) was, Tocqueville thought, a way the young democracy might successfully mitigate its tendency to individualism in order to create and maintain a civil society.

I must admit, Rotary doesn't look like the kind of place where civilization takes root and flowers.

First there'll be a President John, wearing a big tacky medallion around his neck, who will stand and lead a prayer. The national anthem will then be sung astonishingly badly and with touching gusto. President John will hit a bell with his ancient gavel as a signal to receive the weekly report, notable mostly for its extreme blandness. The secretary will announce in a rapid and monotonous tone the success of past events and the progress of future plans. That achieved, the president will then turn to his lukewarm comic sidekick, probably named Sergeant Ken, who will recount a few innocent jokes downloaded off the Internet and pass around a wooden box to extract "fines" from the joshing but generous members. At the conclusion of the formalities, the Rotarians will sit back in their chairs and dutifully listen to a little talk from a guest speaker about, say, birdwatching or the latest accountancy developments, which will be of almost no interest to anyone, and particularly not to that table of toothless old boys sitting in the corner in the battered navy blue double-breasted jackets they've worn to each and every meeting since 1981.

Most of the time everyone manages to stay awake. But to say there is rarely an atmosphere of excitement is a grave understatement.

Looked at one way—well, truthfully, looked at most

ways—Rotary's rituals seem horribly outdated. But whenever and wherever Rotary meets, people are getting things done. Money is being raised for malaria prevention or sheltering homeless youth. Young people are gaining the opportunity to live overseas and to learn about other cultures.

The manners of Rotary, it turns out, are its strength as well as its weakness. The rituals carry them all through, week after week, year after year. Everyone simply turns up and gets on with business, without fuss or clamor, cushioned by the predictable format. You could fly in from Sri Lanka to a Norwegian chapter of Rotary and you would more or less know what is going on.

Rotary was, for a long time, a very conservative organization. Growing up, we Catholics were rather suspicious of this small businessmen's club, as if it were some kind of anti-papist cabal. And yes, Rotary has a conservative air to this day. Some of the more ancient Rotarians still look perturbed when women turn up and take an assertive role.

But last time I was a guest at a Rotary meeting—when I was, in fact, one of those dull guest speakers—I had a sort of mental flash. As I looked around at the Rotary membership—the accountant and the marketing manager and the suburban lawyer and the undertaker—and as they listened to me with courtesy and bought my book and asked after each other's well-being and gave away their money and planned fund-

raising events and made plans to visit some of their ailing older members, I had a sudden insight that these people were the quiet vanguard of modern civility.

Drawing upon the inexhaustible resource of Rotarian etiquette and a store of personal kindness—without personal vanity or social competitiveness—they were doing nothing less than building a civil world over a cup of tea.

That's why I'll always cherish Rotary, in spite of the rubber chicken.

. . . and connect the self to society

America is the first modern democracy. But it is by no means the only exemplar of a great democracy at our disposal. A very long time ago, in the fifth and fourth centuries before Christ, the Greeks conducted a grand experiment. The historian H.D.F. Kitto frames their story this way: ". . . [I]n a part of the world that had for centuries been civilised, there gradually emerged a people, not very numerous, not very powerful, not very organised, who had a totally new conception of what human life was for, and showed for the first time what the human mind was for."

Athenian democracy was the high point of this innovative culture. It was very different from our own. Citizenship was strictly limited—no women, foreigners, freed men or slaves. So it was a democracy with a certain aristocratic temperament.

And it took shape in the polis—a city-state—that might consist of as few as five thousand and perhaps up to a maximum of fifty thousand citizens. The polis was far more than a patch of land or microstate in the modern sense. The citizens weren't intermittent participants in civic life. To start with, in Athens there was no standing army: in times of war—and there were many of them—each citizen was expected to fight. Each citizen was also expected to serve in public office if asked—and a great number were. This put pressure on everyone to stay well informed and ready to participate. The polis, therefore, represented the whole communal life of the people: political, cultural, moral and economic.

Perhaps the best portrait of this exceptional culture comes from Athens's most famous general and leader, Pericles, who in 430 BC delivered a funeral oration in honor of Athenians who died fighting Persian invaders.

The speech is a tribute to the dead. But it is also a celebration, an explanation and a political idealization of Athenian democracy. Pericles describes for his own and future generations the culture, the tenor and the values of his city.

Pericles begins by explaining that Athens is an innovator, setting a pattern for others. Athens is free and open, all citizens are equal under the law, and anyone may advance by merit. Public life and private life are each valuable and free

trade brings in new goods from all around the world. Beauty, art, education and culture adorn the life of the polis. Poverty and obscurity are no shame as long as a citizen makes himself useful. Athenians are generous and openhanded with their neighbors, Pericles explains, not from some small-minded calculation of benefit, but from the confidence of a free and unchained culture. Unlike the Spartans, the Athenians don't spend their time obsessively preparing for war. But Athenians are ready to plan intelligently and act audaciously when necessary. And they have shown themselves to be remarkable warriors.

As part of his word portrait of the polis, Pericles also talks about manners. He explains that in Athens people don't monitor and envy their neighbors, they respect each person's privacy and right to do as he pleases, even when what he does is disagreeable. But this does not encourage lawlessness because an Athenian does not limit himself to observing the written law. The general approbation of his peers is important to him, and to transgress unwritten cultural codes is to risk public disesteem. And, Pericles says pointedly, unlike other nations, in Athens the man who takes no part in his public duties is not considered quiet or unambitious but, rather, *useless*.

This is a democracy in which each person matters, and in which individual acts, great and small, are seen to contribute

materially to the culture. It is a community in which each citizen judges his own happiness in large measure by the quality and extent of his social engagement.

It is clear from Pericles that the Greeks were passionately interested in the formation and maintenance of a civil society, but they were just as fascinated by what it means to be an individual and how to construct a good life. Their achievements in science and art, philosophy and drama, sport and spectacle were all associated with this twin intellectual quest.

Happiness (*eudaimonia*), thought the Greeks, was not a passive state but rather an activity. *Arête*, the term usually translated as virtue, more fully means excellent or outstanding. In the Greek mind, happiness meant the act of living in accord with excellence. And the Greeks understood just how hard that goal was to achieve, which is why life for the Greeks was comic and tragic and heroic, all at the same time.

One of the greatest minds to emerge from Athenian democracy was Aristotle's. Aristotle was many things: empiricist, scientist, logician, rhetorician and philosopher. He was certainly no unalloyed democrat; he had his doubts about the merits of rule by the people. He was also an ethicist and the core of his views are laid out in his portrait of an ideal man in *Nicomachean Ethics*.

Aristotle's ideal citizen is very clearly a product of the sort of Athens that Pericles describes. He is, in total, great-souled.

He is prudent, brave, open-minded, reasonable. He is just. He is truthful, witty and good-tempered. He is generous and civilized. Friendship is very important to him. These are his virtues. And, as you might expect, humility and compassion and guilt are nowhere listed as desirable attributes—these are Christian virtues, not Greek ones.

These qualities seem in some respects very modern. The ideal Greek individual has an air of confidence that would inspire even the most dedicated self-esteem addict. And, as in our own era, the Greeks adored and celebrated individual excellence. They had a vivid celebrity culture, in which heroic warriors and beautiful young male athletes were rewarded for their prowess with prizes and laurels and odes and sculptures and vase paintings.

But there is an important distinction between the Greek individual and modern democratic man. Pericles points it out. And Aristotle makes this clear: he believed that man was essentially a political animal, or as Kitto puts it more accurately, "Man is an animal whose characteristic it is to live in the polis." Aristotle believed that society preceded the individual. And what's more, that no citizen could fully express or fulfill his humanity except through society. While Pericles and Aristotle would have differed on many things, on this point they would have agreed utterly.

Tocqueville found and prefigured our modern world of

social disconnection, in which social competitiveness and self-ish individualism draw people apart. Sometimes I fear we have locked ourselves into a foolish and ultimately doomed quest for personal advancement at the expense of the overall well-being of our society and ultimately, therefore, our own. I don't wonder that there is an epidemic of depression in wealthy countries—I am surprised there isn't more of it. When each one of us struggles to win at the expense of others, we will guarantee we all lose.

But the Greek attitude offers another model, in which we acknowledge the bonds linking us as citizens to each other and to our society. Of course we can't, today, have everyone participating personally in politics and government. Our societies are too big and too complex. We need to delegate our citizenship at least in part to a professional political class, advised by skilled and expert public servants.

But we can still have manners—a small, tangible and practical expression of our civic values. We can still enact our citizenship through them every day.

I think my favorite of all the Greek political innovations is the practice of ostracism. When the Assembly decided upon it, each citizen was invited to write upon a piece of broken earthenware the name of any citizen—anyone at all—whom he would like honorably removed from the city for ten years. No need to give a reason. Goodbye. See you in ten. It was a clever

way to resolve a political bottleneck or remove the leader of a dangerous faction. But the point is, exile was agony for an Athenian. Nothing was worse than being separated from the society of which you were an integral part—and which was an integral part of you. After all, it was contributing to your society that helped you fulfill your human potential.

And even though we're not Greeks, when we choose to exile ourselves, even metaphorically, from our own society, we also exile ourselves from an important aspect of our own humanity. To put it another way, to connect to our community is to dignify ourselves.

And here is the funniest thing. As I was reading about Athens and trying to imagine what it must have felt like to be a citizen in those great days, I kept feeling a niggling sensation at the back of my head. As if I had a memory of this exuberant world, just below the surface; a sort of deep knowledge that I couldn't explain.

Then one night I remembered, and I laughed out loud. Once, in Sydney, Australia, we *were* Athens in 400 BC. It was, of course, when we hosted the Olympic Games in the year 2000. We created, for a brief and shining two weeks, a polis in the Hellenic tradition, with the world's greatest athletes contesting for athletic arête, and all our citizens uniting to make our city a global beacon of affability and goodwill. The city was scrubbed and clean. Public transport was efficient,

and absolutely everyone used it. Most people had some connection with the great event: many thousands volunteered, others paid to go to events or else gathered at sites around the city where large screens were set up. I have never, before or since, smiled with so many strangers.

For once, we were all proud citizens of our polis, subscribing enthusiastically to the greater good. We discovered unexpected personal fulfillment in communal engagement. And there was a veritable epidemic of good manners.

4

Because sovereignty demands self-sovereignty

ONE OF THE DOWNSIDES of manners is undoubtedly that they impose constraints upon our personal freedoms. Rules, etiquette, social taboos—surely they interfere with the free and autonomous exercise of our personhood? Yes, as it happens, they do.

And in our modern era, this is regarded as a very serious drawback indeed because freedom is the twenty-first century's catchphrase and cure-all. It's the dream of every teenager under curfew. It's the hope of every Saturday morning lottery entrant with a mountain of personal debt. It's the slogan of the United States of America as it *liberates* nations from the yoke of dictatorships.

Freedom is beautiful, but it is not the only value. A completely free society would be—is—a recipe for anarchy. Order

is surely just as vital: personal security backed up by strong institutions and enforceable rules. Only within agreed-upon structures and limitations can freedom be safely enjoyed.

Manners are some of the limitations society imposes to prevent one person's rights from infringing upon another's. Sovereignty requires self-sovereignty.

Or, as Sigmund Freud put it more psychologically in 1930: "It is impossible to ignore the extent to which civilisation is built upon renunciation, the degree to which the existence of civilisation presupposes the non-gratification (suppression, repression or something else?) of powerful instinctual energies."

Ah, repression. So sadly undervalued in modern life.

Some years ago I worked for an Australian deputy prime minister who had formerly been Australia's minister for defence. Despite his appointment as minister for finance, the minister retained strong and affectionate links with the Australian military, an institution that he greatly cared about and admired. So he was regularly invited to attend military occasions and to give speeches.

The first time I had a close encounter with the Australian Defence Force was when the minister was asked to address the Australian Defence Force Academy, which is a sort of finishing school for the elite Australian officer class. I recall feeling slightly guilty and disreputable, and my spiky days in the eighties marching loudly for nuclear disarmament and the

eviction of U.S. military bases in Australia came to my mind as I passed through its portals with my minister for a preliminary cup of tea.

To say I was surprised by the experience is an understatement. As we went to the commanding officer's rooms, it was as if I had stepped back in time to the Edwardian tearoom described in one of my borrowed etiquette books. A silver teapot so polished it caught the light. Fine porcelain teacups. A seat pulled out for me, and pushed in behind. An air of respectful, indeed graceful, charm. I felt myself sitting a little taller, as if the elegant deportment of the officers were infectious. I felt myself pulling my feet under the chair, to hide my scuffed pumps. I wished I had smoother hair. But the courtesies were so refined that I quickly forgot my own inadequacies. The tea was excellent; the conversation stimulating; under such tender ministrations, I was charming, too. Like the minister, I came to realize that there were few things more enjoyable than afternoon tea with trained killers.

I also came to realize that the elaborate and indeed old-fashioned manners of the officer class serve a very important purpose. They are part of the overall code of self-discipline and regimentation that is essential to the effective running of any military. It is part of a code of behavior wisely imposed on them to stop them turning their guns upon each other—or mounting a coup. But it is more than this. When English

aesthete and conscientious objector Lytton Strachey was asked during World War I why he wasn't with the troops fighting for civilization, he replied superbly: "But Madam, I am the civilisation for which they are fighting."

We delegate to our military very extraordinary powers. We ask them to make wise judgments that will ensure our safety and preserve our national honor. That's why every day in a democracy the officer class needs to prove to itself and to the wider community not only that its soldiers are fighting for civilization—but more than this, that they, too, are part of the civilization they are fighting for. Their fine manners are a way to demonstrate that they are worthy of this trust.

Of course, fine manners do not automatically lead to goodness. The Nazis were particularly popular with elements of the English aristocracy because their military leaders had superlative manners. Manners are no guarantee against barbarism.

But they do prove that the officer class understands the standard of civilization expected of it by society. If it fails against that standard, then it can be held knowingly accountable.

We give our military so much freedom because we ask and trust them to delimit their actions. Manners are both an instrument to achieve, and evidence of, their self-control.

One night in 1695, a tremor ran through the richest court in the world. At the French palace of Versailles, presided over by the Sun King himself, Louis XIV, an event occurred of such awesome magnitude that the duc de Saint-Simon scurried back to his rooms and wrote that the courtiers were scared to death by what they had witnessed. As word spread of the event, even people who weren't present were reported to have experienced terrors.

The cause of this earthquake? The source of this shock and fear? Quite simply this: the most powerful man in the world had lost his temper.

The story goes as follows. The king had finished his dinner and risen from the table. His hat and cane were handed to him and he made to leave. But suddenly he observed a footman furtively pocketing a sweet biscuit. At that moment, as Saint-Simon said, his "royal dignity forgotten," the king rushed across the room, abused the miscreant and whacked him with his light bamboo cane, which immediately broke on the footman's shoulders. The footman was shocked and ran from the room.

That's it. That's the sum total of the event that reverberated around a terrified court. The royal lapse of manners

was considered so appalling that Saint-Simon could not help but seek extenuating circumstances for the king's actions. It turned out that the king had received personally devastating news from the northern front. His illegitimate son, the duc du Maine, had been cowardly and ineffective in battle and therefore the cause of terrible military reverses for the French army. While the military commander and courtiers were covering up this story to protect the king's feelings, no one had told the plan of deceit to the king's plainspoken bath attendant, who reported the humiliating truth to his sovereign.

But while this certainly explained the king's actions, it did not, as far as Saint-Simon and the other courtiers were concerned, in any way justify them. Indeed, the king himself took the view that his failure to control and repress his feelings was a crime. After the incident, he immediately went first to see his saintly wife and then to see his confessor, père François d'Aix de la Chaise, from whom he sought God's forgiveness for his sin.

Manners were critically important to Louis XIV. As a young boy, he had a terrifying experience when a group of nobles mounted an uprising against the crown. So as an adult, Louis XIV decided to centralize power and exert total control over the aristocracy. He built a magnificent home at Versailles and instructed all his courtiers to come and live with him rather than on their estates where they might develop separate

power bases and plot against him. To make Versailles attractive, he commissioned a nonstop parade of entertainments— Molière's plays and Lully's music, extravagant masked winter balls, gilded pleasure boats floating down long summer canals, hunting, gambling, summer feasting in the light of sparkling fountains and glorious fireworks displays. And to cap this exercise in domination, the king instituted a system of etiquette so rigorous that simply getting through each day at court became a full-time job.

Pleasure has never been better organized, nor put to such powerful political purpose.

And the severity behind the soft codes was well understood. If any independent-minded courtier absented himself, tiptoeing off to the freedom of his estate or sneaking out to the wanton delights of Paris, the king was bound to notice. Even in a room of three hundred people, the king was famous for spotting a truancy. The phrase people most dreaded was the monarch's quiet "I do not see him," which converted almost instantly into the loss of privileges, favors and financially lucrative appointments.

If the king cannot see you, you no longer exist.

Over the course of Louis XIV's long reign, as the court aged and the glamour wore off, the etiquette became excruciating in its detail and dreary in its execution. People were reduced to agonizing over what kind of chair or stool one was permitted

to sit on in the king's presence (if a seat were permitted at all); who had the fortune to receive the small notation (*pour,* meaning for) on his bedroom door that marked the king's favor; and who was privileged to hold a candle at the king's bedtime. The ennui became so extreme that the king's sister-in-law prayed not to have the honor of sitting next to the king at church, because His Majesty would prod her with his elbow to keep her awake. Even the king himself was eventually bored. "What a torture," said his second wife, Madame de Maintenon, "to be obliged to amuse a man who is unamusable."

The curious thing about this world of ceremony is that no one was more bound by it than Louis XIV himself. He lived his entire life in public. Each step in his day had arcane ceremonials attached. Just getting up and dressed in the morning represented an epic ritual. In the morning, a hundred courtiers had the privilege of attending the king's *grand lever.* One gentleman was appointed to drape the dressing gown around the king, another assisted him to adjust the right sleeve and a third to adjust his left. Someone else would have the honor of rubbing the king with orange water and spirits of wine. And so it went on, interminably.

Louis XIV never said, as rumored, *"l'état, c'est moi."* It was redundant. It was perfectly well understood that in Louis XIV, the body personal embodied the body politic. But that did not give him license to behave as he pleased. On the con-

trary, the king's right to rule his kingdom relied upon his ability to rule himself. As it happened, whacking his footman did
not bring about the downfall of Louis XIV's government,
and he retained his title as the most powerful king in Europe
until his death in 1715. But in order to rule this world, he had
to rule himself. That's why his one little slip had the reverber-
ations of a small earthquake.

Just recently, I was woken from fitful sleep at 7 A.M. by the
sound of a cleaner waving a noisy leaf blower around the
parking lot of a building across the road from my apartment.
This was very annoying, but I soon became aware that the
strong southerly breeze was in. That the leaf blower was noisy
was bad enough; that it was almost certainly ineffective was in-
tolerable. I became itchy and agitated at the very idea. I found
that I very much wanted to shout abuse at someone; I was absolutely ready to lose all self-control.

I knew the signs, of course. I'd been there before, complete
with the requisite rationalizations. Damn it, I'm going to go
for it, to hell with the consequences. It's what I really think.
Why shouldn't I just say it? And I've felt the tingling electric
surge you get when you're about to crash through the polite social barricades, when the atmosphere momentarily changes
like the air pressure dropping before a tropical storm, when the

atoms shift and reassemble around you. And then—that brief intoxicating whirlwind as just for once, hotheaded, you say what you truly want to say.

(Which would be something along the lines of: "What the FUCK do you think you are doing? Do you realize how noisy and POINTLESS that thing is? Haven't you noticed there is a gale force wind blowing? And that all you are doing is creating chaos? Are you a TOTAL FOOL?")

Lucky for me, I didn't say any of it. I can't claim that my manners saved me; my intentions were thoroughly malign. It's just that my inherent laziness and addiction to routine, plus a dash of cowardice, sufficiently delayed action. By the time I had dressed, drunk a cup of coffee and scanned a newspaper, the noise had finished and the moment of blinding fury had passed. I was grateful for the hiatus because later I rang the office manager and was able to explain the problem in a relatively calm voice. This met with a positive response and a productive discussion. While I would have ideally liked to hear that brooms and dustpans were thenceforth back in fashion, instead a compromise was reached that leaf blowers would not commence in the parking lot before 8 A.M.

It might have been exhilarating to deliver the outraged blast. But then again, it might have been nothing more than a momentary self-indulgence to be followed, as night follows day, by 3 A.M. self-disgust and bitter recriminations. Manners

always provide the automatic, the healthy, the kindly, the later-to-be-welcomed restraint. They make it possible to resume the conversation. They allow for the possibility of a civilized exchange of views rather than a childish airing of sentiment. They allow for the fact that what you think first thing in the grumpy and uncaffeinated morning may not be quite the same as what you think an hour later.

I am glad I did not give in to my base instincts because I almost certainly achieved a better outcome using good manners than if I had succumbed to my first impulse: a naked and raging Lucinda confronting a handyman peacefully waving his, um, tool.

. . . order is necessary to freedom

Louis XIV found that manners are a way to reinforce order. But manners, in a delightful reversal of expectation, can also nurture freedom. If, in the eighteenth century, you had been a brilliant and progressive intellectual; if you had wanted to explore new frontiers in literature, science, art and politics; if you had wanted to create a liberated, enlightened world, there was only one place for you to go. While Versailles was still the center of power for those who were clinging to the past, nearby there was another center of power for those who were inventing the future: the salons of Paris.

A salon was, quite simply, a gathering of guests under

the auspices of an elegant society lady. A core group would convene once or twice weekly and their numbers would be augmented by various visitors and foreigners. The hostess would act as moderator, chair, mediator and facilitator. She would use her charm, discretion, intimacy, tact and personal authority to guide, shape and manage the conversation. In the salons of Paris, women created the premier school of manners in Western civilization.

The salons began in the early seventeenth century with a deliberate emphasis on changing social culture. Women were sick of the violent habits of their men. So they changed the rules. Instead of having duels outside with swords, the men were encouraged to bring their disputes into gilded drawing rooms where conflicts were resolved by words. Just as cutting as the blade, but rarely with mortal consequences. Many of these innovations were incorporated into the early life of Versailles by Louis XIV.

And many of the words we use to delineate the specifics of manners today still echo the culture of these French drawing rooms: *étiquette; savoir-faire; faux pas; bon mot; RSVP (répondez s'il vous plaît)*. Some of the terms are deliciously subtle, like *mauvaise honte*, which means false shame, an emotion that I am fairly sure no longer exists: when your society no longer has shame, there's little incentive to fake it. Or *amour propre*, the

bubble of self-regard, most tellingly felt when someone has punctured it. Or *l'esprit de l'escalier*, when you think of something devastatingly witty to say to someone, just that infuriating fractional second after the moment has passed.

And while English is now the global language, French still holds an important place in international diplomacy. The evolution from drawing room manners to international diplomacy makes eminent sense: why go to war when you can sort out differences via discussion, negotiation, mediation and agreement between your appointed representatives? The United Nations and the diplomatic corps still use many French words like *envoy, chargé d'affaires, démarche, aide-mémoire, agrément, rapporteur* and *rapprochement.* Although without, necessarily, the same effectiveness as the *salonnières* in their heyday.

For by the eighteenth century, the salons were so important that the Enlightenment basically took place under the guidance of a few very smart, very alert older French women. And it was a school of tough love: if a salon hostess accompanied you to the door, you knew straightaway that you had failed to please and *you were not welcome again.*

The highly mannered environment of the salons did not hinder the new era of free intellectual discourse; in fact it made it possible. The salon became a space where challenging, controversial concepts could be aired, refined, contested

and disseminated. Newtonian cosmology? The demerits of monarchies? The composition of gunpowder? The follies of romantic love? No matter how risqué the subject, the salon was the only place to explore it.

A paradox: the salon was one of the more repressive, contrived institutions in human history. And that's why it played a vital role in the Enlightenment, one of humankind's greatest phases of intellectual liberation.

Baron de Montesquieu spent twenty years thinking about politics and society and contemplating the British political model before he published *The Spirit of the Laws*. This groundbreaking work on government argued for the separation of powers into executive, legislative and judiciary branches so that no single branch could threaten the freedom of the people. These ideas were so politically explosive that the book had to be published secretly. But the salon hostesses of Paris made sure it was a major success, and the Americans went on to use the work as a template for the United States Constitution.

Madame Geoffrin hosted her gatherings on Wednesdays, centering around a young generation of philosophes. They, too, had a daring and dangerous project under way. The *Encyclopédie*. It was a huge undertaking—twenty-one volumes of text and eleven volumes of engravings appeared spasmodically over twenty long, hard years. This tome included everything from how to grow and cook asparagus to the latest theories of

inoculation. All the new scientific discoveries were included, as well as technical information on everything from silk-weaving to metal-pressing.

Today this sounds commonplace but then it was extraordinarily dangerous. It was threatening to the governing classes sitting in Versailles because it took for granted religious tolerance, freedom of thought and the value of science and industry. It proposed to take information out of the hands of an elite few and equip ordinary people with the tools to create the future. Revolutionary idea. All the greats contributed to this enormous exercise, including Montesquieu and also Voltaire, Buffon the naturalist and a succession of scientists, technicians and thinkers.

The editor of the *Encyclopédie*, Denis Diderot, wasn't a natural salon guest. He was bold and outspoken. He lacked the social graces. "A great man," remarked Voltaire after meeting him, "but nature has refused him an essential talent: that of dialogue." In the salons this was, of course, a disaster. Madame Geoffrin certainly never allowed heated discussions. She was willing that the philosophers should remodel the world, said one of her critics, on condition that the kingdom of Diderot should come without disorder or confusion. When the conversation became too vociferous, she silenced her guests with her catchphrase: *"Voilà qui est bien,"* she'd say. That's quite enough.

Today this kind of behavior—a bossy woman directing

the conversation—would perhaps be considered socially unacceptable. In our egalitarian times, how dare anyone seek to take social charge? But the salon hostess expected deference and she got it. She controlled the guests, the topics, the time, the style. The salons were so restrictive that even the writing style of the philosophers was influenced by them. As Diderot said, "Women accustom us to making even the driest and thorniest of subjects clear and entertaining since we are always addressing ourselves to them. We gradually acquire a certain facility of expression that passes from our conversation into our style of writing." Through learning to write in the lucid, persuasive style that appealed to the salon set, the philosophers were also learning to write for, educate and eventually politicize the broader public.

By enforcing standards—in conversational style, in writing style, in manners—the women of the salons were effectively creating a neutral, safe territory upon which the most diverse and daring ideas could be safely discussed. They created a common ground for dialogue, making it possible to bring together individuals holding very diverse and even antagonistic views of the world. Out of manners came intellectual emancipation, the prelude to political change. Manners in this context were not about conformity, not at all. On the contrary, they were simply a means to help very different people ex-

change ideas with one another. Using manners to create the rules of engagement meant that you could debate contested ideas with someone instead of killing them.

In the salons of Paris, manners may have contracted the egoistic individual self, but they expanded the polity. Manners provided the confinement to give birth to freedom.

. . . and manners reconcile liberty to stability

Growing up in the 1960s and '70s, we children minded our manners. At home we said *please* and *thank you*, we did our household jobs, we waited our turn and we knew our place. School was a long, acculturating process of discipline and habit.

But in a curious way, the boring and predictable regimentation of an ordinary childhood protected our privacy and unleashed our inner lives. People always seem to be poking into children's minds these days, encouraging them to express themselves. But a child is often not ready to express. Children need time to absorb, to soak the world in, to dream. I always discovered a creative feeling in myself when I was unoccupied; it was the signal to make something up. If anything, the secret self, the self as yet unknown, could develop in free quietude, in the peacefulness of routine.

And in the meantime I was learning how to live in a society. When we caught the bus or train, we stood up for all adults. This expectation was rigorously enforced. If we did not do so, the adult commuters would not hesitate to berate us, or even ring the school, and then we'd be in dreadful trouble. I remember sometimes feeling resentful, feeling little and weak and tired, with my big schoolbag and weary legs on a long bus ride. But I also knew I was part of a larger continuity, of community. I assumed that one day the young people would stand for me.

No one ever talked to us about freedom. No one ever talked to us about our rights and liberties. On the contrary, we were trained to respect the rights and liberties of others. And of course, the self-respect was deeply implied: this is how worthwhile people behave.

The priests and nuns of our Catholic schools drilled us, quite literally, into order. Weekly marching practice was about taming our individual selves, putting us into sturdy lockstep, and as we wheeled and spun in long even rows, as we sometimes grabbed the chance to step out of line, we always knew we'd have to step back in. And there was a consoling force in this knowledge.

A defined world, a world of contours and shapes and boundaries, is not such a bad thing. "Self-control at least develops a self," said cultural historian Jacques Barzun.

Our ability to control ourselves—or perhaps more accurately, to tolerate controls—is important, because where Louis XIV embodied the state in a single person, the fundamental principle of our modern democracies is that we embody the state collectively. *L'état, c'est nous.* Each one of us carries within us a kernel of sovereignty. And so we each must carry a measure of responsibility, too.

As individuals and as societies, we tread a delicate balance between order and freedom, personal liberty and social stability. Manners are a modest and effective means to help us resolve this complex equation.

And not just to preserve the status quo—but to help us forge a more enlightened future, as well.

5

Because who else can
we call on?

Not so very long ago, we had a group of people in society who carried the banner for manners. We knew them by various names, many of which were not altogether complimentary: the toffs, the nobs, the blue bloods, the grandees, the snobs, the swells, the aristocrats, the upper classes, the ruling classes. Them as opposed to Us. They were society's leaders and they set the style and standard of living to which the rest of us aspired. Whether we liked it or not, they were the elites, and manners were their business.

It didn't matter that most of the population never actually met or socialized with these Olympian citizens. All we needed to know was that the elites enjoyed a lifestyle worth aspiring to, full of glamour, parties, comforts and fun. Their glittering lives—illustrated in the society pages, reported in the

vice-regal columns—provided the carrot and stick for generations of careworn parents struggling to inculcate civilized behavior into their children. Mums would say to their grunting boys: *You'll never get to the governor's table if you eat like that!* Grans would say to their slovenly granddaughters: *You won't get away with grubby hands at the queen's afternoon tea!* Social aspiration was the driving force for the spread and codification of manners.

Of course, it was never the case that manners were solely the preserve of the social elite. Indeed, it may well be debatable whether elites ever had the most desirable manners. But it was certainly the case that elite manners set the broader social tone. In *My Fair Lady*, Eliza Doolittle wants to learn the manners of Professor Higgins's class, not the other way around. And even though Eliza's roguish dad is the most sympathetic character of all, no one asks for tuition in *his* amusing and larcenous working-class manners.

So here we are in modern democratic consumer life without an elite class whose authority we unquestioningly accept. In the absence of aristocrats, which group is in a position to go beyond merely minding their own manners and take on the greater burden of influencing manners across society?

Celebrities might seem likely candidates. They are, after all, the most visibly privileged caste in modern life. Beautiful film actresses, wild rock stars, the latest TV personalities—they gaze down like gods and goddesses from the heights of

magazine covers and websites and movie screens and stadium arenas and glittering advertisements. Their every move and pronouncement is recorded and replayed endlessly. But while gullible young girls may be dazzled by them, I don't think celebrities are seen as realistic role models. Indeed, their elite status often depends upon a simulated rebellion against the codes of civilized life rather than conformity to them, and certainly not leadership in maintaining them. Like the deistic pantheon of ancient times, they play a darker role: they enact our dreams and our nightmares. We like our celebrities to be mixed up, romantically troubled, creatively wacky, drugged out, in rehab, in litigation, anointed, betrayed, restored, humiliated, resurrected and pursued like wild creatures through the streets. We don't look to celebrities for guidance; we look to them to learn how *not* to live.

Political leaders might naturally be referred to as a source of manners; they certainly once played such a role. But in modern life politicians can't or won't admit to the responsibilities of being elite because any hint of arrogance in political life is a neat shortcut to electoral death. So instead they pretend to be regular folks. Ordinary. One of the people. Just muddling through. They don't like to use the patrician language of leadership. Instead, they deploy deeply egalitarian phrases such as: *I'm listening. I share your concerns. The government certainly meant well. That matter was never brought to my attention.* If they are smart, they

pretend to be dumb. Often they *are* dumb, but they act even dumber. And modern politicians are increasingly less likely to act in the genuine interests of their voters than to represent their opinions, which is not at all the same thing. More often than not, our politicians are not leaders but panderers, hostage to daily opinion polls and focus groups. Perhaps the most important point is simply this: too few people aspire to the life of a modern politician for them to be effective role models.

There's another group. As governments have receded from their highly interventionist role in most modern economies, big corporations have become vast engines of wealth-production, employment and influence. And within these corporations we find a cadre of executives who are amassing enormous fortunes. Riding the market boom, flush with stocks and options, accruing vast multiples of the salaries of their subordinates, this new caste is truly a new elite. Barring some major glitch, their children will be rich and their children's children will also be rich. But I recently read a survey that said that even very wealthy businesspeople choose to describe themselves with astonishing and resolute inaccuracy as *middle class* and *on average incomes*. In other words, they'd rather the rest of us took no notice of them and they are not at all keen to take on a social leadership role.

If we accept that our modern elites can't or won't accept the task of shaping our social attitudes and manners, how do we

shape and disseminate modern manners? How do we promulgate courtesy?

. . . rudeness won't make us authentic

But first we must address a problem, because many good people don't accept the premise. They aren't at all sure that manners represent an unmitigated good that should be promulgated.

Which is a shame, because for a very long period of time in Western culture, manners were seen as partners of progress. It was widely accepted that social rules made societies better, happier and more civilized. An interest in manners among the ruling classes developed alongside a love of science, culture, legal reforms, literature and art. Reason and manners sat cheerfully side by side.

But then a new generation of philosophers, led by Jean-Jacques Rousseau, profoundly and permanently rearranged the scale of virtues in the late eighteenth century. A new alliance of values began to emerge. Nature was suddenly better than Culture. Feelings were better than Reason. And Sincerity and Spontaneity were higher, nobler and more moral than cold-blooded, artificial, hypocritical, faking-it, clapped-out old manners. This was Romanticism replacing Classicism and we are all still paying the price: "The worst are full of passionate intensity," said Yeats.

These new ideas coincided tellingly with the publication of a book on manners. Over the course of many years, Lord Chesterfield of England had written a series of letters to his illegitimate son, Philip Stanhope. The letters were never meant to be made public. But after Lord Chesterfield's death in 1773, his intimate missives were issued by a relative. And they caused a huge scandal.

Lord Chesterfield had spent a lot of time in France and his advice is heavily influenced by the French view of the world: it is wise and worldly and sophisticated. It assumes that we all live together in society and that manners enable us to advance our own interests in the world. It treats manners at least in part as a useful tool for material progress. Virginia Woolf described the advice as "urbane, polished, brilliant," as indeed it is.

But Lord Chesterfield's book appeared during a time when society was suddenly suspicious about manners. And one, in particular, of his frank and astute observations gave potent ammunition to the new Romantics:

If you would particularly gain the affection and friendship of particular people, whether men or women, endeavour to find out their predominant excellency, if they have one, and their prevailing weakness, which everybody has: and do justice to the one, and something more than justice to the other. Men have various objects in which they may excel, or at least would be thought to excel; and though they love

to hear justice done to them, where they know that they excel, yet they are most and best flattered upon those points where they wish to excel and yet are doubtful whether they do or not.

Aha! Here, in Chesterfield's own words, was the evidence, the proof, the smoking gun of the appalling immorality of manners. Manners weren't about indifferent courtesy at all, but about the calculated manipulation of others for personal gain. They were plainly no ennobling feature of human society; on the contrary, they were perversions of natural human goodness. The case was once and for all summed up by Lord Chesterfield's onetime friend Dr. Johnson, who declared that the advice "preached the morals of a whore and the manners of a dancing master."

Chesterfield's world is certainly full of subtlety and, yes, flattery. It assumes that human beings are various creatures, and that social intercourse is multilayered. In a way, far from demeaning human interactions, his advice lends gravity and interest to it all. Because to succeed in his world you must also be thoughtful, considerate, charming and reasonable. And that's no small task. In fact, the standard of behavior the lord sets for his son is arduous and exacting. Among his injunctions: You must be well educated, self-disciplined and modest. You must study in the morning, acquire no less than three languages, inform yourself about all good things. You must

observe social decorum, dress soberly but carefully, use perfect grammar, never talk about yourself, never be a bigot or an eccentric or absentminded or a bore.

Now this seems to me like excellent advice to a young person. Indeed, if only there were more of it. I am even prepared to defend Chesterfield *père*'s seemingly Machiavellian recommendations that his son study the strengths and weaknesses of other people and respond to them accordingly. Is that not an ideal way for a young person to discover a great deal about human nature, and perhaps about himself? Often I think the young need time to work out who they are and what kind of person they want to become. What better way than by carefully observing the drives and motives of others? I have no doubt that Chesterfield never intended his son to turn into some shallow or deceitful chameleon. Certainly Chesterfield himself never did. As he lay dying in 1773, a visitor came into the room. "Give Dayrolles a chair," said the courteous lord, and then expired. It's hard to imagine he expected any social advantage from his dying words.

But by then it was all too late, because the Romantic movement was well under way. And in the Romantic worldview, civilization and its attendant baggage—and most particularly manners—came to be seen as a barrier to the expression of natural and authentic man. With Jean-Jacques Rousseau, the

fantasy of the noble savage was born, and we live with the sad consequences today.

When Rousseau wrote his famous *Confessions* in 1770, he boastfully claimed at the outset that it would have no imitator. After all, he no doubt thought, who else but J.-J. Rousseau would be so hungry for notoriety that he would be prepared to expose to the world the most intimate details of his life, including farming his five children out to orphanages, unusual sexual experiences (including his encounter with a Venetian courtesan with a deformed nipple) and urinary problems?

As it turns out, just about everybody. Any day on television we can now see Rousseau's cultural descendants confessing the most gruesome details about their marriages or childhoods or dysfunctional relationships or weight problems. They do so with an air of therapeutic self-satisfaction as if, no matter how gravely they have fouled up their lives, their frankness is a tribute to the healthy connection they have forged with their authentic selves.

But here's the thing: as critics like the historian Paul Johnson have pointed out, Rousseau's claim of authenticity was, in fact, bogus. Rousseau used distortion, exaggeration and selective memory both to misrepresent himself and to avenge himself upon others.

As do his successors today.

There's a horrible new category of reality TV programming like *Big Brother* in which people are locked up together for weeks on end. The drama seems to rely upon placing such stress upon contestants that their codes of civility are progressively broken down. In extremis, each contestant's "authentic" self is revealed, for which they may be punished or rewarded via text message. But these are highly artificial situations and the contestants are explicitly selected on the basis of their narcissism and exhibitionism. As it turns out, you *can* fake authenticity.

Rousseau boasted that he had dispensed himself from the artifice and manipulation of manners. He said, ". . . my sentiments are such that they must not be disguised." He declared he was "rude on principle." He proclaimed: "I have things in my heart which absolve me from being good mannered." I am not sure what those things were.

But it seems to me that Lord Chesterfield's advice almost certainly offers a better path to genuine maturity than Rousseau's agenda of rejecting society in pursuit of some elusive "natural" self.

I just can't see that rudeness makes you real.

. . . manners aren't just the tool of right-wing bigots

And another thing.

Not long ago over dinner at a friend's home, I raised the

topic of manners and asked for his views on the subject. I might as well have grabbed a hot poker and prodded him. With an air of mounting rage, he told me unequivocally that he *loathed* manners. He'd spent his whole life escaping from his *repressed* lower-middle-class family in his *appalling* bourgeois regional town. He had always hated manners and he wasn't about to start complaining about the lack of them now. Manners were a way to create dull, *obedient*, uncritical human beings leading boring *conformist* lives.

At that point I felt I fully understood his views. (*So, I gather you're not too keen on manners?*) But there was more, much more.

Manners made my friend *sick*. They made him think of small-town snobbery and *hypocrisy*, like his gloves-and-hat grandmother with her pseudo-refinements and her bigoted opinions about single mothers. Manners created a *tedious*, stultified, rules-bound society. Manners were for social conservatives who were afraid of change. Manners were about telling other people how to behave. Manners were a way to stop all change, progress or creativity. Manners were just *wrong*.

At least I knew where he stood. His was an updated version of the Romantic antipathy to manners. Plus, he had a point.

Today a whole generation of baby boomers like my friend prides itself on the social reforms that were achieved at least in part through bad manners. People who were young in the

1960s broke through the racist and sexist taboos of their parents to unlock a better world. They grew their hair, massed on the streets, burned their bras, made free love and, by defying the rules of etiquette, exposed the encoded bigotry and small-mindedness of their elders. They threw out tired old protocols and brought in a new era of permissiveness, openness, spontaneity and unconventionality. Anti-manners equaled pro-progress.

And real progress was achieved. Huge political battles were fought and won on behalf of the rights of women and African Americans and indigenous peoples and minority groups. When Rosa Parks refused to give up her seat on a bus to a white man in 1955, she broke the law, and she broke the equally powerful taboo of contemporary Southern manners. Some battles, such as the right to gay marriage, are still being waged, and the push for parity is probably irresistible.

An eloquent reiteration of the suspicious baby-boomer attitude toward manners comes from Michael Hanlon in the August 2004 edition of *Spectator* magazine.

The conservatives argue that our society is the most ill-mannered in history. Really? Let's go back to the 1950s, shall we, the so-called golden age of politeness when gentlemen always took off their hats on entering a building, children minded their ps and qs and women were unfamiliar with the ways of the doorhandle. "No blacks, no

Irish," seen on boarding houses and hotels after the first waves of post-war immigration were affronts to decency and good manners un-thinkable today. People talked, without shame, about "Jewboys" and "nignogs" and the wealthy showed their inbreeding by behaving with grotesque condescension towards the lower orders, a term used with-out irony well into the last century. . . . Now is good; the future, barring some calamitous accident, will be better.

The baby boomers were never on their own, of course, in privileging the dream of a liberated future over a repressive present. The post-Napoleonic generation in France and Germany was intensely Romantic, heavily influenced by Rousseau, with disillusioned young people bucking against their elders and dreaming of the untrammeled exertion of the will. The French writer Stendhal, in his *Memoirs of an Egoist*, raged against the politeness of the upper classes in France and England that "proscribes all energy and grinds it down if by chance it exists. Perfectly polite and perfectly devoid of all energy . . ." The Romantics grew their hair, wore pink waistcoats and espoused the liberation of Greece.

After World War I, another disillusioned generation of Bright Young Things embraced the manners of Modernism. T. S. Eliot wrote poems that reflected the deep disillusion with the older generation that had stolen the lives of so many young men in a pointless war: "In the room the women come

and go/Talking of Michelangelo," Eliot wrote bleakly of English social life. "We are the hollow men/We are the stuffed men . . ." The inter-war generation cut their hair (the women, anyway) and championed abstract art and the cause of socialism in Spain.

But it seems to me the anti-manners posture is more than just an intergenerational issue, more than just tomorrow defending itself against yesterday.

Michael Hanlon clearly believes that declaring yourself pro-manners is equivalent to declaring yourself a political conservative. And it remains true that conservative politicians are more likely to defend manners than socially progressive ones. This means that when someone in public life asserts the importance of manners, a whole generation of baby boomers instinctively questions their motives. Like Hanlon, in fact, they immediately tag a defender of manners as (a) authoritarian and (b) nostalgic for a bigoted past.

Such labeling makes things awkward for someone like me who considers herself socially progressive but who cares about manners. Is this crossing over to the dark side: aligning oneself with abhorrently bourgeois values; stamping oneself as a defender of the old discriminatory racial, class and gender hierarchies; declaring oneself a relic and a reactionary? Let's face it, who among us wants to be the lead fogy, the head

fuddy-duddy, the number one busybody, the annoying, interfering, nosy so-and-so, the oh, God, no, the manners Nazi?

But it seems to me that these clear-cut political demarcation lines may no longer apply.

The progressive approach has always been about creating
a more egalitarian future. In Australia you'll still hear left-
wing political allies greet each other with an only half-ironic
Comrade! And because the left has always favored state interven-
tion, progressive politicians are more inclined to use legislative
instruments like industrial relations and anti-discrimination
laws to bring about a more civil society.

Take what is now called, usually pejoratively, political correctness. At its best, this is a code—sometimes legislated—
of progressive manners. It means you don't offend members of
minority groups through the use of demeaning language or
stereotypes. But it has a very clear downside. At its worst, it becomes a form of censorship over free speech: when people are
too scared to say what they really think for fear of being la-
beled a bigot.

I personally am delighted that it is socially unacceptable to
say *kikes* or *niggers*. And I am quite content that this requires
some people to think privately the ugly opinions they won't
have the courage to say in public. Hypocrisy may be repugnant,
but it is usually preferable to the confident airing of bigoted

opinions. It is, after all, as La Rochefoucauld noted long ago, "the tribute that vice pays to virtue." I am less comfortable with the legislative emphasis of political correctness. Far more effective than the legal sanction is the social one. It's exhilarating to think that community outrage can force radio shock jocks or celebrities or politicians to apologize, or even resign, for vilifying the members of a particular race or social group.

The other day I was on a bus with a friend when we heard behind us vigorous mutterings about the failings of the driver, who happened to be, I imagine, from South Asia. Two little old ladies were in full flight. I turned and saw a tiny ancient thing with her handbag perched on her lap like a shield against foreign invasion as she pursed her lips and summed up the thrust of the exchange: "Well, I suppose I don't mind if they let them in *as long as they learn our manners.*"

My friend bristled. Here was racism plain and simple. Here was another example of that long, dishonorable tradition whereby manners provided an excuse for social exclusion. But I saw it somewhat differently. Perhaps the little old ladies *were* racist. Many people are. Or perhaps they were merely expressing their fear of newcomers and the inevitable changes they would bring. Even so, they had resigned themselves, if reluctantly, to the evolving order. And they had rightly identified the adoption of local manners by the newcomers as a simple concession to make this change more tolerable.

To my mind there is a rather different downside to manners. It's not so much that they provide cover for the bigot or hypocrite, but that they induce a kind of social silence on those who might unmask them. I was reminded of this while watching the film *Borat,* in which a fictional yokel, bigot and philistine from an imaginary Kazakhstan tours America. In one scene, Borat turns up at a classic white, pillared, antebellum mansion for a dinner party where he hopes to practice his newly acquired Southern etiquette. His host and her guests behave with immaculate charm and courtesy in the Southern fashion. Borat progressively ramps up his outrages. Politically incorrect remarks. Ignorance of hygiene. Then toilet antics— including producing a bag of shit and asking the hostess what to do with it. At each step in his downward progress, the Southerners are comically pained prisoners of their etiquette: you can see their unease as they try to humor their appalling guest. The strain on their faces is hilarious and upsetting all at the same time. Finally, a cheerful whore turns up at the front door and when Borat brings her to the dinner table, the Southerners abandon all efforts to redeem the barbarian. They throw him out. But it took some time. They had tolerated Borat's antisocial behavior for way too long because to do otherwise might have appeared intolerant, ill-mannered and even—how cruelly ironic—antisocial.

The political agenda behind Borat's comic antics is an

interesting one. Borat's creator, Sacha Baron Cohen, apparently seeks to do two things—to vividly expose those sexists and bigots who would agree with Borat's ugly views, and to condemn the polite but fundamentally immoral passivity that people tend to adopt when confronted by prejudice. But the film shows, perhaps unintentionally, the positive role that manners can play. It reveals that manners *do* tend to keep the lid on most unacceptable behavior. And when pushed, the decent people in the film firmly reject Borat's racist and sexist worldview.

Now, let us travel to the other side of the political spectrum and consider the idea of manners in relation to conservatism. Conservatives by definition favor the past and resist change. Some still, no doubt, look back nostalgically to manners as a way of reinforcing social inequality, which at its ugliest means those great days when the swinish multitudes, the vulgar masses, the hideous hoi polloi, knew their subservient place. But surely conserving the past is not always and necessarily bad. While people may fondly like to imagine history as a series of unbroken advancements, at worst interrupted by the odd hiccup like the Black Death or World War II, the truth is, it can—and has—gone horribly wrong. Go to Granada and see the tinkling fountains and the magnificent gardens and you want to weep for the demise of that glorious Islamic civilization. Go to Athens and see the crumbling architecture of classical Hellas.

Go to Macedonia and see the Byzantine frescoes disappearing into the stone walls like the culture that created them.

No civilization lasts forever, and it is nearly always a close-run thing. If you were a Roman in the fifth century, the barbarians really were at the gate. And when the curtain comes down on a civilization, it can be a very long time before it rises again. Even the basics can be so swiftly forgotten. After the Roman demise, it was centuries before baths came back into fashion: those years weren't called the Dark Ages for nothing.

There's merit in conserving things. Today we try to conserve biodiversity, energy, heritage buildings, remnant bushland. Just as we look to conserve the best of nature or architecture, surely it's worth remembering our most delightful customs?

Manners can never, of course, be permanently fixed like fossils in amber. They must, and do, evolve and adapt. But at their best they are a species of cultural memory. The things we do today—shake hands, clink glasses—become an affectionate nod to our past. A salute to our ancient humanity and to the funny, anxious rituals of our forebears. Men once shook hands to prove they carried no weapons. They clinked drinking vessels to slop wine into each other's glasses, disproving the presence of poison. Today, as we forgetfully play out the rituals of modern life, we are nevertheless communing with the mysterious and delicate process that is our civilization.

To me this seems very beautiful—and perhaps it explains why I find myself so sensitive to the signals that these links are becoming more and more attenuated, why I am so alarmed by the little signs that we are untethering ourselves from our historical moorings.

. . . and they advance social progress

Here's a thought: What if—in our modern era—manners were not conservative but subversive?

What if those old-fashioned conventions and courtesies that take up time, make no money, serve no commercial utility—what if, far from upholding some ugly status quo, they were in fact a protest against it, a green oasis of gentle civilization in the jungle of consumer capitalism? What if the little gestures that make life sweeter and kinder and more predictable were a wonderful rebuke to the cruel consume-work-die routine of modern life? What if manners were, rather like recycling and community volunteering, a modest way to uphold the values of community in the midst of the rampant commercialization of modern life? And what if, instead of repressing our authentic selves, manners allowed them to flower?

In 1928, one of the founding members of the Bloomsbury group, art critic Clive Bell, wrote and published a little book called *Civilization*. He dedicated his essay to his dear friend

Virginia Woolf, with whom he had already discussed many of his ideas on the subject.

Bell was writing in the aftermath of World War I, spurred by the death of millions of young Englishmen who were sent to fight in the trenches for the cause, their government told them, of civilization. Having lost many of his friends in that war, Bell considered it might be worthwhile working out what exactly was this "civilization" in the name of which so many young men had died. Many of the ideas Bell expressed would now be considered old-fashioned and indeed politically incorrect, which is probably why I enjoyed them so much. Bell considered that the first step toward civilization was "the correction of instinct by reason"; the second, "the deliberate rejection of immediate satisfactions with a view to obtaining subtler."

Bell argued that all civilizations depend upon a small but potent core of highly civilized individuals. A leisured class is essential, Bell said. And he explained exactly what this leisured class required: leisure, of course, but also economic freedom and liberty to think, feel and experiment—no doubt a list all too familiar to Virginia Woolf, who agreed that every artist needs a room of her own.

Bell was writing at a time when the British economy was an inflexible, near-broken machine and British society was simi-

larly rigid and restrictive. He assumed that there were only two possible classes: those living comfortably off capital, and those working hard for wages. The fortunate few who had capital were the group from which the leisured class might spring. In his view, almost all forms of moneymaking were detrimental to intense and refined states of mind, because almost all tired the body and blunted the intellect.

But Bell stressed that leisured did not necessarily mean pampered—the Athenian Greeks, as he noted, lived in great simplicity and yet had the finest of all civilizations. And indeed, Bloomsbury itself was noted for the relatively simple lifestyles of its members. And its progressive politics. Think of what came from Bloomsbury—the feminism of Virginia Woolf, the economics of John Maynard Keynes, the sexually liberated lifestyles of nearly all its members and a legacy of intelligent freethinking that has influenced successive generations.

Of course, Bell's basic point is unimpeachable. Civilization has always been a function of time left over after the necessities of food and shelter have been dealt with.

But in modern life it seems to me that the circumstances for civilization are not necessarily the all-or-nothing proposition that Bell imagined. The truth is that many of us do have the opportunity to create lives that are civilized. The world is no longer divided between capitalists whooping it up on the one hand and workers laboring under the yoke on the other.

Most of us in the modern middle class, with our mortgages and retirement funds and jobs, are both capitalists and workers. We have much greater flexibility. We may work full-time for ten years then take a year off, or obtain our long-service leave, or take a study break. We may choose to work part-time. We can move in and out of jobs, we can work as contractors or consultants, we can telecommute, we can shift between companies and job locations. Never in human history have we ordinary people had such capacity to influence our own working lives.

We live and work in very flexible economies. And while this presents its own challenges and anxieties, at least we are not condemned to work in the same dreary office for forty years before getting a gold watch at age sixty and dropping dead a sad year or two later.

And here's another thing. It costs so comparatively little to be civilized in modern life. It takes more money to buy a CD by a venomous rap artist or this week's dreadful pop princess than three Mozart symphonies or a Duke Ellington songbook. It's cheaper to buy any of Robert Fagles's translations of Homer's *Iliad* and *Odyssey*, or a Flaubert, Conrad or Bellow in a bargain bookshop than to buy the latest chick-lit offering at Borders. The Internet has the most extraordinary free resources available. You can tour the world's wonderful museums, read back copies of the *Paris Review* interviews, download full

texts of out-of-print books or join in spirited chats with experts devoted to European film history. Sometimes I am quite alarmed at how little civilization costs today; in our relentlessly commercial era, this is a saddening sign of how little it is valued.

The one seriously inhibiting factor, of course, is time. Leisure is in short supply in modern life. The irony is that this problem applies most dramatically to our most affluent citizens. Most senior executives toil such long hours they have no time to enjoy their fortunes. The company operatives a little further down the chain are rather like well-compensated slaves: body and soul available at all times to their corporate masters. The significant financial compensations—flashy cars and in-ground pools and new kitchens—are shiny handcuffs to bind the workers to their income and enforce their fealty.

But some of us are changing. We are stepping back from the path of unbridled economic aspiration. Downshifters, part-timers, urban hermits, sea-changers, tree-changers—call us what you will, but we are gently, genially and sometimes necessarily bailing out. We are climbing off the treadmill.

We are now the ones who enjoy leisure—or leisure enough—to take part in and contribute to civilization. We have internalized the delightful paradox that a lower income might grant to us a higher standard of living. If we are

lucky, we have discovered that the redundancy package is modern life's greatest career opportunity. And if multitasking is the enemy of manners, which it is, then a slower, sweeter, simpler life might well be a rich source of manners. With time to think, write, cook, read. We are creating, not lifestyles but life itself.

Of course, for many people the child-raising years will pass by in a necessary blur. They will simply have to juggle all their myriad responsibilities in the messy, sustaining fog of family life. But look at the cultural life of any Western city and you'll see that once their family work is done, many people resume their wider interests. Older men and women are among the most active community volunteers in the soup kitchens and visiting the frail elderly. Women, in particular, are the patrons of the arts, the enthusiasts at writers' festivals, the prime movers at book clubs and library meetings.

Those of us who have stepped back find we can contribute to civility in all kinds of small or large ways. We don't add to the stress and traffic jams of rush hour. We are off-peak users of energy and water. We take up fewer resources than people inhabiting high-rise, air-conditioned office buildings. When I worked in government and business, I was always rewarding myself for my labor. Now I don't need to spend anything like the same amount of pep-me-up money on expensive shoes and

handbags to console myself for all those weekends lost to work. Less shopping, less rubbish. Some of us have the time and energy to collect our neighbor's mail, or talk to the community board about the new arrangements for the local park, or contribute to the co-op board in our block of apartments or make a casserole for a sick friend, or even just to invite someone stressed and busier than we are to go ahead of us in the supermarket queue.

None of these measures are about being a more virtuous person. They are a delightful by-product of time and choice. In fact, it's a privilege to live like this. It's much easier to be nice when you are happy. And being nice makes you feel good.

Clive Bell thought that to be truly civilized you had to be part of the leisured class continuously and from early life. Perhaps our era is different. Perhaps we can draw down on— and contribute to—our civilization with differing intensities, according to the different phases of our lives. And our later years might be some of our most fruitful.

A final thought. The night that my friend told me he loathed manners started out quite badly. I recall slumping back in my seat, wondering if his negative views were widespread. Perhaps people of goodwill, people whom I respected, appeared to have given up on what I considered to be a basic and really undeniable condition of civilization. *What hope is there?* I said to myself despondently.

But then: before his little daughter went to bed, my friend quite unself-consciously counseled her to say good night politely to Mummy and Daddy's guests. She came up close to me and told me solemnly that she was allowed ten minutes of bedtime reading before lights out. She had a good book and she hoped to finish it tonight. And then she was lovingly shepherded by her father upstairs.

6

Because McDonald's doesn't
own manners

In MAY 2004, the prime minister of Australia once again reminded Australians that manners are important. He said that we were living in a less civil society than even ten years ago. He asked parents to bring up their kids with regard to the old-fashioned courtesies. And then, perhaps as helpful guidance, he referred to what he saw as a prime source of civility in modern life: fast-food chains. "Some of the friendliest, well-mannered young people are the ones you find at McDonald's," declared the prime minister.

For reasons I can't quite express, I went into a small decline at this statement and took temporarily to my bed. I must have been in a weakened state because the idea of McDonald's as my prime minister's notion of a civilizing Australian institution was just too much to bear.

It's not that he was necessarily all wrong. McDonald's came to Sydney when I was a teenager. And it was a rare business at that time because it was prepared to employ young people, give them a little training and put them to work in a bright and shiny environment. It seemed a lot more fun to many than washing Dad's car or mowing the lawn for pocket money. Although I must snootily admit that I never took to McDonald's cuisine.

When I was first thinking about this essay I assumed, if I can put it this way, that all social interactions are equal. That civility and incivility have the same quality and effect no matter where they are found. But gradually I came to realize that this is not true.

When we interact with people in a commercial sense— when we pay and buy, when we sell and exchange—the parameters change. One party in the transaction has a motive behind his or her courtesy. In such a case, manners are not sublimely indifferent. They are directed to a specific end. The fact is, when young people are polite to their customers at McDonald's, they are being paid for it. Money changes everything. Not necessarily for the better.

When I was growing up there were two categories of salespeople: hearty and surly. But now I have noticed that people trying to sell me things are becoming more and more polite. It's true. You might not have noticed, but they are all

trying very hard indeed. Sometimes infuriatingly hard. Even the computerized telephone systems are polite. *Thank you for holding. Your call has been placed in a queue and will be attended to shortly. Meanwhile please enjoy your music program. Please ensure you have your account number ready. Thank you for waiting. Your call has progressed in the queue. If you'd like to purchase our new software, please press four. All our operators are currently busy. Your call has progressed in the queue. Your call is important to us.*

This careful courtesy is not, of course, necessarily co-equivalent to good service. But I am sorry to say that commercial manners do not incline me to be more polite in return. On the contrary, these transactions bring out the very worst in me. Somewhere deep inside I simply don't feel the same respect for manners when I am expected to pay for them. I was thoroughly rude to some poor woman calling from God-knows-where in India, just trying to earn a living selling cell phones. I left her saying, *"Madam! Madam!"* in a pleading tone as I slammed down the phone. Another time, after being put through to three different areas of a computer company, I was finally told that no one there could help me with the break-down of my machine—that's when I, too, more or less broke down in a welter of abuse. I have been nastily sarcastic via email when some flowers I ordered online for a friend did not arrive. It's only my natural cravenness that has prevented me from being rude to people in shops. And in each instance of

my rudeness, the salesperson has not been rude back to me but has stoically—almost heroically—retained a demeanor of courtesy.

Afterward I have always felt terrible. I had intended to send a message to a corporation but I just ended up ruining the working day of a human being.

And yet, despite the legitimate or unwarranted abuse of staff by people like me, the trend toward retail politeness intensifies. It is not only a feature of commercial interactions, it is also and increasingly a theme of modern sales. If you look up the websites of big consumer companies, many will have published the equivalent of etiquette guarantees—customer service charters, customer "bills of rights," "ask once" customer commitments. These are all about assuring customers that they are highly valued and will be treated with courtesy and respect.

A major bank is running a series of TV advertisements proposing its superior courtesy as what the marketing companies call its "unique selling point." In each advertisement an ordinary person is subject to a telling instance of the rudeness of modern life. No one will hold a door open for a man carrying a huge pile of documents. A pregnant lady on the bus is pointedly left to stand up by her complacent co-travelers. Cut to our hero and heroine sighing with delighted relief when they

enter a branch of this particular bank. *We won't slam the door in your face! We'll give the pregnant lady a chair!* The bank presents itself to us as a refuge from the incivilities of modern life.

But I fear that this marketing campaign may backfire. Manners in the world of commerce are not a gift, they are a promise of service. And if customers find that the ultimate promise isn't kept, they can get very cross indeed. The finer the manners, the bigger the letdown and the more explosive the response.

True story: In January 2007, *The Sydney Morning Herald* reported on the latest findings about so-called customer rage. Despite the best efforts of so many companies, people were just getting crosser. The findings showed that the trigger times for rage were becoming smaller and smaller. The most serious incidents occurred when there was "a double deviation," that is, when a customer felt that he or she had been treated disrespectfully twice in succession.

- A man who was not allowed to return an unused can of paint drilled a hole in it and carried it dripping around the store.
- A woman who wanted to exchange baby formula at a drugstore became infuriated, returning later to spray the formula over staff.

- A man who was told his electricity would be disconnected when his bill was eight weeks overdue threatened to blow up the power company's headquarters.
- A woman whose light mocha was not stirred properly poured it on the counter.
- A woman was still in tears six months after a department store sold her a faulty air conditioner and refused to replace it.

Yes, I, too, felt that the light mocha incident was an odd inclusion in that list. And why shouldn't the electric company disconnect the power of a persistent defaulter? But if the examples are not particularly helpful, nevertheless the story made me wonder if what people were reacting so vehemently against was not a problem with manners but a problem with service. To put it bluntly: companies shouldn't imagine they can woo you with smooth words and smiles and then, having won your business, treat you like crap. And it must be remembered, it's not just the customers who suffer.

True story: In March 2006, German researchers claimed that enforced enthusiasm in the workplace was making people sick. Psychologists at Frankfurt University discovered that flight attendants, sales personnel, call-center operators and waiters were professionally required to be nice to people.

They discovered that this fake friendliness was causing depression and stress and even a lowering of the immune system, leading to more serious ailments. As part of the study, test students working in an imaginary call center were subject to abuse from clients. Some of the participants were allowed to answer back; the others had to maintain politeness all the time. The admirably named Professor Zapf noted that every time a person was forced to repress his true feelings, there were negative consequences for his health. Professor Zapf's unstartling conclusion was that we should show more respect to those in the service industries.

Waiters and call-center operators are not called frontline staff for nothing. It must seem like warfare to them as they grapple with the gripes of customers, especially if they are not personally responsible for the customer's dissatisfaction or are not in a position to rectify a problem themselves.

Our lives are governed by commerce. That's the reality. Short of living in a tree in the jungle, we can't escape. Even at home we are bombarded with advertising on our televisions, radios and computers. Sales pamphlets and letters of promotion are stuffed into our mailboxes. Even our bills are regularly accompanied by enticements to purchase other products. The phone rings with unsolicited offers for holiday clubs or credit cards or insurance. And we can't attempt to engage with the

culture in the most humble way—go to a movie or a football game or a concert—without pumping music and big-screen advertisements and programs covered with marketing material.

Sometimes I have the creepy sensation that at all times, somehow, somewhere, there's a smiling woman with a headset waiting for my call. It's a feeling of being passively stalked.

So while I would like to agree with the prime minister and argue that the *Have a nice day!* culture at McDonald's genuinely contributes to the formation and maintenance of a civil society, I am not sure it is the case. Of course good manners are always more desirable than rudeness. But the evidence so far is that the fashion for commercial civility is not making more customers any happier—and appears to be making many staff sick.

. . . corporations don't own our souls

Now let's take a peek inside the big and expensive corporations. Here we again find salespeople but this time they sell things for thousands and millions of dollars instead of just the price of a hamburger—and also professionals of all kinds who crunch the numbers, organize human resources, run the supply chain, devise the marketing campaigns, audit the accounts, manage compliance with tax and other laws, design new products and engineer the information technology systems.

Here the atmosphere is a little different.

Last year my friend Aaron graduated from a university with excellent results and started looking for a job as a lawyer. As an older graduate, with a background in community politics, Aaron was eagerly taken up by a prestigious city firm and he conducted a first round of interviews with the associates and partners. Then he received feedback from the recruitment officer to the effect that, while Aaron had all the right professional qualities, he appeared to lack *enthusiasm*. This was something he needed to work on before his final meetings with the senior partners.

Aaron was puzzled by this. He consulted our mutual friend Alice, who had worked for similar companies.

"Let me guess," said Alice. "You said something like, 'I am moderately interested in this job where I propose to utilize my skills and abilities on your behalf, for which you will pay me an appropriate salary.'"

"Pretty much," said Aaron. "What else was I meant to say? Wouldn't anything else sound fake?"

Alice haw-hawed. "Of course! Your job is to offer undying loyalty to the firm; theirs is to declare they'll be loyal to you in return. There is no reason to believe either of you will be speaking the truth."

"So I need to look really excited and say, 'I would *love* to be a regulatory lawyer at your firm and I've dreamed of it for years.'" Aaron blushed at the very idea of such excess.

But Aaron laid it on and got the job. After which he was deposited in an office, handed three hundred pages of documents and left alone for weeks on end. At one point his phone had been silent for so long he called Alice and asked her to ring him at his desk to make sure it was still working. He told her that he could not imagine a job where unbridled enthusiasm would be a less helpful attribute.

Aaron's experience is not uncommon. In the big corporations today it is simply not enough to turn up and do your job. You have to be pumped, you have to be firing, you have to have an edge. It seems they don't just want your body, they want your soul, as well. I do not exaggerate.

A management consultant once boasted to me about the new program his firm was introducing to a top mining company. This was all about engaging and motivating employees and connecting them more closely to the aspirations of the company with, of course, the ultimate goal of increasing productivity and performance. He actually said it was all about "bringing the soul to work." He beamed with pride at the idea. Thinking back, I can't remember whether this was a gaze of pure innocence or unadulterated cynicism—either was possible and both were scary.

And I could have cried. I wanted to say: "It's bad enough for most people to bring their bodies to work. Do you have to have their very souls, as well? And what if they don't want

to bring their souls to the office? What if they'd rather leave them resting peacefully at home?" (I wanted to say this, but in fact, struck dumb by horror, I said nothing.)

I've heard of one advertising agency that has *impact* meetings at 7:30 each morning where loud music is blared out to create high energy and the operatives are required loudly and excitedly to shout their sales targets for the day. *Impact.* As if you are in a high-speed car crash, which is exactly what it must feel like. Another company explicitly tells job applicants that their "attitude and enthusiasm" are as important as their experience—as if ten years in marketing is only valuable if you can emote convincingly about it.

Some of the top professional firms, like management consultancies, demand more than just skill, competence and co-operation. They want a total commitment. While my friend Aaron was sent to his own lonely office, more commonly these businesses put their staff in open-plan spaces so that they have no real privacy but must relate to each other almost as intimately as family members. Casual clothing emphasizes an egalitarian mood and a feeling of belonging. Staff are encouraged to form close-knit teams aided by bonding sessions and boot camps and "away" meetings. To add to the sense of an all-embracing and even domestic environment, bright office cafés, time-out stations, food bars and comfy couches are installed, so that there are even fewer excuses for venturing

beyond the corporate domain, let alone going home. The importance of the commitment to this ideology of work is reinforced by explicit performance measurements such as "contribution to firm culture," as if the firm were a small nation protecting a precious cultural heritage.

Perhaps it sounds as though this would be an environment in which manners might thrive. Where close collaboration would be actively enabled by courteous modes of interaction. But often this is not the case. Aggression, testosterone, high energy levels and a competitive spirit are valued. Big targets, extravagant demands and grueling timetables are admired. Pressure and speed are celebrated. And if a particular individual is making enough money for the firm, then his or her petulant, virulent and rude behavior will be quite rationally excused on the grounds that he or she is contributing to the overall good of the firm.

There are many companies in which no one wants to talk about manners because they employ too many genuinely effective people who don't have any.

It might validly be argued that all this is a matter for individual businesses, and not really relevant to a discussion of broader civility. Who cares if these high-paying companies demand extreme levels of emotional engagement from the staff? Who cares if bullies and pigs are tolerated in these elite workplaces?

But it does matter, because these organizational cultures don't just exist unto themselves. They are a part of the world we live in and they employ many talented people. The way they operate has an impact on broader civility.

Here I am aboard one of those Friday evening commuter flights. The plane is full of up-and-coming young operatives from IT companies and telecommunications firms and management consulting partnerships, heading home after a week on a project. They are all remarkably similar: uniformly thirtyish, male and prematurely balding. They each carry a laptop and an earpiece. They exude the sour smells of lunch, sweat, a few beers and corporate fear.

Three of us nudge into our row, stow our bags, sit down, strap up. I am in the middle. We're so close, we intermingle elbows, shoulders, breath and knees. We do not look at one another, rather into the middle distance of the headrests in front of us. No one wants to engage. This is almost certainly the nearest any of us have ever come to a threesome. Yet we do not exchange a word.

I lean down to extract a magazine from my handbag. The guy on my right puts the volume of his headphones on so loud I can hear the thrashing bass and my heart and breastbone throb in painful and unwilling chorus. I sit upright and cautiously attempt to turn the slick colored pages without jerking my elbows or spreading my hands too wide, and at the

same time the guy on my left throws his head back and immediately begins loudly to snore. He then utters a snort so bone-shatteringly momentous that he wakes himself up. He sits up, sighs loudly, shakes his head for a moment, then carefully places it under my ear and falls back deeply asleep. The man in front of me immediately reclines his seat to the maximum so that my magazine is now pressed up to my nose and the man behind me completes the compression by putting his feet directly into the small of my back.

This is before takeoff.

Pinioned between four men, I reflect on modern life. No one here is deliberately rude, no one is nasty, and yet, to say I feel violated would not be going too far. This is the closest physical contact I have had with any man—men—apart from my husband, for years. I might as well be lying in bed with four strangers, all of whom are ignoring my very existence. This is, to say the least, unflattering. And yet we are all here, now, together. Yes, even you, I think, looking down at the sad depleted follicles of my somnolent traveling companion.

But gradually it occurs to me that these men are weary. Not just bone-weary but soul-weary. They have a sort of emptied-out quality, a telltale post-work flatness. Nothing comes back at me from behind their eyes. And I realize that this airline flight is, in a funny way, a relief, a vacation from affect, a wel-

come escape from the office and its exhausting, complex and passionate interactions. They simply don't have the stock of emotional energy required to be civil on the plane to a stranger. They can't face the stress of nodding and saying, *Good evening.* They don't want to look at me, in case I try to engage them. They want to ignore me as if I don't exist. More important, they want me to ignore them as if they don't exist, either.

Which is true, in a way. They are utterly hollow. If they have any emotional energy left, they are understandably storing it for their wives and children and the few friends they have outside work. That's when the lights will come on again and the outer life resumes.

At the end of the flight we all clamber out and join the glum stream winding down the corridors and escalators and swivel our heads anxiously as the baggage carousel grinds round and round. We finally disperse and I slump into the taxi queue. I feel rather as though I have had very bad sex—a grimy, well-handled feeling without the afterglow.

I appreciate the dignity of labor. I do. And I am glad that these young men are all keen to be successful and make lots of money because I can then enjoy all the useful and beautiful products and services that will flow from their efforts.

But they are achieving these good things in workplace cultures that exaggerate the value of work and downgrade the

importance of civility. They pay a heavy price for this and so do we.

Recently, I came across a book called *The No Asshole Rule: Building a Civilized Workplace and Surviving One That Isn't*, written by Robert I. Sutton, a professor of management science and engineering at Stanford University. I came across it not because I routinely scan the business literature, but because it shot immediately to the best-seller list in my favorite bookshop. As Sutton explains, he wrote the book because a short blurb he penned about *assholes* in the *Harvard Business Review* attracted a massive response. I have to explain here that I am going to use his term because, well, it's his. (And it is, of course, incorrect. The correct term is *arseholes*.)

At last! I thought. The book I have been waiting for. A book that will explain that all the hype in the world can't disguise the fact that a company is still just a collection of individuals gathered to achieve certain commercial objectives—and that the fundamental human things still apply.

Sutton lists twelve everyday actions assholes use: personal insults, invading someone's territory, uninvited physical contact, threats and intimidation, sarcasm, abusive emails, status slaps designed to humiliate, public shaming, rude interruptions, two-faced attacks, dirty looks and ignoring people. It

seems to me as though every single one of these misbehaviors is, at minimum, a matter of manners.

Sutton goes on to consider the economic costs to firms of these behaviors by bullies and jerks, the way dysfunction can spiral through the office and how companies can make an active decision to create harmonious and productive workplaces.

And reading this I became very excited because I was sure that Sutton would go on to explain why civility in the workplace is important and how it can be created and what can be achieved by it. But in these naive expectations, I couldn't have been more wrong.

In an apparent contradiction of his own agenda, Sutton explicitly says that his book is not about the virtues of manners. Not at all. As he says, he truly believes in the virtues of conflict, the right kind of friction and the merits of vigorous debate. He can't stand spineless people. As far as he is concerned, firms mustn't stifle creativity and populate their corridors with dull clones. "If you want to learn about the virtues of speaking quietly and the nuances of workplace etiquette," Sutton concludes bluntly, "then read something by Miss Manners."

And that's it. Sutton defines manners so narrowly as to justify their exclusion from his thesis. He wants to make civilized workplaces, but doesn't want to accept that civility plays any role in achieving this. He does, however, have many good

stories and suggestions about dealing with the dysfunction caused by assholes. Some of them—such as "constructive confrontation" courses—sound to me like fancy terms for teaching people to handle differences using good manners. But Sutton prefers the jargon.

This sensible man from Stanford feels so uncomfortable with the term "manners" that he defines it away as equivalent to spinelessness, lack of creativity and conformity.

. . . and manners are no barrier to greatness

When I was in my early twenties, I went to work in the Australian Department of Foreign Affairs. I thought of myself as young and smart and vibrant—when all I was, was young. When I got together with my new contemporaries, we were scathing of our older (male) supervisors, with their beige suits and their bland courtesies and their infuriating understatements. Bloodless! we thought. Dull! Now I look back on those tepid men with unlikely nostalgia.

One legendary departmental secretary was a tiny colorless egghead of fierce intellect. When a briefing note was returned from his office, there were only four likely responses. If he wrote *Noted*, you were relieved: this was almost always what he wrote. If he wrote *Thank you*, you were very pleased with your-

self. If he wrote *Many thanks,* then you went zooming into joyful outer space: he hardly ever wrote *Many thanks.* When he wrote *This needs further thought,* you panicked.

The egghead had no need for hyperbole. No need for the injection of modern exaggeration. Nor had he any need to yell, throw things or respond to incompetence with abuse. The restricted palette of his reactions only served to intensify the effect of his communications. Everyone knew what he meant and where they stood.

The egghead would never have been deluded into thinking that an idea presented in a loud and intimidating voice was better than one presented quietly. Nor that a personal attack was more effective at modifying employee behavior than a clear and succinct reproof related to the professional issue at hand. He would have supposed there was a time and place for the spontaneous emotional response, but he himself had never happened to come across such a time and place. Ideas were debated, but not in dramatic shouting matches filled with the frisson of testosterone and tension. More usually in a low-key conversation, carefully guided by the chair of a meeting, based on well-prepared notes and followed up by a brief clarifying minute.

It is bizarre and wrong to imagine that manners in the workplace are a cork in the fizzing bottle of creativity, or a

roadblock on the pathway to achievement. Equally, of course, they are no guarantee of competence or a ticket to glory. But they can certainly help.

One of history's greatest statesmen and bureaucrats was the eighteenth-century French foreign minister le duc de Talleyrand. He never left home without white pancake makeup, a wig and an elegant limp (clip-*clop*, clip-*clop*). His exquisite, icy cold manners and ruthless decision-making frightened people: some made the sign of the cross when he walked by to ward off the devil, which was particularly ironic given that he had once been a bishop. Talleyrand's menacing authority was intensified by his air of boredom, his famed pauses, his lassitude and his undying commitment to a long chat with his chef every morning about the menu for dinner.

And there was professional method in this refined and lethargic approach. Talleyrand was so brilliant, his acumen so renowned, his judgment so astute, he served in the successive and utterly oppositional governments of the ancien régime, the Revolution, Napoleon and even the restored Bourbon monarchy. In the history of political survivors, Talleyrand must rank among the greatest.

In his biography of Talleyrand, the Englishman and diplomat Duff Cooper lauded Talleyrand's greatest professional attribute. Cooper noted admiringly:

He discouraged excessive zeal even in his subordinates, and when he relinquished the Ministry for Foreign Affairs, he said, presenting the permanent officials to his successor, "You will find them loyal, intelligent, accurate and punctual, but, thanks to my training, not at all zealous." As M. de Champagny evinced some surprise, he continued, affecting a most serious manner, "Yes, except for a few of the junior clerks, who, I am afraid, close up their envelopes with a certain amount of precipitation, every one here maintains the greatest calm; hurry and bustle are unknown."

As Talleyrand understood, manners permit you to start small and slow. To say: *I'm sorry to hear that.* And: *Events are under review.* And: *It appears to be quite serious.* To keep things formal and calm and quiet. And the pause, the time, the slowness are an aid to truth and to good judgment as much as to style. Talleyrand's famous maxim? *Surtout, pas de zèle*: Above all, no zeal. Cooper explained that this deliberate manner of conducting business was of particular service to Napoleon, who, though he loathed the effete Talleyrand, recognized his admirable foreign policy skills. Napoleon was often glad to find that instructions he had given with too little consideration had not been acted upon several days later when he was already prepared to cancel them.

And it's not as if Talleyrand was never placed under

duress. Throughout his career, he was threatened by some of the greatest challenges any statesman in history has had to face, as France reeled from revolution to war to empire and counterrevolution. He had to have his wits about him at all times. Indeed, he was necessarily a master of duplicity, calculation and thoughtful corruption. And he had his own codes of honor. As far as he was concerned, the governments he served were merely temporary institutions, while the interests of France remained permanent. And it was these interests he served. As well, of course, as his own.

Napoleon, once driven to fury when he heard of Talleyrand's latest plotting, hurled public abuse at his foreign minister, ending with the famous attack, "You are just shit in a silk stocking!" People were shocked, of course. And they naturally assumed this meant the end, finally, at last, of the everlasting Talleyrand. So there was a murmur of amazement when Talleyrand appeared at the next grand ball, utterly unperturbed, and bowed low to kiss Napoleon's hand. Far from seeing this act as one of pathetic subservience, everyone knew this meant that Talleyrand was in fact capable of anything. Napoleon retained Talleyrand's shitful but essential services. And Talleyrand, of course, outlasted Napoleon.

If manners can be of value when the highest national interests are at stake, surely they can't hurt in the design, marketing and sales of the latest high-tech product?

I was disappointed with the *No Asshole* book, but I think it has merit as an advance in the discussion. Even if Sutton disdains manners, manners are what he is really talking about. And plenty of organizations now accept that they can be successful without draining the lifeblood from their employees. These companies are trying to improve working conditions for their staff. Some are putting anti-bullying measures in place to stop the worst offenders against manners in the workplace. And perhaps if they do this, the benefits will flow through to all those stressed-out frontline workers, who then won't have to feel as though they are sandwiched between abuse by their customers and mistreatment by their employers.

And I have made a small resolution. As recommended by Professor Zapf, I am going to try very hard to be polite to people with whom I am having a commercial conversation, no matter how hard this may be. And, on those rare occasions when I come across higher-end operatives away from the office, I am going to be kind to them, too, because they are also part of our polity. And because one day, who knows, they may well return to the world and need to know how to be part of it. Those exhausted businessmen may well be the next generation of sea-changers. I'll welcome them back.

Because manners give us dignity

S OME PEOPLE SEE MANNERS as a veneer, like an overlay of gilt over tin jewelry: strip away the glitter and the cheap true self will be revealed. For some reason, the very people who think this are the ones who most disparage manners—as if we would all prefer to see people at their most base. To me this seems a bleak view of human nature. I see manners more optimistically: the artifice as embellishment rather than disguise. A way to enhance and illuminate the inner self, not to hide it.

Perhaps that's why I find myself dismayed by the comprehensive casualization of modern life. The tradition of wearing your Sunday best was never just about putting on your finest clothes for morning church and Sunday lunch—it was about putting on your finer self, as well. To me an unlit

candle is a sad thing—but lit up it serves its proper function and glows.

George Orwell was a progressive man, a thoughtful man, a deeply moral man. He was certainly not one to focus on human trivialities. In his memoir, *Down and Out in Paris and London*, he unflinchingly portrays the indignities of life as an impoverished kitchen hand.

> *We quarrelled over things of inconceivable pettiness. The dustbin, for instance, was an unending source of quarrels—whether it should be put where I wanted it, which was in the cook's way, or where she wanted it, which was between me and the sink. Once she nagged and nagged until at last, in pure spite, I lifted the dustbin up and put it out in the middle of the floor, where she was bound to trip over it.*
>
> *"Now, you cow," I said, "move it yourself."*
>
> *Poor old woman, it was too heavy for her to lift, and she sat down, put her head on the table and burst out crying. And I jeered at her. This is the kind of effect that fatigue has upon one's manners.*

What I find interesting and surprising about this story is the idea that being robbed of one's manners constitutes an assault on one's selfhood as powerful, invasive and disabling as poverty and low status. Manners were important to Orwell: they were a sign of his humanity. And he deeply resented a system that pushed him so hard that he lost them.

To regard manners as a mask that should desirably be cast off is to misunderstand the role they play. When you lose your self-control, when you explode in rage or anger, when you abandon your manners, you are not proudly revealing yourself, you are losing something, some key element of your personhood.

There's a rebuke that's now out of fashion: *Sir, you forget yourself!* It assumes that one's real self is not necessarily the base authentic creature. Rather, the real self is that artificial self, the thoughtful person who subscribes to higher standards of behavior. And it turns out that to be told you have forgotten yourself is actually something of a compliment—it assumes there's something valuable to remember.

In 1528, at the height of the Renaissance, one of the gentlemen at the court of Urbino, Baldesar Castiglione, sat down and wrote a series of dialogues set over four evenings. It was called *The Book of the Courtier*. There's a portrait of Castiglione by Raphael: it reveals a comfortingly open face, with large blue eyes and a soft and melancholy expression.

The Courtier is a curious book. With its almost magical air of courtly idealization, it has been unfavorably compared with Machiavelli's near-contemporary *The Prince*, which unswervingly examines the harsh realities of leadership. And indeed

Castiglione does adopt a more noble view of power: "... a man who strives to ensure that his prince is not deceived by anyone, does not listen to flatterers or slanderers or liars, and distinguishes between good and evil, loving the one and detesting the other, aims at the best end of all."

But he had some unique insights into courtly life and the aesthetics of manners. There was one vice above all others that Castiglione thought the courtier should seek to avoid. Affectation. He wrote:

> *Affectation is a vice of which only too many people are guilty, sometimes our Lombards more than others, who, if they have been away from home for a year, on their return immediately start speaking Roman or Spanish or French and God knows what. And all this springs from their over-anxiety to show how much they know; so that they put care and effort into acquiring a detestable vice.*

One can only dream of a society in which the main vice is that people actually try too hard to be learned, to be erudite, to be civilized.

But more than this, Castiglione had a very clear and positive idea of the highest virtue a courtier should aim to possess. He called it, in a lovely Italian word that seems to suggest its own meaning, a certain *sprezzatura*. We have no single English

word that does this term justice—it means something like ease and nonchalance and graceful carelessness. Castiglione thought this ease should conceal all artistry and make whatever one says or does seem uncontrived and effortless. He added: ". . . to reveal intense application and skill robs everything of grace."

How lovely, the idea that one might have a high degree of social artistry at all, let alone a desire gracefully to conceal the effort behind it. Though Castiglione was an Italian, his ideas took greatest hold in England, where aristocrats thereafter prided themselves on a certain underplayed and witty persona. When Sir Walter Raleigh spread his cloak over a muddy puddle so that Queen Elizabeth's silk shoes would not get damp—that was *sprezzatura*. Nothing labored or pompous. Just a moment of carefree, joyous, everyday beauty.

And it's true that some people don't just have manners, they have beautiful manners. There aren't many, but if you know such a person, a loving image of them will have already sprung to mind. They are the ones who think of the perfect small gift for the sick friend, or gently draw out the shy stranger, or quietly close the window against the cold draft, or tactfully change the dangerous topic, or subtly reorganize the seating so that the slightly deaf person is able to hear better.

Sadly, I am not one of those people but I know one or two,

and I also know that they vivify life; the prosaic becomes lovely in their hands. I have one friend who graces the world with her manners so lightly, with so much of Castiglione's *sprezzatura*, that I sometimes won't notice at the time but afterward I'll remember and think, *That's right!*

The writer Marcel Proust was famous for his manners. This may surprise those of you who have found it a strain to get through his somewhat inconsiderately long *À la recherche du temps perdu*. But his sensitivity, his delicacy, his refinement were renowned. This was particularly touching because Proust was a lifelong invalid, suffering from allergies, an inability to warm himself and a curious kind of insomnia that meant he could only sleep during daylight hours.

On one occasion, a certain friend of Proust's named Paul Leclercq called to see him at the Grand Hôtel in Cabourg after a hot day's bicycling. The restaurant was full of bare-shouldered ladies and tailcoated gentlemen. But Leclercq was wearing cycling breeches. Proust said to his friend, "Never mind, we'll dine in my room, and I'll serve you myself so that the waiter shan't see you." Sure enough, Proust collected each course from a tray in the lobby of his room, but only when he was absolutely sure the waiter had moved off down the corridor.

Leclercq was touched and amused by this incident. He thought Proust was under the mistaken impression that being

seen by a waiter in the wrong clothes would be as embarrassing to Leclercq as it would clearly be to Proust—and decided that this was true courtesy.

But this story has another level. Proust would have been just as concerned for the feelings of the waiters as for his friend. If Leclercq had paraded his wrong clothes, it may have seemed to the waiters like a snub to their dignity and that of their establishment. Proust was probably even more courteous than his friend imagined.

Good manners lend grace to life, but it must be admitted that bad manners can also be enlivening. Of course, they are only really effective when delivered by those with a special gift for it, with an ear for it, like music. They are the ones who know exactly where the line is drawn between consideration and rudeness—and are skillful enough to lift their knee high above that line and land with malicious precision on the other side. One of these was Beau Brummell, the world's first dandy. He took men out of their patterned silks and breeches and dressed them simply and soberly in beautifully cut black suits, adorned with elaborately tied neckwear. He claimed to take five hours to dress, and recommended that boots be polished with champagne. For a long time, he was great chums with the prince regent, but for reasons that aren't perfectly clear, Beau began to lose favor. At this he became vastly annoyed. One night, as the grossly overweight prince strolled

past with their mutual acquaintance Alvanley, Beau abandoned his usually impeccable manners and remarked loudly, "Alvanley, who's your fat friend?" In the hands of a beginner, this remark might be vulgar. But it's a delicious zinger coming from the most refined man of his day.

Bad manners may not only be amusing, they may sometimes be the occasion for some of the most beautiful manners of all.

In 2005, the great actress Cate Blanchett was playing the lead in Ibsen's *Hedda Gabler* when something terrible happened to the man in the front row, stage left. His cell phone began ringing. In his hurry to extract and silence the phone, he accidentally flung it onto the stage, where it continued to emit a chirpy ring tone in the middle of late nineteenth-century Norway. At this point an actor calmly walked across the stage, picked up the instrument and handed it to the culprit, who sank back in shame. But taking her bows at the end of the play, Cate leaned forward and patted the culprit on the knee.

Oh, yes, the audience swooned.

. . . improve communication

One of the worst implications of the lack of manners in modern life is that it is now almost impossible to convey subtle messages to other human beings.

Once, we all made efforts to develop what were known as social antennae: to attune ourselves to the ebb and flow of society; to render ourselves capable of responding sensitively to the subtle currents of meaning beneath the noisy river of social discourse. If someone just faintly flicked an eyelid at you, or raised their eyebrows fractionally in your direction, or paused just a little too long before replying to your remark, you would instantly be aware not only that a message was being sent but what that message intended to convey. You knew at once whether it was sympathy or disapproval or warning. More important, others around you would also be aware of this communication, because their social antennae enabled them not only to decode their own interactions, but to interpret the interplay taking place between others, as well.

Someone not long ago castigated me for my interest in manners and complained that I was too soft on the snobbery that inevitably goes hand in snooty glove with manners. I replied indignantly that I was not soft on snobbery, I was *nostalgic* for it. How on earth can someone be a snob in the modern era? Who would notice? We have no dress codes. We have no dining etiquette. We have no rules of conversation. We have no class, in all senses of the word. The sheer brutal enjoyment of snobbery relies upon an accepted in-crowd humiliating an outsider. It only works when everyone agrees there

is an in-crowd. And when the outsiders accept they are of inferior status. Maybe I am just moving in the wrong circles, but I am fairly sure an incident that Proust describes in *The Guermantes Way* would be unlikely to occur today. Here are the narrator and the historian being introduced to the duchesse de Guermantes:

> *The historian made a low bow, as I did too, and since he seemed to suppose that some friendly remark ought to follow this salute, his eyes brightened and he was preparing to open his mouth when he was chilled by the demeanour of Mme de Guermantes, who had taken advantage of the independence of her torso to throw it forward with an exaggerated politeness and bring it neatly back to a position of rest without letting face or eyes appear to have noticed that anyone was standing before them; after breathing a little sigh she contented herself with manifesting the nullity of the impression that had been made on her by the sight of the historian and myself by performing certain movements of her nostrils with a precision that testified to the absolute inertia of her unoccupied attention.*

I like to think of myself as reasonably socially alert, but I am fairly sure if someone merely adjusted her torso and flared her nostrils at me, I would be hard-pressed to spot that she was sending me a message about the nullity of my impression.

In modern life it is almost impossible to communicate with people socially. Where once you need only send up a tiny social smoke signal to convey a message about manners, now you have to burn down the whole house.

A friend of mine was once the unhappy hostess at a dinner party where one guest was a bore. Not just any bore, either, but a *home renovation* bore. She tried to distract him, offering more food. She tried to deflect him, turning brightly to another guest, saying, "How is the new job working out, Cecile?" But all to no avail. The offender, absorbed in his own tedious commentary, did not get the message or, more likely, did not care. He continued unconcernedly, unashamedly, to drone on about the rise in the value of his property that was sure to result from the various improvements he was undertaking, despite the assorted sins and failings of his builders, tradesmen, architects, intolerant neighbors and recalcitrant local council.

As the night wore on, my friend's guests began sneaking out one by one, and two by two, casting her either resentful or apologetic glances or both. Of course the dullard remained. My friend got up and cleared the plates. Then she put them in the dishwasher. She stopped filling his glass. Then she took his glass away. She stifled a yawn. Then she didn't stifle a yawn. Then she yawned very loudly. Finally her husband left

the room, brushed his teeth and put on his pajamas. And when he came back he told the bore that it was time for him to go home. He refrained from adding: the one you have been droning on about all evening.

This kind of occasion is very disheartening. It is a strong disincentive to venturing out in society—or inviting society in.

Of course, society has always had its socially inept members. And I have been one myself, on more occasions than I care to remember. But it used to be that if someone was becoming tedious at the dinner table, the host or hostess could deliver a subtle rebuke with little more than a patient sigh and a delicate wave of the wineglass and the other guests would be in a position to observe, with sympathy or malice, the ripple of deflation crossing the blunderer's face as he or she suddenly realized their error and abruptly subsided.

Cruel, yes, but kinder than the modern alternative. Where once the oblique rebuff or reproof left everyone's dignity more or less intact, now one is forced to deliver or receive an unambiguous and wounding rejection. Like: *You need to go home now.*

And on the matter of snobbery, perhaps it is worth noting that the capacity to use manners wonderfully and well is not just a matter for the ruling classes. In Gertrude Stein's *Autobiography of Alice B. Toklas*, she describes one of the most subtle

social rebukes I have ever come across. Please note that the spelling and punctuation are all Ms. Stein's.

> *Hélène was one of those admirable bonnes in other words a maid of all work . . . She was a most excellent cook and she made a very good soufflé. Hélène had her opinions, she did not for instance, like Matisse [author's note: yes, that Matisse]. She said a frenchman should not stay unexpectedly to a meal particularly if he asked the servant beforehand what there was for dinner. She said foreigners had a perfect right to do these things but not a frenchman and Matisse had once done it. So when Miss Stein said to her, Monsieur Matisse is staying for dinner this evening, she would say, in that case I will not make an omelette but fry the eggs. It takes the same number of eggs and the same amount of butter, but it shows less respect, and he will understand.*

. . . prevent premature intimacy

Let us now imagine a meeting between two acquaintances.

How do you do?

Very well. How do you do?

Very well, thank you.

I trust your family is well?

Quite well. And yours?

Well, yes, it is dull. It is long-winded and impersonal and

artificial. It will take a long time before these two people disclose anything personal or private to each other. In fact, if they proceed as above, they may never find out anything. But let's be perfectly honest: most people are dull. The slow-witted will never become more interesting simply because they are let off the leash and allowed to fully express themselves. This is the one irrefutable piece of evidence amassed by TV talk programs and reality shows.

Manners offer us the protection of social constraints. Manners take time, often too much time. But they also confer time. Time to get to know someone, time to think about how we feel, time to consider our reactions and respond wisely and well.

Somewhere there arose the false idea that rapid intimacies bring people closer together. In fact, all too often they simply raise the stakes improperly in the early stages of a relationship. They increase the risks. What if the person from whom you've taken these intimate details turns out to be someone you don't really care to know? There you are, burdened too quickly with their secrets, their private dreams, their hidden stories. The very artificiality of manners protects us from the temptation to enter into premature intimacy.

I once had to stop going to a really good hairdresser because I regretted the intimacies that I myself had foolishly initiated. I realized I had *told him too much*. We'd started kissing

each other hello and goodbye. He talked about having a drink sometime. I just couldn't stand it anymore. If only I'd stuck with a more formal approach. A small artifice can sometimes forestall a large phoniness—or the loss of a great hairdresser.

A friend of mine went on a coffee date with a man she had met at a dinner party. Within five minutes he told her that he had Googled her and discovered she was on the RSVP website—a site that helps people find romantic life partners. Before they had even ordered coffee, he quizzed my friend on whether she wanted children and informed her that he himself had had a vasectomy. This was more information than my friend could cope with at short notice, and she made sure her coffee was an espresso so she could leave in an express fashion, as well.

Every time you read one of those glib lifestyle articles about relationships, it will tell you that the key to a happy relationship is frank and honest communication. This is, on the whole, wrong.

Most of the successful romantic partnerships that I've come across have relied on the considerate withholding of unpalatable truths. A little light deception, you might say, plus a big dash of routine and a great deal of courtesy.

Somerset Maugham once reminisced about the curious marriage between his father and the beautiful woman who was twenty years his junior:

*In Paris they were known as beauty and the beast. My mother was
very small, with large brown eyes and hair of a rich reddish gold,
exquisite features and a lovely skin. She was very much admired.
One of her great friends . . . once said to my mother, "You're so beautiful and there are so many people in love with you, why are you
faithful to that ugly little man you've married?" And my mother answered: "He never hurts my feelings."*

I've seen the forty-plus-year marriage of my own parents
held together by fruit-shop flowers every Saturday and a kiss
every evening without fail. No matter how much they irritated
and even enraged each other, during those inevitable times they
did. And they're still together. It's not too much to say that manners got them through their marriage.

People think manners aren't sexy. Transgression is sexy;
busting taboos is sexy. How can manners be sexy? But as anyone interested in sex will confirm, deferral is the essence of
foreplay. Manners play their delightful role in creating tension, anticipation, curiosity. They respect the essence of each
partner's separateness.

Here's beautiful young socialite Millamant being wooed
by handsome Mirabell in William Congreve's play of 1700, *The
Way of the World*. Millamant is setting up certain strict conditions
before she'll consent to marry this young man with whom, by
the way, she is desperately in love.

Millamant: *I won't be called names after I'm married; positively I won't be called names.*

Mirabell: *Names!*

Millamant: *Ay, as wife, spouse, my dear, joy, jewel, love, sweetheart, and the rest of that nauseous cant, in which men and their wives are so fulsomely familiar——I shall never bear that——Good Mirabell, don't let us be familiar or fond, nor kiss before folks . . . nor go to Hyde Park together the first Sunday in a new chariot, to provoke eyes and whispers; and then never be seen there together again; as if we were proud of one another the first week, and ashamed of another ever after. Let us never visit together, nongo to a play together, but let us be very strange and well-bred: let us be as strange as if we had been married a great while; and as well-bred as if we had not been married at all.*

To Millamant, the preservation of a certain strange and well-bred distance is not a path to marital estrangement but to lifelong romance. She is fighting for a sexy marriage. And the continuation of a certain distance, far from killing off the relationship, is, in her view, likely to add spice to it. He must always woo her; she will always seduce him.

Congreve's play pokes fun at upper-class manners, but at the core of it all is the way love might be expressed in manners—which hold two people gently apart in order to bind them more closely together.

Those magazines and self-help books that tell you to un-load your every little passing thought, feeling and criticism upon your partner are cruelly misleading. When love means never having to say you're sorry, it's nearly always because you weren't unkind to your partner in the first place.

. . . unlock our humanity

The modern conception of great art is that it relies upon tearing down social conventions. But great art, even, and perhaps especially, when it subverts the orthodoxies, relies upon the artist's deep ingrained knowledge of the rules. The greatest artists all started with profound technique, even if like Matisse they ended up making collages of little bits of paper.

The experience of artistry most necessary to me is reading novels. I still remember that my first overwhelming, expand-ing sensation at discovering fiction was one of relief. That there were people out there who could show me how the world really worked. Who could illuminate the strange and mysterious ways in which adults behaved. Novels, or the great ones anyway, take you outside your own tiny boxed-in per-spective and reveal the shades of motive and meaning that guide people in their interactions with each other. Novels make you compassionate, because they show you the deep motivations that drive otherwise indefensible actions.

People have wondered about the rise of nonfiction. But to me it makes perfect sense. Fiction reached its high point in the English language during the repressed Victorian era. It was always a covert way to explore taboo topics—bad marriages, domestic violence, infidelity, larceny, betrayal, treason. But now the taboos have gone. People can—and do—talk openly about the appalling things they have done, or that have happened to them. No topic is off-limits anymore. No subject is too cringe-inducing, humiliating, mortifying or shameful. I was a porn queen, drug fiend, incest survivor, stripper, swinger. I cheated, I stole, I lied, I got away with it, I didn't. We don't need fiction as a way to explore these dirty little secrets anymore. We've got fact.

But this doesn't mean we can do without fiction. The novel is still the art form that most comprehensively grapples with what it means to be human and to struggle along in the world. And many of the greatest novels are comedies—or tragedies—of manners.

Henry James and Marcel Proust and George Eliot and Edith Wharton and Jane Austen and F. Scott Fitzgerald and Anthony Powell are very different authors. But all of them show us people circulating in society: negotiating their way, finding their feet, losing their heads and breaking their hearts.

For me, the greatest pleasures are the revelations of subtle feelings: emotions and sensations that are not normally explored or expressed. When Lydgate in *Middlemarch* slowly shrinks his spiritual aspirations to meet his wife's material ones. When Elizabeth Bennet in *Pride and Prejudice* comes to understand that her beloved father's weaknesses are almost as culpable as her mother's. That terrible moment when Isabel Archer in *The Portrait of a Lady* walks in on her husband and Madam Merle: they are doing nothing more than looking at each other but something in their body language suddenly awakens Isabel to the depths of their complicity. "Society is the stage on which manners are shown; novels are their literature," said Ralph Waldo Emerson.

Sam is a very lovely sixteen-year-old of my acquaintance who likes to watch TV and movies. She also likes to read, but she thinks novels of manners are boring and outdated, preferring fantasy and comedy and action. The problem with each of these genres is that, at their most simple, they are cartoon-like and flattened out. And at their most elevated, they are operatically grand, dealing with heroically inflated figures and black-and-white moral situations. They simply don't deal in the novel's uncomfortable shades of gray.

I once saw Sam's beautiful face ripple with surprise as she experienced a subtle feeling that she could not name, and for

which Homer Simpson's *Doh!* and *Woo-hoo!* or even the grand moral dilemmas facing the hobbits in *Lord of the Rings* offered no satisfactory explanation. Because it was just a simple human experience: the first time she had been socially bested by a skilled hypochondriac. As the conversation proceeded, I could see Sam beginning to realize that no degree of sympathy or boosting would suffice; that offering her limited experience of ill health was not welcome; that the hypochondriac's manipulative self-pity and narcissism were inexhaustible. Sam could do no right. If only Sam had made Mr. Woodhouse's acquaintance in Jane Austen's *Emma*, she might have been better equipped to cope—or at least to recognize simply that here was a familiar human type, and that she was part of a long and honorable continuum of hapless victims.

The phony sitcom half-feelings of *Friends* or *Seinfeld* don't lessen our capacity for real feelings, but equally, they do not enhance our capacity to understand them. When we eliminate literature from our lives, we deny ourselves the wisdom of generations of authors who reveal not only the surface of human nature but what lies beneath. The inner selves that are so hard to find and touch and understand.

The path to those inner selves is always through the outer world. Manners provide not just the formal structure but also the prism through which we can engage with the deepest things.

. . . and make life beautiful

I recently read that a series of ballroom dancing films had stimulated certain schools to teach children how to dance. The aim was to use dance as a vehicle for inculcating civility. Of course. Dance teaches manners. When we hold each other in our hands. When we support and strengthen each other. When we learn to trust. In dance we embrace the separate unity, the distinct wholeness, when two people move as one. And the outward structure provided by dancing is an aid to inward development.

There's an extraordinary moment in the best of all Fred and Ginger films, *Swing Time*. The lovers have met the insurmountable hurdle in their romance. It's over, it's insoluble, they can never be together, although they must, for they are truly in love. Fred sings to Ginger that without her he'll never dance again. "Never gonna dance," he warbles in his thin true voice, "Never gonna dance, only gonna love, never gonna dance . . ." Now, in their evening clothes, they walk across the dance floor. They are close but not touching. Their heads are lowered. They are beautiful and sober and sad as they grieve for the fact that they'll never dance together again. When suddenly you realize that their walking—their non-dancing—has, imperceptibly, turned into dancing. Their last dance.

As Fred and Ginger glide and turn, they pay homage to

their own love story, repeating snatches of dance sequences from other scenes in the movie, as if their whole relationship could be summed up in his swoop and her dip, his lean forward and her lean back, his weight and her flexion, as indeed it could.

Can there be a better metaphor for civilization than two dancers twirling in joyous and respectful synchronicity?

AFTERWORD

Looking back over all I have written, I appear to have made some outlandishly extravagant claims for manners. Such as, for example, healing the planet, inoculating us from a police state, restoring our citizenship, saving our marriages and making our lives richer and filled with meaning. Hmmm.

Perhaps I'll end on a smaller note.

Most Saturday mornings at 9:15 I can be found in a large old hall with long wooden floorboards and high rafters on open black beams where, with a small class of regulars led by our teacher, Sana, I do yoga.

Sana is about twenty-eight years old. When, lying on her stomach, she raises herself up on her hands and rolls her chin and eyes upward in cobra pose, she looks distractingly like a

supplicant Renaissance Madonna—if that Madonna had worn a T-shirt and sweatpants.

The ritual is always the same. Breathe in, breathe out. In, out. In. Out. Downward dog. Plank. Child's pose. Head up. Scoop to cobra. Breathe in. Breathe out. Up again to plank. Back to downward dog. Breathe. Now it's standing poses. Triangle pose. Warrior One. Spear pose. Mountain pose. Hold. Hold. Breathe. Relax.

Of course, the practice of yoga is physically and spiritually beneficial. And then there is the curious diversion of looking at the world via the triangle between your legs. The back of a hall gains a certain interest when viewed upside down. The dust floating on a sunbeam seems still more delicate from under your armpit. You become aware of ancient cobwebs on the ceiling as you lie on your back holding your knees to your chest. And as you lean your body forward and twist your torso to the back of the room, you notice with sleepy affection the unbrushed patches of your classmates' Saturday morning heads.

After years of yoga together, we students know very little about one another's professional qualifications, income, career highlights, domestic arrangements or belief systems—these matters never arise. Instead we know the important things: whose knee is tender, whose back is weak, whose hamstrings

are tight. You get to know another body very quickly when you're pushing a hip or twisting a shoulder or compressing the outer ankles to the floor during partner exercises.

In yoga, sometimes the body takes over—a surprised fart makes its way to the surface, or a snore rolls up to the rafters and expands across the hall. Once, a man began weeping, hard and painfully, and the atmosphere became suddenly very still, as if the class were collectively bearing witness to his distress.

Often at yoga all you can hear, no, all you can feel, is your breath rising in and out in your flesh. And where your body seems, usually, so weak and heavy, as you lunge and lift yourself and pull the air in and push it out and dimly hear the matching sounds around you, you suddenly feel that all human life is as powerful as this—this in and out and in and out. And as frail.

Toward the end of the class we all lie quietly on our mats, and Sana will take us through a relaxation exercise. I rarely comply with her verbal guidance, and instead of emptying my mind or letting thoughts disappear like passing clouds, I let the words and sentences gather and frame in my head.

In its unassuming way, this weekly ritual reminds me what manners require, and can achieve. The way it balances the needs of each individual and the demands of the group. The poise it creates between self-discipline and relaxation, submis-

sion and assertion, privacy and intimacy, order and freedom. The sense of private integrity in a communal space.

Manners do matter. Because, by our individual contributions, our little, petty sacrifices, we dignify ourselves. And we combine to make something bigger than ourselves. A civil society.

FURTHER READING

Aristotle. *Nicomachean Ethics*, translated by Terence Irwin, Hackett, Indianapolis, 1999.

Clive Bell. *Civilization: An Essay*, Penguin, London, 1928.

Edmund Burke, *Reflections on the Revolution in France*, Yale University Press, New Haven, Connecticut, and London, 2003.

Baldesar Castiglione, *The Book of the Courtier*, translated by George Bull, Penguin, London, 1967.

Lord Chesterfield, *Letters Written to His Natural Son on Manners and Morals*, Peter Pauper Press, Mount Vernon, New York, 1936.

Collected Works of Erasmus, Volume 3, University of Toronto Press, 1985.

H.D.F. Kitto, *The Greeks*, Penguin, London, 1951.

Harold Nicolson, *Good Behaviour: Being a Study of Certain Types of Civility*, Constable and Co. Ltd, London, 1955.

Robert Sutton, *The No Asshole Rule: Building a Civilized Workplace and Surviving One That Isn't*, Sphere, London, 2007.

Alexis de Tocqueville, *Democracy in America and Two Essays on America*, translated by Gerald Bevan, Penguin Classics, London, 2003.

ACKNOWLEDGMENTS

I am grateful to Jane Palfreyman, who suggested I address the subject of manners, and to Tim Whiting in Australia and Amy Einhorn in the United States for their support and advice. Special thanks to my editor, Nadine Davidoff, for her support and professionalism. A fellowship at Varuna, The Writers House, gave me invaluable time and space. My writers' group: Vicki Hastrich, Eileen Naseby and Charlotte Wood, has been essential both to joy and writing. Many dear friends helped me greatly with their editorial advice, kind support, book loans and tales of manners. Gratitude deserves individual thanks, but courtesy to readers demands brevity—so I shall simply say thank you all very much. A loving thank-you to the Holdforth family. And to Syd Hickman, who makes it all possible.